THE THIRTEENTH TIME ZONE

David Hess

THE THIRTEENTH TIME ZONE

A novel by
David Jebb

iUniverse, Inc.
New York Lincoln Shanghai

THE THIRTEENTH TIME ZONE

iUniverse books may be ordered through booksellers or by contacting:

iUniverse
2021 Pine Lake Road, Suite 100
Lincoln, NE 68512
www.iuniverse.com
1-800-Authors (1-800-288-4677)

ISBN-13: 978-0-595-36431-2 (pbk)
ISBN-13: 978-0-595-80863-2 (ebk)
ISBN-10: 0-595-36431-4 (pbk)
ISBN-10: 0-595-80863-8 (ebk)

Printed in the United States of America

To my best friend and wife, Maya and the two special angels in my life, Gabriel and Michelle.

Acknowledgements

To my son, the reason the story was started, to my daughter the reason this story was finished and to my wife for being there for me throughout. To the team behind the scenes and the special people of the Torrey Pines Gliderport, San Diego, California.

INTO DARKNESS

"Unit 413, respond to a 415 disturbance at the Dirty Angels Bar, 3700 University Avenue."

"Unit 413, ten-four." I glanced down the street at the herd of gangbangers I'd been watching for the past half-hour, then shrugged and drove away in the opposite direction. Damn it! The call that had just come in didn't have anything to do with drugs or gangs. It was a routine "disturbing the peace" situation, but I was probably the closest unit. Even hotshot Special Crime Attack Team or SCAT officers were expected to do normal cop stuff when it fell into their laps.

Anyway, this was Dirty Angels they were talking about.

I turned and stepped hard on the gas. The first officer to the scene always handles the call, and this consistently earned the respect of his fellow officers. Tardy units had to explain themselves to the other officers. Plus, Dirty Angels was a topless bar. Although not what you'd call a classy joint, it still featured dancers who could make a grown man lose sight of his purpose, especially if the officer ignored the fact that the same women wouldn't glance at him twice if he was wearing his civvies.

Three minutes later, I pulled into the Dirty Angels parking lot and shut the engine off. Music pounded out of the low concrete building. In front, a dozen Harley-Davidson motorcycles stood at the curb like a line of chrome steeds.

A middle-aged, heavyset guy stood in the bar's entryway. He identified himself as the doorman and pointed inside.

"Those guys have been getting rough with some of the customers and several of the waitresses. We've asked them to leave, but they won't."

I peered into the darkness. They were a greasy bunch with dirty jeans, worn leathers, and lots of hair and tattoos—they had obviously ridden in on the Harleys. It was equally obvious they'd been partying for some time. In San

Diego, methamphetamine production was the province of outlaw biker gangs, and "partying" meant consuming a nasty volatile combination of booze and speed.

In a situation like this, policy was to bring in backup. Standing out of view, I keyed the mike on my portable radio. "Unit 413 requesting backup units and ETA."

A response came back in seconds. "Unit 416 responding from College and El Cajon."

I scanned my mental road map. It would take him at least six minutes to get there. "Unit 413, ten-four," I returned.

A savage roar came from inside the bar. I peered back in. One of the bikers had jumped up on stage and was circling the dancer like a bullfighter about to make his initial sword thrust. The dancer continued her performance, a nervous smile glued to her face. But her movements slowed to a disjointed rhythm as she watched the biker move around her, hips thrusting forward and back to a beat of his own. The scene was primordial—the apish, liquored-up biker and the half-naked woman. For a moment, the smoke-filled barroom took on the aura of a cave and a ritual that must have been enacted in an era long gone.

The biker raised his muscular, tattooed arms, and tightened the circle.

I checked my watch. Still five minutes for backup.

The dancer halted when the biker came within a foot of her. She was still smiling, but even from the doorway, I could see the strain and fear on her face.

The crowd started shouting, "Do it, Benny! Do it, Benny!"

Benny's hand flashed out grabbing a fist of hair, yanking her backward. A moment later, the girl was sprawled on her back with Benny standing above her, straddling her, a smile on his face.

The chant changed to a deeper bellow, "Fuck her, Benny! Fuck her, Benny!"

Staring up from the stage, the dancer became instantly submissive, motionless. Benny unbuttoned his greasy jeans and dropped them low enough that even from my angle in the doorway, I could see Hell's Angels tattooed above his buttocks. I could also see that he was hung like a mule. The dancer had an even better view, and her face twisted in panic.

The rest of the bikers were now in a feeding frenzy. One of the bartenders started to approach the stage. But three guys stepped in his way, and he backed off.

I looked at my watch. Two minutes left. I looked at the doorman. He was turned away from me, away from what was happening inside the bar, away from everything.

"Hey," I snapped at him, "get your butt over here. Back me up when I go in."

"No way, man, I ain't going in there. Those crazy bastards will stick a knife in your back before you get on stage."

"Back me up, or you'll have to deal with me when I'm finished."

Inside, Benny had his erect penis in his hand and was masturbating over the dancer. The bikers had all risen to their feet. Their fists pumped the air. "Fuck her, Benny! Fuck her, Benny!"

I pulled out my radio. "Unit 413, cover now at Dirty Angels! Right now!" Then I threw the door all the way open and bolted into the room. Knocking aside a few startled bikers along the way, I reached the stage and leaped onto it.

Benny had no idea what hit him. In a second, I had clapped him in a carotid restraint, the infamous "sleeper hold." Bending him backward against my chest, I had one arm around his neck while the other locked that arm in place, restricting the blood flow to his brain. He clawed at me frantically, but I was a master of this technique. My resolve and arm were like iron.

Within seconds, Benny's body began to shiver, then to shake. Finally he slumped, unconscious. When I dropped him, his head bounced off the stage floor. The sound was clearly audible because the barroom had gone eerily silent. Everyone was staring at me. The bikers were red-eyed. Their mouths gaping open.

I sensed movement and spun around, my baton flying from its holder and cracking hard across the forearm of a biker who had crept up behind me and was reaching for my head. The guy's arm developed a new elbow. He stared at it, rising onto his toes, his mouth forming a scream that never got free before my backswing caught him across the jaw. He was hurled off stage and crashed like a pallet of lumber onto a table surrounded by his fellow bikers. The table collapsed.

Another biker—all hairy, sweaty, and with murderous eyes—lunged onto the stage. I greeted him with a butt stroke to the jaw that sent him soaring unconscious into the audience.

Only then did I get a chance to yell, "Police! Don't anyone approach the stage. It's mine, and I'll kick anyone's ass who tries it!"

They looked ready to jump on board anyway, but before anyone did, a half dozen more cops charged into the bar. Finally! The dancer was still lying on the stage after the altercation. She extricated herself from Benny's limp arm and leg and slid on her butt toward me. By then Benny was stirring, so I rolled him onto his stomach and handcuffed him before he had the opportunity to physically express his innermost feelings.

Being manhandled woke him from his brief slumber, and he was not in a good mood. "You motherfucking pig, let me up!" Blood and mucus sprayed from his beard.

I had often seen the wild-eyed look of a fallen gladiator humiliated in defeat—a pain worse than that of gaping wounds and broken bones. It was in these brief moments that the meaning of my life was defined. I defined defeat as death. At twenty-six years of age, I felt invincible. Yet, I could not explain the wave of anguish swept over me.

"Come on, big guy," I said, and grabbed his thick arm. I hauled him to his feet. He smelled of sweat, beer, and blood and was foaming-at-the-mouth mad. He had no choice but to perform a shackled shuffle toward the doorway with his pants still around his ankles.

The rest of the bikers milled around, growling and grumbling. With one of them still unconscious, another suffering a compound fracture, and more cops storming into the room, the fun was clearly over.

The doorman was still standing at his post, gazing around as if University Avenue had become the most fascinating piece of real estate in the world.

"You piece of shit," I said. "I asked you to watch my back."

He didn't respond. Benny lunged at him like an attack dog on a choke chain. I hauled the biker back although it was tempting not to. He and I both seemed to feel the doorman was about as worthless as a door ornament. As tempting as it might have seemed, the constraints of my position wouldn't allow me to release Benny on this gutless citizen. I reminded myself of the code which I swore to uphold—to protect the innocent against deception, the weak against oppression, and the peaceful against violence. Since childhood, I have been protecting the weak and the sports inept from tyrannical schoolyard bullies. Why? I could not explain it. For a moment, though, I understood Benny's animalistic rage and wondered how much it really differed from my own. I lived in a world of daily death, mayhem, and rage—even in my dreams. My mind twisted looking for an escape from these questions. Yet they were questions that I easily avoided living in the fast lane.

The drive home from work that morning was no different from the usual. Everybody else on the road was getting into fender benders and trying to steal the next lane downtown while I cruised along an almost-empty freeway leaving the city. I left the windows down in my Nissan truck and turned the radio on full blast to keep from falling asleep at the wheel. My body was exhausted, yet the violent encounter at the bar left my mind replaying the scene over and over again like a frustrated movie director displeased with an imperfect take.

I pulled into my garage and stumbled into the house. I placed my off-duty weapon on the nightstand, undressed, and climbed into the shower to wash off the smell of blood and sweat—the perfume of a night's work. After the shower, I then fell into bed.

The alarm shattered the darkness. Over it I heard a calm, familiar voice. "Any unit for a 459 audible ringer in the vicinity of 29th and Commercial?"

I groped for the microphone. "Unit 413 John from—" Speaking into my jangling alarm clock I awoke mid-sentence. I shut the alarm off, set it on the bedside table, and squinted at the burning line of sunlight showing through the bedroom curtains. It cut into my eyes like a dagger. "Never off duty. Twenty-four hours a day on the job. Even in my sleep it never stops," I thought. No doubt, my life was complicated, but I always seemed to thrive in chaos. Mental and physical chaos I could handle, but my emotions were raw. Nothing in my training had prepared me for the life of a pedal-to-the-metal street cop.

I got up and stumbled into the living room, also closed off from the daylight. Even in the darkness I could make out empty beer bottles, crushed corn chips, and spilled containers of salsa and guacamole strewn across the floor. Since my wife left six months earlier, the only social routine in my off-duty life consisted of the occasional predawn "choir practice," where late-shift police officers coming off duty gathered and drank until dawn. Separated from my wife after four years of marriage, I still held out hope that she might return. For the time being, I was a bachelor. Divorce was rampant on the force, a senseless casualty of street warfare. The memory of her swept over me daily like the pounding surf on a desolate beach. Nobody knew how devastated I was at her leaving. My police career was on a stellar path, but my inner being felt burned out.

Some people sit through the entire game of life with their butts on the bench while others never leave the game. I asked myself, "Why?" My exterior life seemed certain, but my inner life seemed increasingly hesitant and conflicted. I was a third-generation police officer. Between me, my uncle, and my brother there were three of us sworn to protect and serve. My great uncle died in the line of duty as a Chicago police officer. Since that time, there had been a tradition of duty—a tradition that weighed heavily upon me with each passing shift. How is it that one's sense of duty could override reason? *Why* was not an easy question to answer, and a constant restlessness pervaded me.

I staggered into the shower hoping the cool water would clear these notions from my brain. After showering, I made some coffee, opened a package of peanut-butter crackers, and glanced at the newspaper. *President Nixon announces Vietnam peace with honor.* Cracker crumbs rained down on the headlines.

Spreading the paper out on the kitchen table, I laid out my on-duty boots and started spit-shining them, as I did every morning. This routine brought me back to reality much quicker than headlines. Nothing like the smell of coffee, peanut butter crackers, and Kiwi boot polish for a quick morning pick-me-up, even if my "morning" began in the middle of the afternoon.

I finished polishing my boots, then stood there admiring them. I had bought them just before graduating from the police academy. Over four years of rubbed-in wax created a glossy black mirror surface. The shine hid the truth of the person looking into it. I paused, thinking for a moment that the boots symbolized me—brilliant on the outside but, beyond the surface, leather worn beyond its age by raging doubt.

This emotional split harkened back to my school days. As a young boy, I played baseball with all my heart. Winning the game meant everything. The few times my team lost, I would usually go alone behind the dugout and sit in disconsolate quiet. Sometimes my teammates came around to try to console me saying, "It's only a game." But at the age of twelve, I thought baseball was life. I never played life to lose. At the age of twenty-six, my heart had hardened after three-and-a-half years of street warfare. I already lost my wife, my family, and most of my civilian friends. I had lost one teammate, killed in the line of duty, and felt as if I were losing myself and my humanity.

Yet the accolades, the department citations, the team cheers, the pats on the back—all this made you believe you were winning. In the heat and passion of duty, I had not yet realized that winning was easily defined by others. The game mantra changed now that I was a cop. The simplicity and idealism of youth, tempered by the will to protect and serve others, would eventually extract its due. Too enamored by the glamour, I could not see that the inner demons of my life were coming at me like a high-speed, out-of-control eighteen-wheel Mac truck.

I set my boots aside and walked into the bedroom. I dressed in a pair of gym shorts and running shoes and headed out the door for physical training before going to work. I ran at least four days a week up and down the Pacific Beach Boardwalk. Homes and shops sat on one side of the boardwalk while, on the other side, the vast expanse of the blue Pacific Ocean stretched to unseen lands beyond.

San Diego epitomized the endless summer lifestyle of sun, beautiful bodies stretched out on the sand, blue waves crisscrossed by surfers, perfect smiles on every tanned face. For many, jogging on the boardwalk was a lifestyle state-ment of health, slim bodies, fitness, and tans. I didn't jog. I ran a six-minute-mile pace, pushing hard—not for pleasure, not for a tan, not to socialize with other cut-and-trim beach bodies. I ran because in a few hours, the sun would go down. I would be in the San Diego that defied the sheen of tourist bro-chures. Running fast in this darker city could be a matter of life or death.

The SDPD was headquartered in a building that could have been an old Spanish mission, except for the parking lot full of cop cars—beige stucco, red-tile roof, and palm trees hanging over the parking lot. I arrived for work as the blazing red-orange sun was setting over the harbor.

I walked to the station's backdoor with gleaming boots in hand and stepped into the musky smell of the locker room, one flight of stairs above the police cafeteria. As always, the locker tops were covered with dust, dry cleaning bags, clothes hangers, report forms, city-issued ballpoint pens, and used D-cell flashlight batteries. The trash receptacle in the corner was overflowing.

"No wonder they call us pigs," I muttered.

The empty locker room represented a place of metamorphosis. I opened my locker and started changing, not just changing clothes but shedding the image that identified me as a regular member of society. I reached into my locker and dragged out a pressed uniform shrouded in plastic that clung to the metal locker. I strapped on my bulletproof vest, still moist with sweat from the night before. Next I donned the pressed uniform and the glossy black boots. Sitting down I began the ritual of polishing the brass badge and nametag. I cleaned my service weapon, loaded it, and placed it on the locker shelf. I strapped on the leather and secured the pistol in its holster. Then I added the baton, nun-chucks, and a can of mace—my metamorphosis was complete.

As I finished my "pre-lineup" routine, Jay Rasmussen entered. Ras was a tall blonde man of Norwegian descent and a fellow surfer.

"Hey, Blue, what's happening?" he said. That was my cop name: Blue. Few officers called me by my real name, Owen Drew, any more. Right after the police academy, I won the California State Police Olympic Gold Medal Surf Championship. I was called Blue Wave Rider and Blue Waterman, but over time, the nickname was shortened to "Blue."

I said, "We're getting raped on beats 624 and 625. That's what's happening."

Jay stopped at his locker and spun the padlock dial. "Is that all you think about? You ever think about getting a life. Christ, Blue, since your wife left you, you've just crawled into this shit hole called police work."

"Ras, maybe you are right. But right now this job and the team are the only things I have left."

"Really?" He opened his locker and started to change. "Well, just take care of yourself brother."

"Maybe we ought to go out and catch some waves one morning after work, Ras."

"Slow down on the late arrests and get out of here at a halfway decent hour, and I'll take you up on that, Blue."

"He's a straight shooter," I murmured to myself, heading out the door. I exchanged greetings with other team members just coming in. These guys made up the team I worked and drank my mornings away with. In the briefing room, I checked over the crime stats for the past twenty-four hours. I stared at endless pages of computer printouts: a murder, rapes, robberies, burglaries, assaults, thefts. How does goodness survive in a world of such darkness, I thought.

Big Mark Demotte entered the briefing room and headed straight for the coffee mess. I studied him. What an animal—six feet, six inches tall, roughly 280 pounds. His nickname was Baby Huey. It was rumored that he once tried out for noseguard on the Buffalo Bills. Even now, most sober men would think twice before trying to take him on, despite the jellyrolls of flesh hanging over his belt.

He caught my stare. "What the fuck you looking at, boy?"

"Your cute waddle, Baby Huey. I love what bulking up on those twelve-pack donuts at Mitch's has done for your figure."

"Fuck you, Blue," he said mildly and joined me at the beat information table.

As he and I discussed the stats, the rest of the team entered one by one. After a bit of verbal jousting, everyone settled into concentrated study of the print-outs and lists, and there arose a profane harmony of "shit" and "fuck." The litany escalated into a full chorus by the time the lineup sergeant walked in and bellowed, "All right, ladies, take your seats!" Sarge was a former Marine drill instructor. He was gruff and resembled the Marine Corps' bulldog mascot, with the bull neck and drooping jowls to match. A shaved sidewall haircut and a red, high-blood-pressure complexion gave anyone the impression that Sarge was running at a high rpm before he even opened his month.

The noise level plummeted instantly, and we surged toward the chairs. Sarge stepped onto the lectern and laid out his announcements, training bulletins, work assignments, and personal comments. He waited for everyone to settle down. The pattern was, by now, familiar. The front-row rookies sat rigidly, ready with pen and paper in hand. In the rear sat the senior officers, many of whom looked as if they were just sobering up. I sat in the middle and to one side of the room near the exit.

Wherever we sat, one thing we shared in common was a desire not to piss off the sergeant, old "Bombs and Bullets." He stood before us ready to brief his squad before combat.

"All right, gentlemen, let's get down to business." In his memorable way, he proceeded to describe particular suspects wanted for robbery. "The goddamn asshole is described as a WMA, five-eleven, 170, brown and brown, having acute dick breath and shit for brains."

Another thing about Bombs and Bullets, nobody felt that he was bucking for lieutenant, which was evident by his non-politically correct attitude. After Sarge finished his briefing, he turned the last ten minutes of the meeting over to other officers. One by one, they got up and talked about suspects, trends, and people to watch out for. As minutes passed, the atmosphere in the room grew more charged. By the time lineup ended, I felt as though I'd been saved at a Baptist revival meeting. Once again I clearly saw the light of duty—a light that seemed to be fading over the rest of humanity. But there was one difference between lineup and religious revival meetings: on any given day for most citizens, death is an abstraction. For us, however, every night could very well be the last night of our lives, and we knew it.

After lineup as I was getting ready to race out to the lot, Sarge approached me and spoke in an uncharacteristically quiet voice. "Blue, I need to speak with you. Come on back to the captain's office."

Shit. If administration had anything nice to say, which they seldom did, they usually said it in front of the whole squad. Only if you were about to get your ass chewed did they take you into the back room. What now I wondered? Surely, they didn't think I could have handled that mess at Dirty Angels any differently.

Things looked worse when we got to the captain's office because the captain was actually there at eight at night. My lieutenant was also present, sitting in one of the chairs across from the captain's battered city-issued metal desk.

"Sit down, Blue," the captain said. As always, his voice gave nothing away, and he wore the face that most cops seemed to acquire after twenty years or more on the job: stony-eyed, one corner of his mouth slanting constantly downward as if pissed off about something he couldn't talk about.

I sat in the chair next to the lieutenant. Sarge took the chair to my right. Hemmed in, I felt as trapped as I probably looked. All eyes were on me. Right then I made up my mind: whatever this was about, I was going to deal with it the way I dealt with every other aspect of my job—head on. No bullshit.

The captain leaned across his desk. "Blue, I've been noticing your arrest reports lately."

I didn't say anything. I waited for the kiss of the ax blade.

"Over the past couple of years, the robberies, rapes, muggings, drug trafficking, and murders in the southeast sector have hit an all-time high," he continued. "Most of the crime appears to be gang-related. Would you agree?"

"Yes, sir," I said. "I would." The line of questioning both relieved and puzzled me. At least this wasn't about last night. The Hell's Angels gang didn't live and work on my beat, so he didn't have to qualify the gangs he was referring to.

"As a cop on the front line," he said, "why do you suppose the gangs are winning and we are losing?"

Actually, I had already given this a lot of thought and even if the captain didn't like my answers, I had already promised myself no bullshit.

"There are a lot of reasons," I said. "For starters, some of these puke-for-brains gangbangers have political connections, especially with civil liberties groups. Every time a cop calls somebody a name in Southeast, we end up writing CYA reports for hours."

His gaze never wavered. "Yet lately, someone's been managing to give them grief out there."

I said nothing.

"You've led SCAT in arrests in Southeast for the past several shifts," he persisted. "What do you attribute your success to?"

I shrugged. "I grew up on these streets. I know most of these bums personally. I don't like what they do. But I know how they think, and that helps me nail them."

For a moment he said nothing. Then he continued, "I think there's more to it than that. Most of the other cops in your sector know the locals pretty well too, but none of them come close to your score of arrests. Not even in the same ballpark. I know that concern about civil suits is part of the problem, but that's not all of it. Give me something else."

"If you're concerned about corruption, sir, I don't think that's it," I said. "I think the real problem is that most of my fellow officers are intimidated by the gangbangers. They're afraid to really take them on."

"And you're not?"

Suddenly and with perfect clarity, I remembered a moment from my first year as a cop. I was attending the funeral of a policeman, a bit older than I was, gunned down in the line of duty. His wife and two children stood in front of his coffin, and their pain and suffering swept over me like a tidal wave. At that moment, I resolved that losing to scum was worse than dying. At that moment, I decided that losing, like dying, was not going to be an option for me.

"No, sir," I said to the captain. "I'm not afraid to take them on."

"I see." He sat back slowly. On either side of me, the sergeant and lieutenant remained motionless. "Tell me something, Blue," the captain said. "If you had the power to really deal with the gangs in your sector, to handle them any way you like, what would you do?"

I hesitated to give the impression that I was carefully considering the question, but this was something else I already knew the answer to. Looking the captain right in the eye, I said, "Most gangbangers are stupid kids that think they're badasses. They're dangerous, but they're not the real problem. The real problem is the leaders, a handful of guys that provide leadership to the gangs. Most of the gang leaders are older guys and have done hard prison time. If given the chance, I'd take those people off the street—one by one if necessary."

"So, what's stopping you?" the lieutenant asked.

I glanced at him. "Well, sir, like I already said, when I'm out there I have to fight both sides of the law. Hoodlums and heroin addicts on one side, and bureaucracy and red tape on the other. Sometimes, it's difficult to know which team you're on when the very people you're trying to protect and serve are also the ones screaming about more humane treatment of criminals. The law is cut and dry with street criminals. But the law, our own departmental regulations, and even certain higher-ups in management play both sides of the line. Politics as usual, I guess."

Stirring on my other side, Sarge snorted, "Come on, Blue, we all know that regulations structure the game in favor of the criminals. If these buckets of shit don't play by the rules, why should you?"

"Because I'm a cop. Following the rules is what makes me different from them."

"Like last night at Dirty Angels?"

"Those bikers came at me first."

"The rules say you should have waited for backup."

"A citizen was being assaulted," I said. "I couldn't wait."

There was a long silence in the office. The three higher-ups looked at one another. Then the captain leaned toward me again. "Blue, what we see here is a cop who's willing to take the initiative when things are tough, who's innovative, who's not afraid. We've been looking for a cop like that. What would you say if we removed your shackles?"

I felt my pulse beating in my neck. The sword I thought was hanging over my head had just been held out to me as a gift. But still I realized that, if I grabbed it carelessly, I could get cut.

"What do you mean by 'remove my shackles?'"

"I mean do whatever it takes to get gang members off the street—get physical with them, put them in jail, and destroy them if you have to. That's what I mean."

You couldn't get much blunter than that. After several seconds, I broke my gaze from the captain's and looked at the lieutenant and then at Sarge. They both gazed back without expression.

"Gentlemen," I said. "You already know I don't mind mixing things up, but would you mind if I gave this some thought?"

The captain raised his palms. "Go ahead. Get back to me tomorrow evening. But in the meantime, don't mention a word to anyone, is that understood? It stays with the four of us in this room."

"Yes, sir, I understand."

Sarge immediately rose to his feet, walked to the door, and opened it. "I'll see you out there later, Blue."

I stepped into the hallway as though I were the only person in the department who knew World War III was declared. I headed to the parking lot, threw my equipment into the first available unit without doing my usual vehicle inspection first, and drove into the night. I even left the radio off, so that I could think.

Twenty minutes later, I parked near a donut shop and walked in. Cops are often immersed in the smell of hot grease and dough between the hours of midnight and six in the morning. Of course it's a cliché, cops and donuts, but the truth is that donut shops tend to be one of the few businesses open around the clock. Cops spend much of their lives working late and graveyard shifts. Besides, full meals make you feel content and sleepy during the graveyard shift. And imagine running a forty-yard dash or being in a five-minute fistfight with a drugged-out whacko on a full belly.

So, donuts are the perfect cop food.

I walked to the counter. There was only one employee there, dressed in the usual attire of his profession—white pants, white short-sleeved T-shirt, white apron. The outfit was mottled with flour and dough stains. Judging by the swell of his gut, he spent too much time sampling his wares.

But his smile was big and genuine. "Can I help you, officer?"

"Do you have anything freshly made?"

"How about some buttermilk bars?"

"That's fine, and a medium coffee, please. For here."

I took a seat in a booth, and he returned to pushing dough.

I started to work on the buttermilk bar although my mind felt more like a cinnamon twist. Did the captain really ask me to go to work as his personal rogue cop? Yes, he had. The choice to participate was mine, and whatever I decided would surely affect my career and my entire future. And that wasn't all. The situation demonstrated just how badly the system had broken down. When the job can't be done by legitimate means, it means the system itself has become ineffective.

So what was my duty here? Where did honor lie?

An admonishment by my old field-training officer came to mind, as it often did in moments of indecision. "Kid, this ain't a baseball game. In a baseball game, you win or lose. On the streets, you win or die."

No, it wasn't a game on the streets. It was a war, and we all knew the criminals were winning. The court system, the civil liberties groups, and the politically correct politicians turned their backs on the officers as the street battles raged.

I stared out the window at the black sky, the stained concrete of the surrounding buildings, the lowlifes slouching around the street corners and storefronts. Having consumed my coffee and donut, I needed to make a decision.

I snapped on my radio.

INNOCENCE AND DUTY

"Any unit for a 415 family disturbance at 7-8-1-4 Skyline Drive," the dispatcher said.

A map of southeast San Diego automatically scrolled through my mind. The 7800 block of Skyline was about eight blocks away. Domestic disturbances, like bar fights, were not primarily what SCAT officers were commissioned to work on, never mind potential under-the-radar rogue cops. The Special Crime Attack Team or SCAT officers were selected for their perceptive nose for hot crimes—robbery, hot-prowl burglaries, murder, and major gang activity. Given my limited time on the force, I knew I was fortunate to be a member of such an elite team. But there was a downside, too. My wife pointed out repeatedly that SCAT officers didn't enjoy a shift change every four months. We worked the high-crime period, 8:00 PM to 4:00 AM, which put us out of sight and mind of the majority of the department's officers and civilian personnel. I didn't care, though.

The dispatcher came on again. "All units responding to Skyline Drive, be advised that shots have been fired. The suspect may have taken his wife and child hostage."

The microphone was in my hand even as I flung open the door of the donut shop. "Unit 413 responding from 7000 Imperial Avenue."

I hadn't driven half a block before a field supervisor came on the air. "All units responding to Skyline Drive, switch over to tactical frequency."

I switched over. The supervisor identified himself as 400 Sam. "Units responding to the Skyline shooting," he said, "stand by and do not go to the residence. Meet me half a block south of that 10–20."

A few minutes later, I rendezvoused on foot with the Sam unit, a sergeant. He was with a second unit, a young cop named Archie. I'd never worked with either of them before, but I knew the sergeant by reputation. He was a veteran of the same head-bashing law enforcement tradition as old Bombs-and-Bullets. He was old enough to be a father figure. His calm bearing instilled confidence and respect. He was tall and one could see that his once muscular physique was gracefully giving way to age. Six stars engraved on his name tag signified at least thirty years of service.

"Communications has the wife on landline," the sergeant said. "She says her husband is despondent, out of his mind on drugs. He's going to kill her and the child."

Drugs, I thought. Out of his mind on drugs, of course.

"Should we call in the hostage negotiators?" Archie asked. He was a young guy, even less senior than I.

"We don't have time." The sergeant was already jacking rounds into a twelve-gauge shotgun. "Blue, I want you and Archie to move in on the house. I'll cover you from across the street. Dispatch thinks this guy is going to make his move any minute, so we don't have time to waste. Get inside and take the son of a bitch out."

Archie's eyebrows rose. "What do you mean, 'take him out?'"

"Kill him, you dumb son of a bitch."

I looked at the shocked expression on Archie's face and suddenly didn't feel so great about being teamed with him. Didn't he realize that we were at war? With no stars on his name tag, it wasn't hard to figure out that Archie was new to this job. What he lacked in experience I hoped he made up for in academy training.

The three of us crept toward the house and slipped behind a car parked opposite the target house. Shouts and screams carried clearly across the street.

"Can't see inside," Archie whispered. "All the lights are off." Unlike most of the cops I knew, myself included, he did not have a moustache to hide the sweat that glistened on his upper lip.

The sergeant ignored him. "You guys, get up there, and don't drag your asses. I'm told this guy has a bunch of weapons, including a carbine rifle."

Archie looked at me and I looked at him.

"Go!" the sergeant shouted.

Halfway across the street, two shots rang out in rapid succession. I dove for the curb, belly-sliding over the pavement. Archie rolled in next to me. We lay on our stomachs kissing the cold concrete in front of a storm drain. Another shot pierced the night. Judging by the sound, it came from the carbine the sergeant mentioned earlier. The slug ricocheted off the curb inches over my head, sending a cascade of concrete chips down on me. Luckily the drain provided slightly higher curbing than usual.

Then another round struck the same spot shattering more concrete. A third round deepened the crater.

Shit, I thought. He's going to chip away until he gets a clear headshot. Doped up or not, this guy could do some damage.

Across the street, the sergeant returned fire, two blasts from the shotgun. The shooter in the house ignored him and kept hacking away at the curb. Archie's head and mine butted together so hard I felt him wince as each new round struck. I also felt a hot trickle of blood cascading down my face, probably from concrete shrapnel.

"Archie, listen to me," I said. "We have to get up and charge that house. If we do it at the same time, we each have a fifty-fifty chance of making it, but if we stay here, we're guaranteed to die. You hear me?"

"Yes!" Archie shouted it even though his head might as well have been fused to mine.

"Okay, we get up together the next time the sergeant returns fire. Then run at the house. We've got to be quick. On the exact moment I say 'go.' Remember, if only one of us jumps up, he's a dead man."

Archie winced as more concrete shot up at us. "Right, right. I'm with you, Blue."

"Okay, on three. One—"

Across the street, the sergeant's shotgun thundered, and I shouted, "Three!"

As Archie and I sprang up, another rifle shot cracked out from the house. I didn't know where it was aimed. I was already in a headlong sprint, Archie behind me as we hurtled toward the house.

I hit the front door with a full body slam, crashing it back into the wall. The woman's screams cranked up and ceased with the crack of a rifle shot that came from somewhere down a narrow hallway across the living room.

We charged across the living room, weapons drawn, and down the little hallway. As I rounded the corner into the bedroom, I saw a man stretched out on the floor with a rifle beside him. A woman and small child crouched in a corner began screaming.

I pointed my gun at the man on the floor. Although the room was dark, I could see a black puddle slowly expanding around his head. I moved closer. A slug entered through his mouth and lifted off the top of his skull. The faint whiff of gunpowder, cauterized flesh, and blood permeated the air.

I kicked the rifle aside, knelt by the body, and handcuffed him, while Archie stood over us with his gun drawn. This might seem cold-hearted, but it's how officers are trained for their own safety. Many an apparent corpse has come back to life and attacked an unwary cop.

A moment later, the supervising sergeant charged into the room with a fourth officer at his heels. "It's over," I said. "The suspect is dead."

The fourth officer hurried over to the woman and child and bent down to console them.

"Blue?" the sergeant said. "You okay? You're bleeding."

I reached up and felt pieces of concrete embedded in my forehead. Blood painted my fingertips. "It's only a scratch," I said.

"Go get it looked at for Christ's sake."

Archie walked out with me. On the porch, I stopped and looked at him. His skin was so pale it seemed to glow in the reflected streetlight. I couldn't tell what he was thinking.

"You know," I said, "if I got up alone on the third count, that guy could have blown me away. So thanks for doing what you did."

He managed a smile. "Well, just lying there wasn't a very good option, either."

Pure understatement. But I knew he'd be thinking all night long about what almost happened to us. We both would. Even though we were trained as cops not to let intense moments of danger horrify us, swimming in nightly carnage has its effect.

There was movement behind us, and we shifted aside as the sergeant and the other officer led the two surviving family members out of the house. Wife and child sobbed, as they clung to one another. I watched them go down the steps and wondered where they'd be in a year. The woman would probably be remarried, very likely to someone similar to the man who had just blown his head off in front of her. The boy would be watching the local gangsters swaggering around, the heroes of his world. Soon enough he'd hook up with them, either as a customer or as a fledgling soldier. He'd forget all about the anonymous policeman murmuring words of comfort. Life followed patterns, and his early young experiences would shape his future. In a few years, I'd be arresting that kid. It was almost certain.

"Guess I'll go and start writing reports," Archie said.

I turned to him and shook his hand. "Take care, brother."

"I will. Better get that scalp looked at, Blue."

When I got home that morning, I showered carefully, washing around the bandage on my head. The ER doctor had dug three chunks of concrete out of my scalp, joking with me the whole time. Like most cops, I felt oddly comfortable in the ER. It was one of the few places where a cop could hang out and have the feeling that those around him understood the mayhem that comprised life. Plus, there was good coffee in a back break room and a quiet spot where you could write up reports while you eyed the nurses.

I contemplated how often that same doctor treated gangbangers for their injuries, knife wounds, bullet holes, blunt-force-trauma injuries, and overdoses. I thought again about the man who killed himself. Nice of him to save the taxpayers the expense of a trial, but not nice of him to try to take out a couple of San Diego's finest.

The next evening, the captain was busy behind a pile of paper as I entered his office. On one side of the office was a sagging bookcase loaded with law books, department policies, and manuals. A few police-related pictures decorated the opposite wall along with a certificate from the FBI Academy for Executive Officers. The room looked more like a bunker than an executive's office. "Come on in, Blue, and close the door. Have a seat."

"Yes, sir."

He put down his pen and gave me his usual stony stare. "Well, are you ready to get our new program started?"

"I've given it a lot of thought, sir. May I ask a question?"

"Shoot."

"It's about why you chose me out of all the cops on the force. I mean, I appreciate the compliment about my arrest record, but there has to be more to it than that. What you're asking me to do would have to be clandestine, right? Something the civil libertarians and Internal Affairs and everyone else would never know about. It would mean making me a rogue cop. How can you trust any cop with that kind of independence?"

He nodded slowly as if to say it was a good question, the kind of question he'd hoped I might ask. Then he answered it with a question of his own. "Why did you become a cop, Blue?"

I looked at him warily. It was the sort of question only non-cops asked, especially if they thought they already knew the answer. It wasn't to prove anything other than to pay back a debt owed to society, to help kids, to make the streets a safer place for loved ones, to even the score against the criminal bullies in our society, or—

I stared the captain in the eye and said, "I became a cop so I could protect and serve, sir. Just like the words on our patrol cars."

He gave another slow nod. "That's a warrior's code, Blue. To protect and serve—most people just see those as words. It's clear that you see them as more than mere words, and I think I know why."

"Sir?"

"Tell me about your great uncle's death."

I said nothing.

The captain folded his hands on top of his paperwork. "The cop grapevine grows right in through my window, Blue. You mentioned your great uncle to a couple of people back in the academy. He was a cop, right?"

It took me a moment to respond. "Yes, my mother's uncle. He died in Chicago in the thirties after twenty years on the beat. But when I was a kid, the family still talked about him like it happened yesterday."

"He was a good man?"

"A good father, a good husband—and a good cop, an honest cop, which was difficult in Chicago during that time." I cleared my throat, thinking about warriors and codes of conduct. "One morning he walked past a bank on his regular rounds, and a couple of armed robbers ran out behind him. They'd just pulled a heist, and they shot my great uncle four or five times in the back."

The captain's eyes tightened. "Nobody killed cops back then."

"The police conducted a massive manhunt, but the killers were never captured. For my family, it's a bleeding wound that has never healed. You know how that goes."

He nodded. No doubt in his career he'd seen it dozens of times in the members of a family victimized by senseless violence: disbelief, anger, self-blame. The emotions were compounded of course when the crime went unsolved, leaving no closure, no sentencing, no revenge, no justice of any kind.

The captain said, "Look, it's obvious that to you, being a cop is more than just a job. It's part of who you are. It's a personal thing. To me, it looks like you're out there on the streets to even the score with the bad guys and that's what we're giving you the chance to do. Only we're giving you the chance to do it even better than you have so far. That's all there is to it."

I nodded. "Then I accept your offer."

He showed no reaction one way or the other. "Hold on." He picked up the phone, and thirty seconds later, the lieutenant came in and closed the door.

"Blue has just agreed to take on our special project," the captain said.

"Excellent." The lieutenant turned to me. "Okay, Blue, forget about the civil liberties lawyers. Forget about rules and regulations. Do whatever you have to do. We don't care if you have to bury these shitheads. We want them off the streets. We want the people of Southeast to have their community back. Is that clear enough?"

"Yes, sir, it's my duty. But you know these bad boys aren't going to roll over easily. I need to know just how far you're willing to back me up if things get ugly."

To my surprise, the captain stood and leaned over his desk, knuckles planted firmly on the blotter. "We'll cover your ass to the limit, Blue, as long as you keep your mouth shut about our agreement and as long as you don't get caught operating outside department policies or the law. If you get caught, we'll deny ever having this conversation. Do you understand what I'm saying?"

I looked at the veins protruding from his neck and shot back, "Wouldn't have it any other way."

"Glad to hear it." The captain removed his knuckles from the desk and drew back into his chair. "Now get your ass out there and do some good."

After lineup, everyone headed straight out to grab a vehicle. My favorite patrol car was equipment number 254, a specially equipped Ford with a 390 cubic-inch power plant. This unit could easily leave fifteen feet of rubber on the pavement in second gear. With sirens and lights going and the four-barrel carburetor kicked in, it struck terror in the hearts of little old ladies and criminals alike.

Besides, unit 254 was outfitted to maintain a low profile—all black with no overhead light bar, a great asset in the kind of police work I did. I was a member of SCAT.

I walked around unit 254 slowly, inspecting her, my chariot on the SCAT battlefield. The city mechanics made a special effort to keep her up for me too because I had found the secret to their loyalty.

It started with my discovery that most run-of-the-mill street perverts usually drove cars full of hardcore sex magazines. The perverts always denied having any idea how such materials got into their cars—or even, in some cases, their back pockets. So being a civic-minded person, I made it my policy to help them out by turning the magazines over to the people most qualified to decide if they were truly offensive—city garage mechanics. The way I saw it, if something was offensive to those guys, it should be taken off the streets immediately. For their part, the mechanics enjoyed setting community pornographic standards, so they gave my unit special treatment.

On one occasion, 254 and I jumped a few curbs to corner a fleeing robbery suspect. The unit sustained significant front-end damage, a situation that would normally have resulted in my receiving a day or two off without pay. But in this case, the mechanics repaired 254 without filling out any paperwork.

Now unit 254 awaited me in the moonless night, ready to take me for a fast ride into the darkness. As the engine warmed up, I inspected the rest of the vehicle. A street cop is like an airborne soldier who leaps out of a plane behind enemy lines: When it's time to jump, he can't take time to wonder if he packed his chute correctly. For the force, it was especially critical to be prepared since the city always bought the cheapest equipment available. So, I tested the car's spotlights, hidden emergency lights, and siren. Then I opened the trunk to double-check for the first-aid supplies, extra ammunition, tear gas, and road flares.

Unit 254 was ready for combat, and so was I.

When I graduated from the San Diego Police Academy in 1969, I was in the top ten percent academically—athletically, I was number one. Although I'd worked hard to maintain good classroom grades, the weaponless defense training I studied for three years before entering the academy interested me the most.

Physical training consisted of a five-mile run everyday. Warm-up before the run usually consisted of several hundred jumping jacks, fifty pushups, a hundred sit-ups, five minutes of stretching—after all this the running began. The instructor always set the jogging pace between seven-and-a-half and eight minutes a mile. The class started in tight formation, but ten or twelve cadets normally got out in front of the pack and ran full stride after two or three miles.

The race to the finish line was always between a former Marine Corps track star named Jerry and me. Jerry was a well-toned, muscular guy—a classic running Marine who gave new meaning to the term "gung ho." But I was not about to let some "Devil Dog" bite me in the ass, so the two of us always sprinted our hearts out to the finish line.

This was more than friendly competition. We ran against one another because we understood something critical. From a cop's point of view, having the most physically fit officer in the department as your backup was a major asset. In contrast, the honor graduate with the highest GPA normally received cool reviews from the old-street cops.

Of course, jogging in shorts and a T-shirt wasn't like the kind of full-uniform running required on the street, and I understood that. Combat boots, bulletproof vest, weapons, baton, utility belt, flashlight, pens, badge, wallet, and keys don't exactly make for a fair race against someone fleeing for his freedom with only a wad of bills in his pocket or a few grams of blow. So for me, pushing myself hard on the track didn't have much to do with being healthy or looking fit. I trained hard so that I would be able to outrun the "runners." Runners referred to criminal gang members who flaunted criminal acts in front of cops and then ran away to escape arrest. This proved their daring to their peers, while the runners believed they would never be caught.

Soon after taking my first beat, I realized that, unless you possessed superior speed in both short- and long-distance running, apprehending gang members would be nearly impossible. Few old-school cops possessed such an advantage, and the famous Hollywood bit of pulling a gun out and yelling, "Freeze, or I'll shoot," usually evoked a response like "Fuck you—go ahead!" A brain floating on drugs or booze does not care or understand the consequences of deadly force.

In fact, the reality of the footrace situation was a well-known part of a young hood's initiation ritual. Commit a crime in the presence of an officer just to entice him into a hopeless chase, perhaps even into a trap. The cops knew all about this. In Southeast, radio broadcasts about running suspects—or "rabbits," as they were called—and "Officer in foot pursuit eastbound in the north alley of 3000 block of such-and-such!" rang out all night long.

The game never stopped and the hoods usually won. Chasing a three-time loser into a maze of welfare apartment buildings and garbage-spewed alleys on a moonless night was like running through a no-man's land into the gates of hell. The fear that the gate might open and swallow you boiled up in every pursuit.

But to me, being a cop was more than a game. My personal mission was clear even if the rules of engagement, by which cops live and die, were passed down by paper-pushing, politically correct, neutered men and women wearing gray suits and sitting at gray desks in gray administration buildings. It would take officers six months to comprehend the department "Yellow Sheets" of rules and regulations that the lawyer designed to keep you in line with the constipated leadership. They sent us into the streets with the cheapest equipment, measly pay, and the lowest per capita police force for a large city in the United States. So many of the administration seemed out of touch with what was really going on in the "War on Crime." The bottom line was that, when the shit hit the fan, the team was the only one you could depend on.

Getting the job done within the constraints of bureaucratic yellow sheets and spineless leadership meant that you would be only marginally effective. How do you play the game yet remain unbeaten, I asked myself. First, finish the standard training period when all the gray-suited eyes watched critically. I used the opportunity to learn from more experienced officers. Then, as I gained more experience, I paid attention to what really worked and what didn't. SCAT forced me to keep learning, thinking, and planning.

Eventually, I developed a very simple two-part strategy to break the backbone of the strongest gangs in my sector. First, I would go after the gang leaders and drug dealers like a half-starved wild dog chasing down the last meal on the African Plains. Second, I would gather more intelligence than the over-the-hill, pencil-pushing, coffee-latte-sipping bureaucrats working upstairs and use it in untraditional ways to leave a lasting impression on lawbreakers.

Gradually, over several months, I'd tested this unconventional attack strategy in the armpit stink holes of my beat. I wanted to make sure it was sound before I committed myself to it entirely.

Finally, I was sure.

I was ready to make the commitment.

And I knew right where to start.

The southeast sector of San Diego boasted the nastiest crimes in the city. In Southeast, practically every street corner with a liquor store was a gang hangout. Liquored thugs on corner lots pimped whores, sold speed, or stole cars for parts. Certain liquor store owners did more than sell alcohol. Their business involved laundering money, running bookies, or working in cahoots with the coyotes smuggling in illegal aliens, drugs, and automatic weapons.

On welfare check-cashing day, most of the storefronts and parking lots stood packed shoulder-to-shoulder with young hoods on the dole, having been bred to get what they could with as little effort as possible or cracked-out punks trying to scrape together funds for that next important hit. You'd think the state lottery was a $100,000,000 jackpot based on the lines outside the liquor stores.

As the taxpayer support funds began drying up later in the month, the gang community would take its clue from capitalism and turned to more marketable services like pimping, whoring, and theft to make up the fiscal slack that didn't cover their mounting drug and booze tabs. As Jerry and Sarge often said, that much of the hustle in Southeast wasn't much different from downtown Saigon on military payday.

Of all the hood hangouts in Southeast, the most popular was Doctor A's Liquor on the corner of Forty-ninth Street and Euclid Avenue. Doctor A's was the happening spot for buying and selling all forms of drugs and merchandise. The parking lot looked like a paranoid congregation of desperados whose sole purpose was to sound the alarm on an approaching police unit. Being spotted didn't suit my purpose, so I usually parked in the shadows several blocks from Doctor A's. Then I settled back to watch the action.

I ignored the small-time hoods. I wanted to slam the bigger drug dealers and those hawking loot from the back of a delivery truck, stuff cleanly lifted off recent burglaries.

Breaking the financial backbone and leadership control of the most hard-core gangsters might seem an impossible task given the structure of laws and regulations governing cops. But someone needed to step up to the plate.

I didn't have to watch long before I saw what I was looking for. I grabbed the radio microphone. "Unit 413 John, I need cover at Doctor A's on possible 11500 activities." Without waiting for a reply, I popped on my unit's headlights and crushed the accelerator to the floor. As 254 erupted onto the street, I pressed the outside PA system speaker key to amplify the sound of the roaring engine and screaming, smoking tires. A four-wheel skid into the parking lot riveted the attention of even some of the semi-comatose gangbangers.

The group broke out scattering in all directions, but I knew who I was after. Before my unit came to a stop, I was out breaking into a full sprint. Several of the young hoods stepped into my path, trying to earn brownie points with the boss, a small reward of dope or booze for interfering with an officer in pursuit.

I knocked them out of the way without breaking stride. No prizes would be doled out on that night, or any other night I was in town.

Behind the store, an open dirt lot stretched toward a maze of housing projects. A half dozen or so runners scampered off in that direction, but I kept my attention fixed on my main suspect—a black male in his twenties, wearing black jeans, a black leather jacket, and white tennis shoes. The shoes at times were all I could see of him as he dodged in and out of the shadows.

As the gangsters scattered across the lot, they didn't even bother to look back. These were young guys full of themselves, not worried for a moment that a lone cop might come up behind them on foot. After all, they'd already out-run the uniforms on many occasions, so why sweat this loner?

The group gradually splintered, and individuals veered off in different directions until it was just homey and me running through the back alleys of the ghetto darkness.

He glanced back, and I saw his eyes flash, surprised. Sirens must have blared in his skull. He charged harder, and so did I. I was gaining on him until I was about five feet back and easily matched his pace.

"Don't stop!" I said. "It's gonna hurt." My words and tone of voice became a chanting cadence in a march intended to set the pace of the encounter. The pace I chose.

Sure enough, homeboy tried to ratchet his speed up a final notch. This lasted a couple of blocks and then came the shortness of breath—the pained, forced breathing and the acidic bite of hard sprinting in the legs. His pace slowed, his rhythm began to break down. I still felt pumped but far from winded. I knew that the more I tired him out, the less resistance he would offer in the end.

Finally, in three strides I closed the gap. With one quick blow of the baton, it was over. Gravity overcame his Jell-O legs, and he hit the ground hard. I grabbed his Afro-sheen hair and pulled him toward me, so he'd know which officer ran him down. His blank eyes turned toward me as he attempted one last punch. At the same moment I landed one squarely across the bridge of his nose. He collapsed onto his back, eyes wide with shock and anger, nose spurting blood.

"Don't get up," I said. "You don't want anymore tonight."

"Fuck you!" He started to scramble to his feet. "Fuck you, motherfucking white piece of shi—"

I kicked him in the ribs. He collapsed and rolled onto his side. "Don't be calling me white," I said.

Strange, I thought, for me to have uttered such a thing. I had worked so long in this sector that I did not view myself as any different from members of the black community. I felt as though we were the same. The community still needed help and protection from the gangster thugs. My war was against crime, not against color. Distinguishing people by color obviously bothered me. Maybe that last drop kick was as much to keep him on the ground as it was my reaction to being called white.

He reached for something in his waistband. By the time his hand came free my baton already connected with his wrist. A knife bounced across the dirt. Jamming both his hands between his legs, he screamed: "The motherfucking pig is killing me! Motherfucker—"

His cries could probably be heard for blocks, within earshot range of the projects. But when I looked around, no apartment lights were coming on. No one was running to the doorways. Nobody seemed to notice at all. Around here, screams in the night were commonplace, and nobody seemed to care.

I bent down, grabbed my casualty by one wrist, and twisted it until he was forced onto his stomach. Next came the clicking as I slapped on the cuffs. "Get up, homeboy, you know the routine."

No snappy comeback this time. I searched his body and found several baggies of PCP-soaked cigarettes. "You're under arrest for possession. I'm taking you in."

"Fuck you, motherfucker, you ain't shit, motherfucker, shit, motherfucker, shit, motherfucker." Diarrhea of the mouth is a disease often brought on when one has physically arrested the body but not the mind. Despite these lively vocal curses, his body language told a story of defeat and disbelief. I suspected that in his twenty-five years of life—perhaps ten of which were spent pushing dust and dealing death—he'd never been run down by a cop and then gotten a good-ass kicking.

But that was all he got, at least from me. I dragged him to his feet and marched him back toward Doctor A's. I'd been taught in my twenty-six years of life that once a man was down, the fight was over. Knowing when to back off was an important aspect of being a warrior. I liked to believe that even though the criminals I brought down were convinced they'd been screwed, they'd still respect me in the morning.

By taking down this guy, I had succeeded in fulfilling the first requirement of my new strategy—going after the dope peddlers, one by one, to break the gangs' financial backbone. The next part of the plan was the psychological aspect. To be effective, this aspect would have to be reinforced nightly, weekly, and monthly. It would create the psychological effect that anyone dealing drugs would eventually be arrested. If the offenders ran and resisted, they would be guaranteed a one-way trip to the hospital and then jail.

As homeboy and I got closer to the Doctor A's proving grounds, I could see that the sewing circle of twenty-five or thirty hoodlums had already regrouped. By this time a half dozen of the good guys, my fellow boys in blue, arrived, questioning the locals about things they hadn't seen or hadn't heard. Always the same bullsh—. "I don't know nuttin, didn't see nuttin."

The moment I came around the building with my new trash-talking friend, a hush fell over the area. We marched into the full glare of the parking lot lights, and the silence erupted into a rumble of disbelief.

"Did you see that? This white boy fucked homeboy up!"

I opened the rear door of unit 254 and helped him slide painfully onto the "hot seat." Then, looming over him, I shouted loud enough for everyone on the lot to hear. "I got one fucking rule, homeboy, and this is it: if you run from me, I will catch you and I will beat you. So in the future, when you or your brothers see me, you stand there like a man, or I'll run you down and fuck you up bad and then take you to jail."

The other officers smiled and kept running field checks on the rest of the assembled vermin, but I knew that most of the heavies were hiding in the shadows waiting for the cops to get on their way. So I slipped into unit 254 and made a slow drive around the lot. Everyone, hiding or not, needed a good look at the young prince cuffed in the back seat, blood running down his face and all. I wasn't showing off my catch. This was psychological warfare. I was etching a message into the minds of everyone there.

As I drove away, I heard grumbling in the background. "How'd he catch that homeboy?"

I booked my catch into jail that evening. He would probably be released before the watch Sergeant signed the finished report at the end of my shift, but that was okay. It meant he'd be out on the streets spreading the word according to the gospel of Father Blue. In fact, I suspected that after a few drinks and a couple of hits on the glass pipe, he'd relate our encounter in a whole new level of gruesome detail. That was okay, too. In some instances, fear is the only emotion a brain hazed by constant drug, booze, and abuse can still understand.

That was why I intended to make fear a key player in my plan. The business of drug dealing was unlike any other business in this one aspect. Fear, paranoia, mistrust, and trepidation were rampant within the gang ranks. But like any business, drug peddling needed incoming funds to survive, diversify, and expand. Gang funds typically came from the sale of narcotics, prostitution, robbery, and auto theft. In southeast San Diego, dope coming across the Tijuana–San Ysidro border fired the engines of their enterprises.

If I really wanted to hurt the gangs, I needed to go after the highest-profile drug dealers. I already knew these people. Countless morning briefings, prior arrests, and word on the street all gave out the same dozen or so names. Now it was time to make sure they knew who I was. Not only were the gangsters battling one another for greater drug turf, now they had to deal with a predator cop and that fear, too.

I began to hunt them with a vengeance. I became the dealers' predator, stalking them the way a lion stalks its prey. I would lie in the shadows and observe the herd, picking out my intended victim and waiting for him to become vulnerable. Then I would spring, the herd would scatter, and my pursuit would begin.

I ran down as many as one or two dealers on a good night. When things got slow, I captured their minions for possession. One evening with the help of a team of officers, we even captured and arrested twelve gang members for assorted charges of possession of narcotics, under the influence, warrants, and resisting arrest. Through it all I remained true to myself and to everyone who ran from me. Once captured, I returned them to the scene, bloodied, and bruised, so everyone could witness a drug-dealer taking a one way to the county jail. Within a period of three to four months, the behavior of the hood rats and gangbangers in southeast San Diego began to change. They actually got better at being more discreet by developing the fine criminal art of rubber-necking. Where a blatant disregard for law and authority ran rampant before, now a new breed of cunning gangster emerged.

But soon, even for other cops, things began to change for the better. Too frightened to run until they were absolutely sure the approaching unit did not carry someone who could run them down and beat them bloody, the hoods would delay the chase so long that even the most flat-footed, chain-smoking cop could run down a gangster or two.

My strategy proved to work even better than I had expected. What I couldn't understand was why I took each robbery, rape, and assault personally. My empathy toward crime victims was so profoundly deep that it made no sense. While I reveled in my keen assertions and figured that this might be the plan that would clean up the city and keep the bad guys out for good, I could not recognize the short-circuiting of my internal emotional wiring.

I arrived home later that morning, about sunrise, and took a shower. As I dried myself off, I listened to the sounds of the city awakening outside from my darkened living room. When I got to the bedroom, I could barely see the framed photo of my ex-wife and me on the bedside table. Still, I stood there staring at it for a minute.

Janet and I had married four years earlier. She'd been my high school sweetheart with beauty and smarts to match. Hell, more than that, she was a hard-body blonde who liked to have fun—the kind of woman who walked into a party and instantly became the center of attention, particularly with the men. She could tell jokes and wasn't offended by four-letter words. The perfect wife for a cop, you'd think.

Truth be told, in my twisted thinking I was more committed to "the job" than to her. A year earlier, I'd staggered in from a late-running choir practice to find her sitting in the living room in her nightshirt. She didn't even look at me.

"This is it," she said. "You either quit the department or you quit me."

I drew myself up. "I can't accept your ultimatum, sweetheart."

The next morning when I came home, she was gone, leaving nothing behind except a picture of herself.

At first, I didn't believe she would really leave, not for good anyway. She'd be back. I could not give up hope that one day she would understand the vows that we had taken together before a priest and the Catholic Church. Hope was the only thing left for me. I decided to stay married even if she was no longer living with me. How could she leave me at this time in my life, I asked. My life was so lonely. There was no one there for me to share my hurt and pain or my dreams. As the days passed, I felt betrayed and my anger and resentment escalated.

Six months into our separation, the department's Internal Affairs (IA) called me into their office to tell me my wife had been seen at several "questionable" social gatherings where drugs were present. The IA sergeant said, "Officer, you're either married or you're not. If she refuses to be married to you, then divorce her ass, because the next time our officers go into a place where she's around illicit drug usage and you're still married to her, you're out of here."

The next day I filed for divorce.

RAMPAGE

I arrested six drug dealers that night. Chased them down, fought them, dragged them back to the car, and took them to jail. The intake deputy looked at me as if I just dropped in from another planet. A war on the dope peddlers had now begun, and soon they would know it.

The security light hung high on the west side of the concrete building, casting a triangle of white light down a graffitied wall. I stood on one side of the light in the deep shadows, looking across the littered back lot of Doctor A's Liquor Store twenty yards away. One side of the store provided cover for a cluster of hoods deep in conversation. I knew their discussion didn't include existentialist philosophy, nuclear proliferation, or pollution in the San Diego Bay because ten minutes earlier I was listening to them from behind a pile of rubbish not twenty feet from where they stood. From there, I had also watched them peddle drugs to people in passing cars. Most of the chitchat consisted of jiving out ways to lure cops into fruitless chases and new escape routes.

All this talk was very familiar to me now. Over the last two months, I had heard it many times from behind that same pile of trash. The homeboys became suspicious, having no idea how this one cop always seemed to know what they planned. After listening to their plans for a while, I'd crawl on my belly back to this spot—this concrete building with the security light. It stood on a slight rise above the parking lot, a short but steep embankment with a worn footpath used by innumerable gang members fleeing from police. The path was a convenient escape route for them and popular because the homeboys knew most cops would fall hopelessly behind trying to climb the embankment.

Raising my radio to my mouth, I said in a low voice, "413—John, units to 10–87 Doctor A's for possible 11–50s."

Back came a reply: "Unit 415—John, responding from Forty-third and Market."

A few minutes later, a police unit cruised up the street on the far side of the liquor store. I watched the gangbangers spot it, huddle for a moment, and then strike various casual poses—as if they were out enjoying the balmy evening air. But the moment the unit lumbered into the lot, the gang let loose with a storm of rocks and bottles. As the junk rained down on the unit, it stopped with an outraged squeal of tires. A cop jumped out.

The gangbangers charged off in all directions, loving every minute of it. I waited. A few seconds later, one of the gangsters scrambled up the embankment in front of me and sprinted through the pool of light and into the welcoming darkness beyond. As he looked over his shoulder for signs of pursuit and stepped into the bleak gloom near me, I swung my baton. A crack resounded through the air. The fleeing drug dealer dropped at my feet.

Seconds later, one of his buddies scrambled up the embankment followed by another and another—five in all. I widened my stance and swung the baton with measured strokes—one, two, three, four, and five. An assembly line. They just kept falling on top of one another.

I called in three separate units to haul them off to jail. The gangsters would wake up, not exactly sure what had happened. Years of booze and drug abuse left them a bit slow in the deductive reasoning department. But by the time they reached the county jail holding tank, they would figure out that they had run into the back end of the Blue baton.

Sometimes my rogue work dovetailed nicely with a project the SCAT team was already involved in. For example, one project involved looking for a suspect named Bullet with an outstanding felony arrest warrant for attempted murder. Bullet was an enforcer, an assassin for his gang. He was the kind of guy who poked an MCA-10 out the open window of a passing car and sprayed everyone on the street just to kill a single rival gangster.

The problem for SCAT was that Bullet's two brothers, within a year of one another in age and similar in build and appearance, were members of the same gang. Bullet was the only enforcer, but the brothers covered for him and made things difficult for law enforcement. They were smart as far as gangsters were concerned. None of them ever carried identification, so they could be whoever they wanted when the police confronted them. Over and over again we'd arrest one or two of the brothers, thinking we nailed Bullet only to find out otherwise later.

But one evening I got lucky. I spotted a group of hood rats standing in front of a liquor store in a seedy trash- and rodent-infested commercial district of Imperial Avenue. I drove by slowly to let them see that I was staring at them. As usual, they stayed in place, pretending to talk with one another and be casual, although I saw them watching me from the corner of their eyes. Then, to my delight, I spotted all three of the Bullet brothers in the back of the group, trying to look inconspicuous.

The heat of the hunt rose up my neck, but I pretended I hadn't seen anything special. I drove past the store at my usual pace, slow and easy. Then half a block away, I stood on the gas and whipped the car around.

The gang members all took off in different directions as the car slid into the parking lot. I jumped out, ran one of the brothers into the ground and handcuffed him while everyone else disappeared among the buildings.

"What you doin'?" the brother roared into the pavement. "I ain't done nothin'. This harassment, man! This harassment!"

"Are you Bullet?" I asked.

"Yeah, I'm fuckin' Bullet. What about it?"

I hauled him to his feet. "I don't believe you. Bullet's a big pussy who has to hide behind his punk brothers."

"Fuck you, man. He'll—" He realized his mistake and shut his mouth.

I hustled him back to my unit and stuffed him in the back and then radioed for backup. Meanwhile I kept a lookout around me and spotted a flurry of movement in the mouth of a nearby alley. Over the tactical frequency I said to the backup officer, "Listen, Mike, park on Forty-ninth and Solola Avenue. I'll bring the suspects there for pickup, okay?"

"Ten-four, Blue."

I clambered over the center console, opened the passenger-side door and slipped out. I kept out of sight and ran down an alley around the corner, and then entered the back side of the alley where I had seen movement.

A moment later, another Bullet brother lay facedown on the pavement, wrists cuffed behind him. "Are you Bullet?" I asked.

"Yeah, pig, I'm Bullet."

"I don't believe you. Bullet's too big a pussy to come creeping back around here so soon."

"Man, he's going to…." This one shut his mouth, too. But again, it was too late. I grinned.

I marched him back to my unit and shoved him in next to his brother. "I know neither of you losers is Bullet, but I'm going to take you to jail anyway for disturbing the peace."

"What?" one of them roared. "You the one chasin' people around fo' no reason?"

"I also smell alcohol on both of you, so we'll have you blow into the Breathalyzer and add public drunkenness to the list. How's that?"

Now they glared silently at me. I started the car, popped on the headlights, and drove slowly out of the parking lot. I could feel a dozen hidden stares following my unit down the street. Just what I wanted.

"Know what's going to happen to you?" one of the brothers said.

"Sure. I'm going to live a long, happy life and die with a smile on my face."

The brother's grin floated in my rear-view mirror. "Think so? Well, one out of three ain't bad."

"Oooh, a threat. I'm really scared. I mean, nobody's ever threatened me before. Now just shut up and enjoy the view, okay?"

"You a dumb white boy that don't have a clue what's happening." He looked at his brother, and they both grinned. "You think just being down here fucking with the homeboys is going to change anything? You dumber than you look!"

A couple of blocks from the liquor store I found Unit 412—John waiting for me, just as I'd asked. I pulled up behind him, and the backup officer and I transferred the two brothers from the back seat of my unit into his.

"Why did you want to meet here?" the backup asked. His name was Mike Wiley, and he was more than just my backup. He'd been a second-unit beat partner with me, at least on the periphery, for the past year or so. He was a few years older than I and a good cop who had been trying to join the SCAT squad. He was also a fairly regular attendee at choir practice.

"Mike, meet two of the Bullet brothers," I said. "There's one more I want to nail. I figure he'll come out of hiding now that he thinks I'm down at the jail processing these two. Get the idea?"

Mike smiled. "Okay, I'll take these guys in."

"Be careful," I said. "They're full of death threats."

"Oooh," Mike said, "pretty scary."

I hung out in the immediate area for an hour or so, then cruised back to within a block of the liquor store, and got out of the car. I knew the gang turf escape routes at least as well as the hoods, so nobody expected to find a lone cop conducting silent reconnaissance in a graffiti wasteland.

The waiting and sneaking around in the dark shadows and watching from a distance seeking to find one man who had eluded arrest for months was a routine that I conducted for hours each shift. I rounded a building and found Bullet standing with his back against a wall smoking a cigarette. Before the surprised shock on his face could wear off, I turned him around forcefully handcuffed him. He didn't have time to spit his cigarette out or ditch the handgun from his jacket pocket.

"Hey, Bullet," I said as we stood on the silent street. "How's it going, man?"

"I ain't Bullet," he said.

"Funny, that isn't what both your brothers said earlier this evening before going to jail. But they're being printed right now, and pretty soon so will you. Then we'll know who's who, and you'll be going bye-bye for a long time."

I saw the muscles clench in his jaw and wondered if he'd try to make a break. Or maybe he was expecting help from one of his cronies in the nearby alleys. He looked at me sidelong.

"You think you can get away with any shit, don't you?"

"Bullet, I'm a cop. I don't get away with shit. I just do my job."

"Well, they's jobs and they's jobs, you know what I mean?"

"No."

"Just don't be surprised you meet up with someone else doin' his job, that's all I'm sayin'." He smiled at me, and his expression was exactly like that of his brothers.

I shook my head. "I'd love to keep chatting with you, Bullet, but here comes your taxi to the penitentiary."

Ordinarily I wouldn't have thought twice about anything Bullet or his brothers said, but at lineup the next night something happened that changed my attitude. Several criminal intelligence detectives stood to one side of the squad room. Looking at them gave me a bad feeling. I noticed Sarge kept glancing over at them, too, even as he conducted his usual profane briefing recital. Finally, he stopped and cleared his throat. "All right, men, we've got a visitor here with something important to say."

One of the suits approached the lectern. "Good evening, gentlemen. A couple of days ago we received information that several of the gangs in southeast San Diego have pooled their resources to put a bounty on a police officer's head." He paused, and then looked straight at me. "That lucky officer is Blue."

"The suits upstairs blindsided me," I told the captain twenty minutes later. As usual, the captain showed no emotion. "Neither did we until it was too late to warn you. How did the rest of the men take the news?" he asked.

"What else? They kidded me about being the gangs' favorite. I just hope this isn't going to compromise our mission. The pencil pushers upstairs don't suspect anything, do they?"

"No. But we're going to have to take precautions for awhile."

"What do you mean precautions?"

"I'm not worried about the brass putting two and two together. I'm worried about losing our means to effect change just when we're starting to do some good on the streets. Listen, Intel's informant says the scumbags plan to set you up with a fake radio call and then snipe you. That will be hard to avoid, especially since it's an open contract. Every gangbanger on the street will be looking to score on this one."

"Come on, Captain. There aren't but a half-dozen gangsters out there with the balls to actually try anything with me."

"You're not bulletproof, Blue, no matter what you think. I want you to lay low for awhile."

I felt heat rising in my face. "What, just because of some bullshit Intel report?"

"From here on out I want you to have backup on any radio calls involving any kind of disturbance."

"Any...kind...of disturbance? Shit, Captain, if I do that, the assholes will figure out what's going on and think they've won. I'd rather get shot than—"

"That's the way it is, Blue. You keep doing what you've been doing, unless you're responding to a disturbance radio call. In those cases, I want you to wait for backup before you do anything. Is that clear?"

"Yes, sir."

On Friday evening, I responded to a radio call to find no fewer than thirty loiterers outside Doctor A's Liquor. As I drove slowly past the store, I spotted a couple of Crips, identified by their preference for the color blue. They were standing together within the larger group. One of the faces looked familiar.

I hesitated and then keyed the microphone. "Unit 413 John, making contact with numerous 11–50s at Doctor A's." I sighed. Reluctantly I added the dreaded words "requesting backup."

The dispatcher said, "Unit 413 John, on a stop on numerous 11–50s at Doctor A's. Request units for cover."

"415, John, from Thirtieth and Commercial." I recognized the voice of Nate Jones.

"411, John, Fortieth and Ocean View." That would be my old compatriot, Baby Huey.

"Dispatch," I said, "have the units responding switch over to the TAC frequency." I keyed the mike. "Mark, Nate, this is Blue. Listen, get down here fast, but do it quietly and with lights out. Stay close, and don't let them see you. If the shit hits the fan, I want you close by. But I want these guys to think my balls are so big that they're dragging in the dirt, you understand?"

"I got it."

"Okay, Bro."

I parked my car close enough to Doctor A's lot that everyone there could see me climb out and stroll back toward them, casual, not nervous about a thing. When the homeboys faced me, I showed them my teeth, raised one corner of my mouth slightly, and then strode into the group with long, deliberate steps.

"Someone radioed in gang members loitering in the area," I said. "Anyone here see any gang members?" I doubted the captain would approve of what I was doing. A lone uniformed cop, even one without a bounty on his head, approaching so many gang members on their own turf was like a bloody hindquarter dropped into a crowded shark tank. Voices rumbled around me.

"What the fuck you here for?"

"Crazy white motherfucker!" The crowd made way as if I were Moses parting the Red Sea.

I headed straight toward Anthony Diggs, the highest-ranking Crip on the lot. He looked at me and flipped a lit cigarette butt at my feet.

"Watch your ass, Tony," I said. "I'm not in a fire-walking mood this evening."

"Say what, motherfucker? You come here to hassle my ass over littering?"

"No. I'm looking for Tyrone. Where he is tonight?"

"What the fuck, you think I'm going to tell you anything?"

"No, but when you see your homeboy, you tell him he's going to get his ass kicked for putting a contract out on me."

"I don't know what the fuck you're talking about, man."

I saw movement across the street as Nate pulled into a dark lot, lights off. With all attention focused on me, nobody noticed him. I figured Baby Huey couldn't be more than another minute away.

"Maybe you don't know what I'm talking about," I said, "but Tyrone will. Just let him know I'm coming after him."

The mass of gangsters was beginning to close in around me. In my experience, alcohol combined with drugs gave birth to at least one loudmouth, confrontational drunk per group. JJ Spikes apparently decided to be the evening's spokesman.

"Hey, Drew, why you fucking with the homeys?"

I looked at him. "Back off JJ, now!" I turned back to Tony. "You better see to it JJ backs off, Tony. He's drunk in public. And if anymore diarrhea runs from that mouth of his, I'm taking him in for the evening."

JJ looked at Tony. At the same time, I saw Mark's darkened cruiser pull into the lot across the street.

When Tony didn't say anything, his silence became JJ's tacit waiver. JJ took pimp steps toward me, working himself up. I sighed and pulled my radio from its case.

"413 John, cover now on 10–16's at Doctor A's." I put the radio away. "JJ, I told you to back off, or you're going in—you hear me?"

He was practically dancing now. "Fuck you, you be out here fucking with us niggers. I'm going to kick your white ass!" Finally he stepped up to bat. At the same time, I thrust one hand into his left shoulder while grabbing his right shoulder and pulling it toward me. He spun in a half turn and in an instant I locked him in the sleeper hold.

Before anyone else could react, the other two units came screeching across the street into Doctor A's lot. JJ twisted and turned in my grip, yelling in a strangled voice, "Get the fucking pig! Get the—"

"JJ," I murmured into his ear, "shut your hole, or you're going nite-nite."

"Fuck y—"

I tightened my arm for a couple of seconds, then laid his limp form on the pavement and cuffed his wrists.

The other two units smoked to a halt, and Nate peeled himself out of one of them. He was a big black man who weighed about 230 pounds, a bit less than Baby Huey. His arms appeared so massive that a pencil would find little space between his biceps and his shirtsleeves. With his baton raised in a defensive position, he barked orders like a rabid drill instructor and created momentary confusion among the gang members. Meanwhile my beloved noseguard, Baby Huey, waded into the group like a crazed elephant among pygmies. He spoke the language of the streets, and within moments, the crowd was backing off and acting like nothing happened out of the ordinary—same old thing. Nobody saw or heard a thing. Everybody was innocent.

By this time, JJ was struggling up from his nap. I yanked him to his feet and patted him down for weapons. I found none. But when I dug into his right front pocket, I discovered a bundle of what appeared to be plastic wrapped cigarettes soaked in angel dust. I lifted it from his pocket, all my instincts instantly heightened. I had never met a drug abuser on dust who was not dangerous.

Originally intended as an animal tranquilizer, PCP provoked severe and unpredictable psychological and hallucinogenic reactions to those who used it. The user sometimes acquired superhuman strength, felt little or no pain, and could be irrational beyond the fear of death.

I opened the rear door of my unit and pushed JJ inside. Behind me, still more backup was arriving. Meanwhile, Baby Huey and Nate questioned several more hoods they suspected of having warrants.

The excitement finally slowed down in the early hours. It was normal, everyday activity for that part of town. It was just another night on the job. But for some reason it felt like much more than the average day for me. Somebody painted a big red dot on my back with concentric circles around it, and I was determined to find out who it was.

By accusing Tyrone of ordering a hit on me, I was just stirring the waters. Although Tyrone may have initiated the contract, so might a half dozen other guys. Leaders of local gangs normally were deadly rivals, but presently they shared a common problem—me. I searched for these players night after night. Wisely, they kept a low profile.

A few weeks later, after I became the guarantee of financial freedom for aspiring hit men, I got a break that put me one step closer to achieving my own goal. I was cruising past the mouth of an alley behind a liquor store when I spotted "Luther the Hunter" shooting craps. At six feet five and 320 pounds, this gang boss made Baby Huey and Nate look petite. Luther's neck was wider than the waists of most men, and his biceps as round as the average thigh. His body was covered with classical prison artwork, including tattooed murals, bright red scars from numerous knife fights, and even the raised circular scars from bullet entry points.

I watched for awhile from the other end of the alley. Ordinarily, street gambling didn't get me hot and bothered, but it was time to take the big man down as a trophy arrest.

I drove into the alley and stopped a few yards from the action. Hunter was playing with two of his esteemed associates. None of them so much as glanced up at me. I got out of my unit, expecting immediate trouble. Instead, the gamblers shot me a quick glance and continued with their game.

I strolled closer as if interested in the game.

Luther finally reacted although he didn't even raise his eyes. "What the fuck you want, boy?"

I didn't answer him. Instead, on the next roll of the die, I stepped over to the wall and picked up the little cubes.

Hunter shot to his full height like a volcano erupting. "What the fuck you doing, pig?"

In one motion, I slid my baton from my belt ring, tossed one of the dice into the air, and slammed it over the back alley fence. I flipped the next dice up and did the same thing. "Two homers," I said. "The crowd goes wild."

The Hunter's enormous face seemed to swell even further. He reached out with one of his mammoth hands and shoved me hard in the chest, forcing me to step back.

"Who the fuck you think you are, boy?"

My baton was still out. As Luther took a step toward me, I lashed out low, giving him a power shot on the left shin. I didn't care how big he is. Your shins are only covered by a thin layer of skin, and a solid maple baton leaves a hell of a dent. Most men drop immediately to the ground. Luther winced, and then pure rage overtook his eyes. He lunged at me like a charging bear.

Shins aren't the only place where bone lies close to the surface. I met Luther's charge head-on and worked my baton across his hands and forearms. I swung left and right with all my strength and speed. Within seconds, the big man earned several serious wounds and retreated, cursing, flailing his arms, and in obvious pain.

One of his buddies picked up a garbage can lid and tossed it to Luther to be used as a shield. Luther shouted, "Leave him to me, I'm going to teach this boy a lesson." I lunged at the buddy who threw the lid, but I didn't dare leave my back exposed to Luther for more than a second.

Sure enough, when I turned back toward him, he'd found his second wind and a new surge in strength fueled by rage. Holding the lid as a shield in one hand, he waved the other in the form of a massive, bloody fist, and charged me.

Again I met him head-on, this time hammering at the trash can lid with my baton. Slowly backing up, I smashed at the lid until it practically wrapped around his forearm and he felt the pain of my stinging baton blows once again. The frenzy of my retaliation was savage and I kept moving realizing that if he were to grab me, the fight would be over due to his sheer mass. In his haste to keep me moving backward, he lost his footing and toppled over in an avalanche of flesh.

I didn't back off. I leaned down and pounded away at his upper body until he rolled over and covered his head with his arms. Then, like a cowboy roping a fallen bull, I knelt on his back and threw on the cuffs. His wrists were so large I had to pressure-push the cuffs to lock them.

By then, the other gang members crept closer and stood watching, mouths gaping in disbelief. I hauled the Hunter up, shoved him into my unit with as much force as I could muster, and slammed the door.

While I drove Luther to the station, I told him I intended to nail every member of his gang. He smiled. It made me think of the Bullet brothers.

"What the hell are you grinning about?" I said. "You're going to jail for gaming, assaulting an officer, and generally pissing me off."

"That's fine with me, man. If I'm in jail, nobody gonna blame me for what gonna happen to you!"

"You mean that paper on my head? I know all about it, Luther, and I know you are involved. Paying somebody else to do me. What's the matter, chicken-shit, can't handle the job yourself?"

His smile widened. "Got us a volunteer!"

"Somebody willing to kill me for free? That'll be the day."

But it was possible, I thought. No doubt more than one young homey looking for fame and glory would be up for the freebie.

Everything began to change. The celebrity-like status made me feel as though everybody was watching—administration, my fellow officers, even the criminals. Now it was especially important that I not hunt too long in a particular area or in a particular way. I needed to keep the criminals off balance, uncertain at all times without letting them think I was compromised.

When gangsters were not on the streets, usually during weekday mornings between 4:00 AM and 6:00 AM, I usually patrolled the back alleys of businesses with my lights out. A rash of burglaries had plagued the division for months. This routine was more to help keep me awake, but I still hoped to get lucky.

I spotted a car sitting with its lights off at the rear of several connected business buildings. As I climbed out of my unit and walked toward the car, I saw a figure duck down in the front seat. I leaped forward, shined a flashlight beam through the open window frame on the driver's side, and shouted.

"San Diego Police! Hold it right there. Place your hands on the steering wheel where I can see them!"

A white male in his thirties sat up and put his hands on the steering wheel.

"What are you doing in this alley at this time of the morning?" I demanded.

The guy wouldn't look at me. Sweat beaded his forehead. "I don't want to talk about it. I don't have to tell you anything, man."

I shifted my grip on the flashlight. "Would you mind showing me what you have in the trunk of your car?"

He snorted. "You're going to look anyway. Go ahead."

"Then open it up."

Climbing out of the car, he walked around back and popped the trunk lid. I shined the flashlight beam on an untidy pile of cameras, electronic equipment, tools, and clothing.

"What are you doing with all this stuff?" I said.

"I don't have to say shit, man."

So while he wasn't saying anything, I stepped back and radioed for backup. Then I moved forward. "Care to try again? What are you doing here behind these businesses at this time of the morning?"

"Fuck you," he said, and suddenly his fist arced around at me, skimming past my jaw by less than an inch. I swung back reflexively, not even realizing I was still holding the flashlight until I felt the steel cylinder pop the man in the side of his head. He stumbled back into the hood of my car, shaking his head and spraying droplets of blood everywhere—scalp wounds are always messy. I dropped the flashlight and tried to grab his arms to make the arrest, but he lunged against me. Moments later, lying on the hood of my vehicle, we both tried to subdue one another. I finally managed to spin him onto his face and struggled to get the cuffs on. His head was still bleeding quite a bit. By the time the cuffs clicked closed, the hood of my unit looked like an avant-garde finger-painting collage in red blood.

As I was putting my prisoner in the back of my unit, a backup officer arrived and got out of his car. "What the hell's going on here?"

I looked up as he approached, and recognized a field sergeant I knew only vaguely. "I was investigating this guy as a burglary suspect when all of a sudden he swings at me."

The sergeant looked at the hood of my vehicle, and his eyes widened. "It looks to me like excessive force."

"Wait a minute, Sarge. This guy tried to punch my lights out for no reason. I swung back, wrestled him to the hood, and cuffed him. That's it."

The sergeant nodded and got on his radio. "700 Sam requesting a field lieutenant."

"400 Lincoln responding.

My prisoner sat quietly in the cruiser, hunched forward, a stream of blood dripping steadily off his nose onto the floor of my unit. Terrific.

"What the hell set you off, fella?" I said.

He didn't look up. All his anger and bravado seemed to have vanished. "I don't know," he said in a soft, almost weepy voice. "My old lady threw me out of the house this evening. I packed my stuff but didn't have a place to go. I was planning on sleeping in the alley tonight. Then you came along and…I just lost it." He finally looked up, eyes damp through a mask of blood. "I'm sorry for what I did."

Dispatch confirmed the car was registered to the suspect, as were all the serial-numbered items in the trunk.

A few minutes later, Lieutenant Russ arrived. He talked with the sergeant for awhile, and then the two of them came over and examined my unit's bloody hood. "What happened here, Blue?" Russ asked.

I told him.

"I think we should file brutality charges against the officer," the sergeant said.

Ignoring him, Russ bent into the back of the car and asked the suspect, "What happened here this evening?"

"I guess…I fucked up. I just lost my head…." He reiterated what he'd told me about his wife throwing him out of the house.

Russ closed the door and looked at me. "Okay, book him, but first stop by the hospital and get him fixed up."

The sergeant stepped forward. "Wait a minute. I still think we should press charges against this officer."

"Forget it."

"But—but I—"

"Sergeant, I said forget it."

"Thank-you, Lieutenant," I said. Then I got into my car and drove off before he could change his mind. Lieutenant Russ was the same lieutenant working under my Captain. He realized I was doing good police work and sometimes people can be in the wrong place at the wrong time resulting in unintended consequences.

After work I met for choir practice with a few of the other officers. "Damn college-educated asshole" was the consensus of the team, as they raised their beers. "Hey, Blue, is it safe to be around you? Never know when a slug is going to come flying out of nowhere and put a hole in you, right?" I was getting tired of hearing about being a "marked man."

The predawn party broke up a half hour before sunrise, leaving Mike Wiley and me to greet the dawn. Mike finally qualified for SCAT, so he had extra reason to celebrate.

"Who's a college-educated asshole?" he asked.

"That traffic sergeant who threatened to report me," I replied. "He's got education, but no fucking sense, know what I mean? I mean, your basic traffic cop takes home a paycheck for writing speeding tickets, investigating accidents, generally helping out where needed, right? At least it's a stepping-stone to becoming a real cop. But a traffic sergeant doesn't even write tickets. He's about as useful as a pair of tits on a slab of bacon."

"Agreed," Mike said, taking another swig of beer while leaning against my pickup truck in the parking lot behind a big warehouse. As the night sky receded into the morning dawn, the security lights glowed through a gray-blue haze. The smell of brine was almost as powerful as the aroma of hops and barley.

"Know what's really funny?" I asked. "By the time I got that guy all sewn up and dropped off at the county jail, we were practically best friends." Maybe the part about being thrown out of his house by his woman gave me reason to connect with the guy. Funny how a woman's scorn makes a guy do crazy things, I thought.

"Think the traffic sergeant is going to report you?" Mike asked.

"I dunno. He might."

"I'm sure it'll slide right off, Blue. You're golden."

"Yeah, sure."

"I'm serious. Nothing can touch you. You're a wild man."

Overhead, a white flicker appeared in the sky and drifted down. At first I thought it was a big, fat snowflake, which was ridiculous in San Diego. But down it came, spinning slowly and landing on Mike's shoulder. A feather, fluffy, gray-white, about two inches long. The feather rested on Mike's immaculate blue uniform shirt. I smiled. Well, I could think of worse things to have drop from a passing bird. He noticed it and brushed it off. "Fucking seagulls," he said. "Nothing but sky-rats."

"Why do you think I'm a wild man?" I asked. That was the kind of talk that could blow the cover off my secret career-within-a-career.

"It's just that you never seem to have any doubt about what you're doing," he said, twisting his head to look down his back. I realized the feather was nowhere in sight. He was probably worried it was sticking to the back of his shirt. "You just go out there and do what needs to be done, no doubts, no second-guessing. I admire that."

I started to say something and then shut my mouth. A couple of months ago what he was saying would have been right, but not now. A couple months ago, I wouldn't have been so quick to swing on that poor guy in the alley. I would have taken him straight to the ground and restrained him the same as I'd done with dozens of criminals. No head wound, no fountain of blood, no undignified wrestling on the hood of my car, and no threats to report me for excessive use of force.

A couple of months prior, in other words, I wouldn't have lost control of the situation. Through all my training and commitment, all the battles on the street, I prided myself on my self-control. But I'd lost it, and I couldn't pretend otherwise.

A couple weeks later I was driving a roadway and noted a big Cadillac swerve back and forth all over Linda Vista Road. It was 3:00 AM on a Saturday, so it wasn't hard to figure out that the driver was on his way home from a bar or party. I could see his silhouette and that of a single passenger.

I could also see that the car's taillight was out—reason enough to pull him over. I keyed the mike, called in my location and the Caddy's license plate number, and then hit the overhead lights. After a few seconds, the Caddy lurched to the curb and stopped. I got out and approached on foot, leaning down to greet the driver with those textbook words, "Good morning, sir. May I see your license and registration?"

The driver was a large black man in his mid- to late-twenties. He reached slowly into his back pocket. At the same time I made eye contact with the passenger who looked to be in his late thirties or early forties. A tattoo dressed his sleeveless upper arm, almost invisible against his charcoal skin. It was a coil of barbed wire beneath a raven or crow with outstretched wings. The guy gave me a flat stare I recognized. Cons are good at hiding their thoughts and trying to play mind games.

Linda Vista wasn't my regular beat. I had wandered up this direction because Southeast was dead quiet. Linda Vista was beginning to get a reputation for gang problems of its own: Vietnamese gangs. The area was known as "Little Saigon" because of the many Vietnamese who settled there. It was an odd neighborhood in which to find two black ex-cons driving around after 3:00 AM.

The driver finally found his wallet and took out his driver's license. As he handed it over, the passenger suddenly said, "You don't have to show him shit! This motherfucker only stopped you because you're black!"

I ignored him and examined the driver's license. "Mr. Jones, I'm going to run a check on you. I'll be back in just a moment. Meanwhile, I suggest that you ask your passenger to hold his tongue."

"Okay, man," the driver said and turned to his right. "Be cool, brother."

The passenger's eyes gleamed in the darkness. "Fuck the pig, man. You don't have to tell him shit!"

I walked back to my unit to radio in a warrant check on the driver. As I sat waiting for the response, I could see the passenger jacking his jaws.

The check came back negative. I walked to the driver's window. "Sir, you have a taillight out. I'll be issuing you a warning to have it corrected. Also, it's apparent both of you have been drinking heav—"

"Fuck this bullshit, man," the passenger said. "This is just harassment."

I fixed him with my flattest, hardest stare. Cops play mind games, too. "Listen, mister, I've already told you to keep your mouth shut."

"You keep your fuckin' mouth shut, moth—" He knocked aside the driver's warning hand. "Fuck this honky, man!"

I wasn't really in the mood for this shit, but some things can't be ignored. "Passenger," I said, "Get out of the car." When there was no reaction, I walked around to his door, speaking into my radio: "413 John, I need cover on Linda Vista Road with a possible 10–16."

"10-4, any unit to respond to 413's request for cover on L.V. Road?"

"415 John responding from 163 and Genesee."

"411 Roger from Mesa College."

Both officers were not right around the corner. For the time being, I was on my own—just the way I liked it.

The two occupants of the Caddy decided to have a pushing contest in the front seat. I leaned forward toward the open window on the passenger side. "Passenger, get out of the car now."

He whirled toward me. "Fuck you, motherfucker!"

"This is your last warning."

"Fuck you! Come in here and get me, you fucking pig!" He reached over and locked the door, even though his window was rolled down.

Later, I could not be sure if I was more upset by his scorn for my authority or the clear insult of his action. Regardless, I lunged toward the window opening and grabbed him by the wrist with such speed that even I was surprised. I dragged him halfway out of the car before the driver latched onto his other arm. A tug-of-war ensued. After going back and forth a few seconds, I managed to raise my size thirteen boot and place it on the door. In an explosion of anger, I pulled back with everything I had. Not only did the passenger catapult through the window, but the driver followed him onto the sidewalk as well.

Before I could regain my balance, the driver jumped to his feet and came after me, punching—left-right, left-right. A moment later the passenger joined in, hammering on the back of my head with his fists. I managed to knock the driver onto the hood of his car long enough to free my baton. In the same motion I swung around 180 degrees and smacked the passenger alongside the head. Blood gushed down his face in a scarlet sheet, and his eyes rolled back. He fell to the sidewalk.

Just then one of the driver's arms clamped around my neck from behind, and he pulled me back onto the hood of his car with all his weight, punching me in the face with his free hand. I punched back as best I could, but I couldn't seem to get him off me. In fact, he managed to pin my arms to my sides. A moment later, I felt his fingertips tearing at my eyes. Whipping my head from side to side, I began to feel something new—panic. If his partner got up and found me in this position, I was finished.

The driver's thumb found one of my eye sockets and began to dig in. Meanwhile, several of his fingers slid into my mouth. I bit down on them with everything I had.

The driver screamed, and his iron lock around my throat eased. We rolled off the car together and fell, becoming lodged between the Caddy's right rear wheel and the curb. The driver landed on top of me. I couldn't move at all, but he could. I felt him groping for my gun with the hand not clenched in my teeth. There was nothing I could do, except bite down harder.

The driver's free hand alternated from pounding my face to trying to grab my gun. I thrashed hard enough to roll him onto his side on top of the curb. With my back braced against the tire, I finally gained enough leverage to get some power into my own punches. The driver's' fingers were still locked in my teeth, which kept him from using that fist, but his other fist kept whaling on me.

The primordial fear of death was upon me. I lost track of time, feeling, sight, and pain. My only thought was to survive—nothing else even registered.

Then I felt his finger pulling away from my mouth, escaping somehow. A wave of panic overcame me. I bit down with the last of my strength. Still his body lifted away from me. No, no, if he broke free, he would kill me. His screams were silenced by my own internal howls.

I registered the sound of urgent voices and screeching brakes. I opened my eyes to see three officers trying to pull the suspect away from me. I opened my mouth and saw the man's partially severed finger hanging from his hand by a thin string of flesh and muscle.

I flopped back in a daze.

"Blue, you okay?" It was Rick, one of the backup cops.

I stared at the sky, wondering how long the cops labored trying to pull the suspect's hand out of my mouth. "Yeah, man, I'm okay. Help me up."

Rick reached down and pulled me to my feet. My uniform was shredded, the shirt soaked in blood. "Hey, man, you need an ambulance?"

"No, I'm okay. I just need a few minutes to pull myself together."

"Shit, Blue, I thought we needed a tire iron to get that asshole's hand out of your mouth. Are your rabies shots current this year?"

I managed a bloodstained smile. "Thanks for getting here when you did, Rick. That guy almost pounded me into unconsciousness."

"Not since we've been here. We were trying to pry him loose from you. Shit, Blue, we're going to have to take him to a surgeon to see if they can reattach his finger. You practically bit it off. And what about the guy laying up there on the sidewalk with his head split open?"

"Oh, him. He was the shithead that started this party."

We stood around for a few minutes shooting the breeze. The other cops laughed and told jokes, and I pretended to be relaxed and calm. I didn't dare let on about the extent of my pain. Like Mike, they thought I was a wild man—invincible.

The driver of the Caddy was yelling from the back seat of Rick's unit. I walked toward the car, and he saw me coming.

"Get that motherfucking pig away from me!"

Everybody laughed. But as I looked into the man's eyes I saw the raw terror there and said nothing.

I thought I had lost it—again.

Then I drove myself to the hospital.

Weeks and month passed by and nobody shot me. The threats about what was going to happen never did. No bullet sought me from darkness. Yet I became, day-by-day and night-by-night, ever more sensitive to danger. At home, I kept my curtains closed at all times. At restaurants or bars, I sat with my back to a wall. The only time I didn't carry my weapon was when I was jogging or sleeping. Why make things easier for a sniper?

Still, I didn't let my fears affect my work—my mission. That continued as before, night after night. I pursued my prey through the streets, down alleys, and across backyards full of weeds, rusting cars, and furious dogs.

I hit full stride on a night I arrested no fewer than six gang members. Most of them I handed off to Mike or another backup officer to take to jail, but the last three I transported myself. When we walked into the admitting area where most of his gang buddies were still being processed, the collective roar sounded like an erupting riot.

Music to my ears! How could anybody snipe me when they couldn't even keep their own sorry asses out of jail?

But one person was not playing in the criminal orchestra. Another gang leader I considered a main candidate for sniper of the year—Tommy Johnson, one of the most feared gang drug peddlers and enforcers in the city. His name was spoken in hushed tones in Southeast, usually accompanied with glances over one's shoulder.

I spent weeks tracking him down, mostly by the use of informants, "snitches." This wasn't as difficult as it might sound. Many rival gangs were eager to see Tommy taken down since he had developed a near monopoly on the drug business in a large part of southeast San Diego. He was universally hated and feared. He had earned a reputation for hurting people and enjoying it.

Bit by bit, my informants told me which hangouts Tommy favored, and I staked out each one. Finally, late one evening, I spotted him. The tall, gangly man wearing a fashionable suit and a fedora might have graced the head of any one of a dozen downtown pimps hanging with street prostitutes outside a dance club. They seemed to be in no hurry to go anywhere, so I called in for a couple of additional officers to meet me several blocks away.

A two-man unit showed up at the rendezvous. The officers, Bob Johansen, with over nineteen years on the streets, and his partner Perry, a rotund guy who went through the Academy with me.

"Guys," I said, "I've got Tommy Johnson, who's got an attempted murder warrant out on him, just a couple blocks down the street."

"Shit, man," Perry said, "that dirt bag has been outstanding for some time now. Let's get the son of a bitch."

"Listen," I said, "don't underestimate him. Tommy's done a shitload of time. He's strong, and he's tough. With half a chance, he won't hesitate to kill any of us."

"He's also a snappy dresser," Bob said.

Perry smiled. "Word is he says he won't let anyone take him back to prison alive. I say let's go test his honesty."

Tommy didn't notice us until we approached, striding fast out of the darkness. He reared back. "Shit, man, what the fuck you motherfuckers doing here?"

"Just checking out the neighborhood, sir," I said. "Have you got any identification on you?"

"I ain't got no ID with me, man...what's up?"

Bob stepped closer. "Tommy, you know there's a warrant out for your arrest."

"That's bullshit. You motherfuckers are just fuckin' with me."

I stepped closer, too, crowding him. He glared at me from under the brim of his hat. A jaunty red feather stuck up from the band, matching the red silk pocket square on his suit coat. I said, "Tommy, you'll have to come with us to get this all straightened out."

He opened his mouth, but before he could say or do anything I slipped behind him and cuffed him. He didn't resist. His shoulders slumped. The red feather fluttered. He was mine.

The prostitutes walked away as though they did not know, or ever knew, Tommy.

Pleased at how smoothly and under control things went, I took Tommy to Central Division, picked up his arrest warrant, and then walked him toward the interrogation room to see if I could get any more information out of him.

"What the fuck you got me for, man?" he said as I led him down the corridor. Despite being hitched along by his cuffed arms, he managed to put a funky spring in his step.

"Tommy," I said, "stop playing dumb ass with me. You've known all along that you have an outstanding warrant for attempted murder."

He grinned. "You fucking pigs aren't taking me in on that charge."

"No? Well, where do you think you're going right now? La Costa Country Club?"

I felt his biceps bunch under my hand, but there was nothing he could do. Except, of course, mouth off. "Drew," he said, "when I get out again, I'll find you. And when I do, I'll shoot you in the back and watch you die begging for mercy."

I halted, dragging him to a stop. "You'll do what?"

"You heard me, man."

"Shoot me in the back? Is that what you said?"

"Damn strai—"

I blinked. Tommy wasn't standing next to me anymore. His back was now pressed against the wall, pinning his cuffed arms behind him. His eyes looked startled, his mouth agape. His suit jacket gaped open to reveal a white satin shirt.

I blinked. My fists had somehow taken on a life of their own, flashing out left-right, left-right, crashing into that white shirt.

I blinked. Tony's fedora was lying on the floor. The red feather had popped off the brim and landed beside it. More red appeared alongside the feather. Then an uncontrollable blur of frenzied punching.

I blinked. Tommy lay curled up on the floor.

I blinked. Tommy was on his feet again, supported against the wall by my hand, but he couldn't seem to stand straight. He swayed, dipped, almost fell. His mouth gasped as if having trouble breathing.

I blinked. Nothing changed.

Suddenly as if a light switch flicked on, I realized the gravity of my actions. I lost it again. Worse, this time I'd lost it in police headquarters where brass and administrative personnel might come wandering down the corridor at any moment. If Tommy started screaming, I was in deep shit. Beating a handcuffed prisoner was a serious violation of department policy, not to mention my own code of honor—the warrior's code to protect and serve.

Okay, so I'd screwed up. I wasn't about to lose my career because of a worthless pile of scum like Tommy Johnson. No way. I leaned close to his ear. "Tommy, what's the matter, you got a boo-boo? Well, why don't you just start crying like the sissy you are? You're a punk. And if you keep running your mouth at me, I'll make sure the entire cell block hears how easy you really are."

He sucked at the blood on his lips but didn't say a word. I could tell he was hurting inside. We both knew that if word got out in jail that he was beat up by a cop, he would be punk bait for the other inmates.

The intake deputy met us at the door of the county jail, looked at Tommy, and raised his eyebrows. "Prisoner, are you feeling okay?"

With an effort, Tommy lifted his head. "Fuck, yeah!"

I smiled. He just talked his way into intake.

As the cell door started to close behind him, Tommy turned and looked me in the eye. He spoke in a strained rasp. "Blue, when I get out, I'll come after you. And when I find you, you're dead meat. Then I'm going after your family. I'm going to fuck your wife and all of your children and your family pets. You got that?"

"I don't have a wife," I said. "And I don't have any children or pets. But I've got a dead houseplant you can fuck if you want." Then I turned and walked away.

QUESTIONING DOUBTS

I grabbed the phone off the bedside table before its second ring, nabbing it neatly in the dark even as I took in the display on the alarm clock: 6:00 AM. "Yeah?"

"Blue?"

"Hey, Mike, how you doing?"

"Not good. Blue. I'm calling to say goodbye."

I sat up. "What's happening?"

I heard the sound of the phone rustling in his hand, nothing else.

"Mike, talk to me, brother. Mike? Hold on, I'm coming right over."

"No, Blue, it's too late. I've already turned the gas on. When I pull the trigger, this whole place is going to blow."

"Mike, you asshole, you wait for me. You ain't going nowhere without your partner." I dropped the phone and bolted out of bed.

Mike's house was ordinarily a ten-minute drive from mine. I made it in eight even through heavy morning traffic. Those minutes ticked by at what seemed like an hour. I screeched to a stop in the alley behind his house, a little bungalow perfect for a bachelor. It was still standing. I found the front door unlocked, and ran in to the smell of natural gas so strong I could barely breathe.

Mike was in the kitchen, lifeless on the table with a gun in his hand and the stove gaping open, hissing, behind him. I stopped and stared, fearing the worst. But there was no blood, just an empty whiskey bottle on the table.

I placed my hand on his wrist, carefully removed the gun, and stuck it under my waistband. Then I tried to lift his head off the table.

Without warning his eyes snapped open. "Let me be!" he screamed, leaping up. He started to topple over backward.

I grabbed him and dragged him toward the front door. "Mike, stop it. Let me get you out of this place."

He sobbed, his body wrenching with each breath. "Let me die, Blue. Let me die."

I hauled him around to his backyard and laid him out in the grass. He curled into a fetal position and just lay there crying.

"Hold on, brother, I'll be right back." I returned to the house and shut off the gas, and then started opening windows. Through the rear windows, I could see Mike lying in the grass and breathing heavily.

Finally I came back and sat down beside him. "You with me, partner?"

He sat up slowly. "Yeah, Blue." The sobs returned. "I feel like the world is caving in on me, man. I want to get out, but I don't know how. I don't have any friends outside the police department, and police work is all I know."

I shifted uncomfortably on the grass. "Come on, Mike. You're coming home with me."

He was still sitting there when I got back from locking up his house. I helped him to my truck and barked, "Get in!" as if dictating commands to a recruit.

And he did. On the drive back to my place, he rested his head against the window and stared, a vacant expression on his face. The air in the cab was thick with the smell of whiskey, sweat, and propane. I rolled down my window. I was tired and Mike was drunk. What a great combination.

I parked in front of my house and got him out of the cab. With his arm slung over my shoulders, I walked him inside and all but dropped him onto my sofa. He said nothing. I found a spare blanket to throw over him. Then I removed my shoes and sat on the easy chair across the room from him. That's where I intended to stay until I was sure he would not try to finish what he had started—at least not yet.

He finally fell asleep, snoring thunderously. At 3:30 in the afternoon, I climbed out of my chair and put some coffee on. "Mike, get your ass up, boy."

As I poured him a cup I saw him stirring. Finally, he sat up and put his head between his hands. I placed the hot steaming mug in front of him. "You aren't going to tell, are you, Blue?"

"Tell what? To whom?"

"You know…what I tried to do…to the department."

"Look, Mike, this has nothing to do with the department, but what were you thinking?"

"I don't know. I guess I was just feeling down."

"Well, next time you feel down, give me a call. I can think of a lot more exciting ways to get you up. Speaking of which, when were you last with a woman?"

"I don't know."

"Know what I think? I think you need to get laid. Get your mind off the job and onto something a bit more upbeat for a while." Only then did I realize I had never seen Mike with a girlfriend. Maybe a female acquaintance or two, but I didn't ever recall him dating. He spent all his free time with his police buddies. "Are you going to be okay, man?"

"Yeah. I guess I just got fucked up on whiskey and got depressed. But I'll be okay. I'll be okay."

"Drink your coffee. Go take a shower, and we'll drive into work together. How's that?"

"Thanks, man. Sounds good."

While he was showering, I prepared a light meal, which we ate while talking copper trash and crime series. Everything seemed fine. Then I showered and changed. We locked up the apartment and headed toward my truck.

I headed out the station that evening thinking that this job was killing us.

No sooner had I rolled out onto the street than the radio came to life: "Unit 413, be advised neighbors report a female screaming at 2-5-1-8 Imperial."

I put the pedal to the floor, and a few minutes later, I was on Imperial Avenue and rolling toward the address. It was a residential area, run-down, and ragged—the kind of place...well, the kind of place where a man might try to blow a cop away with a high-powered rifle from the security of his bedroom. I switched off my lights and pulled to the curb a block before I reached the exact address.

"Unit 413 is 10–97," I said into the radio.

A voice responded, "Unit 411 is also 10–97," and I saw a second police car cruise in at the far end of the street, also without lights.

The moment I turned my engine off I heard the screaming: frenzied, high-pitched, looping endlessly.

Unit 411 was driven by Ben Olson, an older cop, but a good one to work with. He climbed out, and we approached the house from opposite directions, arriving on the porch at the same time. No one seemed to take notice of us. I peeked through the front window. The television was on in the living room, and light spilled in from a hallway to one side. The glass vibrated with the end-less screaming.

"What do you think, Ben?" I said.

"Sounds like someone's getting her ass kicked big time in the back room." He grinned. "Let's go." He crossed to the door and hammered on it so hard it shook on its hinges. The screaming paused for a moment and then returned even louder than before. I twisted the doorknob. The door swung open.

Static from the TV screen flickered like lightning against the walls of a small living room. An elderly black couple sat on a ragged sofa in front of the television set, staring at the tube.

"What's going on here?" Ben yelled over the screaming.

The old gent looked up. "Nothing."

The shrieks crashed down the hallway. "Let's go," I said to Ben.

The hallway was dark and smelled like sour socks and gym sweat. A door at the far end was cracked open slightly. As we approached it, we could hear furniture being turned over and glass breaking.

I pushed the door open with my nightstick. On the bed, a muscular black female clad only in panties straddled a black man sprawled on his back. The woman held a knife in both hands, the butt pressed against her chest for leverage as she screamed furiously and tried to shove the blade into the man's face. The man gripped her wrists with both hands and struggled to shove the knife away.

"Police officers!" Ben shouted, raising his pistol. "Drop the knife!"

There was no reaction from either of them. The tip of the blade eased closer to one of the man's bulging eyeballs. I stepped forward and swiped my baton across the woman's hands, jettisoning the knife to the floor. She turned her screams of rage in my direction and lunged at me like a rabid lioness.

Suddenly I became overwhelmed by a clawing, kicking, spitting, screaming—not to mention naked—woman. Even after I locked arms with her, I could barely restrain her. Together we staggered back and fell over a chair.

As we rolled around on the floor, the smell of PCP was so strong my eyes began to water. Meanwhile, Ben's silhouette shadowboxed with that of the man, who didn't seem very grateful for our efforts to keep a knife out of his eye.

"Kill him, Babe!" he shouted. "Kill the pig!"

Then all at once the room filled with a dense cloud of Mace, and through my tears, I saw Ben take his opponent to the floor. At the same moment, I managed to get the crazy bitch in a scissors squeeze between my legs, her face flattened against the floor. Still she managed to scream, "White motherfucker, I'm going to kick your ass!" Thanks to the PCP, she wasn't feeling any pain.

I released the scissors grip long enough to jump on top of her and force her wrists to the floor. But before I could get the cuffs on, her arms began to rise as if she found 185 pounds of cop to be a warm-up bench press.

Ben was still rolling around on the ground with the guy.

"Bitch," the man called to his sweet darling, "I'm going to kill these mother-fuckers!"

I finally got an arm lock on the wildcat. I pinned her arm to the point that every ligament, muscle, and bone in her arm was as tight as piano wire. She didn't seem to notice at all. She kept struggling. Her body eventually informed her drugged-out mind that the fight was over. The handcuffs snapped on.

Ben just cuffed his playmate as well. He looked at me with sweat pouring down his cheeks. "Well," he said, "aren't drugs just wonderful?"

Backup units had just begun to arrive as Ben and I guided our two PCP-laced lovers through the living room. We reached the door when I spun around and glared down at the elderly couple on the couch.

"What's wrong with you people? Hasn't anyone told you it's your duty as citizens to report homicides in progress?"

They looked at the floor and said nothing.

"Blue," Ben said. "Take it easy. These old folks are too afraid to do anything. That's the way it is around here now."

"It seems like dumping a dead body onto the street in this neighborhood is just as easy as taking out the trash."

On the couch, the old couple stared at the floor and said nothing at all.

The next afternoon I went downtown for a routine traffic court appearance. Afterward, as I walked back to my car, I thought about that old couple on the sofa. What Ben said was true. The old frightened couple were helpless victims. Yet every time I saw the image of them staring at the television, rage billowed inside me. What had happened to decency, people's willingness to help one another? I was not indifferent to the environment and life around them. My heart saddened as I asked myself how people stopped caring for one another. How does one remove oneself from life?

Several days later, the doubts and questions surged within me, overtaking me physically this time. I was off duty and walking past a construction site pro-tected by a fence painted in a black-and-white checkerboard. The contrasting squares began to twitch in the corner of my eye and then to swirl. They merged into a gray blur that floated from the fence and rose directly in front of me. I stopped, swaying. The blur expanded to take in the entire world. I grabbed the fence as everything began to spin. And spin and spin and spin, a blur surrounding a black and widening abyss.

The next afternoon, I visited my doctor. I usually saw him maybe once every two years for a checkup. I had a far more established relationship with the emergency room doctors near my beat.

"The doctor is ready to see you," the receptionist said, and she led me into a big room with a picture window overlooking Mission Bay. I sat down and lost myself in the glitter of light on water.

"Hi there, Owen. I see it's been a while since your last visit."

I watched the doctor come in, face turned down over my chart. "Yeah, doc, how you doing?"

"Great." He dropped onto a chair opposite me. "So, what brings you here?"

I hesitated. "I think I'm losing my vision. Things will suddenly go blurry for a while, and yesterday I felt like I was going to black out."

He got out his torture kit and examined my eyes and ears. He took my blood pressure. Meanwhile, we chatted about general stuff at first, but soon he was asking questions.

"Owen, if I remember, you're a street cop, right? What's been going on with your job?"

I was hesitant to answer, but I finally began to talk. Without mentioning my rogue status, I told him about the hours I was putting in, the stresses and strains of the job, the death threats, and the complete lack of a personal life. Not until that moment, as I put it all into words, did I realize just how dismal my life actually sounded.

The doctor jotted a few more notes and then closed the file. "You like to sail, right?"

"Huh? Yeah, you bet. I did a little racing when I was younger."

"That's what I recall. You know what I suggest? I suggest you take a sailing adventure for a few months."

"What?"

"Or hike the Pacific Crest. Or tour Europe. Just take some time off—real time—and have fun."

"What do you mean? Why would I do that?"

He laughed. "Doesn't it mean anything to you that you don't even understand what I'm saying? Owen, I'm telling you to take some time off from the pressure cooker you work in. The blindness you're having, the dizziness, there's no physical reason for them. They're psychosomatic. Your job stress is getting to you."

"Take some time off. Have fun. That was it?" I asked. He smiled and nodded. I was speechless. How could the doctor, unquestionably a brilliant man with more than a decade of college and medical school who probably earned five times as much as I did—how could he be so sure?

I walked out of his office and stood in the sunlight. Unbelievable. Just walk away from my job for a few months. Relax. Take it easy. Your job is causing you to lose your sight. Impossible. My job was me. How could I walk away from myself? From the war I was fighting? Did a warrior stroll away from battle when things got difficult? Did a warrior turn his back on a tradition that had begun over forty years ago with the death of Blue's great uncle?

I glanced up and down the street. Everything looked clear. No blurriness. No dizziness. A beautiful day. Actually, a day. I was actually up at the same time as the sun. Maybe I would take a stroll. Not a jog but a stroll. Look at the tourists, some ordinary taxpaying human beings.

But not on the boardwalk today. Instead, I drove over to Mission Bay and pulled up to the guard kiosk of the San Diego Yacht Club. On the far side of the gate sprawled an exclusive country club-type setting bristling with masts and banners and wire stays. When the security guard stepped out of the kiosk, I showed him my badge. The guard issued me a guest pass and allowed me to go inside.

I parked my vehicle and walked down to the docks. The scent of ocean air was invigorating. The sun stood bright and hot in the sky. I walked to the end of one dock and sat down, dangling my shoes over the water. Amazingly, I didn't feel sleepy. I should have been in bed at the moment to prepare for another shift.

Later, on the way back to my truck, I passed the yacht club dock master's building. Posted outside was a bulletin board fluttering with notices and pictures of boats for sale. It reminded me of the board in the briefing room at work, so I paused to read a few of the messages. Nothing about car theft, murders, rapes. Most notices were requests for employment or services: crew hands asking for work on yachts, yachtsmen asking for crew hands heading for exotic ports. I smiled. What the hell. I'd leave a message. It would give me something to smile about while I was busting heads in a few hours.

Inside the office I found a note pad and pencil and wrote: "College-educated male, with years of sailing experience looking for a crew position. "Willing to travel to exotic ports in exchange for room and board. References upon request."

When I left the docks, I was smiling. I even momentarily thought that a break from my police routine might be good for me.

The next morning when I woke up, I found a message on my phone recorder. "Hi there, this is Bert. I got your number off the yacht club bulletin board. I plan to sail for the Marquesas Islands in a couple weeks, and I'd like to talk to you about the crew position."

I sat down in the nearest chair. I hadn't really expected anyone to call. Now what? Obviously, I couldn't go off sailing across the Pacific Ocean for God only knew how long. Still, I didn't want to be rude, so I picked up the phone and called the yacht club to leave a message for Bert.

"Tell him I'll come by the club tomorrow at nine in the morning to introduce myself and explain what's going on." I asked the club staff to see that he got the message.

I arrived at the yacht club at exactly 8:50 the following morning, freshly showered and dressed in shorts and a T-shirt. In the office I found the location of Bert's sailboat, *Eros*, berth B-14. I headed down the appropriate dock, filled with apprehension. Of course I was just nervous about telling the poor guy I wasn't going to be able to be a crew member on his boat. It wasn't as if I were really considering the job or anything.

When I arrived at B-14, I found myself looking at a beautiful thirty-five-foot cruising yacht, sloop-rigged, with a hull of fiberglass and wood. A high-class vessel with the word "*Eros*" painted in gold across her flat stern. As I approached the bow, I saw a balding middle-aged guy kneeling on the deck, doing some touch-up paintwork.

"Excuse me," I said from the dock. "Are you Bert?"

He stood and smiled. His teeth were very white and contrasted with his sun-tanned face. "I sure am."

"Hi, I'm Owen. I hope you got my phone message from yesterday."

"I did. Come on aboard, Owen."

I stepped onto the deck, and we shook hands. "Beautiful boat," I said.

He grinned as if I had complimented him on his favorite child. "She was handmade in Norway about ten years ago—not your typical fiberglass pop-out. Some of the best sailing vessels in the world came out of Europe in the last fifty years. It's getting to be a lost art. Price wise, old-world craftsmanship can no longer compete with the Hong Kong and Taiwanese builders."

"You know your boats, Bert."

He shrugged, but he was clearly pleased. "Europeans have been building ships true and tested in the North Atlantic Ocean for over a thousand years.

Makes me feel good about the little jaunt across the Pacific we've got planned. Speaking of which, how much sailing experience do you have?"

Now was a good time to tell him I wasn't going to be sailing with him after all. Instead, I told him about my sailing background, which consisted mostly of maneuvering small boats near the shorelines of Hawaii and California in years past.

"Nothing long-distance?" he said.

"Not like what you have in mind," I said, and I felt mysteriously disappointed.

He nodded. "Well, would you like to inspect the boat's interior?"

"Sure."

Below deck I met his wife, who was washing dishes in the galley. She looked to be a very homely Midwestern type. In fact, she was from Wisconsin. She had short brown hair and a wide smile. Her very light skin and heavy frame made her look the part of farm girl.

"Hi, I'm Linda, or as Bert says, the second mate of the *Eros*."

While the three of us sipped coffee at the galley table, I learned that Bert had retired from the construction business at the age of thirty-six. Linda may have been four years younger, but they both acted much older than their age. Linda met Bert in Hawaii a few years after finishing graduate work in anthropology at the University of Hawaii. Bert sold his business, and they both decided to take a few years off to do a South Pacific cruise. "What do you do for a job, Owen?" Linda asked.

I hesitated. "I'm a police officer with the city of San Diego."

"That must be pretty interesting," Bert said.

For a moment, I was actually too surprised to respond. I wasn't used to having strangers smile and show curiosity when I told them what I did for a living. "It has its moments," I said.

Bert and his wife exchanged a glance. "Owen," Bert said, "if we hired you for this cruise, how soon could you be ready to go?"

I won't be able to go at all, I thought, but what came out of my mouth was, "I could be ready within the next two weeks."

ESCAPE

Two weeks later, the *Eros* motored out of its berth in Mission Bay harbor at six o'clock in the evening. As we glided past the Mission Bay breakwater into the open sea, I hauled up the sails and Bert killed the motor. The thump of sailcloth swelling in the wind and the thrum of water splitting across the bow filled me with an overwhelming sense of relief, an exodus. Standing on the forward deck or bow, I looked toward the western horizon and wondered where this journey would take me.

I already knew what I had left behind for the next twelve months: my job, my police friends, and my pledge to fight crime. The captain understood remarkably well that I needed to get away from the streets for awhile.

"A yearlong cruise, eh?" he said. "Well, I can't give you an official leave of absence for that long, but I promise you'll be considered for rehire when you come back."

"Thank-you, sir," I said. "I will be back."

"Just make sure it's before twelve months are up." He peered at me over his bifocals. For a moment, I thought he might actually smile. "Hell," he said, "I wish I were going with you."

The SCAT team guys were just as gracious and, perhaps, a bit more drunk than usual during the big farewell party in my nearly empty apartment. Special close-knit teams usually turn their backs on a member who would quit, but I was not quitting. Everyone, including me, believed that I would be back in less than one year.

The week turned into one big blur of packing, storing, taking trips to the dump, and moving onto the boat with only a single duffel bag. We shoved off to docks by late afternoon and soon were under sail on a southwest heading.

I licked the taste of the ocean off my lips.

As the shoreline disappeared astern, Bert turned the wheel. We headed southwest toward our first intended stop, Ensenada on the Pacific coast of Baja California.

As night approached, I took the first watch, which basically meant manning the helm until six in the morning. Since I was still attuned to the hours of a night shift, this was a cakewalk for me. At sunset, the winds all but disappeared, and the ocean became smooth and flat. We could not be making more than two or three knots headway under the swollen stars. Every now and then, a fish left a phosphorescent streak in the water around me.

I thought about the SCAT team I had left working a few dozen miles to the east. Baby Huey, Nate, Mike. How would they do without me? Fine, no doubt. And what about the gangsters? How would they do without me? Probably even better.

We spent the next day in Ensenada, our last outpost of real civilization on the northern coast of Baja California. We cleared our paperwork for the remainder of the trip down the length of Mexico. Since bureaucracies work slowly everywhere, but especially in Mexico, we killed time ashore. The stop in Ensenada was a first for Bert and Linda, but I remembered it from numerous surfing trips in my youth, so I showed them around. Change was slow in Mexico. There was the harbor with its nearly lifeless fishing fleet, the cantinas, restaurants, and curio shops catering to gringos.

The next day we charted a course that would take us into the open sea before turning south again. We expected to lose sight of land for almost a week. It would be good practice for the transpacific leg of our journey yet to come.

Days passed. When I sat watch after dark, all was black except for our running lights, the stars streaming overhead, and the flash and glitter of fish in the water. During the day, the blue-green ocean blended into blue sky in every direction. I became aware of how insignificant we were in the watery palm of the Pacific.

As an open cockpit vessel, the *Eros* ensured that whoever was at the helm or working the sails was constantly exposed to the weather. It didn't take long before the results of this began to show up as sunburns and salt lines on all our faces, especially Bert's and mine. I also noticed that my appetite seemed to become bottomless. How could I get so hungry just hanging around on an open deck or at the helm? Maybe it was the fact that about all there was to do out there was eat, but I preferred to blame it on the influence of fresh salt air and cool water.

By day five, I felt quite comfortable on the open sea, and so did Bert. Linda acted as if she was enjoying the cruise, but her body language told a different story. I could tell she had never been much of an athlete or an outdoorsy person. For her, sailing out here was like being in a vast wilderness. She seemed to be okay in the current gentle seas and light winds, but I wondered how she would handle things if they got rough.

That night, I got a hint because the winds began to rise and the *Eros* climbed up and down steeper swells. In the morning, the sun floated on the horizon like a blood orange. Bert climbed out of the cabin and looked around.

"Red sky at morning," he said. "Sailor, take warning."

"What are you talking about?" I asked.

"It's an old sailor's saying. It means something is brewing out there."

"Have you mentioned it to Linda?" I asked.

"Not yet."

"I heard that," Linda cried from below. "This boat is smaller than our living room back home, you know. Secrets are hard to keep."

Bert smiled sheepishly. "Could get a little rough later, sweetheart, that's all."

"Well, I didn't expect it to be a picnic every inch of the way, boys."

Over the next twelve hours, the winds rose even more, swaying between twenty-five and thirty-five knots. The seas washed over the bow from one direction and then another. I retired below and tried to sleep, figuring I might need all my energy for the night shift. But just as I was dozing off in my bunk, the hatch flew open to show Bert's tense face.

"Owen, jump up here! We've lost our rudder!"

"What?" I leaped from my bunk and stood, thrusting my head and torso through the aft hatch.

Bert slapped the wheel with his hand and it spun freely—no resistance. "We're drifting sideways. We need to drop some mainsail and pull in the jib. I'll check the rudder linkage."

I scrambled onto the deck while Bert jumped down through my sleeping quarters to get to the little compartment that housed the engine and rudder linkage. In less than a minute I had the mainsail down and reefed to its lowest point. I rushed forward to drag down the forward sail and the jib, and then stuff it into a big bag lashed to the deck. Spray slapped me hard in the face, and the sea broke knee-deep around me.

As I was working my way back aft, I looked into the galley to see Linda storing things away. The boat was starting to really roll from side to side. She gave me a quick smile, but her face was pale.

Bert popped up through the aft hatch. "Owen, I think the steering linkage is broken."

"Can we fix it?"

"I don't know. I'll need some time."

We both stuck our heads into the bilge. Soon we decided that the broken fitting would need to be fabricated from scratch. There was no way to jury-rig it.

"Goddamn it," Bert said. "I didn't count on needing a machine shop on this trip." He rubbed his hair and looked at me. "There's a sea anchor in the forward cabin. Let's get it out and see if it will hold for the evening, then we can figure out a way to limp back to shore."

"Sounds like a plan," which made me realize I didn't personally have a plan at all out on the seas. I was just reacting to things. I didn't know if that was good or bad, only that it wasn't like me at all. From the forward hatch I pulled out a thirty-pound stuff bag marked "Sea Anchor." Bert came forward, pressing against the wind and waves that washed over the bow at a fairly steady rate. He reached into the bag.

"Tie this end off to the bow cleat there." I nodded, pulled out three or four feet of one-half inch rope called a "sheet" by sailors, and started knotting it around the bow cleat.

"Hold on!" Bert shouted, his voice rising in fear as a sound like thunder rose around me. I instantly grabbed the rail and hung on as the sea submerged the entire bow, plunging into the depths like a submarine, then the bow heaved into the air, and I realized I had somehow managed to hang onto both the *Eros* and the sea anchor bag.

"You okay, Owen?" Bert was on the cabin roof, drenched hair in his face, arms wrapped around the mast. "Quick, we got to get the anchor out before the next set rolls in."

He jumped down, yanked the bag from my hands and heaved it over the side. The boat, shoved backward by the wind, drifted as the sea anchor started to unfold beneath the water like an undersea parachute.

Several minutes passed before the anchor reached the end of its 100-foot tether and the line became taut. The *Eros*'s bow immediately turned straight into the wind and stayed there. Now, although the breakers continued to slam us up and down between peak and trough, at least they couldn't climb so boldly on board.

Bert grinned through a mask of water droplets. "Great! She's set and holding."

"Now what?" I said.

He shook his head. "About all we can do is get down below and wait it out until morning."

We hustled into the cabin and closed the hatch. Linda was talking on the CB radio. "This is the *Eros* calling any vessel in the vicinity of Cedros Island, over. *Eros* calling any vessel." She looked over at us, eyes wide. "Bert, no one's in the area."

Bert put an arm around her. "The sea anchor's out. We'll be okay. We'll just keep calling through the night."

Over coffee, Bert and I sat at the little fold-down table and looked at the charts. "The way I see it," I said, "we're 350 to 400 miles south of San Diego, and fifty or sixty miles off the Baja coast. Sound about right?"

Bert nodded. "This means we should be pretty darn close to the Cedros. That worries me. I'd hate to get blown into an island during the night."

"Let me get into some dry clothes," I said. "I'll go out and keep watch."

When I climbed out on deck, a steady rain was falling. I decided it didn't matter that I changed my clothes. The wind and waves hurled more water on me than a thunderstorm ever could.

Despite the chaos, there was even less to do than usual on this watch. The boat was drifting, so all I could do was try to keep water from sluicing down the buttoned collar of my rain gear while I watched to see if an island popped out of the darkness.

By the time the sun started to show itself through the early morning mist and fog, I was exhausted. Bert came out of the cabin with two steaming cups of coffee in his hands. "How'd it go?"

I took a cup gratefully. "I froze my balls off. About the only entertainment was trying to piss over the side without falling overboard."

He laughed and slapped my shoulder, and Linda stuck her head out to announce that breakfast was ready. I ate and, fifteen minutes later, lay in my berth wrapped tight in my sleeping bag. An hour passed before my shivering eased enough so that I could fall asleep.

I dreamed I was running after criminals I could neither see nor catch.

I woke at two in the afternoon. "A fishing boat picked up our distress call," Bert said as I popped out on deck. "It should reach us within the hour."

"Great!"

"Thank Linda. Who can resist a woman in distress? They're going to give us a tow into the Cedros Islands. The captain of the fishing boat said there's a village there that can fix just about anything that goes wrong on a boat."

Getting towed, rudderless, behind a rust bucket Mexican trawler was no treat. Bert worked to keep the *Eros* on a straight heading, but that proved almost impossible without a rudder. We basically inscribed an endless series of S curves all the way to Cedros.

There, the fishing boat released us about a hundred yards from the beach. Bert shouted to the captain, "Thanks! We'll meet you on shore!"

"Shore," Linda said from the cabin. "Now there's a word I like."

Cedros was a rough-looking, treeless island inhabited only by fishing people and their families. The little cove featured a small pier and a rocky shoreline littered with debris and old broken-down skiffs. As we rowed in on our rubber dinghy, the stench of decomposing fish grew to almost overwhelming proportions.

Still, the sensation and sound of the rubber bow grinding into the pebbles of the beach were welcome ones. I jumped out and hauled the raft firmly onto the beach, then looked around. The entire village, a line of ramshackle wooden huts, appeared to be built around the cove. The sun was going down, and the warm glow of kerosene lamps flickered in the windows. Clearly there was no electricity here.

We found the crew of the fishing boat that towed us in, sitting at a table outside what appeared to be a combination of a residence and a restaurant. Bert walked up and introduced us. The skipper of the fishing boat, Gus, appeared rough-skinned, large-framed, and unshaved for at least a week. Forty years at sea gave him the bearing of a pirate.

Bert and Linda sat down with him and began thanking him profusely for his help. He waved them off with a casual hand scarred by fishing lines and hooks. I eased down at the other end of the table with Gus's three crew hands, all Mexican nationals who spoke fairly good English, especially after a few beers and tequilas Bert bought for everybody.

When we left hours later, the drunken crew bid us a grudging farewell. Outside, the night was beautiful, the sky full of stars. The sounds of lapping water and stones shifting against the nearby shoreline and the smell of dead fish and salt air seemed a perfect end to an eventful day. I rowed the dinghy out to the *Eros*. In silence, Bert and Linda sat staring up at the stars.

In the morning, we returned to the village to find a welder. Fortunately, we didn't have to remove the rudder itself, just the steel pins that attached the steering linkage to the rudder. One sheered off and needed to be welded. We found a welder, and in my limited Spanish, I explained what we needed. He told us to come back in several hours. When we returned we found the part repaired and reinforced. We spent the rest of the afternoon repairing the rudder and making ready to get underway again for the following morning.

After finishing our preparations, I lay in my bunk and started reading. I had brought along a small library of books on history, philosophy, religion, and archaeology with me—these were stories of seekers and searchers of truth. Lying around and reading a book was a new experience for me. Until this moment, there never seemed much time in my life to be quiet and just contemplate. I was already learning that there was a lot of time for introspection on a small boat floating in the midst of the ocean.

By seven the next morning we charted our course, finished breakfast, and started motoring away from Cedros. The Mexican trawler was already gone.

Outside the cove, I hosted the mainsail and jib. It felt good to get underway again.

Nightfall found us surrounded once again by nothing but open ocean and darkness, and soon I was alone on deck with the wheel in my hands. This would be the regular pattern for the next few days and nights. I would steer the boat for two three-hour shifts during the day and resume the helm from 10:00 PM until 6:00 AM the following morning. Sitting on the deck alone at night gave me plenty of time to reflect on my life—something else I had not done much of before. Most of my life I believed in God, but never worshipped him in a church after seventh grade. My relationship with God was most blissful when riding waves as a young surfer. The ebb and flow of the sea had been my greatest and most consistent comforter during adolescence. The ocean had always been there for me. My life direction was never more uncertain than the present—even in the midst of the great sea.

These thoughts kept returning me to "What Winds," a poem by Frances Adams Moore:

What winds blow through the long night watch?
What stars fling fire abroad?
What waters shift beneath the sloop?
What speaks the night of God?
What silences renew the heart?
What image fills the mind?
What dreams, and hopes and fears, and loves?
O, winds of night be kind!

The poem reflected the questions that absorbed me on those long ocean nights: what am I running from, and where am I going? I didn't have the answers other than I'm sailing south by southwest to Magdalena Bay. For now, that would have to do.

Apart from the night of the storm, every late shift I spent at the helm of the *Eros* was the same as the one before: quiet, peaceful, disturbed by nothing but the rasp of the wind, the slap of the water, and the occasional splash of a fish passing beneath in darkness. Then, early in the morning on our fourth day out from Cedros, I noticed a bright cluster of lights on the far horizon. I stared at them. It was the first time I had seen any ship's lights at sea. The little constellation seemed to be growing rapidly as if the ship were heading directly toward us.

I tilted my head back to search for the *Eros*'s topmast light. There it was, gleaming thirty-three feet above the deck, with red and green bow lights and a white light on the stern. In theory, these markers would not only help an oncoming vessel spot us, but they would indicate our boat's size and orientation. According to international maritime convention, more maneuverable vessels are required to give way to less maneuverable vessels like sailboats. But first, we had to be seen, and our small navigational lights could be lost in the vast ocean darkness. But really, what were the odds that the only two vessels in a thousand square miles of open water would actually collide with each other?

Thirty minutes or so passed. Odds or no odds, it became increasingly clear that the oncoming vessel was on a direct course toward us. And she was a big vessel. I did some mental calculations. The *Eros* was easing along at three to five miles per hour. At that speed there was no way to accelerate or brake with any suddenness. Even maneuvering would take considerable time. Judging by how rapidly the oncoming vessel's running lights approached and rose into the sky, she was moving at a very rapid clip indeed.

I opened the galley hatch. "Bert, you better get up here."

He shot out of the forward berth. "What's happening?"

I pointed. The oncoming ship was lit up like a Las Vegas casino and was now close enough that I could see the giant winch and swaying nets characteristic of a fishing trawler. But unlike the boat that towed us to Cedros, this vessel was easily 200 feet in length.

"He's not changing course," I said. "We'd better get lit-up fast."

Bert was already dodging back into the galley. In rapid succession, all the interior and exterior lights snapped on. I kept an eye on the trawler. Estimating its exact course was difficult in the darkness, and so was calculating the best way to avoid a collision. It would be just as easy to turn directly in front of it as out of its path.

"Owen," Bert shouted, "start the engine!"

I did so and then turned the *Eros* away from the trawler as hard as I could. But the sailboat's motor was designed for casual, low-speed cruising. The trawler continued to gain on us like a guided missile.

"Oh, my God," Linda said. I hadn't noticed her come up on deck.

Despite the brilliant lighting on the trawler's deck and bridge, I saw no sailors or deckhands moving about. The *Eros* was now crawling along at her topmost speed of seven to eight miles per hour. The trawler lunged toward us at easily three times that pace.

I felt a moment of pure panic as the trawler loomed over us, and then sliced past the *Eros* at a distance less than one hundred feet. The name *Sea Bird* was painted on her bow. She appeared to be on automatic pilot, and no one stood at her helm. Probably no one on board would have noticed if the trawler's bow sliced the *Eros* in half.

The wake of the passing ship loomed out of the night and rocked us hard over, but within a minute the sea was calm again. The trawler's shining cluster of lights receded across the ocean.

"First, a big storm out of nowhere, and now we almost get run down by the only other ship on the ocean," Linda said. "Do you ever feel cursed?" She was trying to joke, but I heard a tremor in her voice.

"Think of it this way," I said. "We must have gotten the worst of it out of the way by now."

"Crap, this stuff is as thick as pea soup," Bert said in the morning when he opened the galley hatch.

"It came up a couple of hours ago," I said. Fog condensed all around the boat, including its helmsman, like dew. The *Eros* was barely making headway over a glassy sea, where visibility could be counted in yards.

Bert consulted a chart. "According to my calculations we should be approaching Magdalena Bay within the next couple of hours. The bay opening is only about one mile wide, so we'll have to keep a sharp lookout. Otherwise, we could run aground."

"Well, that's one thing we haven't tried yet," Linda said from behind him.

Bert returned to the galley to switch on the Fathometer. "We're in 180 meters of water."

"Then we must be coming up on land," I said. "I sure am looking forward to anchoring, so we can relax a little."

"I'm with you." Linda came out on deck to give me a cup of coffee and some company.

Bert stayed below, talking to himself and his sea charts. Then he raised his voice. "The way I got it figured, we should just about be there. You guys keep your eyes peeled up there!"

A half-hour later, the Fathometer read fifty meters, and a bed of kelp appeared through the fog. Then, to my relief, the fog began to dissipate and soon thinned into a morning mist that cut off visibility at no less than a mile. I spotted the tops of two mountain peaks rising above it.

Bert saw them too. "This is it! We're dead-centered on the opening to the bay."

"Good job, honey," Linda said.

We spent three days and nights anchored in Magdalena Bay, a desolate place with a rocky, uninhabited shoreline. While the shore may have been uninhabited by people, it was hardly lifeless. The air was filled with noisy seagulls. The clear waters teemed with bass and grouper. Armies of lobsters sat on rocky shelves even during daylight hours. Tide pools littered the ocean shore. In one tide pool, I discovered a stranded lobster as long as my arm. It took several minutes for me to wrestle him out of his refuge onto the sand and dispatch him with Bert's knife, but it was worth it. He provided us with fresh meat for the entire length of our stay.

The troubles encountered so far—the storm and the near miss by the trawler—now seemed like a distant memory. We left Magdalena Bay two days later, not without regret. Our next stop was to be the very tip of Cabo San Lucas, Baja California.

The inlet to the harbor of Cabo is guarded by a pair of what looked like enormous, prehistoric McDonald's arches rising from the blue of the ocean. As we came around them, the harbor itself swung into view. Cabo was huge but almost as barren, occupied by only a few boats moored off the beach. Village homes were clustered together near the water's edge.

"Wow," Linda said. "This is unbelievably beautiful."

The harbor was so deep the Fathometer did not register the ocean floor until we almost reached the beach. We dropped anchor less than fifty feet from the shore. The water was as clear as blown blue glass. Listening to the lap of tiny waves and the cry of seagulls, I decided that Cabo San Lucas was paradise.

We lowered the dinghy into the water and rowed ashore.

It took all of twenty minutes to complete our tour of the town, which consisted of one main street and a couple of side alleys. Beyond that was a vast desert—hot, dry, and sandy with no green vegetation anywhere.

I couldn't figure out how the villagers earned a living. Without commercial fishing boats in the harbor and nothing resembling farmland beyond the town, business seemed to consist of a few small stores and a couple of restaurants.

We returned to a lone beachside cantina with its palm-leaf roofing and whitewashed adobe walls. A rug served as a door. Pushing it aside, I was surprised to step into a beautiful little sport-fishing bar. With only a few windows and no signs of electricity, the place was full of light, thanks to the loosely thatched roof and several rectangular holes cut in the wall. The walls were decorated with photos of grinning men standing beside enormous marlin and sailfish dangling by their tails.

I gestured to the bartender. "*Cervezas, por favor, señor.*"

"Okay, man," he said, and within minutes three ice-cold beers stood at attention on the bar in front of us.

Linda hoisted the first bottle and said, "Sunny skies and smooth sailing!"

As I downed my beer, I noticed three salty-looking Americans sitting at the far end of the bar. One of them waved at us. "You guys just get in? Where you from?"

"Our last port was San Diego," Bert said, and we moved over to join our countrymen.

Bud and Millie appeared to be in their mid-thirties and looked like hippy dropouts. They told us they lived in a homebuilt forty-foot trimaran sailboat. Joe was in his mid-twenties, with shoulder-length brown hair and glasses. His hair was held back by a bandana. Judging by the things he said and how he said them, I could easily picture him in a wool sports coat and tweed slacks, puffing on a pipe as he carried his beat-up leather briefcase across the quad of some Ivy League campus. Like me, he was a crew hand.

The trimaran's crew dropped anchor in Cabo about a week earlier.

"How long do you plan to stay?" I asked.

Bud laughed. "We don't really have any plans. We just go with the flow." Millie and Joe smiled. Everyone seemed comfortable with the flow, so I smiled too and downed another beer.

By three o'clock, the place was crammed with several dozen people, mostly Spanish-speaking locals. Where they had all come from, I did not know, but they were thirsty. The stock available at the bar consisted of beer, tequila with salt, beer, tequila with lime, beer, and tequila with salt and lime—or beer. No one drank anything plain in Mexico, I noticed. The lime peels and drifts of salt on the floor seemed to be part of the decor, along with the strong smell of Mexican tobacco.

Late in the afternoon, Bert and Linda asked if I was ready to return to the *Eros*. I figured they could use some privacy, so I said, "You guys head on back. I'll hang here for the evening. I can find my way back when I need to."

Bert gave me a grateful wink and escorted his wife out the door. The cantina was full of smoke, flies, and boisterous chatter. With no television, music, or other distractions, all there was to do was share one another's dreams, stories, and aspirations.

The drinking continued late into the night. I left and swam back out to the *Eros*. The next morning, Bert and Linda decided to get underway. Although our one-day stay was pleasant, I personally felt a burning desire to continue the journey. Of course, part of this urge was pushed by the fact that I had promised the department I would be away for only a year, and a month had already gone by. It seemed as though I were traveling at warp speed, but to where? Not to Cabo San Lucas. That much I knew.

We were under way by dawn, heading into the rising sun toward the Mexican mainland across the Sea of Cortez.

On the third day of the crossing, I decided to try something new. The Sea of Cortez was known for its abundance of sea life. When I wasn't manning the helm, I spent time sitting on the bow, watching for dolphins, enormous manta rays, and man-sized sea turtles sunning themselves near the surface. Usually, when the *Eros* drew near a turtle, it would just dart away.

On that third morning, the sea seemed especially crowded with sea turtles. I watched one after another go by, and then I scrambled back to Bert. "I have an idea. See if you can cruise up close enough to one of these turtles for me to jump in and grab him."

Bert's eyebrows rose. "Hell, Owen, they're too big to eat. What are you going to do once you get one?"

"I don't know. Maybe just take him for a drive around the block."

"You're crazy. Let me know when you're ready."

It took a couple of hours before I saw a suitably large enough specimen sunning itself, its green-brown shell exposed like a miniature island. I hollered at Bert, and pointed, and he started letting off the sheets. The *Eros* slowed, and we came about ten feet from the turtle I dove into the water and onto the animal's back. Before he knew what was happening, I grabbed his huge shell just behind his neck. But I had barely grabbed the animal when it dove with such power my arm almost tore from its socket.

A pocket of boiling bubbles followed us down for a few seconds and then dissolved. The turtle's shell was slick with algae and hard to hold onto as the animal propelled us downward with a galloping rhythm. The temperature dropped fast even as the pressure on my eardrums increased to the point of agony. Then I remembered my free hand. Stretching it behind me, I found the trailing edge of the turtle's shell, grabbed it and pushed it down with all my strength. This pushed the animal's tail downward and pointed his head upward. A moment later, the animal was heading for the surface with the same urgency it had shown in the dive.

When we erupted into the air, I saw Bert and Linda gaping at me from the rail of the *Eros*.

"I got him!" I shouted just before plunging back into the depths.

That turtle dragged me around for two or three minutes before I tired him out enough that he stopped trying to sink me. After he surfaced, it was like riding a prehistoric Jet Ski. The turtle and I took a couple of laps around the *Eros*, where Bert and Linda stood laughing.

Finally, I let the animal go and watched him swoop into the depths and vanish. Then I swam back to the *Eros* and wearily hauled myself aboard.

"That," I gasped, "was harder than chasing down criminals."

We pulled into Mazatlán that afternoon. Despite being one of the largest ports on the Pacific Coast of Mexico, Mazatlán was basically a dirty seaside harbor town, thick with the stench of rotting fish and diesel fumes.

We anchored about a hundred yards off the beach.

"We're expected to go into the customs office here and clear our papers in order to continue our trip," Bert said. "Linda and I will take care of that. Owen, would you mind hanging out here to keep an eye on the *Eros*?"

"Not a problem," I said, although I was aching to get my feet back on land.

With nothing better to do, I sat on the deck in the sun, closed my eyes, and listened to the sounds around me—the never-ending seagull talk and the steady lapping of water against the hull. Suddenly I realized how lonely I was. Bert and Linda were terrific people and wonderful company, but a couple. They had each another—what did I have? Everything that once meant so much to me was gone. My wife and lover since high school, my job, my family and friends—all were stripped away from me. My worldly possessions reduced to a single backpack of books and clothing.

Tears began to slide down my face, salt into salt. With no one around, I spoke out loud, "Lord, if you can hear me, please give me the strength to go on. Please help me find my way."

The darkness behind my eyelids was like the ocean depths—endless, mysterious, and frightening. But then, a glimmer of light appeared in my mind's eye and slowly grew brighter. I imagined it must look the way the sun did to a creature deep in the sea as it rose into the warmth. The light grew more and more intense, consuming the darkness until there was nothing left—no shadows, no fear, no loneliness, no me.

When I opened my eyes, the sun was heading toward the horizon. Jesus, hours must have passed, I thought. Bert and Linda had not returned, but I didn't care. For the first time, I realized I was not alone on my journey. I was connected to a much greater force, and it was this force that would provide my life with purpose. What that purpose would be, exactly, I didn't yet know. But that didn't matter. What mattered was that I was filled with a sense of peace and tranquility I had never known before. Something wonderful was in the offing for me. I knew it. Something was waiting for me to find it, grasp it, and ride it into the unknown like a man clinging to the shell of a sea turtle.

HOT PURSUIT

Several days later, we dropped anchor in shallow water about a half mile off-shore from a village called San Blas. The harbor was little more than a cove with sandy beaches, the water too shallow to allow for the anchorage of large ships or commercial vessels. San Blas itself was a decent-sized village nestled at the water's edge with a dense jungle backdrop.

We rowed ashore and walked into town. The largest building was a Catholic church that dominated a square whose bustling open-air mercado appeared to be the center of trade and barter.

I was really taken by the place, which seemed stuck in a time from a hundred years back. Late that afternoon, when Bert and Linda said they were ready to head back to the *Eros* for the night, I said, "I think I'll just hang out here for a while."

"How will you get back to the boat?" Linda asked.

"I can always swim."

Bert took his wife's hand. "Take your time. We'll probably hang out around here for a day or two. Just make sure you get back to the boat within forty-eight hours, okay?"

"Done."

I wandered around, taking in the sights of the village, feeling like a visitor from the future. I wasn't sure what I was looking for, but I kept scanning the crowds for...something.

As the sky turned indigo, a young Mexican guy approached me. "Hey, man, are you an American?" he asked in English.

"Yeah, I am."

"What's your name?"

"Owen. What's your name?"

"I am Roberto." Sharks would have been envious of his toothy smile. "What are you doing in San Blas?"

"Just hanging out, looking for women." That was when I realized that was exactly what I was doing. I hadn't been with a woman in months, and my loneliness became a hunger gnawing at my center.

Roberto offered his teeth again. "All right, hombre, you have come to the right place!"

"Have I?" The truth was that the only women in San Blas—or so it seemed—were baby-laden Indians, most of whom were still in their early teens. And this was a very Catholic country and a backward-looking village. My chances of hooking up with an attractive young lady for the evening didn't look too promising.

Roberto seemed to read my mind. "Don' worry, man. We just walk around the plaza until we see some nice girls. Then we go up and introduce ourselves. That's it." His eyes shifted down to my wrist. "Hey, nice watch you got. That's great. The ladies will really like it."

I shrugged. The watch was an ordinary Timex, but I had noticed that in poorer countries, even a mediocre wristwatch was a status symbol. Still, I wasn't convinced of its power as a chick magnet. On top of that, Roberto was no Mexican Casanova, so he appeared to be banking on his newfound relationship with me to impress any eligible women we might run into. But what the hell! He was a local and knew his way around. I let him tag along with me.

We circled the plaza until sunset but without success in impressing the few eligible young women. Finally, I wandered toward an open-fronted cantina, Roberto tagging along like a lost puppy. Sitting outside where I could keep an eye on the plaza, I ordered several beers. When the waiter arrived with them, Roberto explained to him that he, Roberto, was my guest. I wasn't surprised and didn't even mind paying for his beer. His Spanish was better than mine.

On the other hand, I was beginning to understand that my new companion was more interested in my wristwatch and the free beer than in my quest to find female companionship. He talked a mile a minute, and I couldn't get him to shut up long enough to permit me to enjoy the circus-like setting before me.

San Blas clearly came alive on a summer evening. The number of people roaming the streets more than doubled since sunset, and many of them appeared to be single, childless women. I decided to get back onto the street and see if I could shake free of my host.

Roberto came right out with me. I stood on a street corner, enjoying the diminished heat and humidity, if not Roberto's ongoing monologue. Soon I saw a blonde, longhaired woman walking toward us. Like me, she was accompanied by a Mexican guy, although hers was expensively dressed and manicured, and he wasn't talking.

As they came closer, I stepped out and spoke in English, "Hi. I'm new in town and lost. Would you mind helping me?"

The woman smiled. "Sure." Her accent was plainly American. "I'm Judy from Seattle. Where are you from?"

"San Diego. I'm Owen."

Her escort stepped forward, his hand outstretched. He spoke in English with an upper-class Spaniard accent. "My name is Marco. Where are you going, Owen?"

Before I could answer, Roberto jumped in. "Hello, I am Roberto. My friend Owen and I have been painting the town tonight."

I said, "Actually, I'm looking for a good cantina, good beer, and good music. Does such a place exist in San Blas?"

Marco smiled. I noticed that his wristwatch was at least four times as expensive as mine. "Actually, that's where we're going right now, if you would like to join us."

"Of course!" Roberto cried.

As we all walked down the crowded sidewalk, I stole sidelong glances at Judy. She was dressed like a California beach girl in a tropical wraparound skirt and a tank top that looked to be concealing the headlamps of a 1957 Chevrolet. While she was built a bit on the heavy side, her smile stirred something warm inside me.

A block off the main street we came upon a large cantina where a Mexican band played to a packed house of locals. Judy and I were the only gringos in the place, and, as far as I could see, Judy was the only woman. All eyes turned on us as we sat at the only empty table.

Marco said, "What do you have to drink?"

"I'll have a beer," I said.

"Me also," Roberto said.

"Me, too," Judy said.

"Do you like a shooter with it?"

We all did.

With the first rounds served, Marco turned to Judy. "Would you like to dance?"

She smiled. "I love to dance."

She and Marco shared the dance floor to themselves—although as far as I was concerned, Judy was alone out there. The music was fast and she moved like an Egyptian belly dancer. I also noticed that, rather than looking at Macro, she kept staring across the room at me. Heat rushed into my head.

"Wow, Owen," Roberto said in my ear, "she likes you man. She wants you. I can tell. She's hot for you, man." I couldn't shut him up. All I wanted to do was watch Judy laugh and move to the tunes of a broken-down, five-piece Mexican band.

After the song, she and Marco returned to the table. Judy took a sip of her drink when the band started their next number, a slow tune. I jumped to my feet.

"Judy, shall we?"

She smiled and took my hand, and I walked her to the dance floor. I held her close. "Mind if I ask you what your relationship with Marco is?" I murmured.

"I just met him this evening. I'm staying at a little village just outside San Blas. He's a nice guy, and he offered to take me out tonight. That's all."

"Good," I said.

For the next four hours, Marco and I took turns dancing with Judy in what amounted to an undeclared war. Each of us gave our best moves on the dance floor and whispered sweet words into Judy's ear. While Marco plainly had more money, better clothes, and a better wristwatch than I—and the band seemed to play more slow songs when it was his turn on the dance floor—I was certain that Judy would see through all that superficial stuff and take me home at evening's end.

At one o'clock, the crowd finally began to thin. I suspected most of the patrons stayed so late just to watch the dance contest between Mexico and California. At the moment, Marco and Judy were on the floor. She was at least three inches taller than he, so he needed to tilt his head back to whisper in her ear. She smiled and laughed. They returned to the table. "Marco and I are leaving," Judy said.

My jaw sagged. Marco shook hands with Roberto and me, smiled into my eyes in a good-natured way and escorted Judy out the door. I dropped my head to the table and tried to ignore Roberto's drunken nattering. What the hell was I going to do now? I lived on a boat that was anchored a half a mile off the beach. I was too drunk to swim, and I had spent all my money on the bar tab. Unless my good buddy Roberto offered me a place to crash for the night, I would have to sleep on the beach.

Roberto had apparently come to recognize the depth of my defeat as well as the emptiness of my wallet. He shot to his feet. "Mr. Owen, thank-you. I have to leave now."

A moment later I was alone, except for a bartender stacking chairs.

I sat there. And sat there. Staring into my empty bottle of beer. Then I felt a kiss on my cheek. I looked up. Judy grinned down at me.

"Wha—what the hell you doing back here?" I asked, lurching to my feet.

"When I got to Marco's hotel room, he no sooner closed the door than he started trying to rip my clothes off. I ran out, and here I am."

"So I'm what, second choice?"

She put a hand on my shoulder. "I was with Marco first this evening. I didn't feel right about just dumping him for someone else."

"Oh."

"So, do you hate me, or can we go back to your place?"

I considered that. "How good a swimmer are you?"

"What do you mean?"

"My place is anchored about a half a mile off the beach."

She laughed. "Well, unfortunately my place is about fifteen miles outside of town, and the only way to get to it is by bus, and the buses stopped running around midnight."

I sat back in my chair. I couldn't believe the irony of it. I had won the evening's prize after all, but I had nowhere to take her.

Judy sat and took my hand. "I've got an idea. I've got a girlfriend who lives in a dormitory here in town, but she's gone for the weekend with her boy-friend. We could go there. At least there's an empty bed."

At that point I would have accompanied Judy anywhere. I got back to my feet.

"There's something else I should probably tell you about the place we're going," she said.

"What?"

"The dormitory?" Her smile lit up the room. "It's for girls only."

The dormitory was a large, single-story building that looked like a cross between a hotel and a private residence.

"How are we going to get into this place?" I whispered. The whole town seemed to have gone to bed.

"Well, the building's not usually locked, but they do have a midnight cur-few, so we'll have to be quiet."

"Great."

We walked around to the back and passed through a gate into a large courtyard. At a darkened doorway, Judy turned and whispered. "Okay, this is it. She has about eight roommates, so we'll have to be real quiet."

"Eight?" I had to clamp my lips to keep from laughing. "You mean, there are eight other girls in the same room? Where we're going?"

Somehow Judy managed to look serious. "They should be asleep by now."

The door opened, and we stepped into a dark room that appeared to be about thirty feet square. Scattered around it I counted eight single beds, one of which was empty.

Judy took my hand and led me to the bed, and we sat quietly. Within four feet on both sides was a sleeping woman. Judy removed her sandals, stood, and, without ceremony, dropped her skirt to the floor. I stared at her, dumbfounded. I couldn't believe we were going to do it right here in a fully loaded women's dormitory. But I didn't care, either.

I barely got my sandals off before she was unbuttoning my jeans and ripping off my T-shirt. A moment later, I was on the bed—on my back—straddled by Judy. We started kissing, and I felt her lovely breasts pressing against my chest. She began to grind against me. A moment later, she grabbed my cock and pushed it into her hot center with a sigh.

I began to thrust, slowly at first. She moaned. Her eyes closed. Clearly, she was in a world apart from this small room full of sleeping women. I pushed faster, harder. After all these months, the sensation was beyond description.

Judy quickened both the pace and the intensity of her moaning. I placed one hand gently over her mouth to try to muffle the sound. She didn't open her eyes, but she didn't miss a beat in the rhythm of her hips either. And she just got louder.

I glanced left and right. On each side a girl lay on her side, facing us, eyes closed. Dear Jesus, don't let these girls wake now.

The bedsprings started to ring out rhythmically. Judy was a big girl, and she was clearly flying on autopilot now. I tried to pull her down to my face to quiet her, but she was reaching climax and nothing could contain her. Some of the other women began to stir. A sound of disgust came from across the room, but there was nothing I could do now. At this point, I was just along for the ride.

The girl on the bed to my right blurted, "This is disgusting!"

Without missing a stroke, Judy said in a matter-of-fact voice: "Shut up, bitch."

Then she started her climax. I had never heard anything like it before, but I forgot about our audience as I came too, both of us flying off into a separate place. My orgasm lasted for an eternity, every last drop of my essence releasing within her. Then she dropped and lay on top of me, quivering. Our blended sweat ran down my sides to the sheets.

The afterglow was short-lived, however. A chorus rose around us, "I can't believe it." "It's disgusting." "Who are these people?"

"Judy," I whispered, "we've got to get out of here. The sun will be up soon, and I don't want to face these ladies in broad daylight."

Back in the main square, the vendors began setting up for the day under a sky just beginning to brighten. Judy breezed through the mercado, picking up a few bags of fruit and some sweet pastries. She then led me to the road out of town.

"Where are we going?" I asked.

"To my place."

Soon we were standing at a bus stop alongside a dirt road, watching a broken-down bus pull up. The bus driver greeted Judy with a grin as we walked to the backseats and sat down. Judy opened the bag of fruit.

The bus drove along a bumpy dirt road for about half an hour, or the time that it took to consume two bananas and a mango. Then Judy grabbed my hand and led me off the bus and onto a path descending into the most lush undergrowth I had seen in Mexico so far. In a few minutes, we came to a lagoon decorated by a tiny village of circular buildings called yalapas constructed only of wood and palm leaves.

Judy led me to one of the shacks. Inside was a dirt floor roughly twelve feet across beneath a high, conical ceiling. A king-sized hammock stretched across the room.

Before I knew it, Judy had disrobed and was standing before me without a stitch of clothing on her lush body. She was even more beautiful in daylight. I took my clothes off and she pulled me down to the hammock. She smiled and closed her eyes, and this time I made love to her without restraint or self-consciousness.

Judy was a schoolteacher from Washington, who had come to San Blas for the summer. The yalapa rent was twenty dollars a week, and the bus ride to and from town each day came to about twenty-five cents.

As we lay on the hammock, I told her about my past, including my life as a cop and the breakup of my marriage. She listened without comment, and afterward, we made love again. By late afternoon, we had exchanged addresses and mailing information.

"Judy," I said, "I'm not sure if Bert and Linda are planning to ship out tomorrow or what. If we're still here, I'll be back to see you."

"Why don't we plan to meet in the village plaza at, say, around noon?"

I kissed her. "If we haven't lifted anchor, I'll be there."

She walked me back to the bus stop and gave me some Mexican pesos and a long, lasting kiss. A few minutes later, I was back on the bus, staring out the rear window and waving good-bye.

When I got back to the beach, I found the dinghy parked on the beach, which meant Bert and Linda were in town, so I swam back to the *Eros* after all. It was twilight when I awakened from a long nap to the sound of Bert and Linda climbing aboard.

I got up to greet them. "Hey, guys, you have a nice afternoon?"

Linda looked at me sidelong. "I notice you didn't make it back last night. Did you have a good time?"

"Just fine." While helping unload supplies, I gave them a slightly edited version of the events of the past twenty-four hours.

"Well, I'm glad you had fun," Bert said, "because we're heading out early tomorrow morning. Two days in San Blas and we've seen everything."

My shoulders slumped. I wouldn't be able to tell Judy good-bye. That had sure been a quick romance, the fastest one I had ever experienced. And the most intense. I wondered if I would ever have another one like it.

We sailed southward, stopping briefly at Puerto Vallarta before heading on toward the famous resort town of Acapulco. "That's our last stop before we head for the Marquesas Islands," Bert said. "I want to make good time getting down there, because…" He glanced around, obviously seeing if Linda was in earshot. He then continued in a lower voice, "Hurricane season begins in just over a week."

"Hurricane season? I thought that was a few months off yet."

"That's because everything is backward this far south. In the states, it's summer, but down here it's the start of the rainy season. That's when most of the bad weather starts. Don't worry. We'll beat it out of here."

We reached Acapulco early in the morning. The approach was beautiful. The large, well-sheltered harbor was lined with sailboats and yachts everywhere. Hotels crowded the waterfront, with mansions overlooking them from the hillsides. The wealth on display was unlike anything I had witnessed so far in Mexico.

We made our way to a yacht club where we tied the *Eros* at a guest mooring less than one hundred feet off the club dock. The yacht club was within walking distance of downtown Acapulco. We checked in at the club and strolled down the main street toward the center of town. I said, "Why don't you guys look around for a while? I'm going to take off by myself." I figured they should have all the alone time they could get before we took off for several cramped months at sea.

Linda gave me a wink. "I hope you won't mind swimming back to the boat if we return before you?"

"A mild punishment for staying out late, but I can take it," I said jokingly.

Six blocks down the street, I came upon a cantina stuffed with English speakers sitting at tables out on the sidewalk. One of them spotted me and waved me over to his group of a half dozen gringos. "Hey, where you from?"

I grabbed an empty chair and pulled it up. "California, how about yourselves?"

"We're Canadians. My name's Dennis. Dennis Storch." He introduced the rest of the bunch, and I gave them my first name. The whole thing was so casual that they might have been a bunch of my buddies just waiting for me to show up.

"Where you off to tonight, Owen?" Dennis asked.

"Hell, I don't know. I'm just finding my way around town."

Steve, a long-haired guy sitting tilted back with his feet up on the table, raised his beer and cried, "Here, here, another round for our brother from California!"

"How long have you guys been down here?" I asked.

"Most of us left Canada this past winter to come down south like snowbirds," Dennis said. "We've been having such a great time we haven't been able to leave. What about you? How long ago did you leave San Diego?"

I hid my dismay. Had I mentioned San Diego?

"Hey, guys, look!" Dennis said. "We've got more company." I turned and saw a couple of uniformed Mexican police officers standing at the corner of the building, glaring at us, undoubtedly because the group was surrounded by so many empty beer bottles and because they were the loudest patrons of the cantina.

Steve leaned toward me and winked. "Watch this." Raising his voice, he called to the policemen, "Hey, señores, come here."

The two officers walked toward the table. Both small men, no more than five and a half feet tall, and rather portly. Neither had shaved in three or four days. Their pastel blue uniforms were ill-fitting and dirty, with sweat stains running from armpit to waist. Their gun belts might have been taken off Poncho Villa, although most of the bullet loops were empty. Nothing was polished or shined.

Dennis got the waiter's attention and soon a cold beer sat before each officer. "A toast!" called Dennis. "To our fine friends in uniform who live by the gun and die by the gun." He wasn't looking at the officers, but rather at me. Everyone, including the officers, laughed. I thought it was clear the cops didn't understand a word said. They understood free beer, though.

I was bothered. His toast had a more ominous meaning to me. Maybe this was the Canadian's way of just teasing cops, but the whole situation made me uncomfortable. In fact, my cop senses, blessedly dormant since I left San Diego, were beginning to resonate. I saw no reason to disobey them just because I was not on the job.

I pushed my glass away. "Well, guys, the heat and humidity have got me longing for the nice cool waters of the bay, so…nice meeting you."

There was a momentary silence at the table. One of the policemen asked: "*Qué?*"

Steve took his feet off the table. "How long you planning to be in Acapulco, Owen?" It became apparent they wanted more details than I was willing to provide. I knew better than to reveal the truth.

"Oh…about two weeks. You can bet I'll be back to hang with you guys during the next few weeks. In fact, I might be sitting out the entire hurricane season right here in Acapulco." I knew better than to tell them anything truthful.

"Great. We'll see you again. We're here at this time every day, so stop by whenever you want."

"I'll do that," I said, and gave the group a nod. As I walked away, I knew I would never drop by again.

I wandered deeper into the city and found myself looking over my shoulder constantly as if expecting to find myself pursued by a grinning Canadian or decrepit Mexican police officer. Ridiculous. Still, I meandered in and out of quite a few empty backstreets before I felt comfortable I was alone.

As I walked, I realized that the yachts in the harbor and the big villas up in the hills did not reveal the whole truth. Like most other coastal Mexican towns, Acapulco was essentially a few blocks of tourist window dressing surrounded by a Third-World slum. Crumbling buildings and makeshift shacks crowded narrow streets just a block or two from the city center.

Raising my gaze to the jungle-draped hills looming above me, I decided to try something new. I hiked to a lofty ridge and just relaxed for a couple of hours watching over the city. At sunset I strolled back into town via the back door in a part of the city tourists would seldom visit willingly. Walking down the slope toward the harbor, I deliberately stuck to back streets to avoid tourists, especially Canadians.

At the bottom of the hill on a particularly gloomy street, a Mexican guy sidled up beside me. "Hey, mister, you want some good dope? It's the best—Acapulco Gold."

This was almost too corny to believe. The guy persisted and would not take no for an answer. After a few blocks of pestering, I finally stopped. "Show it to me," I said.

He reached under his serape and surprisingly pulled out what looked to be a small shopping bag and handed it to me. I opened it up and reached inside and sifted some of the contents through my fingers. I pulled some out and raised it to my nose. No question it was unrefined, fresh-cut marijuana. While momentarily examining the contents, I had not noticed the Mexican cautiously backing up. Standing in the darkening street, crumbling brick buildings rose all around me, leaving a narrow band of purple sky overhead. A couple of pigeons flapped from one side of it to the other. I heard more pigeons stirring in hidden places. What the hell am I doing? I suddenly thought. An ex-cop pretending to be on an undercover dope-scoring mission? Am I insane?

As if conjured up by the thought, two men appeared on the street ahead of me. They didn't move at a typical Mexican *mañana* pace. In fact, they angled toward me fast. My cop radar instantly started flashing. To my right was a narrow alley. Casually, I turned toward it, dropped the bag, and bolted.

Behind me, voices shouted, "*Alto, Policía!*"

Shit!

Not halting and not even slowing, I glanced over my shoulder to observe two men in full pursuit with drawn pistols less than one hundred feet behind me. Shit, shit!

Gunshots rang out. I spotted another cross alley and scrambled into it, skidding on damp cobblestones and found myself in a long, even narrower alley. The far end was blocked by a six-foot adobe wall.

I kept running, head down, arms pumping. I heard more gunfire. Christ, it sounded like three or four guns now, and chunks of plaster flew off the wall in front of me. I gathered myself and vaulted the wall like an Olympic athlete, landing in the rear courtyard of a residence. Without breaking stride, I vaulted a second gate and found myself on another deserted street. From all sides came shouting voices. No more police whistles, no more commands to stop. Something was very wrong here. I was not being pursued—I was being…hunted.

The game had turned violently. The mighty hunter was now being hunted. Who was chasing me, and why were they trying to kill me?

I continued running down the hill, and the streets around me became a blur. The pounding of my heart grew louder than the shouts that pursued me. I ran and ran, jumping over parked cars, fences, and walls. Finally, I bolted onto a street I recognized—a busy street with bright lights, traffic, and tourists. Lovely, lovely tourists. I slowed to a normal walking speed and joined the mob, letting it sweep me toward the harbor.

Luckily, Bert and Linda were still gone when I got back to the yacht club. Although the *Eros* dinghy was parked at the club dock, I eased into the night waters and swam to the boat. I climbed over the *Eros*'s stern, dripping warm salty water all over the deck. I retired immediately to my bunk to think about what had just happened. On the one hand, it was humiliating to picture myself running away from cops, fleeing up and down alleys and over fences—the great Officer Blue, running from the police just like all the criminals I had pursued through the streets of San Diego.

On the other hand, I had clearly been set up. Being arrested with that huge bag of pot would have made me eligible for prosecution as a dealer, not just a user, which in turn meant the cops could have demanded a much bigger bribe to let me go. Or was something else more ominous being played out here? Mexican officials don't shoot tourists. Could this have been a rogue cop hit team?

The more I thought about it, the more sinister the situation became. Whoever these guys were, they unloaded at least a dozen rounds. The other thing that didn't make sense was the first two guys I spotted walking toward me were not wearing uniforms. I heard the word "*policía*," but I never saw a uniform, a badge. My thoughts kept drifting back to those Canadians. I had not told them that I was from San Diego. How had they known? Who had told them? And why? At the time, I had had the feeling they were waiting at that cantina for me.

I was pretty sure no one had followed me to the hillside during the late afternoon, but how hard would it have been for someone to tail me?

But that still brought up the biggest question of all—why me?

"Drew, when I get out again, I'll find you. And when I do, I'll shoot you in the back and watch you die begging for mercy."

Tommy Johnson's threat came to mind. Maybe he had been released from jail? And there were the others, too—a whole crew of hardcore gangbangers eager to earn money and prestige by killing me. But did any gang leaders in San

Diego really have a long enough reach to touch me here in Acapulco? It was a stupid question. After all, how did half the dope sold in San Diego get into the city, except by working its way up through Mexico? Contacts, contacts everywhere.

I could actually hear my heart beating in the darkness. The yacht club no longer seemed such a safe haven. Of course, capturing or killing an American in some back alley with only pigeons as witnesses was one thing—doing it among the sailboats in the Acapulco harbor was another.

I was still thinking about that when Bert and Linda got back, moving quietly, trying not to wake me. I recognized the noises they were making.

Still, I fell asleep only after the sun came up.

RED MORNING

When I crawled out of my berth in the morning, Bert was bent over a chart on the kitchen table. "Listen," he said, "I talked to the harbormaster at the club yesterday, and he advised us to leave immediately."

"Sounds good to me," I said.

"Really? I thought you'd been enjoying yourself."

"Oh, I have...but there are too many Canadians around here."

"Huh?"

"Nothing. I thought you wanted to stay a couple of days."

He glanced around and lowered his voice. "Turns out I was wrong about when hurricane season starts. It's earlier than I thought—around the first of June."

"But...today's the third."

"Exactly. That's why we did all our shopping yesterday." The sly look turned to a grin, eyes brightening in his suntanned face. "We're ready to roll."

"Great! Show me the route," I said.

He traced his finger along a straight line, more or less a west-southwest direction for more than two thousand miles to a tiny pinprick of land. The Marquesas are part of the South Sea island chain generally referred to as Polynesia. They are the exposed peaks of a range of underwater mountains.

"Linda was an anthropology major specializing in South Pacific Islanders," Bert said, "so she really wants to spend some time with the natives there. I figure we'll stay in the Marquesas a week and then sail on to the Tuamotu Archipelago, French Polynesia, the Society Islands, Samoa, Tonga, Fiji, New Caledonia, and then to our final destination in New Zealand. That's where we'll spend the winter."

I gazed at the great blank space that lay between Mexico and that first tiny dot of land. "How long do you estimate until we get to New Zealand?"

"I figure about six months under sail should do it."

My grin cracked the skin of my sun-baked lips. "Let the adventure begin!"

A few minutes later, we were motoring out of the bay. This was it. Looking over my shoulder, I bid farewell to the beautiful resort city beloved by millions of people and the contract killers who might be searching a cold trail leading to the water's edge. Then I turned my back to the land and gazed westward, where my future lay. Happiness rushed over me. My joy was caused, in part, by what I was leaving behind. But far more important was what I was heading toward—a future of unknown, unexplored possibility.

The Pacific was so calm we had to motor several miles off the coast before raising the sails. Bert returned below with Linda while I sat at the helm, keeping us on an easy west-southwest heading. Behind us, the coastline sank into haze and then vanished entirely. The *Eros* tacked across a blue backdrop that, at some indeterminate distance in all directions, became the sky. The thought that this would be my living environment for the next half year filled me with awe.

"Owen" Linda called, "you coming down for breakfast?"

We sailed on our new heading for the next five days, and every day the wind grew stronger and steadier, shoving us at a good clip over long, muscular swells. The *Eros* charged onto each wave and then leaped over the top to look for her next conquest. At this rate we would shave at least a couple of weeks off our transpacific time.

But in the art of sailing, there's a fine line between optimal conditions and conditions being too strong, between the boat attacking the swells and being trampled by them. By the end of the fifth day, we had crossed that line. The *Eros* shot along as fast as she could go, but at the price of being constantly keeled over at a thirty- or forty-degree angle—too steep to make sitting around below decks comfortable. And the swells grew ever taller, so we met each one with a staggering thump followed by a fan of blinding spray.

At sun down the fifth day, its light seemed to extinguish much quicker than usual. Typically, I would sleep at that hour, resting for my night shift, but on this occasion I happened to be on deck. I gazed west just in time to see the sun drop behind a black wall—a wall that stretched both north and south as far as I could see. Then a bucketful of spray hit me in the face, and twilight settled over the ocean. I wasn't sure that I had seen anything out there at all.

That night, I pulled my windbreaker on before going up to start my shift. Even warm ocean water hurts when it sprays into your face all night long.

"Weather's still picking up," Bert told me as I took over the wheel. "It usually lets off a bit at sunset, but tonight it's just gotten worse."

I looked up at a star-filled sky. I had to raise my voice above the hum of the wind in the rigging. "I might have seen some ugly-looking clouds ahead of us earlier. I'm not sure. Have you heard anything on the radio?"

He shook his head. "It's been malfunctioning ever since we left Acapulco. Don't tell Linda." He hesitated. "What kind of clouds did you say you saw? Remember what the port captain said?"

"You think we are heading into a hurricane?"

"I don't know, but definitely some rough weather."

Linda shouted cheerfully up the companionway: "Owen, I made a jug of coffee for you."

"Linda, you're a doll." I ran down, grabbed a Thermos and some snacks, and then returned to the helm. "Bert, odds are this is just a squall or summer storm we're coming up on, but no matter what, we'll be safer farther out at sea than closer to shore. I'll do my best to make good distance tonight. I suggest you get below and relax with your first mate."

He turned the wheel over and flexed his fingers. "Okay, see you in the morning. Remember, don't go for any long walks. And no uninvited guests or parties while we're away."

"You got it, Skipper."

He dropped into the galley and shut the doors.

Alone, I situated myself for a long night. The wheel felt as stiff as steel in my hands. The *Eros* crashed ahead, taking on wave after wave and throwing back spray that hit my face like the snapping mane of a running horse.

I pulled my windbreaker hood over my head and knotted it tight.

By 2:00 AM, an hour at which the wind usually dozes, I could barely hang onto the wheel. The *Eros* flew along at twelve to fifteen knots, which would have been terrific if the boat were rated for that speed. As it was, I kept listening for something to snap. Still, I didn't have much choice but to let her run. With the sails all up, the only way to slow the boat was to let off tension on the boom, to maintain just enough momentum to plow through the waves that were now more than fifteen feet high.

As daybreak approached, the weather did not let up. Looking behind me, I watched the sun rise in a blood-colored smear. "Red sky at morning," I said, "sailor take warning." Then I looked west, and my breath stopped. I hadn't imagined that low black wall yesterday. It was still there, only much taller, looming over the ocean ahead of us.

Just then Bert opened the galley hatch, and when he saw where I was looking, his face blanched. "Ah, man, that can't be a hurricane. Can it? I mean, we couldn't possibly be unlucky enough to catch the very first hurricane of the year...could we?"

I licked salt water off my lips. "Well, we should probably plan things that way."

"Christ, Linda is going to freak out."

"I guess you'd better talk to her and get her prepared for some rock-and-roll."

"I'm not looking forward to turning the boat around in these conditions, either."

I shook my head. "I still think our best bet is to keep going. It's like flying a glider—the rougher the air, the more distance you want between you and the ground. If this is a hurricane, we don't want it pushing us back into the coast."

"What a reassuring idea."

Even as I watched, the wall of clouds began to arch overhead into a roof. I felt like we were sailing into the jaws of hell. Still, I managed to make my voice light.

"I'm going to do a quick walk around the boat to check the rigging and then go below for a little shut-eye before my watch. Can you handle it for the next four hours?"

"Yeah, go ahead."

I hooked a safety line from my vest into the rigging, then climbed onto the deck, and made my way up to the bow and back. Along the way I inspected every fitting and cable for fraying or looseness. I was satisfied now more than ever that the *Eros* was a well-constructed craft. Still, when I returned to the cockpit, I said, "I think we better drop the jib and replace it with our smallest sheet. And we might consider reefing down the mainsail. Better to do it now than wait until the winds are blowing fifty miles per hour."

"Jesus. All right, let me get Linda on deck, so I can help you out." Bert hollered into the galley, "Linda, can you come topside?"

The look in his wife's eyes was that of a small child expecting to be spanked. Bert gave her a smile and put her hands on the wheel.

"Just keep her pointed on this course, not quite into the wind, just enough to keep some forward movement. We're going to drop the jib."

Bert clipped on his safety harness and we both moved up to the bow. As Bert released tension on the jib sheets, I grabbed the jib itself and pulled it in as fast as I could. It slapped at me like a creature just wrestled out of the ocean and eager to return. As we fought, the bow hit a particularly big swell and I found myself knocked to my knees with water gushing around my waist. I hung on, desperately stuffing loose coils of rope under my body and pulling down the jib until finally Bert worked his way up to me and helped haul in the remains.

At last we stuffed the jib into its bag, opened the forward storage compartment and jammed it in. Then we pulled out a smaller bag containing the undersized storm jib. After we secured the jib sheet to one of the eyelets in the storm jib, Bert went back to the cockpit and started pulling on the loose end of the sheet. As it came taut, the jib flew up from my arms and inflated with a crack like a gunshot.

I moved back to the stern where Linda was drenched but hanging onto the wheel as though her life depended on it—which it did.

"Okay, Linda," I said. "Bring her straight into the wind now. We're going to partially drop the mainsail."

"Are you sure you want to do that?" Linda asked.

Bert hollered back. "In strong conditions, a fully extended sail can be blown to pieces or snap the mast off. Reefing just means reducing the sail's surface area so it catches less wind. Owen's right. We better do it now."

Bert and I lowered the mainsail, which also thrashed me thoroughly as I tried to hold its folds against the extended boom. Finally, Bert and I fastened the sail to its lowest reefing points, small holes that allow you to tie rope through the sail and tighten it to the boom. By the time we finished I was exhausted, but at least the mainsail was now reduced by two-thirds and ready for the increasing winds.

Bert relieved Linda at the helm, and for a moment we all sat there in the cockpit, glistening with spray as the wind howled and water washed over the decking around us. This was about as ready as we could make the *Eros* for a storm. We could only hope it would be enough.

I stretched my arms over my head and yawned. "Well, guys, have room service wake me if you need me. I'm off to catch a few winks." My attempt to make light of the situation failed. I could see the fear on my friends' faces, especially Linda's, as I crawled down into my bunk.

Although I was soaking wet, I covered myself with my sleeping bag and tried to fall asleep. It seemed an impossible goal. I felt every lunge and slam as the *Eros* climbed a wave, dropped down the back side to crash into the face of the next wave, and then rise again. Even down here the wind howled.

But within minutes I was asleep.

"Owen, can you get up?"

I opened my eyes to a gray, sickly light and Bert's face. His expression told me all I needed to know.

When I opened the hatch, it was as if someone turned a high-pressure water hose directly on me. The waves passing now grew twice their original height, like giants marching at a quick pace through gray gloom.

"Christ, Owen," Bert gasped, "if this isn't a big fucking hurricane we're going into, I don't know what it is."

I used the calm, soothing tone of voice I used to reserve for victims of violent crime. "Why don't you go ahead and get below with Linda and take a little break?"

Without a word he stumbled into the galley and shut the hatch.

I looked at my watch—two in the afternoon, not that you could tell by the dark gloom around me. I figured the winds were now blowing fifty to sixty miles per hour. Swells thundered over the *Eros*'s deck—one after the other, each time burying the boat in water several feet deep. I knotted a safety line around my waist and clipped it to the cockpit railing, hoping that would be enough.

As I rode the bronco, I imagined Bert and Linda down below. Bert would be his calmest, reassuring self, hiding his own worry. Linda would be fighting the terrified realization that she feared most from the beginning of our journey. As time passed, fear and doubt would have a debilitating effect on them both, especially since there was nothing for them to do right now but hold on to each other and get thrown around like BBs in a matchbox.

The seas kept growing until I could have sworn they matched the height of *our* mast. The sloop leaped like a ski jumper over each crest and then soared in breathless freefall for a second before flopping down on the backside. Each time this happened, I became temporarily airborne in the cockpit. But I hung on, and the sailing continued.

Just before nightfall, the reefed mainsail exploded into rags. Instantly, our steering was compromised and so was our headway into the waves. From here on, the situation could only worsen.

I jumped to the hatch and opened it a crack. "Bert, get up here quick."

A minute later, he came out in his foul weather jacket and shut the hatch behind him. "What the hell happened?"

"The mainsail just blew out! We need to take it all the way down, now!"

"Get the engine started so we can keep her pointed into the wind," Bert shouted. Then he hollered, "Linda, we need you on deck!"

Linda was reluctant to come out and take the wheel again, but she recognized the seriousness of the situation and did it anyway. Bert and I made our way to the mast and began grabbing torn sheets and pulling down the sail. This was no easy task, with water rushing knee-deep over the top deck every ten to fifteen seconds and the boat lurching unpredictably at the mercy of the waves.

Whipped by torn sailcloth, Bert and I managed to haul in what was left of the sail and lash it to the boom.

I shouted, "We have to take down the jib, too! Go release the line. I'll bring the jib down and stuff it in the bag."

When Bert released the tension on the sheet, the jib engulfed my body like a huge jellyfish. I dropped to my knees and began pulling and stuffing fabric and sheets close to my huddled body, gathering everything away from the wind so I could get it into the bag. Bert came up to help me, and we slid back and forth over the deck as waves smashed over us. Finally we got the bag stowed and managed to crawl back to the cockpit.

Linda was shaking all over, her legs planted in almost a yard of standing water. "You guys get below," I said. "I'll take her from here."

"You sure?" Bert asked.

I nodded and cut my gaze at Linda. He nodded back and led her below.

With only the engine to drive the *Eros* forward, her speed eased back. But at the same time both the wind and the swells continued to build. Now, each freefall down the backside of a wave seemed to last for minutes and threatened to throw me out to the end of my lifeline. I knew that if I fell over the side, Bert and Linda would never know I was gone. When I got the chance, I slid a rope over my shoulders and tied the ends to cleats on either side of the cockpit, anchoring myself more firmly.

I reminded myself that I'd sailed in rough weather before and always survived. All I needed to do was relax and hang on tight.

And, of course, hope that the repair on the rudder held up.

The arrival of night was signaled only by the fact that the sky darkened to something indistinct and lightless, like a black void. The mountainous waves still just visible, though, rising as high as two and three-story buildings and pouring tons of ocean over the *Eros* every few minutes. Each time the *Eros* rose over the crest of a sea I throttled the engine down to keep the boat from racing even faster into the trough. Then, at just the right time, I poured on the power to drive the *Eros* safely up the next wall of water.

Higher, bigger, blacker. The wind blew at eighty or ninety miles per hour now according to our wind meter attached to the top of the mast. Each wave that broke over the *Eros* drove the boat's deck completely under water. When this happened I held my breath while the sound of wind vanished in a world of violent churning foam. Then my head would pop above the surface again. How long could this possibly continue?

Hour after hour, toppling crested waves consumed the *Eros* under tons of churning water. The yacht would rise like a whale to breathe life again through the backside of the wave, surfing the water in the giant wave's trough followed by the next toppling wave. The rhythm of submersion was constant and unwavering. Above the water, the hail of pelting rain swept across my face with the intensity of hailstones. I hoped that the little engine would hold on, pushing us into seas that sought only to push us under into a roiling black abyss. The wind howled through the rigging like a siren.

Back in San Diego, every night became a blur full of small, intense battles. Creep up on a felon, break into a sprint, bring down the prey, and subdue it. A burst of energy, a flood of adrenaline—then it was over. A bit of a rest, and then repeat.

This was different. There was no rest. Every muscle was at full power every second. The adrenaline demands did not abate. And conditions grew steadily, inexorably worse. Soon each oncoming breaker hit me with such force that it drove most of the breath out of me, leaving me sagging limp underwater until the *Eros* could fight her way back to the surface. It held me down longer and longer each time.

Eventually there was no doubt that if I remained on deck much longer, I would drown.

Then, the biggest wave yet found the *Eros*.

I didn't see it coming. One moment I was blinking spray out of my eyes, and the next I was underwater, trapped in the churning chaos. I could not gasp for air. All I could do was hold on as the boat swung and jerked, utterly at the mercy of the sea. Finally, she resurfaced, but the foam was so deep that I pushed it away from my face just to inhale.

That did it. I lashed down the wheel, untied myself from the deck cleats, removed the safety line and turned off the engine. Instantly the *Eros* was adrift. I rushed to the hatch and vaulted down into the galley, shutting the hatch just before the next wave crashed over the *Eros* and turned her broadside to the storm.

I braced myself and shouted, "Bert, Linda, can you hear me?"

Bert came out from the forward berth. "What happened? Did the engine quit?" He braced himself in the doorframe as the *Eros* rolled hard to starboard.

I was thrown against the galley bench, then the bulkhead, and then dropped down to the floor where I braced my back against the lower cabinets.

"I couldn't hold up out there any longer," I shouted. "We're adrift now."

"Adrift?"

"The waves were drowning me." I felt my lips part in a wolfish grin. "Well, you've always said this boat was the best ever built for its size, Bert. We're about to put her to the test."

Bert returned to Linda in the forward berth. I could hear him talking to her, trying to reassure her. Meanwhile, I lay flat on the galley floor, arms and legs extended, bracing myself for the next hit. With no forward momentum of her own, the *Eros* was completely at the mercy of the storm, which turned her sideways and proceeded to slam its fist onto her deck and shoved her onto her side.

Over and over and over again.

Looking out the windows was like looking into the porthole of a front-loading washing machine.

It didn't seem possible, but with every minute, the storm grew stronger. Dishes and pans flew out of the cabinets and crashed around me like pebbles in a rock polisher. On top of that, I gradually became aware that I was lying in about six inches of water. That was interesting. As I recalled, there was at least six feet of space between the bottom of the keel and the floor where I was lying. This area, the bilge, was where excess onboard water was supposed to go. So if the bilge was full, that meant…let's see…that meant the boat had taken on almost seven feet of water and was slowly sinking.

I thought about that for a moment. Then in an interval when the boat momentarily righted herself, I rolled onto my knees and pulled up a section of the galley floor. Sure enough, the bilge was flooded.

Christ, I thought, we're sinking.

There's nothing like the thought of death to clear your mind. If I didn't get some of this deadweight out of the boat, the ocean would soon get a good grip on the top half of the *Eros* and rip it free.

Lying on my belly, I groped around in the bilge until I felt the handle of the built-in pump. It was a manual mechanism. With one shoulder partially submerged and my face turned to the side to keep it out of the water, I braced myself against rollovers and began to work the handle.

The *Eros* staggered through the storm throughout the night, her long mast flailing into the water as sky became sea and back again. I hung on and pumped until I couldn't feel my arm anymore and then kept on pumping. The water receded to the galley floor, then farther—a foot or two down into the bilge. At least that was my guess. The problem was that every time the *Eros* fell on her side, bilge water gushed all over the galley. Paper plates and foam cups drifted around me like mocking reminders of what floating was supposed to mean. I didn't call for help, though. It seemed to me that it was my job to keep the *Eros* afloat and Bert's job to keep his wife secure.

Daybreak, when it came, was barely noticeable. I lay on the floor, barely conscious, cold, soaked, and shaking all over. Pumping until I could no longer move. My bare feet and hands, wet for two days now, looked like giant pale raisins.

Yet the *Eros* was still afloat. I didn't see how. Each time she was struck by a wave she shuddered so hard she seemed about to explode, and Linda screamed at the top of her lungs from the forward berth. To me it sounded like the *Eros* was screaming.

Finally, it happened. I could pump no more. My arm simply stopped working. It was over. I rolled onto my back and lay there, staring at the deck head above me. The shuddering, the rolling back and forth, the water pouring over my body, the siren-like howl of hundred mile-per-hour winds. It all seemed to fade away. I lay there braced against the bulkhead, waiting for nature to do her worst.

But bit by bit, the howl and scream of the storm faded away. Water continued to rush back and forth over me the same as before, but I didn't feel it. Like the *Eros*, I was adrift, but my inner sea was calm and warm, a place where I was mentally at rest.

Then I became aware of a different sound. Not the howl of the wind or the thunder of waves or the sobbing of Linda. Something else. A slow, rhythmic thumping, quite distinctive. Footsteps. Slow and measured, crossing the deck above me. Even though that was impossible.

I lay there, listening. The footsteps started on the bow and moved toward the stern, paused, then returned forward again. Then back. Then forward. Back. Forward. Taking their time. Not hurried, not unsteady, not concerned. Patient.

"I know who you are," I said.

The footsteps halted directly above me.

"You're the Angel of Death," I said.

The wind made the faintest sighing sound like a breath exhaled in another room. Then I heard a voice, strong and resonant in the darkness. "Yes." My panic heightened. I was momentarily speechless, and then my mind shot back.

"Have you come to take me?"

"Yes."

I would have never imagined it happening this way. Getting shot on the job, stabbed during a brawl on the street, struck by a passing car—all these common incidents seemed to promise me a death in action on the streets. But not this, this powerlessness, this exhausted resignation. There seemed to be no way for a warrior to die. I was about to go down for the final count, without even swinging.

"Come to me," said the voice.

I fought long. I fought hard. And I fought nobly. When death comes under those circumstances, a warrior neither snivels nor crawls. I was afraid of death. And though I lived my life without fear, my entire being was consumed by the fear of dying at that moment.

I sat up, braced my hands on the bulkheads, and rose to my feet. Even the rolling and pitching of the *Eros* seemed distant and unimportant now. I made my way to the hatch like a zombie and stood at the base of the ladder to the deck.

"Come to me," called the voice.

I placed my hand on the hatch handle and took a deep breath. Then, with all the strength left in my body, I slammed the hatch open.

She stood before me, the Angel of Death, disguised as a great black bird. A thick ebony cloak covered with indigo feathers. Her face was black, with the blackest eyes I had ever looked into. But these eyes were not placed directly to the side of its face like most birds. Both eyes were directly in front of its face peering directly into me, into my soul. My mind was gripped by the startling image as curtains of raging water swirled and a horrid piercing sound of wind, like the melody of a dirge, played in the background.

"It is time," I said. It wasn't a question.

I stared deep into her eyes. It was like looking into infinite blackness. Then I heard a resounding, "Yes."

For the first time in my life I realized I was about to cross over the threshold of death, not fighting, but resigned to surrender my being with dignity. What other choice was there, I thought.

"What makes you think you have a choice? Death and destiny are one. The only choice you have is to accept your destiny."

I stared at her, trying to understand. There was a long pause. I was in a timeless state. The storm raged in near silence beyond the Angel. All I heard was the gentle rustling of the feathers on her cloak. Then she nodded.

"I shall take you. Yes, I shall take you…but not now."

At that moment I realized that by totally surrendering to my fear of dying, a part of my life was reborn. My destiny was not to die. For the first time in a long while, I was given hope. I shut the hatch and dropped to the floor.

The wind screamed through the halyards. The *Eros* shuddered as she pitched onto her side with each broadside wave, the heave and crash as she rose and dropped. I lay in the belly of the boat, waiting out the rest of the storm, no longer concerned about what would happen. I went beyond the fear of dying and returned. I closed the hatch on the Angel of Death but not to my destiny.

As I lay there, my body was completely exhausted, but my mind was at peace.

The wind began to diminish by mid-afternoon, and the skies grew somewhat lighter. Bert stumbled out of the forward berth, his face green.

"Is it over?"

I turned back onto my belly and was pumping out the bilge again. Without breaking rhythm I looked up. "Hurricanes have two sides, Bert. I think we're entering the eye right now. This leaves the other side to go through."

"Oh...shit."

"We have a little time before then, though. We should check the rigging and deck and secure everything as much as we can," I said.

Bert looked at me without expression.

"Don't worry," I said. "We're not going to die. Not in this storm, anyway."

He didn't seem to hear me. Standing with his limbs braced in the doorway, he watched me pull and push the pump handle. "How long have you been doing that?"

"Pretty much all night."

"You mean—" And suddenly his voice was a shout in a quiet world. The wind dropped to zero as abruptly as if someone turned a switch.

Bert looked at the main hatch and licked his lips. "Okay, let's see if anything out there is still intact."

High above the *Eros* hung a gray, hazy sky filled with dim pearlescent light. On all sides rose the black wall, now forming an enormous barrel with us in the bottom.

Although the wind stopped, the sea was a churning mess. Bert and I fastened our safety lines moments before a mountainous swell toppled over the deck, submerging us for a good minute. But when we surfaced, we saw the unbelievable good news: the halyards and rigging were all intact, and most importantly, the mast still stood straight and true.

"You were right," I said to Bert. "This is the best-built boat around."

We scrambled back into the belly of the *Eros* before the next mountain of water avalanched down on us. Bert searched for something around his charting desk, but everything was either scattered around the main salon or soaking wet, or both.

Somehow he managed to find a weather book and turned the page on hurricanes. "Oh shit, Owen. It says here that the second half of the hurricane is the worst. Oh, my God...." He glanced at the forward cabin.

I put my hand on his arm. "Bert, don't worry. I'm telling you we'll make it. I'm manning the bilge pump, so the *Eros* will keep afloat. We'll just ride this out. The best thing you can do is to get back to Linda and hold her."

"Yeah, you're right. Okay, I'll get back to Linda."

"I'll see you on the other side of the storm."

He looked into my eyes for a moment, seeming about to say something, then just nodded, and climbed back into the forward berth. I could tell he was carrying the weight of two lives on his back.

As for me, I felt renewed and full of life. I felt that I could carry both their lives if necessary. I was beyond the reach of exhaustion and pain. I was the heart of the *Eros*, to stop pumping now would mean death. My life was spared so that I could keep the *Eros* afloat and for other reasons not yet known.

True to the word of Bert's book on hurricanes, the second half came upon us with the wrath of a savage beast. Within minutes the wind speed increased from mild to a 110 miles per hour. Once again we were in the clutches of darkness and the shrilling scream of the *Eros*'s halyards. I realized that my encounter with the Angel of Death did not guarantee my immortality. It gave me the understanding that the only power that death holds over us is fear. By surrendering that, I had released the grip that fear once held over my heart and mind. Now my duty was to live, even if only for the next moment, without fear and with honor and dignity.

The wailing winds continued to rise. The boat shuddered and rolled, sometimes beyond ninety degrees to more than a hundred. Sometimes I looked up and saw forks and knives on the ceiling of the *Eros*. Then, as the boat came back to an upright position, these things would fall all about me. My body ached, but I knew I couldn't stop pumping.

In the front berth, Linda's occasional screams grew less frequent. I doubted she was less afraid, though. She simply had surrendered to exhaustion.

The storm lasted another full day and night before it began to dissipate.

At sunrise, I made my way to the aft cabin. Below was the engine room. Not a room really, just a space large enough to allow my upper torso to hang down over the engine. It was fortunate that this area was separate from the main bilge. While it was wet inside, it seemed to be the least affected part of the boat.

I checked the engine fluids, determined that everything was good to go, and returned topside to start the motor. It fired on the second attempt. Immediately, I turned the *Eros* into the wind, and the boat resumed her previous pattern of climbing, freefall and crashing. It seemed almost comforting now.

Bert came up and looked around. "I can't believe it. It looks like it's clearing. We made it!"

"How's Linda?" I asked.

His smile faded. "She's hanging in there," he said, and went back below.

He relieved me at midmorning, and I dropped into the galley to see if there was anything to eat. Everything in a bag or box was soaked, so I opened a can of tuna and ate it with my fingers. Then I stumbled back into my cabin and pulled a wet sleeping bag over my cold and shivering body. Within seconds I was asleep.

"Owen, it's time for your watch."

What a funny thing for the Angel of Death to say, I thought, looking into her unblinking black eyes.

"Come on, Owen, it's time to get up."

I opened my eyes and saw Linda, holding a cup through the hatch to my cabin. Behind her, the sky was dark, but the smell of freshly brewed coffee got me sitting upright in a hurry. I grabbed the mug and took my first sip of anything warm in four days. "Wow, that's good. What time is it?"

"About eight o'clock." Despite the dark rings around her eyes, Linda looked almost relaxed.

When I got up on deck, Bert and Linda were sitting together in the cockpit, Bert with one hand on the wheel and Linda with her arm around Bert's waist. I smiled at them and then glanced at the compass. "What—where are you heading?"

"We're heading back," Bert said.

"What do you mean—back to Mexico?"

"Yes, back to Mexico."

"But why not continue to our original destination?"

"Are you kidding, Owen? We lost our mainsail and we don't have a replacement with us."

"But we have some extra jibs. Let's just haul them up. We can do it. It's not a problem."

He shook his head. "No. Linda and I have decided we have to go back to Mexico. We can have some sails made there and continue across the Pacific after hurricane season. To attempt it now without a mainsail would be foolhardy."

My heart sank. Of course, it was their right to decide where we sailed, but I knew we were finished with hurricanes now, and the *Eros* could cross the Pacific on only jib sails. Going back would be like…surrendering to defeat. But I could see from the look in both their eyes that they discussed the matter and that the decision was already made.

Traveling under power at night and sailing during the day, we reached Puerto Vallarta on the afternoon of the fifth day after the storm. It was amazing to be moored inside the harbor, to hear the sounds of cars and commerce. The water was motionless, the breeze soft and gentle. The aromas of land, of sand and jungle, while not new, seemed more potent than ever before.

But I wanted to stay here. I wanted to stay with the *Eros*.

Bert and Linda returned early in the evening, loaded with supplies. When I saw the quantity of bags in the dinghy I was relieved. There was plenty here for a sustained voyage.

Then Bert said, "Tomorrow Linda and I are flying back to San Diego."

"What?"

"We're going to have two mainsails made along with some other supplies we'll need to finish our transpacific trip."

"Okay. How long you plan on being gone?"

"It shouldn't take more than a couple of weeks."

Linda made a fresh, hot dinner that evening, and laughed a couple of times. The three of us sat out on the deck, ate, and relaxed for the first time in almost two weeks.

The next day I rowed Bert and Linda ashore and saw them into a cab, then headed downtown. It was siesta time. The streets were all but deserted, so I found a napping spot on the beach. The sand felt soft, the sun warm, and the sounds of the sea gentle. My thoughts drifted back to the Angel of Death, or the great black bird…was it an exhausted hallucination? Its physical reality didn't matter. The impact and meaning of the encounter were all that mattered. It struck me deeply and defied all reason or explanation.

Yet, lying there in the warm sunshine, I tried to rationalize the change in me. The overwhelming conclusion of the encounter made me realize that as a warrior on the streets of life, fear dominated my life. In childhood, it was the fear of losing the game. In manhood, it was fear of losing my life. In relationships, it was the fear of losing love. But the Angel, coming to me in the hurricane winds and rains while I was absolutely certain that I would drown, showed me my greatest fear—the fear of dying. And in surrendering to that fear, I began a new chapter in my life.

I sat up and looked around.

Time for a beer.

A FOUR-LETTER WORD

About a week after my patrons flew back to San Diego, I headed to the market to buy some fresh fruit and vegetables when a young American woman stepped out of nowhere and started talking to me. She introduced herself as Delores. Delores from New York City.

"What are you doing down here, Owen?" she asked, walking along with me. She was a small woman with beautiful curves and moved with the strength and agility of a dancer. She wore jeans and a cropped crew-top shirt that exposed her tummy. It was muscular, a solid foundation upon which her chest stood out almost disproportionately.

I tried not to stare. "Just passing through. I live on a sailboat. What about you?"

"I'm here with some friends for a couple of weeks, just having fun and hanging out." She brushed back a sheath of black hair that hung in long curls to the middle of her back. Her eyes were dark and her complexion a Mediterranean olive.

"How did you find your way to this marketplace?" I asked. "Most Americans never see this part of town."

"Oh, one of the guys we're visiting lives a few blocks away. I came down to pick up some limes. We're having a party. If you want to join us, you'd be welcome."

"You know what?" I said. "I think a party is exactly what I'm ready for."

We walked to a big two-story house that overlooked the entire village. Delores pushed open a heavy, hand-carved door and led me into the sounds of music and conversation. Someone shouted, "Hey, the nurse is back with the medicine!"

The host walked up and introduced himself as Bruce. He was in his mid-thirties, a bit on the hippie side and had a loose, lingering handshake.

"Delores," he said, "I'll take the fruits, which is about all I seem to attract, and you take the guy. How's that?"

"Just the way I planned it," she said.

At nightfall, the party moved to a nearby club. I could hear the music well before we got there. Obviously, the nightlife in Puerto Vallarta had no defined legal noise limit.

The bar was nearly packed, but the waiter escorted us to a large table. Delores dragged me onto the dance floor the moment the drinks were ordered.

She didn't just move like a dancer—she danced like a dancer. Swaying here, shaking there, and looking into my eyes. I swallowed and tried to think about things that would keep me from getting an erection right here in front of everyone. It wasn't easy.

We barely sat back at the table when Delores leaned over and whispered in my ear, "Owen, can we leave?"

I swallowed and nodded. Nobody seemed to notice as we walked away.

Bruce's house was quiet as I followed Delores up the stairs to her bedroom. She walked to the bed, turned, and started taking off her clothes. I watched, unable to move or speak. When she was naked, she pulled me close and unbuttoned my shorts. Before they reached the floor, I flung my shirt against the wall, and we fell into bed.

Under the sheets, Delores was as passionate and sure of what she wanted as she was on the dance floor. She shoved me into her like an addict sliding a needle into her arm. Her hips thrust to the rhythms of a woman totally given to the moment. The bed bounced with such force it should have activated the seismographs in Pasadena, California. When she came, her expression was of more intense relief than I had ever seen before. When I came a moment later, it felt as if my whole being got lost in her.

We woke at about eight in the morning, kissed, and climbed into the shower together. She soaped me down and I did the same for her. She spent an inordinate amount of time cleaning my genitals. After she rinsed the soap off, she dropped down to her knees. Afterward, I could hardly stand. Delores, on the other hand, was wired and ready to go.

I wobbled out of the shower, got dressed, and collapsed on the bed. I was starting to wonder if I wasn't some kind of love slave, taken hostage by a woman whose only mission was to make love to me until I was immobile. I lay there smiling. Whatever she was willing to dish out, I was determined to take.

We spent the afternoon in the sun and the sea. This woman loved the water, loved the sand, and most of all loved to play.

Later we returned to her place and found Bruce sitting and painting on the balcony. It was a landscape, and it was beautiful. I watched him work while Delores went to the kitchen.

"I would love to paint you, Owen," Bruce suddenly said.

"Really? Why?"

He looked back at me with a critical, analytical look. "I don't know. It's something about you. I'm not sure I can explain it."

"Well, I'm not sure just how long I'll be around. But I don't see why not. I've never been painted before."

He smiled. "I paint what I see, and I see beauty all around me here in this Mexican paradise."

"How long do you plan on being here, Bruce?"

"Until my money runs out. Then it's back to New York City."

"Where he can show off his beautiful tan and still not get a boyfriend," Delores said as she came back into the room.

Bruce laughed and continued his painting.

"You hungry, Owen?" Delores asked. "I could fix up something in the kitchen if you'll promise me dessert later."

My legs got weak again. "It's a deal."

Watching her make dinner wasn't much different from watching her dance. Every movement, every gesture was designed to turn me on. Every moment with her seemed to be erotic. By the time she was ready to serve the food, I was aroused to the point that I needed to adjust my shorts just to walk out to the living room. Delores noticed, of course, and smiled with such delight that I was embarrassed.

She called Bruce to the table, but he was so involved in his painting that Delores and I were already fifteen minutes into the meal before he joined us.

"It smells delicious, Delores. You could make a tire taste like a gourmet meal."

"I agree," I said. "I'm going for seconds."

"I hope I get seconds of dessert," Delores said. I felt my face heat up, but Bruce was a gentleman and acted as if he heard nothing.

After dinner, Bruce lit a joint. He passed it to Delores, who pulled on it like it was going to be her last hit. She then handed it to me. I wondered if it was Acapulco Gold as I drew in the acrid smoke.

The joint passed by three or four times, after which everything suddenly seemed funny. Finally, Bruce interrupted the laughter to announce he was going out. "Have a good time, folks. I'm going back to the dance floor." He paused at the door. "Delores, try not to beat him up too badly. I do want to paint him."

The door had no sooner closed than Delores reached inside my shorts and grabbed me. Then she removed her panties and bra and straddled me. She rode me like a little cowgirl, gripping my forearms, her head and shoulders thrown back. I could barely hang onto her.

We came together as if it were the first time for both of us, and she fell on top of me. Our bodies were soaking wet. I held her against me and felt our hearts pounding together.

The next morning when I woke, Delores was already in the kitchen making breakfast. I walked in wearing shorts and a T-shirt to find two of her friends, Cathy and Leslie, sitting at the table. The girls both looked at me and smiled at one another.

"Hi, Owen," Delores said. "We were just...having some coffee."

Cathy, a pretty blonde in her mid-twenties, said, "Care to join us?"

"Sure." I pulled up a chair and sat down. "Say, you two ladies are nurses. Maybe you can help me. These past couple of days I've been experiencing wobbling and buckling of the knees, and I was wondering...."

"Vitamin E," Leslie said. "Better start loading up on it."

"And lots of water," Cathy said. "Replace those precious bodily fluids."

We all laughed. Apparently the mentality of nurses wasn't much different from that of cops. Of course, each group was, in its own way, paid to deal with trauma and suffering. Each worked around the clock when normal people were sleeping or celebrating holidays with their families. Each wore uniforms as a symbol of the trade.

The women questioned me about my sailing adventure. For once, nobody seemed baffled by my desire to explore unknown parts of the world...and myself.

Delores announced, "Owen's going to take me on a sailboat ride this afternoon."

This was a surprise to me, but it sounded like a good plan.

I raised anchor and hoisted the mainsail, thinking that this would be a fine day for Bert and Linda to come back. I could imagine their panic to find the *Eros* gone.

After we got under sail, Delores removed her bikini top and lay back in the cockpit seat with her long dark hair flowing over the stern in the wind. I looked at her in amazement. She was like a wild horse with an unbreakable spirit. Still, despite the love and respect I felt for her as she sat there so blissfully, I knew that she was just one step on a journey that was only beginning. Soon she would be back in New York, and I would once again be out on the open sea.

At midday, we dropped anchor back at our original mooring spot. Delores seductively climbed below, found the forward berth and jumped into Bert and Linda's double bed. I followed and within minutes began to realize that being on the water only heightened Delores's passion. Her hunger for satisfaction was almost insatiable.

When I mounted her, her moaning grew louder and louder. I teased her with long, deep strokes, and she responded with screams that amplified as I picked up the pace. "Owen, I'm coming!" she shouted and then let out a continuous scream of delight.

We were sprawled on the sheets recovering when I heard voices speaking Spanish somewhere out over the water. They got louder fast, and suddenly something banged against the hull of the *Eros*.

My first thought was that they found me again. I sat up, grabbed my bathing suit, and pulled it on awkwardly as I hopped to the galley hatch. I opened it and peered straight into the bore of an M-16 rifle in the hands of a Mexican soldier.

I froze. Behind the *Eros* floated a couple of small military launches, each carrying about a dozen armed soldiers.

"Stand, hombre!" the soldier shouted in my face.

I raised my hands and slowly walked up on deck. At least ten more rifles pointed at me now. The soldiers gestured for me to lie down on the deck. I quickly complied. They were all speaking Spanish so fast I couldn't understand what they were saying, but I recognized the meaning of the heavy boot that planted itself in the center of my back.

I tried to twist my head around. "Do you speak English, *señor*? I am an American. Does anyone speak English?"

One of the other soldiers stepped forward. "What is your name, *señor*?"

"Owen, I'm a crew hand on this boat."

"And what are you doing here now?"

Lying on the deck with a boot on my spine, you idiot. "Nothing. Why?"

"We heard screams."

I started laughing. I couldn't contain myself.

"What is so funny, *señor*?" The English-speaking soldier knelt by my face. He didn't look amused.

"I wasn't hurting anyone," I said. "That was my girlfriend you heard. Delores. She's okay. Please let me up. I can explain."

The soldier barked out a command, and the boot was lifted off my back.

I sat up, crawled to the galley hatch and cried, "Delores, can you put a towel around yourself and come up here, please?"

The soldiers were all watching me over their rifles. Then Delores rose up the galley ladder with a beach towel wrapped around her torso. Her hair was wild, black crashing waves reaching almost to her waist. Her dark eyes and olive complexion gave her the look of a fair-skinned Mexican.

"Delores," I said, "please tell the commandant you're okay."

Five minutes ago, she'd been screaming out in sexual ecstasy. Now she blushed and batted her eyelids. "Oh, yes," she said, "I'm very okay!"

The commandant stared at her for a moment, then lowered his rifle, and grinned at me. "Oh, *sí, señor,* now I understand!"

He laughed and rattled something off to his men. The entire unit broke into an uproar. It was instant male bonding, every soldier looking at me as though I were the Mexican National Soccer champion. I must have heard the words *muy macho* repeated a dozen times before they got back into their boats and pushed off.

I helped Delores pack on the morning she was to leave. She gave me her address and telephone number.

"You know I'm heading to New Zealand," I said. "I hope to get to New York someday, but I don't know when that will be."

"I understand. Will you write to me in the meantime?"

"Sure, but the letters will probably be few and far between. The mail service in the middle of the Pacific sucks."

She smiled and touched my cheek. "I understand. We've still got a few minutes before I have to leave. Want to fool around?"

I spent the next several days on the *Eros* lost in reflection. From Delores I learned that you can't hide passion and can't hide from it. And if there was one thing I had denied myself as a married man, it was the friendship and experience of many women.

The following week I visited Bruce several times so he could paint his portrait of me. He was pleased with the result, and so was I. To see the radical change in my appearance over the last few months was shocking. My hair was almost white-blonde from the daily dose of sun, and it reached, wild and uncut, to my shoulders, with a beard to match.

Looking at the completed painting of me was a shock. I hardly recognized myself. The mold of military appearances was broken forever.

"I paint what I see," Bruce said.

On the first day of the sixth week, I was sitting in the galley sipping a morning cup of coffee when I heard the hum of a small outboard motor and then a thumping against the side of the *Eros*. Topside I found Bert tying a rented skiff to the sailboat's rail.

"Bert, you finally made it back! Where's Linda?"

"She didn't come back with me, Owen." He'd lost a lot of his tan, I noticed.

Then I realized what he said. "Why not?"

"She…decided to stay in San Diego."

"Okay, so when do you expect her to get down here?"

"I don't. She's not." He gazed out to sea. "We've decided not to continue on, Owen. You and I are going to sail the *Eros* back to San Diego."

We headed to town and ended up in Carlos O'Brien's bar and restaurant, sitting at a nice oceanfront table. Bert ordered drinks. It was only eleven in the morning.

"We can't go back," I said. "After all we've been through…."

"Linda decided she can't go on sailing, Owen. That hurricane took it out of her." Bert was wearing slacks, a dress shirt, and shoes. He looked relaxed and renewed. "I know you're disappointed, but I'm going to need help taking the *Eros* back to San Diego. Name your price."

I looked into my drink and then shook my head. "Thanks, Bert, but I can't go back. I set out to take this journey, and I have to finish it. And I only have nine months left."

He nodded and continued ordering drinks, obviously hoping that the alcohol would weaken my resolve. But I knew that nothing short of my total destruction would stop me now. I renounced my life, my job, and my family for it. No amount of money could persuade me now to give up my pursuit of new experiences and self-knowledge.

We returned to the *Eros* late in the afternoon. Bert intended to set sail the next morning, so I packed what few belongings I owned: a sleeping bag, a jacket, one pair of jeans, a swimsuit and a couple pairs of under shorts, some socks, a knife, a swim mask, and a canteen. They all fit in a small backpack and weighed a total of twenty-three pounds. With regret I left the dozen or so books I owned on the boat.

The next morning, I watched the *Eros* motor across the glassy waters of the harbor, sliding back toward the open sea. Back toward home. Its home, anyway.

I waved once and then turned inland and started walking.

PATHWAY SOUTH

It took me almost a month to walk, hitchhike, and ride the occasional over-crowded peasant bus from Puerto Vallarta to Mexico City and then to head southward to the Guatemalan border. As I crossed the border, it occurred to me that at this rate of travel I'd be lucky to reach Panama in fewer than two more months, at which time the hurricane season would be over. So what was the point? I could have stayed in Puerto Vallarta sitting in the sun and drinking margaritas and would have accomplished just as much.

Except that would have meant sitting there. Sitting there where San Diegan drug lords could possibly find me for one thing. But also just sitting there. Not moving on, encountering new experiences. No, it was better to walk in a circle a thousand miles around and arrive back at my starting point than to never leave at all.

Day by day, the terrain became ever more mountainous, the jungle denser, the traffic sparser. Often I would walk for hours without seeing another person. But I was certainly surrounded by life, the evidence of it flooding endlessly from the jungle around me. Bird songs and cries, buzzes and screams and hoots, the thunder of millions of insects. Then there were times when that racket faded to almost nothing, which told me I was nearing the home of a different kind of animal—human beings.

On occasion, I came across Indians. They were dark-haired men the size of adolescent American boys often dressed in white cotton pants and shirts with exotic feathers hanging from their necks and shoulders. But it wasn't the mere existence of people that silenced the forest—after all, the commotion didn't drop off when I walked past. What shut the jungle up was the native villages, where many mouths meant many stomachs. Apparently, the natives ate everything that moved. Insects, reptiles, birds, any animal of any type—all were fair game.

This worked to my advantage. Ordinarily I had never set up camp near a river because I had heard that alligators could crawl onto the banks and drag grown men away. But if a village was near, that was no problem. Not even alligators were safe from Indian cooking pots.

One afternoon, as I was walking along in silence, I came around a corner and found myself surrounded by an entire band of Indians, ten or twelve strong. They did not slink away into the jungle. In fact, they seemed fascinated by me. They gathered close, gabbling in a tongue I didn't understand, but their gestures and body language made it clear they wanted me to go somewhere with them. Like many Indians in the high mountains, they spoke neither Spanish nor English. I couldn't explain that I was in a hurry to go elsewhere. Instead, I allowed them to lead me along a path deeper into the jungle. Several men ran ahead, presumably to announce our arrival.

Ten minutes later, we came to a village—fifteen or twenty small wood-and-straw dwellings around a central clearing. The entire population came out to greet us or to stare at me, or both. Most of the men wore only cotton breechcloths. The women wore skirts and blouses.

In the center of the village stood a large, wooden table. The Indians insisted with gestures and body language that I be seated there. Shortly after that, a remarkable woman walked up to me. Although she was less than five and a half feet tall, she weighed at least 300 pounds. She had dark brown skin and long, black, straight hair. I could not tell if she was the head of the tribe or some kind of medicine woman, but the locals treated her with great respect.

With a big smile on her face, she sat at the table across from me and spoke to me in her dialect. I replied in Spanish. She said something to the surrounding people, and one of them ran off and returned shortly thereafter with a young Indian man. He listened to the woman speak for a moment and then turned to me. "What is your name?" he asked in Spanish.

"Owen," I replied.

He repeated this to the woman, who spoke again. He nodded.

"Where are you from?" he asked me.

"America."

He repeated that to me as if he had never heard it before, then turned and said this to the woman, who, at this point, I figured to be the tribal chieftain, and then turned to the entire audience and said it to them. There was no reaction. Apparently, no one in the tribe had ever heard of America.

The interrogation continued for some time. Gradually, people began creeping up to me and tentatively touching my hair and skin. I just smiled, and soon everybody in the village was taking turns. A few actually touched my eyes. Obviously none of them had ever seen a white man before, especially a blond-haired, blue-eyed man.

After about an hour of this, a couple natives placed a big gourd on the table in front of the chief-woman. She pulled the top off and dipped into the gourd with a coconut shell, which she placed in front of her. She dipped in a second shell and put that one in front of me. Then she picked up her shell, raised it to me as if in a toast, and drank down the contents.

I glanced apprehensively at the liquid in my coconut shell. It looked and smelled like something scooped fresh out of the swamp: thick and brown-green, with a muddy consistency. Still, I smiled, took a mouthful, and fought not to spit it out onto the table. I forced it down and smiled.

The chief raised her shell, gulped down the rest of its contents, and then pounded it down on the tabletop. The villagers cheered as if she had just scored first in a big soccer game.

I knew a challenge when I saw one, so I raised my coconut shell and swallowed what was left in it. Actually, the process was more like taking two swallows and throwing one back. After ten seconds, I managed to force the elixir down and slammed my coconut shell onto the table. Again, everybody cheered.

Unfortunately, the shells were immediately refilled. The natives began bringing food and placing it on the table. The first plate held what appeared to be giant, unwashed eggs. Maybe alligator eggs or from some large bird. Whatever their source, they clearly had been buried for a long while. A villager wiped the grime off one egg and cut the top off with a knife, then handed the egg to the chief. She raised it the way she raised the coconut shell, then sucked the contents down in one big belt. I was beginning to understand why she was the size of three regular citizens.

A second egg was decapitated in the same manner and handed to me. Although the smell of it was enough to make me puke on the spot, I was aware that the natives were enjoying this neck-and-neck dining extravaganza, especially since the chief was currently leading the competition by the score of one rotten egg to zero. So, taking a deep breath, I chugged down every last drop of rotten slime in that eggshell. For a moment, I was certain it was all coming back up, but I fought valiantly and was rewarded by the cheers of the crowd.

More exotic tidbits came to the table, including something that might have been monkey testicles and corn mush. The chief gobbled everything down, but she was clearly more interested in drinking the stuff in the coconut shell. Our caterers gave her plenty of refills. As for me, who was I to look down on this beverage? I'm sure the locals would have felt the same way about a shot of Kentucky whiskey.

I struggled to keep the dining-and-drinking score even.

I was a bit concerned about paying the bill, though. I didn't have much in my backpack to give these people in return for their hospitality. I had none of the standard gifts seen in old movies: food, cigarettes, beads, or shiny trinkets. All I could think of to pull out was a diving mask I had kept from the *Eros*. I kept it in case I needed it when I got back to the ocean.

The Indians looked at it and passed it around, mystified. I tried to explain its function to the interpreter, but he didn't understand. So I took it back, got up, and walked unsteadily to a stream that flowed no more than fifty feet from the table. With natives standing all around me, I got on my knees, put the diving mask on my face and started to bend to the water.

But before I got that far, most of the natives shrieked and ran back to the table. For a moment, I thought that an alligator had surfaced and was about to grab this non-native man off the riverbank. Then I realized the mask itself frightened my new friends. I quickly took it off, and everyone returned as if nothing happened.

When I left an hour or so later, my hosts waved goodbye with smiles. I walked away thinking about their culture, their remoteness. They were primitive people, and yet they knew how to live in the moment. For them there was no rush, no hurry. No destination. Were they worse off than I, or better?

That night I camped by the same stream that flowed past the village, sleeping serenely because the jungle was still and quiet. With the village nearby, the forest and streams were practically striped of animal life.

In San Salvador, the capital of El Salvador, I stopped just long enough to visit the embassies of the next two countries to the south, Honduras and Nicaragua to get the relevant visas. At both locations I was warned that their countries were unofficially at war with one another, and it was dangerous to travel outside the major cities of either nation.

Days later I arrived at La Unión, the southernmost town on the Pacific coast of El Salvador. It fronted the Golfo de Fonseca, a large bay shared with El Salvador's less-than-beloved neighbor to the south, Honduras. From what I could see, my best bet for crossing the frontier unmolested was to do it by boat.

A twenty-foot fishing boat with an old beat up forty horse-powered Johnson outboard motor pulled away from the dock. It was so heavily loaded it almost shipped water. I sat near the bow, feeling all eyes on me.

An hour later, I climbed onto a dock in the Honduran town of El Zopa. Each day I walked until afternoon, then stopped at a village to buy a potato, an onion, a couple of carrots, and a handful of beans or rice. In the evening, I would make camp in the countryside, start a small fire, boil up a vegetable stew, and eat it—ordinarily my only meal of the day. Sometimes, when I was lucky, I might come across an additional food source alongside the road. At a cornfield, for example, I could break off a few ears to munch raw as I walked. In the countryside, I would sometimes see fruits that I recognized as edible and gorge myself.

Several days down the road I found myself approaching sunset with no campsite selected. This was a problem because, at night, the land would be so dark I could hold my hand in front of my face and not see it. On that night, there was a half moon in the sky, but it provided barely enough light to show me the dirt road under my feet. Also, there seemed to be a farm every few miles, each one guarded by a mob of mangy, barking dogs. Thanks to them, I had become a good rock thrower.

Finally I came upon a cornfield alongside the road, with no dogs in earshot, and decided to just walk into the field a few rows in, lie down, and go to sleep.

I was about a hundred feet into the field when I was startled to hear gun-fire—rifles by the sound—erupt back by the road. I dropped to my stomach and listened as a dozen or so shots cracked off. A moment later, the more urgent chatter of automatic weapons erupted from my other side, farther across the field. Holy shit, I was caught in a crossfire.

Slugs ripped through the corn above me as I crawled deeper into the field, angling away from what now sounded like a full-blown battle. Between exchanges of gunfire, I heard shouting in Spanish.

I crawled low to the ground for about ten minutes as shredded leaves and blasted corncobs rained down on me and then gave up and dropped flat on my belly again. I couldn't tell which way the combatants were moving, if I was getting closer to them or farther away. The battle appeared to be mobile, surging all around the field.

After an hour or so, the shooting declined and finally stopped. I didn't move. I lay on my belly in the furrow and waited. Finally, I dozed off—only to awaken to the sound of furtive rustling. I opened an eye and saw movement in the next furrow. As I watched, a skunk waddled past. I didn't move and doubted the animal even realized I was there. Or perhaps it was just used to coming across motionless bodies in the fields.

At daylight, I made my way back through the field, keeping low and out of sight. When I reached the last row of corn I peered out warily. No one moved on the road in either direction. I stepped out and began walking briskly south like a man with a mission.

My mission was to get to Panama in one piece.

Three days later I passed into Nicaragua. The Border guards gave me some advice as I passed. "Be careful. The mountains are dangerous. Much rebel fighting there." After another week of walking, I reached Managua, the capital city of Nicaragua. To me it looked like every other big city I had seen in Central America—overcrowded, dirty, and ready for demolition.

Early in the morning a Latino man riding a 1965 Triumph motorcycle cruised up alongside me. "Hey, mister, where you from?"

"California."

"Where in California?"

I stopped walking. "San Diego."

"All right! I lived there for a couple years. Where you going now?"

"I'm headed for Costa Rica."

He grinned. "Come on, then. You can ride with me. I'm going a little bit farther down this road in your direction."

He introduced himself as Juan and added, "I am the motorcycle-racing champion of Nicaragua" as if that should reassure me about anything.

I jumped on the back of the bike, and we were off. Juan drove quickly but calmly around the mountain curves, turning his head frequently to tell me all about his racing history. Maybe he didn't need to see where he was going. When he asked if I minded stopping off at the house of a friend of his, I was more than happy to agree.

We pulled up to an old wooden building on the roadside. The front yard was littered with broken-down refrigerators and washing machines, spare parts, and miscellaneous junk.

Juan pulled his motorcycle right up to the front door and shut off the engine. A heavyset guy wearing only a pair of greasy pants stepped out onto the porch, and Juan spoke to him in excited Spanish I couldn't follow. The man nodded and gestured us inside.

His name was Carlos, and Juan described him as "the best refrigerator repairman in all of Nicaragua." The inside of the house featured plywood floors decorated with a couple of pieces of battered furniture. Several small children played in the back part of the house, and occasionally a woman walked down the hallway to carry clothes to an outside extension of the kitchen that contained a washboard and a metal tub. The house did not have indoor plumbing, electricity, or running water. It appeared that most of the refrigerator repair work was done in the front yard or living room.

Still, Carlos was a gracious host. Juan and I barely arrived before he entered into the kitchen and returned with two glasses and a bottle of some liquid. He poured us drinks and made a toast. Juan and I held our glasses up and Carlos drank from the bottle. I figured he didn't own a third glass.

He and Juan spoke gunfire Spanish, but I was able to discern that Juan was trying to persuade Carlos to take us both out for the afternoon. Juan admitted he did not have any money. By the look of things I didn't think Carlos did, either, but after another drink he retreated to the back of the house and soon returned dressed in a clean shirt, pants, and sandals.

Juan grinned. "All right, let's go!" he said.

"Sure," I said, "why not?"

We walked to the front yard, and for the first time I noticed a broken-down car parked among the broken-down refrigerators and washing machines. Carlos climbed behind the wheel of the car and just sat there. Juan said, "We have to push the car to get it started."

Juan and I got behind the car and, after a few groaning steps, were enveloped in a cloud of blue smoke and backfiring. Then I jumped into the backseat, and Juan got in front next to Carlos.

After riding on the back of Juan's motorcycle, I felt as if Carlos's car barely moved at all. Eventually we reached a small town. Carlos parked on a side street, and we walked a short distance to what Juan proudly called a restaurant although it looked more like a bar to me—a crowded bar, even at midday. Inside, we sat at a table where a window frame devoid of both glass and screen offered a view of the street. Carlos ordered a bottle of alcohol, and we were brought something in the eighty- to ninety-proof range.

A short time later, the bartender came out with a platter of food. Not chips and salsa. This was a huge plate of broiled beef and various finger foods. I was surprised, but Juan explained, "It is the custom in my country to bring food with the drinks."

I calculated that the entire feast cost about four dollars. When I offered to pay, Juan and Carlos were adamant that I was their guest. As we sat there eating and drinking, I became aware of at least a half dozen women standing on the far side of the room. I nudged Juan. "Are those girls prostitutes?"

It was a casual question, but the next thing I knew, Juan invited all the girls over to our table. "Owen, pick," he said. "Which one do you wish?"

I was speechless. "No, that's okay, Juan, not right now."

But he insisted, pushing each of the girls toward me. He was trying to be a perfect host, but to me the women looked like typical long-term entrepreneurial flesh-peddlers. That's a hard-time business anywhere and, judging by the girls' faces, even tougher in Nicaragua.

I was finally able to convince Juan that I might take him up on his most generous offer later, and he excused the girls, who drifted back to their original hangout area.

Carlos and Juan fell into a discussion about where we should go next. They were a few minutes into it when Carlos glanced out the window and abruptly fell silent.

Outside I saw a military vehicle parked in front of the bar. Several soldiers stood around it, automatic rifles slung casually around their shoulders. Juan and Carlos began a new and even more earnest debate. This time there was no question what it was about: the best time and route to get out of there.

Carlos finally stood and said in Spanish, "It is time to leave."

We walked outside and turned onto the side street where we had parked. Carlos got behind the wheel. After a brief push and a pop of the clutch, Juan and I jumped in. The car growled off into the countryside, away from the bar.

Fifteen minutes later, we arrived at a huge public park swarming with people. As we got out of the car, I looked closer at the park and saw a concrete dance floor. Nearby, a live band tuned up.

Juan rubbed his hands together. "Owen, this is scheduled to be the biggest dance of the month. We're going to have some fun!"

He was quick to point out that many of the girls were staring at me. "They want to dance with the gringo," he said with his usual grin. He gestured at a small group of girls who were smiling and making every attempt to be noticed by the three of us, and we walked over and introduced ourselves.

Once we started dancing, it seemed like a continuous line of women waited to dance with us. The three of us were out there, nonstop, for over an hour and a half.

During one of the interludes, Juan sidled up to me. "Owen, do you see all the soldiers over there?" He pointed with his eyes toward the rear of the crowd. I looked over the mass of heads and out on the fringes. Sure enough, there stood a dozen or so soldiers. "They seem very interested in the three of us."

At that very moment, one of the soldiers pointed at us. Behind him, several jeeps pulled up. The crowd eased away from them.

"What's this all about?" I asked.

Before Juan could answer, Carlos appeared at his side and whispered in his ear. Juan nodded. "Owen, we are in trouble. During the next dance, we'll each leave as quietly as possible in a different direction, and meet back at Carlos's car. Understand?"

"Sure...."

I watched for the cue. When Juan nodded, I headed across the dance floor through the crowd and off toward the parking lot in the opposite direction of the soldiers. Carlos was already in his car, Juan waiting behind it to push. Moments later, we took off in a cloud of blue smoke.

Carlos looked in his rearview mirror. "They saw us," he said.

Glancing back, I saw the soldiers running toward their jeeps. "Where are we headed Juan?" I asked.

"We'll try to lose these soldiers, then get back to Carlos's house."

"I still don't understand why they're after us," I said.

He shrugged. "I don't know. I suspect they were checking Carlos and me out just because we were with you. Perhaps they think you are a drug smuggler."

"Terrific."

Carlos's car was no longer such a snail. Carlos now drove like a cabbie in a demolition derby. Behind us, the lights of the jeeps disappeared whenever we took curves and turns, but they reappeared on straightaway sections of the road. Carlos whipped his car onto the lane to his home, slid in among several trashed refrigerators, and shut off the engine and headlights. We jumped out and ran into Carlos's house.

The house was lit by candles. Carlos hurried to the back room and spoke to his wife while Juan and I sat at the kitchen table. "Did you have a good time at the dance, Owen?" he asked.

"Sure, it was great. Especially the part where we slipped out before the automatic weapons started firing."

He laughed, but behind that I heard the sound of several vehicles approaching the house.

Juan ran to the door, Carlos right behind him. "Well, the soldiers are here."

I walked to a window and pulled back a tattered curtain. Three army jeeps pulled up next to Carlos's vehicle, which was now surrounded in the dim moonlight by a group of soldiers. Several of them lit cigarettes. "They don't seem to be in any hurry to arrest me," I said.

"Maybe they just want money," Juan said.

I laughed. "Look, if they want me, I'll just go out and surrender to them. I can't put Carlos's family at risk."

"No, no, you must not go outside. Stay here. We are safe here for the time being."

Carlos returned and began talking with Juan. I grabbed my backpack and slung it on, ready to go at a moment's notice.

Several hours later, the soldiers were still milling about in the yard. I didn't understand it. If they wanted me, why didn't they just come and take me?

"Look, Owen," Juan said, "you're an American, and they know it. They want you, perhaps for questioning, but you can make big trouble for them with the American Embassy, especially if there are witnesses. We've got to get out of here before they change their minds. It's just a matter of time."

"But this isn't your problem, Juan. Yours or Carlos.'"

He ignored me. "Here's my plan. My motorcycle is parked just out by the front door. We will run to it. Once I get it started, you jump on and just hang on. Remember, I am the motorcycle-racing champion of Nicaragua. No one can catch me."

I nodded, turned, and thanked Carlos for his hospitality. He grinned as he shook my hand. I doubted his wife was very fond of me.

The front door creaked behind me. "Okay, now!" Juan cried. "*Vamanos!*"

The next minute or two passed in a blur. We were on Juan's motorcycle, and then the engine started with a roar. The soldiers ran madly toward their jeeps. The Triumph's rear tire spun dirt and rocks across the yard and against the side of the house, and we took off like a slithering snake. Headlights bounced behind us in pursuit.

"Where are we heading?" I shouted.

"Into the city."

"Are these guys going to start shooting at us?"

"I don't think so. You're an American. If they shoot you, it will be big paperwork."

We reached the city after midnight. Parked cars lined both side of the narrow streets, but no one was out and about. That was a good thing, because we shot down those streets at over sixty miles per hour, going airborne at each intersection. I kept looking over my shoulder and giving Juan a running update on how the army jeeps behind us were doing.

Juan had not exaggerated about his motorcycling skills. I never before experienced anything like a high-speed chase through narrow city streets. The Triumph's engine roar reverberated off the building walls, and my peripheral vision became nothing but a blur.

After about ten minutes, it was apparent that we left the soldiers far behind. The next thing I knew, Juan was braking hard and pulling into an alley. He shut off the engine and we dismounted and hurriedly pushed the motorcycle into a wooden shed with a rear wall that backed up to the alley. Adjacent to the shed stood a small adobe house.

Inside the shed Juan said, "You can sleep here for the night. I'll be in my house next door. If you hear anything outside, whatever you do, don't leave this building. In the morning, you'll have to leave as early as you can."

"I understand. Juan, thanks for your help."

His grin was visible even in the near-total darkness of the shed. "*Buenas noches, Owen.*"

I laid out my sleeping bag and crawled into it. No more than two minutes later, I heard the rumble of several vehicles driving slowly along the alley. I froze, certain that the soldiers found me after all.

As the jeeps rolled past the shed, I felt the rumbling of the motors through the floor. The only thing separating me from the soldiers was a wall of one-inch-thick boards. The sound of their voices carried plainly over the pounding of my heart.

Then the voices and rumbling continued down the alley and faded away. I covered myself with my sleeping bag. I fell asleep listening for noise.

The next morning I got up just as the chickens began scratching in the yard behind the home of Nicaragua's motorcycle champion. On foot again, I headed toward the center of town, keeping an eye out for any military vehicles. When an old, broken-down bus rumbled toward me, I flagged it down and for the equivalent of twenty-five cents was soon heading out of town with a lot of silent locals.

About an hour later, the driver announced we reached the last stop where I exited and began to walk down a long, two-lane blacktop with rugged countryside on both sides of the famous Panamanian Highway.

I hiked south for several more weeks, passing through Masaya, Granada, Linotype, Madame, Pica Pica, and Rivas. Whenever I came to smaller towns and villages, I tried to creep around them to avoid curious stares. When I arrived at the Costa Rican border, a guard approached me and said, "Your passport, please, *señor.*" He looked at it for a full minute, carefully checking each page. Then he looked up. "How much money do you have with you?"

"About $350."

"Put it on the counter." After verifying my net worth, he nodded and said, "You may not enter our country."

"But…all I'm trying to do is get to Panama, so I can sign on as a crew hand on a sailboat. It's the next country down. I'm just passing through here."

"Yes, I have heard this from many people who enter our country and never leave. You may not enter." He walked away.

I hesitated a moment, then dropped onto a nearby chair, and got comfortable. People walked by and looked at me, but I just sat there, doing nothing, going nowhere.

An hour passed. Another hour, and another. A different guard came in, hesitated, and disappeared. I didn't move. Later, another guard appeared and said, "*Señor*, you can enter my country—but only if you purchase a one-way bus ticket straight through."

"Deal," I said. I gave him fifty bucks and sat down again until he returned with my passport stamped for a one-way ride to the far border, along with a nonstop bus ticket to the same destination. From the windows of the bus, my impression of Costa Rica was that it was a beautiful place, considerably richer than the other Central American countries I had seen. Still, I reached the southern border late that afternoon.

I reached Panama City several days later after almost three months on the road. I decided to stop somewhere for a couple of cold beers, the first since the ones I shared with Bert back in Puerto Vallarta. I walked into a dingy, almost deserted little cantina just off the main street and ordered a beer from the bartender, who spoke no English. I downed the beer and ordered a second. After I had taken two swallows, a pair of big, fat uniformed police officers walked in and parked themselves on either side of me at the bar. They leaned toward one another, literally putting the squeeze on me.

The cop on my right had a machine gun draped over his shoulder. The one on my left had a couple of pistols hanging on his belt. I continued drinking my beer as if I were used to overweight, over-armed Panamanian policemen leaning on me every day of my life.

Finally, the guy to my left threw an elbow to my ribs—hard. I coughed and spewed beer all over the back bar, and reflexively spun toward him. "What the fu—"

The second officer's baton smacked me in the kidney, driving me into the bar. There I held my position, gasping, knowing better than to offer any further resistance.

After I caught my breath I said, "What do you guys want?"

"You an American?" one of them asked in English.

"Yes, I am."

"Give me your passport. Now."

He examined it and tossed it back. He and his partner interrogated me for the next ten minutes. "Where you come from and where are you going?" they asked without any apparent interest in the answers as they emptied my backpack on the floor. I watched their expressions as they rifled through my belongings: a sleeping bag, a space blanket, some soiled clothing, a shaving kit without a razor, a cooking pot. They looked disgusted and most displeased. No gringo treasure here.

Finally, the machine gun-toting cop turned to me and said, "You better leave town. Do you understand?"

"Of course I understand, officer."

They glowered at me a moment more, then turned, and stalked out the door. The few other patrons in the bar returned to their discussions as if I were not even there.

I gathered my belongings from the floor, paid for my beers, and left the bar. Outside, the officers were nowhere in sight. As I walked down various side streets, I noticed anti-American graffiti smeared on the walls and buildings. Finally, I came upon a building that should probably have been torn down fifty years earlier. The sign in front proclaimed it to be the Hotel Azul. *Azul* is Spanish for "blue." It's got my name on it—that's good enough for me, I thought.

Inside, the reception clerk could have been a double for one of those shady characters out of an old Humphrey Bogart movie. He told me I could have a room facing the ocean for five dollars a night, and I handed him a twenty.

The inside of the room didn't look any newer than the outside of the building: a rusty metal-framed bed, an antique wooden desk, and a rickety chair next to the balcony. The bathroom and shower were down the hall. An ugly and decrepit place, yet an upgrade from the wilderness I had been sleeping in for the last few months.

That night I took the longest cold shower in history and gave my clothes the same treatment I gave to my own skin. After all, I was about to go job-hunting.

The next day I walked down to the harbor and located the only yacht club in Balboa. Not surprisingly, it was named the Balboa Yacht Club. Most of the vessels sat empty. They appeared to be a part of the local boating community rather than long-range vessels in transit.

Then I spotted a larger, ketch-rigged sailboat anchored off the docks and smiled. It looked to be the biggest, most expensive yacht moored at the club's visitor's dock. (In fact, it was the only yacht.) I set my slights on her and decided to find out if they needed a crew hand. I was quickly rebuffed. Disappointed, I walked to downtown Panama City, located a bus station, and purchased a ticket to the Atlantic side of the country, to the big Caribbean seaport of Colon.

The Port of Colon was old and elegant, its colonial architecture dating back to the seventeenth and eighteenth centuries. The docks of the Colon Yacht Club were full of expensive vessels. I made my way from one to the next, talking to anyone who seemed to be on a cruise. But almost no one needed a crewmember, and the few who did were heading back up the Mexican coast toward California.

Three days later, while in downtown Panama City, I happened to see a poster advertising a cheap airline flight from Panama to Houston, Texas. I stared at the numbers. Nobody was shipping out to exotic ports, so I figured I had two choices. I could hang out for another month and risk getting stranded with no funds and no means of income. I could also fly back to the States, find a job, and then continue my trip around the world from the east coast rather than the west. Why not? It was the voyage that mattered, not the direction.

Funny how quickly I could make up my mind when the goal was clear. A few hours after this epiphany, with backpack in one hand and ticket in the other, I boarded an airliner bound for cowboy country, USA.

DETOUR

The flight to Houston took five hours, or looked at another way, the equivalent of half a day's walk. Upon arriving, my senses and disorientation heightened as I stepped into the standard rushing American lifestyle: planes, buses, cabs, trucks, cars, even the way people walked. Everything moving faster, faster, faster.

At first, it was disorienting, and then I realized there was an important lesson to be learned. Although my journey was almost half over, I could not waste any time.

Twelve hours later, I arrived in New Orleans, the next major city on the way to the East Coast. I figured I could get a job and save enough money to continue my journey. A trucker dropped me at the edge of Bourbon Street at four o'clock in the morning. I stared around, a bit amazed and befuddled. Even at that hour most of the businesses seemed to be open and busy. It was difficult to absorb all the activity after so many months of near isolation in the jungle and on the ocean.

Finally, I got my feet moving, carrying me toward a coffee shop where a bunch of college students and hippie types gathered in an outdoor seating area. I ordered a cup of coffee and sat down. Music poured out of open bars and restaurants. People strolled the streets, and conversation filled the air. Of all places to end up in the United States, New Orleans had to be the craziest. With its apparently unending Mardi Gras mentality, its aboveground graveyards and voodoo history, New Orleans was a place that celebrated death and the spirits of the dead. I wondered if that was why I had been drawn there. Maybe I, too, felt the need to celebrate death—the death of the parts of me that I once held so dear.

"Hey, man," a voice said behind me. "Where you from?"

I turned and saw a young, bearded man with a big roll of what seemed to be posters under his arm.

"California."

He extended his hand. "I'm Brother Richard. Did you just get into town?"

"I just arrived this morning to find a job and a place to stay."

"Cool. I'm staying in a home with some friends. We've got a vacancy. You interested?"

"I don't see how I could pass up your offer."

"Okay, let's go. I have to finish hanging up a couple more of these posters. If you don't mind giving me a hand, we can head over to the house when we get done."

I followed him into the heart of the Garden District, where we tacked up posters announcing a big anti-Vietnam War protest later that week. Brother Richard told me he had been a Catholic priest for three years and left the priesthood to become more involved with the antiwar movement.

After the posters were distributed we walked six blocks off Bourbon Street to a big, ramshackle Victorian home in a run-down neighborhood. Richard led me upstairs to a large salon where five young hippies sat on the floor, deep in discussion. They looked up and eagerly greeted Richard, who introduced me as "Owen from California. He's looking for a place to hang out for a while before heading for New York. Would any of you object to his staying with us for a while?"

No one objected. Clearly they respected their friend's kindhearted gesture. There also seemed to be an immediate bond of brotherhood between them and me, and why not? I looked as radical as anyone in the room. My hair was beyond shoulder length now, and my beard full. Also, I was from California, which was considered the American trendsetter for the antiwar movement. How could I not agree with their cause?

I sat and listened to their conversation. They came from all over the country and with very diverse backgrounds. Yet, they were bound together by anti-Vietnam War activism and dedication to the legalization of marijuana. I wondered what they would think if they knew that just six months ago, I would have been rounding them up at a demonstration or antiwar protest—just doing my job.

Later that afternoon I happened upon a pizza joint quite by accident. It was having its grand opening. I ordered a slice of pizza and a beer and sat down. Soon I was talking to one of the owners, a guy named Bill. On the spot he offered me a position as assistant pizza-maker. It paid only a couple of dollars above minimum wage, but it included all the pizza and beer I could consume while on duty. The restaurant was staffed by nothing but young people who all seemed to be enjoying themselves.

Fifteen minutes later, I was in the back room learning the art of pizza making. That afternoon, I began work and finished up at about three in the morning. Then it was time for everyone to go out on the town. I didn't get back to the commune until dawn. And that was life in New Orleans.

Every night was an adventure. Late one evening after dancing at a local club, the pizza experts went out on the street to cool down. Across the street was an old New Orleans cemetery. The evening was exceptionally hot and humid, and several of the girls came up with the idea of hanging out at the cemetery.

Soon we were walking through the cool, wet grass. We took off our shirts and shoes and sat down, drinking beer and conversing until sunrise. In any other part of the country, a graveyard would have been a strange place to spend the early morning hours, but in New Orleans, it seemed the right thing to do.

Because the water table is so high in Southern Louisiana, graves are not dug into the ground. Instead, bodies are placed in mausoleums, sometimes stacked several high. Ornate stones and monuments are common. That night as I sat with my friends, I found myself looking up at one of the grave markers looming over me—a great marble angel, stained with age and weather. She seemed to be weeping tears of moss.

At sunrise, I left the group and walked to the banks of the Mississippi River to watch the sunrise. Just as it burst over the horizon, a diesel train came down the railroad tracks below me, drumming slowly along the riverfront. The ground vibrated beneath me.

And I knew that it was time to leave.

I returned to the house and found Brother Richard in the attic printing up some posters. We talked for a while about his involvement with the movement. I was truly touched by his nonviolence and commitment to get the country out of Vietnam, and I found myself unwilling to judge him by my previous standards. He was a kind and gentle soul. Even though our paths may have been heading in different directions, we were both committed to a higher purpose. I think we recognized that in one another.

"Owen," he said, "I wish you the very best on your journey. It's probably good you're leaving now since I've been told that we're under FBI surveillance. We're likely to be raided any day now."

"Richard, I'm sorry to hear that, but I know you'll carry on." I hesitated. "A warrior is committed to the end result. I know that losing your war is not an option for you. I pray your adversaries will be moved by your compassion and love."

"Thanks, Owen. If you ever get back to this area, you're welcome to stop in for a visit—if we're still here."

That night I returned to the pizza shop and let Bill know that after my shift I was leaving for New York. "It's been fun. I honestly don't remember having so much fun working a shit job before."

He laughed. "Get out of here, you hippie."

The next morning I was on the streets at six o'clock, hiking out of New Orleans. Now I had a bit of money back in my pocket but less than six months to finish my journey.

On the outskirts of Florida, a college student picked me up in his Volkswagen Bug. "Where you going?"

"I'm heading for Jacksonville."

"Great, I am, too. Hop in."

I threw my backpack into the back seat and climbed into the front. On the narrow dash rested a tape recorder blasting Pink Floyd music. Over the din, the driver and I introduced ourselves. Within seconds, he shifted through all four gears, and we were roaring down the highway at sixty miles per hour.

"Did you know that Pink Floyd music is outlawed in South Africa?" he asked. "The government considers them revolutionary provocateurs."

It turned out that my student was a political science major studying the Apartheid movement in South Africa. It was all he talked about right up till he pulled over to drop me off just outside Jacksonville. Everything he said made me glad that South Africa wasn't on my travel itinerary.

As the Bug blasted away, I walked along the shoulder of the interstate in the waning daylight until I found a vacant wooded area where I set up camp for the night. Except for the roar of nearby traffic and the lack of monkeys shrieking in the treetops, it was almost like being in Central America again.

In the morning, I caught a ride with a long-haul trucker heading north. In South Carolina, he left the freeway. And at midday, he dropped me off in a tiny town. After shopping, I hit the road again, wandering through the backcountry of South Carolina.

At four o'clock, I passed a wooded area like many others I had seen in that part of the country when I noticed something interesting: a small wooden sign standing next to a narrow lane that disappeared behind the trees. The sign read St. Benedictine Monastery. Staring at the sign for a moment, I wondered if it were really possible that a group of Catholic monks erected a retreat in the middle of the American Bible Belt. The next thing I knew, I was walking down the lane.

A half-mile down the lane stood an old, rambling building of wood and stone. Surely no one actually occupied such a desolate structure, although the grounds appeared to be neatly maintained. I walked under an arched portico and knocked on a pair of large, rustic oaken doors. A minute later, one door opened to reveal an older man of medium stature, wearing a brown robe with tennis shoes peeking from under the robe's hem.

I cleared my throat. "Brother, I'm a traveler passing through. I was wondering if it would be possible for me to spend a few days at the monastery."

He smiled. "Please, Brother, follow me." Turning, he walked away down a long hallway. I followed him to another room where another older monk looked up with a smile.

"Blessed Father," the first monk said, "this young man is a traveler who has asked to stay with us for several days."

The senior monk turned to me. "How is it that you have come here, my son?"

"To be honest," I said, "I'm not certain how I happened to end up at exactly this place. I've been on the road for over six months now, and I've been in some very strange places." The head monk didn't respond to that. He just kept looking at me.

The next words from my mouth surprised even me, "Father, this journey I'm on has been a search to find truth and purpose for my life, my destiny. I snapped my mouth shut before more unpremeditated words might escape.

The father just smiled. "You may be our guest. Brother Gregory will take you to your room."

Brother Gregory led me down a stone hallway to the end of a building where he showed me a tiny room with a single bed, a small table, and a chair. There were no windows. The place looked like the kind of prison cell Amnesty International would have outlawed.

Brother Gregory briefed me on the monastery's schedule: times for prayer, for Mass, for meals. "Brother Owen," he said, "these rooms are very quiet and without distraction to give time for uninterrupted prayer and meditation."

"Thank you, Brother," I said. "I'll try my best to be true to the Benedictine way of life."

He bowed his head and quietly closed the door behind him as he left.

Silence.

I dropped my backpack to the floor and sat at the table. On it rested a Bible and some literature about the monastery and the Order of St. Benedictine.

On the latter was printed the Rule of Saint Benedict: "If someone comes and knocks at the door and is persistent in his request, he should be allowed to enter and stay in the guest quarters for a few days. After that, he should live in the novitiate."

A shiver shot down my spine. I didn't know if I was ever going to be a novitiate, but I had certainly come and knocked on the door. I was nothing if not persistent. I sat on the hard, narrow mattress of the bed, removed my boots, and leaned back against the wall. I closed my eyes. "Dear God," I said silently. "Blessed Father who has looked after me upon this journey, I give you my humble thanks and gratitude for the love and grace of your sweet blessings and pray to be worthy of your guidance on the road of life."

I prayed almost nonstop for the next two days and nights, the constant litany interrupted only by brief, involuntary bouts of sleep and an occasional mouthful of the bread and cheese I bought in the last small town. In a way, the ritual was familiar, like being on a two-day stakeout. But it was very different, too, because instead of waiting for something to happen, I was praying for something to happen. Nothing did happen. No illumination or transformation—at least not that I could detect. So, I decided it was, once again, time to get on the road. I stopped by the senior monk's office and thanked him upon leaving.

He smiled. "Go with God, my son." He then handed me a small silver cross encircled by the symbol of a heart. "Keep this with you, my son, to remind you of your destiny."

I thanked him, turned, and walked away. Within minutes, the monastery vanished in the woods behind me.

Once I reached the road, the hitchhiking was good and at three in the afternoon I found myself at a Howard Johnson's restaurant alongside Interstate 95. I stopped inside for a cup of coffee and hung out at the counter with my eyes and ears open, listening for any trucker who might be talking about a trip north.

No luck. After about an hour I went into the restroom and cleaned myself up so that I might appear more presentable to passing motorists, then slung my backpack over my shoulders, and headed out to the interstate on-ramp.

Less than a half hour later, a green four-door Chevrolet pulled up alongside me. The passenger rolled down his window and said, "Hi, where you going?"

"New York City."

"So are we. Hop in."

I climbed into the back seat and within seconds we were roaring down the northbound ramp of I-95. I was a little surprised to have been told where my benefactors were destined. The usual protocol, I had noticed, was not to give that information to a hitchhiker. That way, if they didn't like you, they could just drop you off at the next exit. Of course, most of the time, there was only the driver, so he would have reason to be concerned. In my case, however, there was safety in numbers.

The driver looked at me through the center mirror. "What's your name, and where are you from?"

"I'm Owen, and I'm originally from California."

"No shit? You're a long way from home. What the hell are you doing in North Carolina?"

"Just passing through."

The driver nodded. "I'm Joe, and this is Frank. We're on our way back from a week's vacation in Florida."

They appeared to be in their mid- to late thirties: ordinary guys, clean-cut, casually dressed, with short haircuts. Both smoked endlessly and kept up a running dialog, mostly with each other, so I just sat back to enjoy the ride. For once, I would not have to provide interesting discussion and company the entire way. Twenty minutes into the ride, Frank turned and asked, "You got any dope on you?"

"No, sorry."

He turned away, clearly disappointed. Strange, he didn't look the druggie type. Even stranger was the fact that he just up and asked me, a stranger, for dope. I chalked it up to my appearance, which wasn't exactly that of a model cop anymore.

The front-seat conversation carried on. I could not quite figure what these guys did for a living, nor did I ask. As long as they kept each other engaged in conversation, there was no need for me to jump in. Both were very animated in speech, gestures, and posture. Joe kept his foot on the gas, maintaining a speed of eighty miles per hour. He did not seem bothered by the fact that the speed limit was sixty-five. I figured he and Frank were just in a hurry to get to New York, which was fine with me.

Then the rain began. It hit without warning, a massive torrent that reminded me of the first blows of the Mexican hurricane. Traffic instantly slowed to no more than forty-five miles per hour.

Within moments, my patrons' anger management skills flew out the window. Frank started bitching about the rain, the fogged-up windows, and the amount of time they were losing. Joe turned and shouted, "It was your fault that we got ripped off in Miami." The rain and screaming continued for about half an hour when Joe announced that we were making a gas stop at the next exit.

Frank turned and asked, "Owen, do you think you could help us out a bit with the gas money?"

"Sure, I can help." I had never been asked to share expenses before, but a direct ride to New York was certainly worth a donation.

The car flew down the next interstate off-ramp. In minutes, we stopped at an Exxon gas pump. Joe and Frank headed into the store to buy cigarettes. I pumped the gas and then returned to pay the cashier. Joe and Frank happened to be snacking down on junk food. I paid for the gas and a Coke for myself.

The moment my transaction was finished, Joe and Frank were out the door. I followed quickly to make sure they didn't drive off without me. Once in the car, the pair opened a fresh pack of cigarettes and filled the car with smoke before they even got the ignition turned on.

No sooner were we back on the interstate and its creeping traffic than Joe and Frank resumed screaming at each other. Bit by bit, I caught enough of the conversation to understand finally what was really going on. Both Joe and Frank were heroin addicts. Evidently, Joe had promised Frank that they would be able to score heroin in Miami, so they had not brought much of a supply along with them on their trip. In Miami, they had been burned, ripped off. Now they were low on funds, getting strung out, and had no choice but to rush home for a fix.

Terrific. Sitting back I assessed the situation. Due to the dense smoke and moisture on the insides of the car's windows, I could barely see outside. Neither could Joe. Assuming we did not get in a ninety-car pileup somewhere along the way, we would probably pull into New York City at around four or five in the morning. It was 10:00 PM now. I intended to stay awake for the next six or seven hours. Who knew what to expect from these two guys as their conditions worsened?

The rain kept thundering down, and Joe and Frank kept arguing. Nothing changed while we drove through Virginia and Washington DC. Just outside Baltimore, the rain stopped and traffic thinned. Joe and Frank did not settle down until we were in New Brunswick, New Jersey, caught in the beginning of rush-hour traffic. My junkie buddies finally quit, too exhausted to fight anymore.

At 6:00 AM when we reached the outer limits of New York City, Joe asked me where I wanted to be dropped off. I had Delores's address, but I wasn't sure what part of the metropolis it was in. Also, I didn't really want to put any more stress on Joe and Frank. "Just let me off anywhere close to the city," I said. "I'll walk from there."

I knew I had made the right decision when they pulled over to the shoulder near no particular off-ramp and let me out. Clearly, they could not even spare the time to deliver me to a surface street.

"I appreciate the ride, guys," I said as I climbed out. "Good luck to you both."

"See ya. See ya." They roared off into the darkness.

At sunrise, I found myself walking through a Jewish area of town, followed by a black area, and then an Italian neighborhood. I could not believe that I was in America. The signs, the shops, the people—all looked to be from many different countries.

Examining my map and comparing it to the address Delores had given me, I climbed aboard a subway train for a while, then a bus, and by one in the afternoon I had arrived at her apartment building. Outside, I hesitated a moment. She undoubtedly thought I was somewhere in the South Pacific right now. Not having her phone number, I was unable to call her and warn her I was coming. Maybe she wasn't home? And how could I even be sure she would welcome me now that we weren't at the romantic Mexican Riviera?

Only one way to find out. I walked up to the building and rang the outside doorbell with her name next to it. A female voice scratched out of the speaker, "Who is it?"

"Delores, this is Owen from Puerto Vallarta."

"Oh, my God, I can't believe it! I'll be right down!"

So much for not welcoming me. A minute later the door swung open, and Delores was standing there with a big smile on her face. She looked just the same—black hair, dark eyes, olive skin. Beautiful. I reached out and embraced her.

She led me down the hallway to her apartment and closed the door behind us. Before I could say a word, she wrapped herself around me and kissed me savagely. She pulled me to the living room couch, and we both fell onto it. "Owen," she said, "if you want to fuck me you can, but we'll have to hurry because my boyfriend will be home any time now."

I stared at her. Maybe it was the fact that we were in a New York City apartment instead of a sunny bedroom overlooking the Pacific Ocean. Maybe it was the fact that I had been through so much since I last saw her. Maybe it was the fact that she was offering herself to me the way someone might toss a Kleenex to a friend with a runny nose. Or perhaps it was the little detail of the boyfriend—but somehow, nothing felt right about this.

I touched her cheek. "Delores, you're special and I care about you. But I can't make love to you—not this way." I smiled. "Besides, I'm on my way to Europe, and I might not get out of here for days if I took you up on your offer."

She laughed. "What happened to you Owen? How did you end up in New York?"

"It's a long story, and I won't go into the details just now. But essentially the *Eros* had to go back to San Diego, and I couldn't catch a boat to the South Pacific. So I decided to make my way to the far side of the Pacific through the backdoor, via Europe and Asia. I figure to be flying to Europe within the next few days, so I just came to say good-bye."

We talked for about an hour. She held my hand and looked into my eyes, and I felt her attraction and a sexuality that was beyond description. But I had changed, and she knew it. When I stood to go, she embraced me and placed her head close to my heart.

"Delores, I wish you well. I can't tell you when or where I'll see you next, but take care and be happy."

"Thank you, Owen." She kissed me.

The realization of how superficial our relationship had been caused me some sadness on the one hand. On the other hand, we really had some crazy fun together. And what was wrong with that?

I left knowing that I would probably never see her again.

That night I slept at a nearby YMCA. I then rode the subway to JFK International Airport and started shopping around for the cheapest fare to Europe. This turned out to be a no-name airline flying into Luxembourg. Departure time was five o'clock that afternoon.

Outside was a little grassy area where I spread my damp clothing out to dry. Repacked, the backpack weighed less than eighteen pounds. It contained one sleeping bag, a space blanket, and one change of clothes. There was also the little Tupperware container I used to keep my matches and passport dry. In Central America, the jungles were wet and hot. Europe would be wet and cold, so I kept the container.

On the plane, I sat back in my seat and thought about my childhood philosophy. As a kid, my mother used to tell me not to get dirty, or I could expect a spanking when I got home. Usually having fun meant getting dirty, so the moment I got that first smudge I just reasoned there is no sense in stopping now. If I was going to get a spanking for a little dirt, I might as well go all the way.

And why was I thinking about this? Because as I sat there in a metal tube hurtling through the lower atmosphere on its way to Europe, I knew there was an excellent chance I wouldn't get back to San Diego on time, in which case I figured I might as well be really late instead of a little late.

On my mother's birthday, nine hours after leaving New York, I stepped off the plane in Luxembourg, rested and refreshed. Picking up my backpack, I checked through customs and strolled out of the airport with no fixed plan of where I was going next. All I had was a vague sense of geography. My initial plan was to visit some of Western Europe, then walk or hitchhike east through the Iron Curtain and Turkey, and then descend through the Middle East and into India. I wanted to spend a little time in India, believed by some to be the foundation of where much religious and metaphysical thinking originated. I would then continue to Bangladesh, and from there to Burma and Malaysia. When I reached the Indian Ocean, I figured I could find work on any number of ships or boats heading east.

Walking away from the airport, the ancient buildings, narrow streets, and small cars captivated me. It was a perfect summer day as I hiked out of the city and into the countryside, which was marked by tumbledown outbuildings and old stone houses that often looked deserted.

Finally, I came upon an apple orchard. Apples lay all over the ground. Clearly no one was harvesting them, so I stopped and picked up a dozen big apples and put them in my pack. I planned on eating anything I found along the way, short of road kill. In a newsstand at JFK, I had seen a book called *Europe on Five Dollars a Day*. I decided I could do it on one dollar a day, or less.

I hiked into Paris on a cool, misty morning five days later. Four hours later, I walked out of Paris by a different route, heading toward the English Channel.

SECRET GARDEN

I left France from a coastal town called Boulogne sur Mer, crossing the English Channel to Dover. The hovercraft ride was fast, loud, and full of vibration. In less than an hour the beautiful white cliffs of Dover eased into view against the setting sun. The hovercraft hurtled into the harbor, then lumbered up the launch ramp, and settled down in a big parking lot. We exited the craft, and suddenly everyone around me was speaking English. Funny-sounding English, true, but at least I could understand it.

Although I was getting a late start, I walked on out of Dover and made my way to some distant, rather desolate foothills. It was full dark by the time I arrived, so I rolled out my space blanket and sleeping bag in an area surrounded by low brush and lay down for the night. As I dozed off, I thought about how lucky I was that not a drop of rain had fallen so far on this leg of my trip.

On the *Eros,* I had read a book by the Indian philosopher Krishnamurti, a spiritual man known for bridging and combining Eastern and Western philosophies. I remembered that he lived in a town called Brockwood Park in Surrey, England. I decided that Surrey would be my next destination.

Several days later I arrived in the County of Surrey, where I learned that Brookwood Park was not on any map of Great Britain. When I mentioned Krishnamurti, people would point me in vague directions. Finally, I spotted a postal deliveryman and flagged him down. I figured this guy to be the ultimate authority on directions. After all, who ever heard of a lost postman?

He pointed me down a narrow country road. "You'll come to an old Victorian three-story farmhouse on the left side, and a forest on the right. I think that might be the place you're looking for."

I walked down the road, and sure enough I soon saw a three-story, early Victorian-style farmhouse on one side of the road with a barn standing behind it. I walked up the walkway to the house and knocked on the door. A woman in her early twenties appeared. "Hi, I'm looking for the Krishnamurti Spiritual Retreat."

"This is the Sufi farm," she replied.

"What's a Sufi farm?"

"We're a spiritual commune that follows the teaching of a Sufi, Master Mashaik Fazal Inayat-Khan."

Could be interesting, I thought. "May I stay and visit with you folks for a couple of days?"

"Please come in and wait. I'll get William so you can talk with him."

She escorted me to the kitchen—a large, sunny space where about a half dozen young people stood around. A few minutes later, the young woman returned with a straight-looking man in his early thirties with short black hair, a pasty white complexion, and thick black-rimmed glasses. He held out his hand.

"Hi, I'm William."

I shook his hand. "Nice meeting you. I'm hitchhiking around England and wondered if I could hang out with your group for a few days."

He looked me over. "Do you have any experience with construction or farm work?"

"Yes, to both."

"Well, we don't really have much room at the moment, and the main house is pretty full. Would you mind sleeping in the barn?"

I laughed. "Not at all. That would be like hotel accommodations to me."

"Fine, then you can stay for a while. One of the folks here can take you out to the barn and show you around. We usually eat dinner around five o'clock. You're welcome to join us."

He turned and asked one of the nearby girls to take me out to the barn and show me to the hayloft. A young blonde came over and in a strong French accent introduced herself as Genia.

"I'll show you around, Owen."

She was a petite Swiss beauty with an accent so pronounced it was all I could do to understand her. But she was a gracious tour guide. "This is our barn," she said as we entered the old wooden two-story structure. She pointed at several stalls. "We keep our livestock here, and this is the milking area. Back here the roof leaks, so we are in the process of reroofing the barn." At the rear of the building she pointed up. "And here is your hayloft. This will be where you will sleep. I hope you are okay out here."

"Thanks, Genia, I really appreciate the tour, and don't worry. This looks just fine." She gave me a long look and said nothing. She didn't have to. I recognized the expression on her face as a longing interest to exploring possibilities. I turned and climbed a ladder into the loft.

"Owen," Genia said from below, "if you wish to come inside to get washed up before dinner, you are welcome."

"Thanks, I will."

I climbed to the top of the hay bundles, removed my backpack, sat down, and took a deep breath. I loved the smell of hay and fresh cut alfalfa.

After spreading out my sleeping bag, I kicked back and relaxed. It occurred to me that this was the first time since the monastery that I had been able to just lie still, with nowhere to go in a cozy shelter instead of staying in a jungle, in a desert, under a bridge, or in a storm drain. I would enjoy it while I could. Summer was coming to an end in England, and I knew that soon I needed to prepare for the next, and probably harsher, part of my journey.

Later that afternoon, I walked into the kitchen with a razor, some soap, and shampoo. As I would learn, there seemed to always be people milling about in the kitchen. It was the social center of the commune.

I approached a couple of guys. "Hey, I wonder if one of you could point me to the men's bathroom?"

One of the men introduced himself as Joe.

I extended my hand, "Where you from Joe?"

"Well, I was born here in England, but I spent most of my life in Canada. Just head down the hallway and to the left, mate."

The bathroom turned out to be something right out of the 1920s—a gravity-fed toilet, a claw-foot bathtub, and the kind of deep porcelain sink you might see in an old black-and-white photograph.

I cleaned myself up and walked out into the kitchen to visit with the folks.

Gradually the kitchen grew more crowded than I would have believed—at least twenty-five people, including a large cluster of women working around a large kettle of stew containing potatoes, cabbage, and turnips.

"We're all vegetarians," one of the women told me.

"Great," I said. "Then we should get along just fine, I'm an allgetarian."

"An allgetarian?"

"It means I eat all and everything that's placed in front of me. Why limit yourself when you can be open to all types of cuisine?"

Soon a line formed and folks began helping themselves from the pot. I joined in and then moved into the dining area—a big carpeted room without table or chairs. Everyone sat on the floor.

When William came into the room, everyone fell silent. He said a brief blessing over the food, after which eating and conversation began in earnest. Genia came over and sat down next to me, and I asked her to tell me a bit about herself.

"I have been here for about six months," she said. "I first started following the teachings of Fazal several years ago."

"What is his teaching?" I asked.

"Do you know anything about the Sufis?"

"No, not really."

"Sufism is a practice of seeking divine love and knowledge through a personal experience of God. There are several paths to this enlightenment. One is the Dervish order, which maintains that enlightenment comes through song and dance. Our order is different. We believe that spiritual enlightenment comes through the psychological understanding of ourselves and those around us."

"So, you guys don't play music and spin around until you get disoriented, fall down, and then say you've reached Nirvana, right?"

Genia laughed. "I'm a terrible dancer."

After dinner, William and a few other men approached. "Owen, let me introduce you to some of the guys you'll be working with tomorrow. I think you've already met Joe. This is Heinz, and this is Thomas."

Heinz extended his hand. "How do you do?" His accent was South African.

"Hello." Thomas's accent was German. This Sufi group was quite multinational.

Heinz said, "We're going to do some work on the barn tomorrow. Let's meet here for breakfast and then get started."

"Sounds good."

I awoke the next morning hearing someone moving around in the barn. Peering down from the loft, I watched a stout young woman escorting the cows from their stalls to the milking area. As the cows lowered their heads to the feeding trough, the girl pulled up a milking stool, wiped down the udder of one of the cows, put a stainless steel bucket between its hind legs, and started drawing milk. She knew what she was doing. The white stream struck the sides of the bucket with a racket like water coming out of a high-pressure hose.

In about ten minutes, the woman shifted down the line to the next cow, then the next. Just as she was finishing the last milking, I climbed out of the loft. "Hi, I'm Owen. You look like you've done that once or twice."

She was a sturdily built woman wearing a long dress under several layers of shirts and a wool knit cap. Her handshake was strong. "Yes, I have done this once or twice. My name is Catalina."

"Where are you from?"

"I am Belgian." She reached into a shirt pocket and pulled out a pouch of tobacco and some rolling papers. "Do you care for a cigarette?"

"No thanks. I don't smoke."

She removed a cigarette paper and poured some tobacco and then rolled the cigarette one-handed while stuffing the pouch back in her pocket. The whole process took her about fifteen seconds. She lit up and peered at me through a blue screen of noxious smoke. "Come. It's just about time for breakfast. I got to get this milk inside."

She lugged the milk bucket back to the house. I was smart enough not to try and take it from her. Clearly, she had worked hard for most of her life.

On the walkway just outside the house she tossed down her cigarette butt and then led me into the kitchen area where several people were standing around in conversation. Catalina lifted the bucket onto the counter and then pulled a large pitcher and some paper filters out of a cabinet. She placed one of the filters in a wire strainer and started pouring milk through it into the pitcher. "The breakfast of the day is raw oats," she told me.

"That's always the breakfast of the day," someone else said, and there was general laughter.

Catalina smiled. "If you want to add anything to it, Owen, like fruit or nuts, then you will have to supply that yourself. We usually go to town every week for supplies."

"This will be just fine. I don't usually eat much."

Soon, almost the entire community was standing in the kitchen. I counted twenty-six people—only ten were men. I thought, wow, with these odds it must be really easy to fall in love around here.

Everyone helped themselves to fresh milk and oats. This was my first experience drinking milk still warm from the cow. It was rich and tasty. When I spotted Joe and Heinz conversing to one side of the room, I joined them.

"We were just discussing our project for the day," Heinz said. "We're going to have to tear out about a quarter of the roofing and replace it. It's a big job. Have you done roofing before Owen?"

"A little."

"Great! I think Joe and Thomas are new to this, so we can really use your help."

"I'm new to anything constructive," Joe said with a grin.

"What did you do before you came here?" I asked.

"I was a bank robber."

"A what?"

"I was a bank robber. Then I got caught and spent five years in a Canadian prison. When I got released, I was deported back to England."

I nodded. His background explained the muscles bulging through his snug-fitting shirt. "How in the hell did you end up at the Sufi farm?" I asked.

"While I was in prison I started a correspondence with some people here. After I was deported, I figured this was as good a place as any to make a new start."

I turned to Thomas. "What about you?"

"My story's not that exotic. I was working with computers in London and got bored with it. I used to come here on retreats and liked it, so I finally decided to give up the fast-paced life of London for a more laid-back life on the farm."

Nobody asked me about my background. Maybe I wasn't enough of a member of the commune just yet.

After breakfast the four of us headed out to the barn and climbed onto the roof. It turned out to be covered with slate, a material I was unfamiliar with. I'd only worked with asphalt shingles before. While Heinz surveyed the damage and pointed out the areas that needed to have slate replaced, I looked out across the landscape.

The view was magnificent. A forest grew surprisingly close on all sides. There were probably not more than twenty acres of cleared land surrounding the house and barn, and most of that was uncultivated. Interesting. There was no way the Sufis could be creating an income stream off a handful of cows and the garden I saw behind the barn. How did they support the farm?

We worked on the roof the rest of the day, stripping off broken slate tiles and rotten wood slats, then replacing tiles starting at the outer edge and moving up toward the peak. Once I got the hang of handling the unfamiliar materials, I moved along quickly.

In fact, within three days, I was directing the entire operation. Joe and Thomas lacked roofing experience, and Heinz, who was apparently one of the head guys on the farm, took on a supervisory role with occasional visits only.

On the fourth day the work was complete. After dinner, William and Heinz approached me together. "Owen," William said, "you did a good job on the roof, and we want to thank you."

"Well, it took a day longer than I expected," I said. "But I figure it should last another sixty or seventy years."

They both laughed. "How are your typing skills?" William asked.

"Oh, I type around fifty words a minute."

"Do you? The reason I ask is…would you be willing to stay around here for a while and help us in the office?"

I grinned. "I'd love to stay a bit longer. I like it here."

"Then let's see if we can find you a room inside the house. Heinz, how about if you show Owen the attic?"

On the second floor, Heinz and I climbed a ladder that rose from the hall-way to a one-room, steep-roofed attic with four beds in it. "One person gets each corner," Heinz said. "Three others already live up here, so this corner is yours if you want to get your stuff from the barn."

"A penthouse apartment. How could I refuse?"

I returned to the barn and retrieved my belongings. A warm, dry place to sleep, two steady meals a day, and nice people around me at all times. I felt as if I had just gotten a big promotion. Although I knew I wouldn't be staying here forever, I found myself unwilling to think much about where I might go next. Or when. In fact, as I carried my backpack from the barn to the house, I realized that for the first time in longer than I could remember, I felt truly happy.

The next morning after breakfast, Heinz took me to the office. It occupied a small outbuilding adjacent to the main house, what had probably once been a carriage house and then a garage. The Sufi farm possessed only one vehicle, a truck parked outside in the driveway.

Heinz escorted me to a woman sitting at a desk with her back to the door. "Genia," he said, "here's one of America's fastest typists and business wizards, Owen."

Genia looked up and smiled. I wondered if she had anything to do with my promotion from farmhand and roofer to an inside job. She dragged me by the arm to introduce me to the other office staff members, all women: Jill, Connie, and Joan. Jill and Connie were both beautiful and in their mid-twenties. Joan was far less attractive and in her mid-forties. She had the classic old-maid appearance.

But Genia was clearly in charge of the office. Immediately after the introductions were complete, everyone started back to work.

"So what's the nature of this business?" I asked.

"We run a book distribution business from here, sending books throughout Europe and England."

"Books about Sufism?"

"Actually, they're mostly scientific and business publications. It's kind of a niche market that we serve. This is one of the primary sources for funding the farm, along with Fazal's lectures and workshops."

"Where's Fazal now?"

"He lives in Europe and lectures all over the Continent. When he's not lecturing, he comes here to do workshops. He probably won't be back for another month. You just missed him by a couple of weeks."

Genia spent the next few hours patiently going over my job tasks and responsibilities. I would basically be the shipping clerk in charge of responding to both written and telephone orders. Genia was very knowledgeable about all aspects of the enterprise and, despite her hippie attire, quite an able business executive.

The only problem was following Genia's accent. Although I was becoming used to the many different accents used here—half a dozen flavors of English, Swiss, German, French, Belgian, Dutch, Spanish, Italian, South African, and Brazilian—Genia's speech was the most difficult to follow. But in the end it didn't matter because she remained gentle and patient, and conveyed a great deal of affection toward me.

After several days in the office I was pleased with my new job. At first, I doubted that I would like it since I enjoyed working outside, but the cold English rains I had been expecting had finally begun to fall, which made me appreciate my new position all the more.

About three weeks into my time on the farm, William approached me and said, "We're expecting some guests from London this weekend for a workshop. You're welcome to participate if you like."

"Of course. I'm grateful for the invitation. What's the workshop about?"

"Fazal himself will be here, providing lectures and lessons. On occasions like this we usually get about a dozen people from outside who pay to participate in the workshop and live on the farm. In your case, you might say that free attendance is a fringe benefit of your living and working here."

"Great." I was very interested in hearing Fazal speak. The longer I was surrounded by these good people and their way of life, the more I realized that my personal journey was no longer just about getting away from my job, my life of continuous violent confrontation, and my own fears and doubts. It had evolved into a journey toward something. I was discovering that I suffered from a terrible imbalance inside my life. I realized that being a warrior, a real warrior, meant a lot more than just having the resolve to bust heads and make arrests. It even meant more than simply protecting the public from bad guys. It meant conquering the darkness within.

Late that Friday afternoon, new faces began showing up at the farm, and at seven o'clock everyone gathered in the main parlor, a crowd that included the resident Sufis and about fifteen guests. I noticed that the gender ratio remained consistent. Of the guests, ten were women, and five were men. Why, I wondered, were more women attracted to spiritual philosophy than men. I had not seen that many females in one place since my ex-wife's wedding shower. I deliberately chose a seat in the back of the room, so I could watch all the guests.

When Fazal entered the room, everyone fell instantly silent. I couldn't help but remember Sarge's effect on the officers in the briefing room back in San Diego. The head of the Sufi order was a short man in his forties. He had a slight paunch, long hair, and a beard. He wore pajama pants and a shirt under a dark vest. Watching him, I remembered something else from my earliest cop days: my training officer telling me of the importance of appearances. "If you want people to think you're a good baseball player," he said, "you have to dress like a good baseball player." Fazal wore his uniform well. And not just the clothes. Although he clearly hailed from Europe, he had the deep, dark eyes of an Indian mystic.

Fazal stood at the lectern for a moment, looking around the room. Then he began talking about the weekend's program and some of the wisdom that he hoped to impart to the participants. Most of what he said was familiar, even to me. Since coming to the farm, I had done some reading on Sufism in order to discuss the religion intelligently with its devotees. Sufism had begun as a mystical Islamic belief system devoted to discovering divine love and wisdom through a direct personal experience of God, not unlike the teachings of charismatic Christian sects in the United States. And like any other religious sects that had been around a while, Sufism had itself diverged along a variety of paths. Each path was designed to help its adherents experience divine love and spiritual wisdom in the world by developing both their divine and human natures, but the techniques differed. The famous "dancing Dervishes" Gina had mentioned represented a branch that emphasized attaining ecstatic states through song and dance while Fazal's more modern sect emphasized understanding oneself psychologically as a means of forming a direct personal relationship with God.

I listened as he spoke while allowing my gaze to wander around the crowd. My attention kept coming back to one of the visitors, a beautiful young blonde in her mid-twenties. She sat by herself, and every time I looked at her she seemed to sense my gaze and looked back with a smile. At first, I was embarrassed by how often she caught me looking at her, and then I just gave up and stared. Our eyes locked. The sound of Fazal's voice and the presence of other people became distant. Instead, I was completely absorbed by the young woman's eyes. Oddly, the sensation wasn't sexual as with Delores. It was warmer and deeper as if this woman were someone I recognized from long ago.

After the lecture, everyone moved toward the exits. In the surge of the crowd, I lost sight of the young woman and got up to hurry toward the doors. As I got to the parlor doorway, there she was, standing in the next room with her back against the wall.

I walked up to her with my hand extended. "I'm Owen. What's your name?"

"I am Anna," she replied in a heavy German accent. Her eyes were a piercing blue, and she turned them down suddenly as if afraid their light might hurt me.

I took her hand gently and then placed it on my heart. "I am Owen," I said again. She raised her intense eyes. "Why are you looking at me like that?" I asked.

She blushed. "Because, I want to have your baby."

I must have looked like I was about to fall off a three-story building. She pulled my hands against her heart, and for the first time in my life I was totally speechless, partly from stunned embarrassment and partly because my brain was having a milkshake moment, blending thoughts with utter confusion.

Finally, I just pulled myself against her warm body and laid my forehead against hers. Our hearts raced together. "Anna," I said, "where are you staying tonight?"

"I don't know. I arrived just before the lecture, and they haven't given me a room assignment yet."

"Would you care to stay with me?"

I knew what she would say, and I was right. "Yes, I would."

We retrieved her suitcase from the hallway, and she followed me up to the attic. By now I had personalized my space with a carpet, mattress, a wooden box for a nightstand, and a couple of candles for late-evening reading. I had hung a bed sheet from the ceiling to the floor as a room divider for some privacy. It looked all right.

Anna and I sat on the bed and talked. She told me she was born and raised in a small village near the Black Forest in Bavaria. She wore little or no make-up, yet even up close she was unbelievably beautiful and sensual. She had some of the qualities and appearance of my ex-wife. I was very uncertain about so much and held so much fear and apprehension with relationships. I talked about it and she listened.

It was difficult to say when or why, but we soon reached a moment where nothing more needed to be said. Anna drew me toward her. The moment our lips touched, the love making began.

Although we existed in different bodies, at the moment we climaxed there was no sense of separateness. There was only oneness and union in a world far removed from an attic on a Sufi farm in a country called England on planet Earth.

The next morning I woke to Anna lying in my arms. Although the light in the windows told me the hour was early, none of the other attic denizens were there. As I wiped blonde hair from Anna's face, she opened her eyes. We kissed and she said, "Owen, was that a dream last night or what? It seemed too good to be true."

Although I was pretty much ready to stay in the attic all day, I was now completely devoid of fluids and figured we should get up to replenish ourselves.

While Anna was cleaning up in the upstairs bathroom, I strolled down to the kitchen. Catalina was already there, pouring the morning milk through the filters. "Catalina," I said, "you're amazing. You already got the morning milking done?"

She shrugged her broad shoulders. "With the guests here for the weekend, I wanted to have everything ready early."

"Can I help?"

"Nay. Just go ahead and help yourself to some oats."

I did as she said and then backed to one end of the kitchen and started eating. In a few minutes, Anna came down and immediately got her food. She seemed to know the routine, presumably from previous visits to the farm. She came over to stand next to me and began eating.

Soon the room began to fill with people until it looked and sounded like Grand Central Station. The visitors in particular were excited and full of anticipation of the rest of their visit. With breakfast finished, most of the people poured out into the living room. I squeezed Anna's hand and then slipped to the back of the room while she stayed up front with most of the paying guests.

As Fazal entered, the chatter subsided immediately. On this day, there was a podium for him to stand on, which served the purpose of elevating him above the majority of the audience. This time I really paid attention to what he said. I was a bit ashamed to acknowledge that I had not listened much to what he had said the previous night. I was too busy focusing on Anna. That was bad because, apart from the basic idea that he believed psychology was the key to spiritual awakening, I had a very weak concept of what Fazal actually believed or taught.

Fazal's discourse continued throughout the day, but by the time we broke for dinner I still was not sure what he was preaching. What, exactly, did the other people in this room find so compelling about his beliefs? Or was it more a fascination with the man himself? It was not easy to understand. Here he stood, a short pudgy man, bearded and long-haired, dressed like he had just finished shopping at a backcountry Indian yard sale. Why was everyone staring at him with such rapt attention?

As everyone got up to move around at the break, I moved to Anna's side. "Anna, how about you and I take a walk before dinner?"

"That's a great idea."

I was constantly amazed by how the English and Europeans could stay locked up in a room all day long without going stir-crazy. Maybe I had spent too much time on the open ocean or hiking the mountains, always going somewhere. Staying cooped up inside a building for long was difficult.

Outside, darkness had already fallen, so Anna and I returned to our room to get our jackets. We walked hand in hand into the forest. To me, the sounds and impression of an English forest were very different from those of an American forest, quieter and more still.

Anna, on the other hand, was far from quiet and still. She chattered on and on about Fazal's lecture. I just nodded, not wanting to bring down her energy by saying that Fazal sounded like an ordinary guy talking about ordinary things. Or maybe I wasn't spiritually evolved enough to grasp the depth of what he had to say. Either way, I was better off holding my own counsel. After dinner we climbed up to our loft and talked for hours and then made love. The next day we repeated the same routine as the day before.

Again, Fazal lectured all day. When it ended, everyone gathered their belongings and headed back to London and various awaiting trains, planes, and ships. Anna and I kissed and hugged, and she gave me her address outside Köln, Germany. "I will write you the moment I get there," she told me.

Then she turned, walked out the door, and was gone.

I spent the rest of the evening in my room reflecting on the events of the weekend. Not just the weekend but the last seven or eight months. Up until my journey began, I had always been a one-woman man. It was beginning to seem as if I were falling madly in love with every woman I met. I had never considered the possibility that I could truly love more than one woman during my life. Now it seemed more than true. It seemed fundamental.

I had started my journey with so much anger, hurt, and resentment toward my ex-wife in particular and women in general. Now I realized that there were many beautiful women out there who longed to be listened to, shared with, and loved. In return, they would nurture my wounds with all the warmth and love that they could give.

I had never before considered that promiscuity could have redemptive power, but it did. This knowledge opened my heart in a way the words of all the philosophers I had ever read or heard did not. I wondered what the brothers of the Benedictine Order would say about the idea of promiscuity as a path to Enlightenment. They would hardly approve, but it seemed that my paths were always the ones less traveled. My task was not to turn aside from where my own heart led me. No matter where the path went, I would have to keep myself open to every possibility.

After breakfast the next morning, I went up to the office to work. Within a few minutes, I got the feeling that something was wrong. The women in the room were acting a bit strange toward me. By the end of the afternoon, I realized that some of the single, unattached women on the farm considered me in-house fair game and were disappointed that my first relationship here involved an outsider.

The farm women were all unique and, for the most part, quite beautiful. The high ratio of women to men made life for a single guy very interesting. But the weekend with Anna made me realize that a new batch of guests would be coming here for classes and lectures every few weeks. It would be foolish for me to get tied up in a farm relationship with so many beautiful, unattached women coming and going. Besides, I was just passing through—before long my journey would carry me to new parts.

It was common for many of the Sufis to hang around in the living room after supper, sharing stories and experiences. I soon learned that it was also common for singing and dancing to break out spontaneously. These weren't

Dervish moments. The Sufis here did not dance and sing to attain enlightenment. They did it for fun. Music seemed to create a kinship and bond between them just as effectively as discussions about Enlightenment.

One evening after such a session, Genia came to me and asked, "Owen, do you play any instruments?"

"No, I'm afraid I'm in a minority here."

In fact, I had decided that Europeans as a whole had a much greater appreciation for music and the arts in general than the typical American did. In a way it made sense since Europeans shared a thousand-plus-year tradition of high art, and most of the great classical musicians originated in Europe. In Europe, training in the arts began in early childhood.

Genia said, "I found an old guitar in the basement the other day. Would you like it?"

"Sure, I'd love to try it out." I said with plenty of eagerness but not much hope. I had never even tried to play a guitar before.

Shortly thereafter, Genia brought me her gift, an old classical guitar. It was missing one of its six strings, but other than that, it looked beautiful. Heinz, who had played in a band before turning his life to a pursuit of spiritual understanding, tuned it for me and showed me six or seven chords. "With these simple notes, Owen, you can just about play any song."

I realized he was oversimplifying things, but I was thankful for his counsel and decided I would master this thing immediately. That night I played my five-string guitar until dawn.

Somehow, the spirit of Sufi thinking took hold of me through that guitar in ways it never had through intellectual discussions. It was as if a floodgate of creativity opened within me. Strumming my handful of chords, I wrote lyrics, developed melodies, and sang every night into the early hours of dawn.

I did all this despite the fact that I was a terrible musician. My voice was lousy. I sang so off-key that even I could tell. My sense of rhythm was poor. Even after several weeks of practice, my guitar playing sounded like the picking of someone without fingers. But it didn't matter to me. The music I made in the Sufi attic lifted me beyond my worries, my problems, and my fears. It elevated me into another world. The more I played, the more baffled I became that so many Sufis living on the farm had left behind careers in music. How could a psychological approach to enlightenment possibly surpass what I felt making the worst possible music?

When people down below began hammering on their ceilings with broomsticks to get me to stop, I toned it down a bit. It was like being in love for the first time. No matter what anyone says or thinks about your first girlfriend, you don't care. Love turns a blind eye to anything not of the heart.

Also, there was a culture clash involved. Europeans generally display much more refined and restrained behavior than Americans. No doubt many of the Sufis viewed my unrestrained musical talent, or lack thereof, much like they viewed the typical overweight American tourist walking the streets of Europe in his aloha shirt and Bermuda shorts, with his belly exposed and camera hanging from the neck. To them, my music was totally outrageous and immune to all criticism. But then, they could not have known that one of my inspirations was the country-western singer Hank Williams, Sr. Therefore moaning, yelping, and other heartfelt sounds were more important to me than adherence to the musical classics of Europe.

A couple of weeks rolled by, and a new ground of people began showing up for another weekend retreat. It was a small group, and the weekend was intense since it seemed that everybody who came to these retreats was generally looking for something. People searching with great intensity for their inner spiritual connection. These weekend retreats tended to leave you with the feeling of a wild rollercoaster ride. There were plenty of emotional ups and downs that sometimes left you physically drained.

During the first evening, I noticed that one of the participants was an unattractive blind woman. Somehow, during the second day I ended up having lunch with her. Her name was Nadia. She was about ninety percent blind and wore huge coke-bottle glasses. When I introduced myself, she raised her hands and placed them on my face.

"I am very happy to meet you, Owen." She began going over every inch of my face with her hands. I could see that she was drawing a picture of my face in her mind by using her hands. At first, I was surprised. But when I saw the expression on her face as my face became a picture in her mind, I was pleased that she took the time to see me with her hands.

Nadia was from the Netherlands and spoke several languages fluently. She was about twenty-seven years old but looked and acted much older. Her complexion was pale, and her hair was straight and appeared to have not been washed in a week. Her clothes were as unkempt as the rest of her. Her teeth were crooked, and she had the hairiest legs that I had ever seen—even for a European woman. To be blunt, her exterior was strikingly unpleasant.

But she was unique. We talked for a good hour, and it became clear that, like me, she was on a spiritual quest. Her blindness merely added another dimension to the journey.

Saturday evening after dinner, I returned to the attic and started playing my guitar. I was beginning to find the unrelenting discussions about spiritual matters repetitive and tiresome. Strumming on my five-string allowed me to drift to a place of simple peace and quiet. I was humming along with the chords I played when I heard someone coming up the attic ladder. Whoever it was made a ton of noise. Then Nadia's head appeared above the floor. "Owen, is that you?"

I stopped playing, surprised. "Yeah, Nadia, it's me. How did you find me clear up here?"

"I heard you playing your guitar. Can I come up and join you?"

"Sure, why not?"

I got up and approached the attic ladder and she handed up her white cane and a narrow black box about twelve inches long. Then I grabbed her hand and helped her up. "What's in the box?"

"My flute. It's what I play."

I escorted her to one corner of my bed and sat on the far end to watch her assemble the flute. She did it deftly and with loving care. Then she held it in both hands as if to warm it.

"Would you care to start with something, and I will follow?"

Nobody had ever asked me to play for them. For the first time in my musical career, I became self-conscious—but only for a moment.

I started strumming a slow, soft melody. Nadia placed the flute to her lips, and suddenly the attic filled with the sweetest sounds I had ever heard. I was almost too overcome to continue my part of the duet, but I continued on. After the song ended, I put my guitar down. "Nadia, that was really beautiful. Would you play something else for me?"

She removed her glasses and placed the flute against her lips. As she drew out the first pure note, her entire face transformed, radiating a soft and lovely glow. I closed my eyes and swayed back and forth like a cobra to the sound of the music.

We took turns playing for one another and playing together and didn't stop until midnight. By that time, I had moved so close to her that our crossed legs were touching. A couple of burning candles threw a soft glow on her that beckoned me toward her. I reached up and touched her face. She immediately grabbed my hand and held it to her cheek.

The next thing I knew, she was bringing my hand down to her breast. Her face moved toward me, and the moment our lips met she pulled me into her as though I was a limp washcloth. She heaved me down along her side and unleashed a flurry of passionate kissing upon me as though the floodgates of a dam had broken. I was completely shaken by her passion.

Within minutes, she had removed all of her clothing, and I mine. We were both in my sleeping bag. My mind flew through a whole array of questions centering on what the hell was I doing.

But if I couldn't see clearly where I was going, Nadia advanced with the surefooted pace of one gifted with perfect sight. And just as when we were making music, she held nothing back.

The next morning, I awoke early. Nadia lay sleeping next to me. Oh, my God, I thought, what have I done. In the unrelenting light of day, she was no longer a flute-playing nymph, but rather, the last-round draft pick in a bar-room closing up at two in the morning. She was beyond unattractive. What would everyone else think of me now?

I carefully extracted myself from her arms and the sleeping bag and crept downstairs to the kitchen. It was already crowded with people, particularly weekend guests preparing to get started on the day's spiritual development.

About twenty minutes into my morning oats, Nadia entered the room. I froze. She looked her same old befuddled, groping self. What if she started telling everybody that we had spent the night together making love?

She moved through the crowd, occasionally raising her hand to touch a face. No question she was looking for me. I walked outside and sat on the grass to think.

At that moment I despised myself for my shallowness and hypocrisy. How dare I be ashamed for spending the night with Nadia, for making love with her? Last night, she had shared a beauty that transcended physical form. Her beauty was deep and her gifts precious.

And here I sat, betraying that beauty because I feared what others might think.

When I walked into the lecture hall, classes were well under way. I found Nadia sitting in the middle of the floor, surrounded by guests and Sufi farm residents. I edged into the group and sat beside her. When I touched her hand, a smile came over her face that seemed to lighten everything around us.

I sat with her for the remainder of the afternoon. During the breaks we talked, but there was no physicality to it. I realized she lived utterly in the moment and seemed to accept the flow of life around her with perfect ease and grace.

When classes ended that evening, everyone packed up and got ready to go to the Farnham train station. I helped Nadia to the van and waved to her as it pulled away even though I knew she could not see me.

But she knew, I thought. She knew.

That evening I didn't play my guitar at all—no doubt to the delight of my downstairs neighbors. Instead, I thought about Nadia and the fact that she—and not Fazal or William or any other spiritual leaders on the farm—had taught me the most fundamental lesson of a spiritual warrior. One should never presume that something is what it appears to be on the outside. Love comes in many disguises.

The next morning, William approached me. "Owen, how would you like to take one of the cottages in the woods for your own private quarters?"

I had seen the cottages before, a half dozen tiny structures in the woods about a hundred meters from the main house. These were usually reserved for visitors attending the weekend retreats. "That's fantastic," I said. "Let's go take a look at the place."

William led me to the remotest cabin. The inside consisted of a single room with a double bed, a nightstand, a kerosene lamp, and windows on opposite walls facing the forest. Like a Benedictine cell with a view. I grinned. "This is really beautiful William. It's perfect."

He looked relieved, no doubt thinking that this solved the farm's problem of Owen's late-night singing and lovemaking. On top of that, it meant he was pleased with my work in the office and around the farmyard, and the fact that I seemed to fit in well with the rest of the group.

I went back to the attic and retrieved my backpack and sleeping bag. Now I could really sing to my heart's content. Yet, deep inside, I knew that this comfort was only temporary.

Two weekends later, new groups of people began arriving from London. Anna was in the first batch. The moment she got out of the van, we made eye contact and without a word she ran up and embraced me. I walked her back to my cottage in the forest. It was a perfect setting, the sun setting through autumn trees, our footsteps crunching in ankle-deep, crispy leaves.

When Anna walked into the little building and looked around, her reaction was the same as mine, "This is perfect."

She unpacked her things and soon the room was full of burning candles and incense. We sat and talked for hours. We had a lot more in common with one another than physical chemistry. We were both searchers on a quest for knowl-edge, understanding, and love. We had both become dissatisfied with the status quo and set off on quests to define ourselves in new ways. Anna's journey periodically took her 500 miles across Germany and the English Channel while mine stretched to a destination yet unknown.

Of all the things we talked about, these were unspoken. In our companionship, though, we somehow found reassurance and comfort in a world without meaning.

We skipped the usual first-night group meeting, and settled in for an evening of lovemaking in my little candlelit cabin under the forest canopy. Lovemaking usually focuses one's energies and thinking into the moment, and it was in those moments that Anna and I experienced peace and tranquility.

When the birds began to sing at sunrise, Anna decided to head up to the farm to get washed up and ready for the day's events. After she was gone, I lay in bed wondering how it was that most marriages are devoid of the most precious thing Anna and I shared—the magic of living in the moment. How could that happen? Reflecting on the destruction of my marriage and all the other things I once held dear to my heart, the answer seemed important, yet I had no immediate solution.

Finally, I got up and left the cabin. It was still very early so in the golden light of dawn, steam puffing from my lips with every breath, I walked to the barn to see if Catalina had started the milking. She wasn't there yet, and the cows were still in their stalls. I put feed and alfalfa in the troughs and released the cows. They immediately charged into the milking stalls and started eating. I grabbed a bucket and started milking.

I was on the second cow when Catalina walked in. "Owen, you are up early this morning."

"I decided to get the milking started. I hope you don't mind."

"Of course not. I'm delighted that you like to help." Catalina leaned against the wall, pulled out her tobacco pouch, and rolled a cigarette one-handed as usual in the time it took most people to remove a store-bought cigarette from the pack. She lit it and the smell of tobacco smoke joined that of cow dung.

When I finished milking, my fingers were so numb, I could hardly move them. Trudging toward the kitchen with the bucket in my hand and Catalina smoking along beside me, I wondered how the hell she did this every day, year in and year out, in all kinds of weather.

While Catalina began straining the milk, I stood to one side with my hands in my pockets and watched.

"Are you big hungry this morning?" she asked.

"Yeah, I guess I am. I missed dinner last night."

"Oh, is your girlfriend here visiting this weekend?"

"Yeah, how did you know?"

"It's not like you to miss dinner." She smiled, and I thought it strange that she didn't have a boyfriend. As rugged and tough as she appeared on the outside, she was all woman inside. But then I had spent more time with her than most people on the farm. I had seen her speaking softly to the cows and even singing to them during the milking. I could imagine how tender she would be with a man.

Soon the breakfast area was set, and the weekend guests and residents began filling the kitchen. Anna came along, looking awesome, especially considering how little sleep she had gotten the night before.

"Shall we get in line for some breakfast?" I asked.

"Sure, what's on the menu this morning?"

We both laughed.

By the time Fazal arrived, a steady hum of excitement and anticipation was running through the group in the main hall.

As always, Fazal continued on at length without ever mentioning divinity, peace, or even enlightenment. His words stressed the importance of understanding of one's self psychologically. I listened, and as before, heard nothing profound. Talking about stuff that needed fixing did not appeal to me. No doubt my years on the streets of San Diego had provided me with plenty of character defects that needed fixing, but I did not think psychobabble had the power to unlock any magical doorways to peace of mind. I was searching for something I had lost within myself. Once I found that, I could always fix the other things. Anyway, the closest thing to peace of mind I had found so far was a woman's warmth and sexual friendship.

Then I heard Fazal talking about pain, pain of all kinds, and how to endure it. I remembered the night I was beaten nearly to death by a gang member laced out of his mind on angel dust. His gang name was "Big," and for months he had sat around the proverbial tribal campfire after his release from prison, describing how he would fight to the death rather than go back to prison. Big was tall, with an overblown prison-yard build. Few hoods—never mind cops—cared to tangle with him unless they were armed with an equalizer of some sort: a baton, nunchucks, or a semiautomatic weapon.

The night Big and I had our confrontation, I had received a radio call to meet a citizen at a housing project. It was a routine call—nothing urgent, just something to handle when I got around to it. That's what I thought. At around eleven o'clock on a moonless night, I parked my unit and walked up to the front door of the house. The interior lights were off. I rang the doorbell.

A shadow lunged toward me from the side. Before I could turn, Big had driven me off the porch and onto the pavement. Gripping my neck with both hands, he began pounding my head against the pavement. The smell of PCP was so strong that my eyes watered as if I had been pepper-sprayed, and I could not break loose from that superhuman grip. My holster was underneath me, and I couldn't reach my weapon. I fought back as best I could, but my position was awkward. He was so amped that I probably couldn't have hurt him with my fists even if I had been standing with him toe-to-toe. I felt myself drifting away with each head slam.

So was this how it was going to end for me? Some gangster punk smashing my brains out on the pavement? With a sudden twist of my shoulders, I managed to break free of his grip enough to fling him half off me. We rolled together across the lawn and into the street, exchanging vicious punches to the face and body.

Suddenly I saw my service weapon clatter across the pavement, knocked free of the holster. Big reached toward it. I swung around him and got him in a sleeper hold, but he started crawling, dragging me toward the pistol. He would surely kill me the moment he grabbed it. I tasted the blood dripping from my nose and mouth. I felt its warmth oozing down the back of my neck from open head wounds. I felt it splattering against me as I repeatedly rammed my fist into Big's face. Blood ran so profusely from both our bodies that soon its smell overcame the reek of PCP.

Big got to his knees. With his hand twelve inches from my weapon, his body abruptly dropped, crashing powerlessly to the pavement. I handcuffed him and radioed for a cover unit and then sprawled out on Big's body—too exhausted and hurt to do otherwise. Eventually Big was carted off to jail for attempted murder, and I drove myself to the hospital. I couldn't allow anyone on the street, not even other cops, to know how badly I was hurt.

It turned out to take fifteen stitches to close the wounds on my scalp. Add those to the fifty or so others I had accumulated in the previous three years. And I thought I understood pain very well. What could a quasi-Indian mystic teach me about pain?

When Fazal asked for a volunteer, I raised my hand. He smiled. "Come on up, Owen. Have a seat on the floor. Now, what I'm going to do is pull your hair together and tie it to a rope. Then I will pull you up to the rafters and let you hang suspended by your scalp. All I want you to do is relax."

I nodded, conscious of a lot of stares on me.

Two residents gathered around to give a hand tying my hair up as if this wasn't the first time Fazal had demonstrated this awe-inspiring demonstration.

Soon I felt my scalp tighten, and a moment later my body began to leave the floor. My scalp also began to pull away from my skull, but I just relaxed with it. In a minute I was dangling several feet off the floor. I felt no pain at all.

Judging by the wincing faces around me, others felt the pain for me. After a few minutes, I was lowered again, and Fazal stepped in front of me. "How did that feel, Owen?"

"It felt like I was hanging by my scalp. But it didn't hurt—if that's what you're asking."

I returned to my seat and watched as almost everyone else took a turn at being hauled off of the deck by his or her hair. Not everyone succeeded in the art of surrendering to pain. For those who did, I supposed this was a mental victory comparable to walking over a bed of hot coals. For me, it was kind of a farce. If there was one thing I had learned from being a cop, it was that letting go of pain—or anything else, for that matter—was easy when you knew the consequence was not going to be death.

I already understood the point that Fazal was trying to make. Knowing how to surrender to the powerful forces of life resulted, ironically, in the ability to live a painless existence. Suddenly, I flashed back to the storm and the Angel of Death. Could Fazal's demonstration have been the final missing piece that provided meaning to that event? I wondered.

Sunday morning, I lay awake in the cabin with my arm around Anna, watching the cool light grow in the room until I felt her stir awake. "Anna," I said, "do you want to see me again after I leave the farm? If you do, I'll stop and visit you on my way east."

"Leave? You're leaving?"

"Yes. It's time to continue on." I paused. "It's been more than a year since I left San Diego with a plan to travel around the world. I was supposed to be back by now, and I'm not even halfway done."

"But Owen, winter is coming. You're a California beach boy. You have no idea what winter on this Continent can be like."

"Anna, I've been through a hurricane and a firefight in Central America. I've been chased by soldiers with automatic weapons. I've seen the Angel of Death face-to-face. I'm not afraid of a little snow. I've decided to head for India. The sooner I leave, the sooner I'll get there."

"India…I have always wanted to visit India." I felt her cheek flex in a smile. "You really intend to walk halfway around the world?"

"Well, that and hitchhike. From India, I'll head down to Burma or thereabouts and look for a berth on a ship heading east. Basically, take the reverse route home from what I originally planned."

She rolled on top of me and kissed me deeply. "If you do not come to Köln and visit me on the way to India," she said, "I will be very angry."

"I think you need to work on that emotion psychologically," I said, and kissed her back.

Sunday evenings were usually quiet on the farm, especially after a group of guests left. I walked into the main lecture room and found Genia sitting in the corner reading a book. "Genia, could I talk with you? I have a revelation I would like to share."

She lowered her book. "Sure. Sit down."

I sat on the floor facing her. "Genia, this place has been great for me, and the people are awesome. But I've come to the decision that it's time for me to leave."

Her face fell. "Why?"

"It's hard to explain. Everything is perfect here, but maybe that's the problem. I think I'm getting too comfortable. It's making it difficult for me to complete the search I began."

"What are you searching for?"

"I don't know. But whatever it is, it's not here."

I could see the hurt in her eyes, but she managed to smile. "When will you leave?"

"Tomorrow morning."

She leaned closer and hugged me. She was soft and gentle. Despite her beauty and the fact that we had worked together for months, this was the closest we had ever been physically. I never had a sister, but Genia had become one to me.

The next morning, I packed in the dark and walked out to the barn before the sun rose. I wanted to help Catalina with the milking one last time before I left.

She was already busily at work when I arrived. "Hi, Owen, you're up early, aren't you?"

"Catalina, I wanted to help one last time with the milking. I'm leaving this morning."

"Leaving? What do you mean?"

"I'm heading east."

"But, Owen, you're my relief. I need you here!"

I smiled to myself and said nothing. Catalina was the most independent woman I had ever met.

She handed me a bucket and I started milking and as usual she was done with her cow before I was half-finished with mine. She set her pail aside and rolled a cigarette. "So you're back on the road," she said. "You started out on the farm here in this barn, and now you will finish here in the barn."

"Actually, I was hoping to finish in the kitchen with one last bowl of oats and milk if that's okay with you."

She laughed, dropped her cigarette to the ground, and carefully stepped on it. We walked back to the kitchen without saying anything else, but I could see the melancholy on her face.

In the kitchen, I walked up to William and asked if he had a moment.

"Sure, what's up?"

"I wanted to thank you for all the kindness and hospitality you and the others have shown me here, but I've decided to leave the Farm."

He blinked. "This is rather sudden, isn't it?"

"Yes, it is. But my visa is going to expire shortly. And if I don't leave now, I'll have to leave in the dead of winter."

He nodded. "I understand. Does Genia know about your decision?"

"I spoke with her last night. I was just about to go say a last good-bye to her."

"She'll miss you. You've been a great help to us, especially in the office. We appreciate what you've done. I hope you'll stop by when you're in the vicinity."

"Thanks, William. I certainly will."

After eating that last bowl of oats, I returned upstairs and found Genia seated at her desk going over some documents. She rose and embraced me. "Owen, be careful, and try to write if you can. Take care of yourself. I hope to see you again."

I kissed her on the cheek and tasted a tear. She pulled away and moved briskly to her desk. "When you get to London, go to this address. You can stay there if you need a place. The woman who lives there visits here all the time. I don't know if you actually met her, but I'm sure you'll recognize her." She slipped the folded piece of paper into my pants pocket and hugged me again. When I released her, she returned to her desk and sat staring at me through flowing tears.

"Thanks, Genia," I said, and left.

I returned to the forest house and grabbed my backpack. Once again it contained everything I owned and now one additional sleeping bag, thanks to the generosity of a Sufi resident. There was also a space blanket, a map, and a few toilet accessories. All the clothing I owned, I wore. Fully packed, the bag weighed twenty-two pounds. Perfect.

One of the farm residents offered to drive me to the train station, and I accepted even though I knew I wouldn't be taking the train. I carried $500 in currency, and that would have to take me a very long way.

After the farm van drove away from the train station, I turned and headed toward the motorway on-ramp.

I got lucky with rides, and reached London that same afternoon. It was raining when I arrived at the address Genia had directed me to. A tall, very slim brunette woman answered my knock. As Genia had predicted, I recognized her immediately from her visits to the Farm.

"Hi, Owen, I'm Diane. Come on inside. Genia called and said you might be stopping by."

"Thanks." Stepping into the foyer, I removed my backpack and followed her to the back of her apartment where she showed me an empty and cold room. It looked like her meditation chamber with a couple of pictures on the wall, a small table decorated like an altar, and a window looking down on a busy street.

After washing up and combing my hair, I found Diane sitting at her kitchen table. She was perhaps twenty-five years old and built like a cross-country runner, tall and lithe. Her face showed lines of strain, but her smile was warm and genuine.

"I hope that you don't mind, but I took the liberty of pouring you a glass of wine."

I grinned. "That's the best offer I've had all day."

I sat and we raised our glasses. "To your journey," Diane said.

It felt nice—a warm, cozy home, the company of a pretty woman, good wine to drink. "Tell me about yourself," I said.

It was like opening a dam. A monologue began and ran through that bottle of wine and the next one, with only a slight pause when she sliced some cheese and bread. When the second bottle of wine was empty, Diane took my hand and led me to her bedroom. Evidently being a good listener and not putting out an "I want sex" vibe was an aphrodisiac to her.

She lit candles and disrobed. I followed her lead, not so much out of lust, but rather curiosity.

From some of the things Diane had told me about her past relationships, I suspected she was a difficult woman to please, but it turned out I had no idea what I was getting myself into. She wanted to skip all foreplay and simply climax, which she did the moment I entered her. From that point on she never stopped having orgasms. Even after I climaxed, she still wanted more—and immediately—so she worked on herself for a while. After twenty minutes, she came back to me again. The moment I was ready she continued with her orgasms.

I had never been with a nymphomaniac before, but it was clear that no amount of sex was enough for Diane. Three hours later, I was completely worn out. She threw herself back on the mattress and slipped her hand between her legs again. "No man has ever completely satisfied me," she said.

When I rolled over and started dozing off, she was still deep in the throes of satisfying herself. As I fell asleep I decided that the common male fantasy of being with a sex-starved nymphomaniac wasn't all it was hyped up to be.

I got up early the next morning and was relieved to find Diane sleeping deeply. My clothes were scattered all over the bedroom floor. I got dressed as quickly and quietly as I could, then bent over Diane, and kissed her on the cheek. She opened her eyes.

"Diane," I said, "I've got to go. Thank you for sharing your evening with me."

She started to sit up. "Can't you just stay for a couple of days?"

"Sorry, I can't. But if I get back this way, I'll be sure to stop by." I picked up my backpack and, in seconds, was on the streets of London, walking fast in case she came after me.

An hour later, I was standing on the on-ramp of the northbound motorway out of London. Although I knew I needed to turn east soon, I wanted to head up the west coast of England first. I had always wanted to see Scotland and figured that with a bit of luck I could get there in a day or two.

Fortunately, hitchhikers in England weren't uncommon, and my experience on the road had thus far been good. In fact, once the drivers found out that I was an American, they usually went out of their way to help me. By late afternoon, I had reached the southwestern tip of Scotland—350 miles covered in less than seven hours, which was a New European hitchhiking record for me.

A trucker on his way to Ireland dropped me off in the center of Dumfries, a cozy little village nestled along the coast which was also the ferry landing for traffic going to Ireland. I entered a local truck stop and asked for a cup of coffee.

"Are you American?" the waitress asked.

At least that's what I thought she had said. I could barely decipher her accent. "Yeah, how did you guess?" I asked.

"Well, it was your accent of course," she replied. I think that's what she said.

"I wonder if you might know where I could get some work?" I asked.

"Well…" She glanced from side to side and then leaned across the counter as though she were about to divulge a secret stock tip. "There's the Newton Steward Castle just outside of town that they've been working on for some time. You might try there."

I finished my coffee and headed down the street the way the waitress directed and, at sundown, arrived at Newton Steward Castle. The mossy stone structure was under major renovation, with scaffolding and heavy equipment everywhere. No one was around.

Still, I walked around the castle ruins. A dog barked in the near distance, and a few minutes later, a gentleman approached me through the growing gloom. With a Scottish accent, he said, "Good day, sir. May I help you?"

I examined him. He was wearing a Sherlock Holmes deerstalker cap, a plaid wool jacket, and rubber knee-high boots. To top it off, he gripped a bent briarwood pipe in his teeth.

"Good evening," I said. "My name is Owen. Could you tell me who's in charge of this castle renovation?"

"I am. I'm Doctor Belbray."

A doctor in charge of construction? That was a first. "I heard you might be looking for volunteers to help with the project," I said, embellishing a bit on what the waitress had actually said.

"Really? Where did you hear that?"

"There was some talk in town at the coffee shop."

"I see. Well, why don't you come inside for a spot of tea, and we can talk."

He turned and headed toward a small stone building that looked like a detached part of the original castle. I followed him.

I can always recognize an authentically ancient building, not so much by the architecture or rustic appearance, but by the fact that I have to duck when entering. That was the case here. The doctor led me into a combination kitchen/living room and said, "Please have a seat." He busied himself making tea at a cast-iron coal-and-peat-burning stove.

I pulled out a wooden chair and sat down at an antique table. The only window in the room glowed with soft pink light from the sunset, and the fire on the hearth flickered orange and gave off a pugnacious smell of burning peat and coal. I felt as though I had stepped back in time several hundred years.

The doctor set a big steaming cup of black tea in front of me. "By the way, what did you say your name was?"

"Owen."

"And where are you from?"

"From the States, but I've been living and working for the past several months on a farm in Surrey, England."

"Do you have any construction experience, Owen?"

"A bit, sir."

"Well then, tell me what experience you have with rebuilding castles."

I smirked. "In this lifetime, none."

He smiled back around the stem of his pipe. "Well then, tell me what you have in mind to do around here."

"Looking at the rock pile you have out there, I figured you might need a good strong back and someone who's good with a pick and shovel. I know you can't hire me for wages since I don't have a work permit, but I'm willing to work for food and lodging."

The doctor appeared to consider my proposal as he struck a match and lit his pipe. "As you can see, we have a very big project here. How much time are you willing to commit?"

"Well, honestly, my visa's about to run out, so I have to be out of the country in less than a couple of weeks."

"Where do you intend to go then, if you don't mind my asking?"

"I'm heading east—perhaps as far as India."

He nodded and then gestured around himself. "As you can see, we don't exactly have five-star accommodations here. But we could certainly use your help if you're willing to offer it."

"I am."

Dr. Belbray gave me a brief historical overview of the castle. Constructed over 1,500 years ago, it had fallen into ruins in the last 200 to 300 years. The British Government had taken on the task of restoring many old structures for both historical reasons and as a means of providing work for some of the unemployed laborers across the United Kingdom. It seemed like a worthwhile endeavor to me, and I said so.

Dr. Belbray grinned. "Well, then, that's splendid. We usually get an early start. So, why don't you follow me, and I'll show you to your sleeping quarters?"

We walked to the center of the living room, where he pulled on a rope hanging from the low ceiling. An overhead doorway slid open, exposing a pull-down ladder. He hauled it down, and I followed him into a room with an even lower ceiling. This room had just enough room to stand up and was about one hundred square feet, with one mattress, a nightstand, and a lamp. It looked like a cross between my attic space at the Sufi farm and my cell at the Benedictine monastery in South Carolina.

"This will be perfect, Doc," I said. "I appreciate your hospitality."

"Right, I'll call from downstairs in the morning when breakfast is ready. Be prepared to heft some stones?"

In the morning, the first hint of light was met with rustling sounds from down below, so I rolled out of my sleeping bag and climbed down into the kitchen.

"Good morning," Dr. Belbray said. "And how did you sleep?"

"I slept very well. I didn't realize how tired I was, and it's pretty cozy and warm in the attic."

"Yes, it's probably the warmest room in the entire house."

I sniffed the air appreciatively. "What's for breakfast?"

"Eggs, bacon, toast with marmalade, and tea." Soon I learned not to ask. This morning's menu proved to be the same breakfast served from today until eternity, with only slight variations in the way the eggs were cooked or the degree to which the toast was burnt.

The doctor and I sat together and ate while discussing everything from the weather and politics to the local neighborhood. It was clear that the doctor was not only well educated, but that he had the analytical mind to go with the Sherlock Holmes appearance.

While clearing the table, I glanced out the window and saw a line of a half dozen men forming in the front yard. Dr. Belbray noticed, too. "Well," he said, "we might as well get started by checking in the men who are here to work for the day."

They turned out to be a rugged, weather-beaten bunch, and no spring chickens at that. I estimated that the youngest man in the group was sixty years old. They looked more like attendees at a senior citizen revival meeting than a work crew. No wonder the doc was so eager to sign me on.

By seven o'clock the crew was all checked in and ready to begin work. Overhead, the sky was filled with black and gray clouds that strangled off every bit of sunlight. Nobody seemed to notice but me.

"Owen," Dr. Belbray said, "if you follow these gentlemen over to the castle, they'll get you going."

He returned to the house, and I followed the ragtag crew of geriatric laborers to the castle. We reached the castle where the men stashed a small cache of picks and shovels. They moved slowly and didn't talk at all.

The day was young, and I wanted to tear into the job with a running start. But I feared I was a wire charged with 120 volts surrounded by a group operating on twelve volts. The group split into teams of three men each. My team ended up in a six-foot-deep ditch. One of my partners turned to me and said—as best as I could understand it—"Do you wish to pick or shovel?"

I grabbed the pick. "How deep do you want the trench?" I asked.

"About six feet, lad," answered a guy whose hands and face looked like the bark of a weathered tree.

I turned and began swinging the pick at the hard-packed earth, moving like a rabbit chased by a pack of hounds. My intention was to blow these old guys away. I was young, strong, fit, and fed. It was me against them, new against old, free enterprise versus socialism, west versus east, American new against Scottish old. I was going to wear these old guys down to nothing, so I thought.

Two hours later, I stood in the beginnings of a rain that would last all day, my arms quivering, the breath sawing in and out of my lungs. I realized I was in way over my head. These guys were heavy hitters in the big league of moving dirt. They not only were able to keep up with me, but they put in extra licks just to keep the earth moving. When the rain came down cold and heavy, they didn't miss a beat.

Finally, one of the men offered to give me a break on the pick, and I gladly traded for a shovel. I marveled at these guys. They were relentless and untiring. By giving up on competing with them, I soon found myself in their rhythm. It was not one of hyperactive motion, but rather steadfastness and will.

At lunchtime, we all gathered under a roofed portion of the castle and built a small fire in the dirt to boil water for tea. When the water began to boil, the kettle was passed around and cups were filled. A few of the men had brought brownbag lunches with them while others just took flasks out of their back pockets and fortified their tea.

Lunch was over in thirty minutes, and we were back in the trenches, digging steadily away in the rain. At the end of the day, it was all I could do to drag myself out of the trench. None of my fellow laborers had altered their pace from the start of the day to its finish.

My coworkers rarely spoke. By the end of my ten-day stay in Scotland, however, I felt I was an accepted member of their distinguished earthmoving club. And I felt duly honored. Moreover, the backbreaking work and the daily rhythm I experienced helped me develop a new strategy for the next portion of my journey—find an unflagging rhythm and stay with it, no matter what.

With fewer than two weeks left on my visitor's visa, I would leave the United Kingdom in the middle of winter. My timing could not have been worse. Scotland was very cold and wet. I could only imagine what the winter would be like on the Continent where there was no ocean to moderate the temperatures.

I started hitchhiking south. By nightfall, I was in the small village of Glastonbury, which seemed to be composed primarily of historical ruins. While looking for a place to set up camp for the evening, I came upon a stone tower called Tor located on a small hill overlooking the village. I had heard a bit about it in town. According to the local people, it was a very old structure that the ancient people built for the gods.

I set up my sleeping bag that evening on the tower's damp stone floor. No windows or doors were intact. As the wind and rain howled around the tower that night, the impressions that came to me in my sleep were old and powerful. I had a feeling as though an initiation into the ancient mysteries of Tor danced around my unconscious while I slept. I left that morning not really certain I could explain the sense of awe that overwhelmed me.

I hitchhiked and walked the remainder of the following day until I arrived in Chatham on the east end of London. At sundown, I purchased a ferry ticket for my trip back across the English Channel.

Early the next morning, I arrived at Vissingen, Belgium, and started walking. After three days, I reached Germany near the city of Köln. Knowing that Anna lived outside Köln, I wanted to see her one last time before I started my trek to India.

I called and told her I was only a few hours away. Delighted she begged me to stop by her place. By the time I reached the farm-like countryside where she lived, it was already dark, and snow had been falling for an hour. I walked up to a large, two-story farmhouse with the porch lights on and knocked on the door. Moments later, Anna was standing before me. The smile on her face was pleasant enough, but tense.

Before I could ask what was wrong, a young man crowded into the doorway next to her. He looked me up and down. "So, this is him, huh?" he said with disdain. Then his expression softened, and he said to Anna, "Well, are you going to invite him in, or just let him stand out there in the rain?"

I stepped in.

"Owen," Anna said, "this is my ex-boyfriend, Christian."

Be cool, I thought.

He reluctantly extended his hand toward me, like a boxer who has entered the ring knowing he's about to get the living shit kicked out of him.

I shook it politely. "What's up?"

Christian released my hand and walked away. Instantly the tension left Anna's body, and she threw her arms around me and kissed me. "Come on up to my room."

The moment we were there, she closed the door and I dropped my backpack to the floor. "Anna, why don't we sit down and talk? I need to know what's going on."

She pulled up two chairs and we sat. "Owen…this house belongs to Christian. I broke up with him after meeting you at the farm."

"How long did you live with him before?"

"About seven years."

"Ooh," I moaned. Christian certainly had every reason to hate me. I realized I was responsible for some of his pain and suffering. I knew all too well the anguish that comes from losing a loved one. "Anna, maybe it would be best if I slept in a different room."

She nodded and took me to a spare bedroom near Christian's and then returned to her own room. I tried to make enough noise setting up my sleeping bag that there could be no doubt in Christian's mind that I was not sleeping with his ex-girlfriend while in his house.

I closed my eyes feeling like a lowlife. If Anna had explained the entire situation to me earlier, I would not have shown up at all. But since I was there, I had to make the best of it.

The next day, Anna and I ate a late breakfast together. Christian came down a little later. When Anna briefly left the room, I said, "Hey, Christian, why don't you and I go for a drink someplace where we can talk more in private?"

"There's a pub just down the street." I got up and let Anna know her ex and I were going off to the local tavern. She smiled.

A few minutes later, Christian and I were walking in freshly fallen snow toward an old village. No surprise, the tavern we entered was empty at eleven o'clock in the morning. The barkeeper approached us and said something in German. I didn't speak the language, but I knew what he'd said.

"Christian, how about a good German beer?"

In German, he asked for two rounds. I had never tasted German beer before, but I swallowed the first beer like it was a Rocky Mountain Coors Kool-Aid. I wiped my mouth. "Christian, I'm really sorry about showing up like this. Anna never told me about you."

He hunched over his mug. "Things started falling apart between us a couple years ago. I guess we were both looking for a way out of the relationship, but neither of us had the courage to face the truth." He shrugged. "Perhaps you unknowingly became the instrument for our breakup."

A few hours and six beers later, I stepped out of the bar, dropped to my hands and knees, and suddenly started puking in the freshly fallen snow. Christian laughed. "I can see you never drank German beer before, right?"

"I guess the doggy position in the snow was a dead giveaway," I said, and laughed along with him. Male bonding is a simple thing. Christian and I had established respect for one another, and I had acquired a reverence for German beer.

We returned to the farmhouse and found Anna in the kitchen. I put my arm around her waist and said, "Anna, I better leave now. It was good to see you again, but I'm sorry if I brought you and Christian further pain by showing up."

"Let me at least accompany you to the bus and ride far enough to make sure you take the right direction out of town."

"That would be great."

She left the room and returned minutes later dressed for the cold.

We walked for several blocks to a bus stop and stood together in companionable silence.

As the bus arrived, we jumped on board, paid the fare, and walked to the very last seat. "I'll make sure you take the right transfers to get out of Köln," Anna said.

We changed buses once, twice, three times. On the last one we sat in the back of the bus again. Slowly the bus began to fill with new passengers. The windows were locked shut and the heater fans blasted hot air. My stomach began to twist, then to kick. I turned to Anna. "Please, tell the driver to stop the bus. I've got to get out."

"This isn't where we get off. We still have a ways to go," she answered.

I stared at her. Of course she didn't realize only an hour earlier I was kneeling in the snow on all fours puking my guts out.

Seconds later I was doing it again, vomiting in an immaculate German bus with such force it looked like a small tsunami wave of beer rolling down the aisle. A chorus of screams permeated the air, and the bus driver hit the brakes so hard the big vehicle took a nosedive—the wave slammed against the front of the bus.

I stood up and wiped my mouth. "I feel like I've just given birth."

"Let's get off." Anna looked disgusted as she pulled me toward the door. The bus driver, screaming unintelligibly, charged toward us down the puke-soaked aisle.

"What's he saying?"

"He wants you to pay money before he opens the door to let you out."

"Tell him I'm feeling sick again—even more than before."

The next thing I knew, a vigilante group of riders had pitched me off the bus.

Lying in the snow wreathed in diesel fumes, Anna looked down at me with disgust. I rose to my feet. "Sorry for making such a scene. In my country I have never heard of a bus driver demanding money for puking on a bus." Then, as an afterthought, I added, "Of course I've never heard of anyone puking on a bus, either."

"Paying for cleanup is the custom in Germany." The stern look remained on her face.

I put some snow in my mouth, swished it around, and spat it out. "Well, I guess this isn't exactly the kind of sendoff either of us expected. I'm sorry to have to leave like this."

There wasn't much else to say. When a bus heading back to Köln pulled up, Anna stepped on and waved farewell to me through a window. The bus withdrew and I stood alone in gray daylight, snow tumbling from the sky all around me, I realized that my search for love through the endless cycle of relationships had only served to damage me. I needed to take a breather between relationships and renew myself. Time would empower me and allow me to make better choices in relationships. Time was taking me to places and people unknown.

THIRTEENTH ZONE

I spent the next couple of weeks moving eastward although with ever-increasing difficulty as rides got fewer and harder to catch. I stayed fairly close to the highways since truckers were my best hope for covering long distances, and I traveled mostly at night because truckers tended to avoid daylight hours when the roads were congested. Still, the pickings were slim.

It didn't help that the weather remained cold and wet. I had no proper winter clothing, so I wore every piece of clothing in my backpack, including a heavy windproof sailing jacket I had since my time on the *Eros*. My protection against rain and snow consisted of wrapping my space blanket around my head and torso.

Trucks and cars, when they did stop, were the only semi-warm and dry places I could find to sleep. The nights I had to camp out, I always looked for barns or bridges to provide shelter. Sleeping in the open invariably meant waking up either soaking wet or covered with snow, or both. Then it would take days to get my sleeping bags dry again.

At the Hungarian border, the agents took my passport, frowned, and told me to have a seat. I had no objection to that. The building was warm and cozy while outside a heavy snow was falling.

Eight hours later, I felt differently and asked what the holdup was. Actually, I had a pretty good idea that a bit of cash would expedite the next few yards of my journey, but I felt about bribery in Hungary as I had in Central America—no way.

In the end, it took the Hungarians eighteen hours to process my paperwork, which ended up consisting of simply rubberstamping my passport. Either the agents finally admitted to themselves that I had no money and nothing in my backpack worth confiscating, or they resented my use of their office as a Laundromat to dry out my sleeping bags and clothes. At midday, I set off toward Budapest in the plunging snow.

My experience at the Hungarian border should have been my first clue that things were going to get more difficult now that I had entered the Communist Bloc. The people here were almost as poor as Andean peasants, so commercial truck traffic lightened significantly as I made my way toward Romania.

Again, I was flagged into yet another customs house where the officials asked to see my passport and then told me to sit in the lobby and wait. This sounded familiar, so I immediately spread out my drenched sleeping bags and sat back in the warmth to wait.

The entire day passed, and the next. By that time, I was completely dry, warm, rested, and hungry. I knew that, eventually, the customs agents here would have to acknowledge that I was not what they considered a typical American. I carried no big roll of cash, traveler's checks, camera, or magazines. What valuables I did possess I hid on my body, leaving just a few dollars in my wallet.

Thirty-two hours after I entered the office, a customs official finally returned my passport and said in broken English, "You are clear to go."

I frowned. "Do I have to? I like it here. Perhaps I could get a job here. Are you hiring?" I started to unroll my sleeping bag on the floor. The agent looked worried. A few minutes later, several other officers came up and insisted that I leave immediately. This time they acted as though they were willing to use force to make sure I complied.

I rolled my sleeping bags up again, thanking them profusely for all their assistance, kindness, and patience. By the time I left, they looked thoroughly bewildered, and I felt at least a little vindicated.

Several days later I was walking toward nightfall through a howling blizzard in rugged mountains somewhere outside the town of Cluj-Napoca. I trudged into the wind, squinting, almost blinded. Even breathing became difficult as the cold stole the power of my lungs. I began to get concerned that if I didn't find shelter soon, the Angel of Death would come to me in the form of a snow owl.

Although I was walking on the shoulder of a major road, I hadn't seen any vehicular traffic for hours. There were no visible houses, farms, or towns around me—just an empty road vanishing into driving snow. I felt numb all over, but I knew that if I stopped moving I would freeze to death in minutes. Thinking about Genia's warnings back at the Sufi Farm and my own flippant disregard for them, I forced myself to walk on…and on.

All at once, a large truck loomed before me, parked on the opposite shoulder of the road with smoke whipping out of its exhaust stack. I stumbled up to the driver's door and pounded hard on the frosted window.

A second later, the glass dropped down a half inch and a voice said something in German that probably meant, "Who are you, and what the hell do you want?"

I shouted back, "Please, can I come inside? I'm freezing to death out here!"

The driver rolled the window down a bit more, presumably to get a better look at me. My desperation was undoubtedly not hidden by the icicles hanging from my beard. The man's eyes widened, and he waved for me to come around to the passenger side.

I did so, flung the door open, jumped into his cab, and thanked him profusely. He pointed at a gauge on his dashboard. A thermometer registered an outside temperature of minus twenty-eight degrees centigrade (about minus nineteen Fahrenheit), and that did not include the wind-chill factor.

The driver was stretched out in a sleeping bag he had extended across the cab's front seats. I unpacked my two sleeping bags, spread them on the floor, and covered myself up.

The diesel engine ran throughout the night, but only to keep the engine from freezing. There was no heater inside the cab. I lay on the vibrating floor and watched a water bottle near my head freeze solid. My body did not stop shaking until dawn, but at least I lived to see the night end.

By then, the driver was ready to get back on the road, unfortunately in the opposite direction from me. I thanked him with all my heart before climbing out of the cab.

To my relief, the blizzard had ended, and the morning sky was clear and sunlit. Shouldering my backpack, I once again set out on the road.

Just north of Bucharest in the small town of Sibiu, I was standing on a highway on-ramp when a truck pulled off the road in front of me. As I ran toward it, I noticed a "GB" decal on the left rear bumper.

"Wow," I said as I climbed into the passenger seat. "Sure is good to see an English truck out here!"

"What the fuck is a bloody Yank doing in these parts?" the driver demanded. "Where the fuck you headed mate?"

"First, Istanbul. After that, India."

"I can't believe it. Jump in. I'm heading to the great gateway to the East myself."

The truck started rolling. After the driver finished working through the gears, I extended my hand and introduced myself.

"I'm George Lee," he said, "hauling out of London. You might as well sit back, relax, and enjoy the ride, mate."

English lorries are not like American semis. They are equipped with a small cab and bench seat behind, with a gap for storage. George had filled his with canned goods, a suitcase, and some tools. The lorry was the most comfortable place I had been in for weeks.

George did not say exactly how far he was willing to take me, and I didn't ask. I resolved to be on my best behavior.

The clouds had closed in again, and snow fell hard for most of the afternoon. Road conditions grew so poor we didn't go faster than twenty-five miles per hour most of that day. But at least I knew why George had decided to burden himself with a passenger. He had been on the road for more than a week and welcomed some company, especially since I spoke, more or less, the same language.

Late that afternoon, conditions got so bad we had to pull over. George explained that his driving situation was rather unique. The lorry belonged to a friend called away on an emergency even as the truck waited, fueled, supplied, and ready to go with a shipment of machine parts bound for Iran.

Iran. I doubted anybody would be willing to share this little cab with a stranger for the length of time it would take to get that far, but I was more determined than ever to become George's best buddy.

We had at least one thing in common. George was recently divorced. He gave me all the details of coming home from a long haul to catch his wife with another man she had met in the pub. He grabbed a shotgun and held it to the guy's head. Although he didn't pull the trigger, something in his life changed at that moment. It was another bond we shared. I, too, knew what it felt like to nearly take a life.

That first day with George became two days, then three, then four. We usually pulled off to the side of the road each evening, built a fire, and heated some of the canned goods from behind the seat. George said he had packed enough to last the eight to ten weeks he expected the roundtrip trek between Tehran and London to take. Knowing that my appetite was cutting into his supply, I took charge of the fire-building, cooking, and cleanup duties. Fortunately, George was low maintenance. We ate every meal right out of the cans.

Although the truck was equipped with a radio, it rarely picked up a station. George had planned for that by bringing along a tape player. Unfortunately, he had only one tape, "The Best of Tammy Wynette." It never stopped playing. Throughout half of Eastern Europe, I listened to the First Lady of Country Music accompanied by the English lorry driver and background vocalist George Lee. He knew every word to each song, and soon I did, too.

As we sang our way down from the higher mountains, mud replaced the snow on the roadway—slippery mud, growing thicker the more we descended. Fortunately, George's skill at the wheel was remarkable. Many times his rig began to slide, but the perfect combination of acceleration and braking kept us on the road.

One evening, as nightfall approached, I was certain George had taken a wrong turn somewhere. We were out in the middle of nowhere churning through a river of mud six to eight inches deep. Only the trees on either side of the roadway and an occasional passing ravine hinted at where the pavement might be. George explained that we had to keep going. If we stopped, we would never get the rig moving through the mud again.

When we finally reached a safe, dry area, George pulled over and parked. We each ate a can of cold beans for dinner. I rolled out my sleeping bags on the floor of the rig and lay down while George took his place on the bench seat.

And the farting began.

George launched the war even before I had finished zipping up my sleeping bag. Not to be outdone, I responded in kind. Soon the cab sounded like a concert studio. Between gaseous rebuttals we both laughed like children. The flatulent duel continued for several hours before we finally ran out of, well, gas.

Still, I lost. Farts are evidently heavier than air. Lying on the floorboards felt and smelled similar to sleeping on the floor of a public restroom next to an overflowing toilet.

On the fourth day of our journey together, George and I arrived at the gateway to the East, the fabulous city of Istanbul, Turkey. It was like setting down on another planet. Instantly everything changed: people, language, culture, religion, food, street signs. Istanbul was a big city, with the conveniences and vices of any modern metropolis. But in many parts of town—particularly the markets—I felt as if I had stepped back into the past.

George announced that we were looking for a truckers' stop he had heard about. Finding it just outside the city on the main road going east, it amounted to nothing more than a restaurant surrounded by a large parking lot. Still, we were happy to see two other lorries from Great Britain. George parked his rig close to them, set the brake, and turned to me with a big smile. "Well, shall we go inside and meet the other blokes?"

"Cheers," George said when we found "the other blokes" seated at a table in this third-world restaurant.

His countrymen stood and everyone shook hands. John was a bearded, middle-aged gent with a heavy Scottish accent. The full beard made up for what little hair he had on top. He explained that he was also on his way to Tehran. Daniel was an Irishman driving for an English company and was on his way back from Tehran. In his middle thirties, he had a slight build and looked rather weathered for his age.

The waiter came up and asked in broken English, "What food like, English?" It became apparent that this was the total sum of the waiter's English-speaking ability. After some back-and-forth we realized that the only items on the menu were stew, bread, and tea. Tea was about the only social beverage available throughout the Middle East, a fact that Daniel complained about bitterly.

"From here on out mates," he told the rest of us, "you can forget about finding any alcohol. Bloody Muslims."

When the stew arrived I attacked it as if it were my first real meal in weeks, which of course it was. The ferocity of my appetite surprised the English, who had the waiter return three times before I was full.

Meanwhile, John and George grilled Daniel about the road conditions they should expect farther up the road. Daniel answered and then grinned. "One more thing. I counted almost two hundred lorries crashed and abandoned alongside the road between here and Tehran. These fucking Arabs graduated from riding camels and donkeys to big rigs, and not one of them can drive worth a damn!"

There was no hurry to finish the after-meal conversation since it seemed the only place to go back to was our trucks. But after a while I began to squirm. "Hey, do you have any idea where the loo is?"

Daniel hooked a thumb over his shoulder. "Go outside and hang a right. The outhouse is in the back."

John added, "Bring your own toilet paper 'cause these locals don't use anything to wipe their ass."

After stopping at George's lorry long enough to grab a roll of toilet paper, I walked behind the restaurant and entered a detached stone building. To my dismay, the facilities consisted of nothing but a hole in the floor with a pitcher of water beside it. I closed the door. So, this was a modern Turkish restroom.

Not that I had any option after three helpings of stew. I unbuttoned my two layers of jeans and dropped my two layers of under shorts. With all the tight-fitting clothing bunched around my calves, the trick became to squat low enough to hit the hole without falling into it.

Once I got aligned, I let loose. It must have been something in the stew, but I felt as though I were having an Ex-Lax attack. I was afraid I was going to cause the hole to overflow, but it seemed bottomless.

I stood and pulled up all my garments and was trying to kick toilet tissue into the shithole when the outhouse door flew open and there stood a middle-aged Turkish man dressed in traditional clothing. He looked at me, at the shit-hole, and then back at me. A look of disgust drew over his face, and he turned and left. Clearly, everything he had ever heard about filthy infidels had just come to life in that outhouse.

Later, I learned that the water jug on the floor wasn't used for quenching one's thirst.

"Well," George said when I returned, "we've decided to hit the town tonight."

"That's great," I said. "What do you have in mind?"

Daniel spoke up. "I know an underground place where we can get whiskey and women."

John slapped a hand on the tabletop. "I'll go unhook my cargo and we can pile inside my cab, if one of you guys will park in front of my trailer so nobody steals it."

A few minutes later, we all crammed into John's cab and headed off to some nightspot apparently known only to a handful of English lorry drivers.

Soon we drove up to a large, windowless commercial building. John parked across the street, and we exited the cab. Reaching the door of the building, we found ourselves staring at a tough, burly-looking Turkish bouncer. He was dressed traditionally in pajama pants, shirt, and turban and was armed with a rifle and bandoliers of bullets wrapped across his chest.

Daniel approached him and started talking. He appeared to be a recognized customer because the Turk stood aside.

Two steps inside the building, I halted in shock. The dimly lit interior was roughly the size of a city block. There had to be at least a hundred tables scattered across the floor, and nearly every seat was taken.

We walked through the crowd toward an enormous bar. As far as I could see, we were the only Anglos in the entire joint, but no one seemed to care. A waiter seated us near the center of the room.

I studied the place. It felt like going back to a saloon in the Wild West if you ignored the sheer scale and the fact that most of the cowboys wore turbans.

The room was filled with noise and so much smoke I could barely see the back wall, but everyone seemed to be enjoying the libations forbidden by Islamic law.

Soon a waiter approached. While he spoke no English, ordering was no trouble. Daniel told us the bar served only whiskey, soda, and tea.

Four glasses and a bottle of whiskey were placed on the table. We must have looked like a bunch of salivating dogs ready to pounce on a bone. The waiter no sooner removed his hand than John grabbed the bottle, tore off the cap, and poured us each a large tot. Staring at mine, I leaned toward George and muttered, "We ain't going to have to take any bus ride back to the lorry, are we?"

"What the hell you talking about, mate?"

"It's a private joke. The last time I had a drink I had a fairly exciting bus ride," I said.

John overheard me. "Now there's a good reason for a toast!"

The glasses were raised "to the Yank's safe and exciting journey," and the contents emptied.

I sat back and looked around again as the next round was poured. My eyes were adjusting to the gloom. For the first time I noticed a dozen or so women, all dressed in low-cut tops and short dresses—garb totally unheard of in a country where women were typically kept wrapped and packed in public, without skin showing. These women strolled through the crowd, stopping now and then to speak to a man, then leading him off behind a wall of bed-sheet curtains to one side of the large hall. A short time later they would reappear—the man returning to his drink and the woman going off on a new prowl.

I realized after a while that all the women were damaged goods in more ways than one. Some had only one arm, or one leg, or one eye. In every instance, there was terrible mutilation or scarring. Still, the longer I sat there and the more whiskey I consumed, the better the women looked.

Time passed, and the bottle emptied. Occasionally, a patron would pass out on the floor, or a small fight would erupt. As the hours wore on, these disruptions became more frequent. Still, no one bothered us, which was a surprise. Given the presence of prostitutes and the fact that everyone here was violating strict Muslim religious law concerning the consumption of alcohol, I had no doubt we were in the company of some of Istanbul's worst outlaws and thugs.

The girls worked the floor throughout the evening and eventually got around to our table. Daniel, the most seasoned driver among us, got up and walked toward the curtain rooms with a slim one-handed girl about thirty years old. In addition to the missing hand, she had a thick scar running across her face from one ear to the corner of her month. It looked like an old knife wound stitched together with baling wire.

Daniel returned in no more than ten or fifteen minutes with a grin on his face. Evidently, he had gotten his money's worth for the equivalent of ten dollars. But I personally suspected the going rate was half that amount. And sure enough—within a few minutes, six or seven other working girls congregated around our table to haggle.

Within a couple of minutes, John had disappeared behind the mysterious hanging sheets. The woman who accompanied him had an attractive body but looked as if someone had poured a pot of boiling water over her face and shoulders.

By the time John returned, George was trying to barter the price down to six dollars. Perhaps he counted on a group discount. Two women were hovering around me. One was missing a hand and the other an eye. Both seemed fascinated by my hair, running their hands through it and chattering to one another. Perhaps it was the color or just the quantity. Most of the local men shaved their heads.

Soon more prostitutes gathered around, attracted like flies to sticky paper. All of us Anglos were feeling no pain at this point, having downed nearly two full bottles of whiskey. The rest of the bar seemed just as loud and out of control even though it had to be well after two o'clock in the morning. Every time one drunk fell off his chair, another showed up to take his place.

I noticed that some of the prostitutes had gone behind the curtains at least a dozen times. It seemed that the only men in the building who had not been back there so far were George and I, which made me realize that not even my golden locks were responsible for all the attention I was getting. The truth was that George and I had become leftover meat to be devoured by the destitute whores of Istanbul.

Daniel and John, recognizing this, began to encourage the women to bid on us. Soon George and I each had three whores competing for us. George's settled first, and in a moment, he was walking toward the hanging sheets. My ladies were less genteel. Their bidding turned into arguing. Suddenly, the one-handed girl reached down with her good arm and bodily hauled me out of my chair. The one-eyed opponent grabbed my other arm, and they began yanking me in opposite directions. Only when Daniel and John convinced the second one that she could have me next did she let go.

The next thing I knew, I was being dragged toward the sheets by the one-handed woman. I meekly followed.

We walked through a slit in the sheets. A big, ugly Turkish man sat on a wooden chair nearby. My one-handed tour guide spoke to him briefly and then pulled me along a corridor consisting of ten cots separated from one another by sheets.

Coming to an empty cot, she pulled me in and slid one of the sheets closed behind us. She briskly slipped off her panties and straddled the cot, then pulled me down opposite her. She started unbuckling my belt and yanking at my many shirts, clearly eager to get down to business. As my pants fell around my knees, she raised her dress and pulled me onto her. She didn't want to kiss. She didn't want to talk.

I wasn't used to making love without feeling some degree of passion. But this wasn't lovemaking. It was a race to see how fast I could get in and out. To my shock, in less than five minutes I was expended. She pulled her dress down and dragged me back down the sheeted hallway.

As we passed the gatekeeper, she muttered a few Arabic words, and the next thing I knew we were both back at my table.

So was George. I poured myself another whiskey when my one-eyed woman friend grabbed my right wrist and two other incredibly mutilated women fixed onto the other. They began arguing. The shouting attracted still more prostitutes. Before I knew it, the situation had dissolved into a full-blown cat-fight—screaming, punching, scratching, and kicking. Hair and blood flew in all directions. Whores knocked over tables and drinks. The spilled drinks seemed to be more than the patrons could bear. A group of Turkish men leaped onto the girls in an attempt to break up the fighting.

Instead, the battle spread to the nearest men and then radiated out through the remotest room until everybody in the place seemed to be running over to join in. Again, I thought about the Old West. This was like a satire of *Gun Smoke*.

The other Anglos and I managed to slip away from the fighting until we were pressed against a wall. Tables and chairs flew. Bottles, glasses, and furniture shattered all around us.

"We got to get the fuck out of here!" Daniel shouted over the chaos. "Now!"

There was only one door to the joint, and we worked our way around to it without ever taking our backs off the wall. The doorman was gone, undoubtedly participating in the fracas.

Once outside, we bolted to John's rig and leaped inside.

Dawn had arrived by the time we got back to the truck stop.

"Time for me to hit the road for jolly old England," Daniel said. "After a night like this, what's there to stay for?"

George laughed and looked at me and John. "What do you think, mates, shall we hit the road, too?"

"Why not?"

Daniel shook our hands. "You guys have a good trip to Tehran. Who knows? Maybe I'll see you on your way back."

Traveling as a two-vehicle caravan, we headed south. Four days later, we came to the little mountain village of Agri, thirty-five miles from the Soviet Union border. As we pulled into town, the first thing we noticed was a string of twelve commercial vehicles parked on the main street.

"This doesn't look right," George said. "Let's pull over and see what the hell's going on."

We joined a bottleneck of German, Dutch, Italian, Swede, Swiss, and English Lorries sitting at a tollgate. George and John got out and talked with other drivers. Returning they looked grim.

"Sounds like the next mountain pass is blocked by heavy snow," George said. "Worse, there's a rumor the Kurds have taken over. People say they're killing drivers and stripping their trucks, so they can survive the winter."

"The villagers say the Turkish soldiers won't go into the mountains to fight the Kurds until the snow melts," John added.

"When will that be?" I asked.

"Next spring."

"What, you mean we might not be able to get out of here for months?"

The two drivers looked bleakly at one another. "Well," George said, "what do you say we go find a restaurant and have a real Turkish meal?"

"Bloody right," John said. "Stewed goat balls and chicken feet would be better than the shit you guys have been feeding me these past few days."

We found a little restaurant that seemed the focal point of the village. Locals occupied most of the half dozen tables.

A young boy came up to us at the door and bowed. "Please, misters, follow me."

He seated us in a booth in the back of the room and then fetched a pot of tea and three glasses. The scalding temperature of the tea was reassuring. I knew that only boiled water was safe to drink in Turkey. There was also a plate of rock sugar on the table. The Turks dumped a lot of sugar in their tea. It was the closest thing to a soft drink that you could order in most of the Middle East.

Soon flatbread was placed on the table. By the time the bucket of stew arrived, the bread and tea were all consumed. Without asking, the young Turkish waiter returned with another pot of tea and more bread.

Our bunch ate as if it were our last meal. I had no idea what was in the stew and didn't care. I swallowed it before I could possibly taste it. My friends did the same, not that eating slowly would have mattered to George anyway. As far as I could tell, his taste buds were about as refined as those of a rat in a garbage dump.

For the next couple days, George and John mingled with the other drivers, trying to sift fact from rumor. Meanwhile, I explored the town, such as it was. There were several blocks of businesses on each side of the main street, but most of the establishments never seemed to open. The streets themselves were a mess, thawing into mud each afternoon only to refreeze after sundown. It was a bleak and silent place, the residents keeping to themselves. Women were practically nonexistent. I heard no radios or televisions playing anywhere.

A week passed. All there was to do was play cards, drink tea, and hang out. I began to feel like a caged animal. Then, to my surprise and delight, the young Turkish waiter came out to George's lorry and called, "Hey, mister, the village elders wish to talk with you in the restaurant."

George and John learned earlier that there was actually a mayor in this place, a man who controlled the information flow to and from the village. Each evening, he and the village elders met for tea, smoking, and conversation at the same restaurant John, George, and I frequented.

George grinned. "Okay, we'll be right there."

"What do you think this is about?" I asked.

"I'm not sure, but it's going to cost us. That's for sure."

"What do you mean?"

"Oh, I put the word out that we would pay for information if it helped us get over the pass. I also heard the village elders could bribe the Kurds to let us through if the proper palms are greased."

I laughed. "You are a wheeler and dealer."

"Do me a favor, Owen. Go get John and that Swiss driver, Hansruedi. I'll meet you all at the restaurant."

At the back of the restaurant sat six elderly Turkish men at a longer table.

The young waiter escorted John, George, Hansruedi, and me to the front group of tables. Hansruedi was a young man, no more than thirty-three. He was on his third trip to Tehran and very impatient to move on.

The waiter walked back to speak to the elders. When he returned he said, "You give me fifty pounds."

"What for?" John asked.

"They want whiskey. You give me fifty pounds."

The drivers all pitched in to generate the bribe. The waiter's eyes bugged out at the sight of what was probably more money than passed through the restaurant in a week, and he sprinted out of the restaurant.

I looked at John. "Where the hell is he going to buy whiskey in this little village?"

John shrugged. "This entire country runs on bribes. Every time I come out here I bring a case of scotch with me. You pass out a bottle here, a bottle there, and you can usually get anything you want. I once had troubles in Istanbul, and what would have been a hefty fine ended up costing me a couple bottles of whiskey."

"But I thought drinking alcohol is against Muslim law." I snorted.

"That's why it's worth its weight in gold in the Middle East. Most of it gets out here from guys like us who have to make a living moving shit through this stinking hellhole. I bet over the past six years I've paid out fifty bottles' worth of bribe whiskey."

He looked over at the other table and sneered. "These little rinky-dink rag head village elders are no different from all the others."

After twenty minutes, the kid returned with two packages. He placed them in front of the head elder, bowed his head, and backed away from the table. The elder, who really fit the title with his ancient-looking, weatherworn face, reached into the bag and pulled out the first bottle of whiskey. Everyone laughed with delight. The other elders began jabbering, and soon the kid returned with a tray of teacups.

"If this is all it costs to get our travel pass over the top of the hill, I believe we got a pretty good deal," said George.

In moments the cups were filled and passed around the table. The senior elder stood, raised his cup in our direction and said something in Turkish.

The waiter translated for us. "He says, 'To your safe travels.'"

"I'll drink to that," George said, and we raised our cups in return.

The drinking continued for a couple hours. George and John, who had no doubt been raised on good Scotch whiskey, showed no signs of intoxication while I was definitely feeling the effects of 80-proof spirits. Hansruedi's face burned with suspiciously bright color, too. Regardless, we all got more relaxed and laid back with each sip.

Across the room, though, the effect of the alcohol was different. The elders fell into an emotional discussion about something. Every time one of them wanted to raise a point he stood and shouted his opinion down the table. The volume increased a notch with every empty round of teacups.

When asked about the argument, the waiter said, "They discussed when is the best time to go over the mountain pass. One of the elders has contact with the Kurds, you see, and there is much argument over how trustworthy this man is."

The first liter of whiskey was nearly empty, and a second bottle sat beside it waiting to be opened. One of the elders stood up, waving his arms and raising his voice in furious disagreement with something said. Then he collapsed face first onto the table. The table rocked and everyone watched in silent horror as the second liter of scotch flipped down and shattered on the floor.

They screamed at their unconscious comrade, but in my opinion it was good fortune that the drinking had ended. The ancient gang would have been under the table before the second bottle was consumed.

George, John, Hansruedi, and I stepped outside into the fresh night air. "What a fucking bloody mess those blokes made of things," John said.

"At least we were able to learn that we should leave tonight around midnight and hit that pass after two in the morning," George added. "It's still a gamble, but the way I see it, we can either go tonight or sit around here until spring comes and the snow melts."

We all stood silently in the cold air for a while until Hansruedi said, "George, John, if you guys are thinking of pulling out of here tonight, then I'm in, too."

"That's fine," John said, "but I think it's a crapshoot getting over the pass."

Hansruedi shrugged. "I know that it is dangerous, but I can't stand sitting here for another two or three months, waiting for spring to come."

"It's now or never, gentlemen," George said. "What's it going to be?"

Another silence fell. The decision had to be unanimous.

Finally, John pulled out a matchbox and withdrew three matchsticks. "Okay. I'm going to break each of these matches into different lengths. The long stick leads the convoy, the short stick takes the rear."

When the drawing was finished, John had won the lead and Hansruedi the middle, with George and me taking the rear. Even in the darkness, I saw

George swallow. The element of surprise would be greatly diminished by the time his truck roared through the Kurdish camp.

"Okay, gentlemen," John said, "it's a two-hour drive to the top. "We've got less than an hour to get our rigs ready to go."

With over one month of living in George's truck, the mud and trash inside the cab did not really look much different from the outside. I started packing utensils and sleeping bags while George checked tires and exterior items around the truck.

When he jumped into the cab, blowing on his hands to warm them, he said, "You don't have to ride with me tonight. If you want, you can probably jump in the lead lorry with John."

"Shit no, man," I said. "I ain't about to leave you now. I came this far with you, and I'm hanging with you all the way."

He almost smiled. "Right. We're going together on this one, you crazy bloody Yank. I'm glad to have you along for the ride."

John leaped onto the running board. "You lads ready to roll?"

"Right," said George.

The sound of truck engines running during the night was not unusual here, but as soon as George put our lorry into gear and started moving down the street behind John, the entire essence of the night changed. I was certain the other dozen lorry drivers parked alongside the road were listening, perhaps sitting up to look out their windows, wondering what the hell was going on.

On the two-lane asphalt just outside town, we all pulled over and got out to huddle in the middle of the road.

"Okay, gentlemen," John said, "this is it. Nobody stops from here on out for any reason until you reach the bottom of the mountain on the other side. You got that? If somebody has to stop, the rest keep going. And remember to hit the pass in as close a formation as you can. We want to go through like a train. The element of surprise is the only thing we have going for us, so make the best of it. Right?"

We all shook hands and returned to our lorries.

Within an hour, as the three trucks labored up the road, snow began to dust the surrounding rocks and grew steadily heavier. There was no other traffic on the road. All was darkness, swirling snow, and the straining roar of hardworking engines.

When the pavement began to flatten and the lorry to accelerate, I was so surprised that, for a moment, I thought we were breaking down. Then I saw

John's rig tearing away ahead of us and realized we had reached the mountain pass.

Looking farther ahead, I saw a fire blazing on the roadway 300 or 400 yards in front of us.

"This is it," George said. "Hold on."

The speedometer needle crawled up to forty, fifty, sixty, as the lorry raced into the mountain pass behind John and Hansruedi's rigs, tires slamming through pothole after pothole. The roadway was no more than one lane wide between head high banks of snow. Ahead, three men, each carrying a rifle, leaped away from the fire burning in the middle of the road.

We shot past them, and I glanced into the rearview mirror as the men knelt and took aim with their rifles. Suddenly, Hansruedi's rig veered sideways and plowed into the snow in a blue-white spray. Instantly, the bandits lowered their weapons and ran toward the rig. George was screaming something at the top of his voice—exactly what, I wasn't sure. My fists opened and closed on my knees. *Nobody stops from here on out, for any reason, until you reach the bottom of the mountain on the other side.* All my instincts screamed at me to leap out of the lorry and go back to help Hansruedi. But a warrior has a brain as well, and it was clear that Hansruedi was finished. Stopping to help would only be suicide.

Ahead, John's rig smashed through the bonfire, and then, amazingly, the cab reared into the air. A moment later, it bucked down so violently the rear wheels also left the road. I glimpsed the massive hump of snow and ice the truck had just driven over—a speed bump of sorts, no doubt constructed by our Kurdish friends.

George didn't slow for it, either, and we hit it so hard the spare tire ripped off the undercarriage and skidded away into a snow bank. That was the last thing I saw before we turned a corner and left the Kurds behind...that and Hansruedi being dragged from his truck and hurled face first onto the road.

Four hours later, our two vehicles reached the foot of the mountain where the land flattened and stretched out into a vast open plain under the rising sun. John guided his rig to the side of the road, and George and I pulled in behind him. We all climbed out and stood together in the cold morning sunlight.

"Could you see what happened to Hansruedi?" John asked.

"I looked back just before we rounded the bend," I said. "They were pulling him out of his truck."

"Jesus. Poor bastard, he didn't have a chance. Let's just hope they didn't kill him."

There seemed to be nothing else to say. Sad and subdued, John returned to his rig and pulled back onto the road. George and I followed, driving in silence over the first straight road I had seen in a very long time.

At sunset we reached the Iranian border and stopped at a place called Bazargan. To my surprise, trucks lined up already, sitting motionless. The drivers, most of them Middle Easterners, lounged around on fenders and bumpers.

George shook his head. "It's amazing how no one in this part of the world seems in a big hurry."

I nodded. It was true. Time seemed to have little control over these men's lives. I wondered if that was good or bad.

Four hours later, I was leaning toward "bad" because we hadn't moved. John's face appeared at George's window.

"All right," he said, "enough of this. I don't know what these blokes are waiting for, but let's drive up to the border and not wait any longer."

"Sounds better than just hanging out here," George agreed.

John returned to his truck and pulled away from the end of the line. We just started to follow when a dozen Middle Easterners rushed toward us, screaming and shouting. Some picked up rocks and cocked their arms as if to throw. Others leaped onto our running boards and pounded on the windows. George hit the brakes fast, but the assault continued.

I watched for a second, and then something inside me snapped. Maybe it was pent-up anger and frustration about what happened to Hansruedi. All I knew was that I was suddenly in no mood for this shit. I pushed down my door handle and slammed my shoulder into the door, blasting it open and knocking the guy standing on the running board to the ground. Before he could get to his feet, I was leaping onto him from the truck. I grabbed him by his collar, lifted him to his feet, and started punching him in the face, over and over again. Two of the rock carriers ran toward me, yelling, arms swinging back. In moments, they too were laid out on their backs, scrambling on heels and elbows to get away from me. Still more guys charged forward. I grabbed the abandoned stones, took aim, and started throwing. One man took a rock in the upper chest and bowled over backward with a wild scream. The rest of the mob finally turned and ran away.

"You crazy fucking Yank!" George yelled from the cab. "You scared the hell out of those poor bastards!" The grin on his face stretched as wide as a barn door. "I can't believe you took those guys on single-handedly!"

I climbed back into the cab. "It's the least I could do to repay you for all the cans of beans and sleepless nights we've spent together in your fart-infested cab."

"Crazy fucking Yank...."

A few minutes later, we pulled up to the border crossing just behind John. It looked like a military outpost with all kinds of uniformed personnel standing on both sides of the border. George turned to me. "I'm going inside with John. Wait here by the trucks, will you? If any of these bloody Arabs come around, crack them with a stone." Laughing, he joined John, and the two of them headed toward the office, papers in hand.

I got out of the truck and stood leaning against John's front bumper. Nobody approached. Suddenly, one of the border building doors flew open, and a group of soldiers marched out leading a lone man in handcuffs not more than fifty yards from where I was standing. They hustled him to a stone wall and pushed him against it. They moved back a few steps, formed a line, and raised their rifles. I watched in disbelief as the rifles fired as one, and the hand-cuffed man dropped to the ground, his shirt turning red.

Without ceremony, the soldiers turned and marched back into their building. A few minutes later, two guys—one pushing a wheelbarrow—approached the wall, loaded the corpse into the wheelbarrow, and rolled it off. When George and John returned I described what just took place.

John responded, "That is how customs deals with Iranian drug smugglers trying to cross into Turkey."

As we reached Tehran, I was surprised at how beautiful and modern the city was. We drove behind John to a truckers' camp located on the outskirts and parked side by side. John jumped out and approached us.

"What do you say if I take you around and introduce you to some of the drivers?"

We followed John into the nearby restaurant where we found a few Europe-ans sitting at a table drinking beer. John and George introduced me, and George proceeded to tell everyone how I single-handedly took on six Middle Easterners to protect his cargo and him from certain harm. By the time the story was done, beers were lined up at the table—compliments of the many truckers who seemed to appreciate my good deeds, as told by a very animated George.

I spent the next few days washing clothes and stocking up on supplies for the next leg of my journey. There was no hurry. While in the camp, I had a place to sleep and food to eat as long as the supply of canned goods held out. Truck camp living was almost like being on holiday.

Within three days, George unloaded his freight and announced he was heading back to London, piggybacking his lorry on a fellow trucker's flatbed rig. This would save George fuel and wear-and-tear on his vehicle. His company would reimburse the other trucker for hauling him out, a win-win situation for both drivers.

The evening before he left, just before dozing off to sleep, I reflected on all the Tammy Wynette country western songs that we had sung together during the past month. No doubt we sounded like two drunken coyotes howling at the moon compared to Tammy. But still, through song and fart, we shared a special bond.

The following morning, I watched George wave good-bye from the passenger window of the flatbed rig. Then I grabbed my bag and got ready to hit the road.

John was still in camp, waiting to pick up some cargo to haul back to London. When I stopped off to say good-bye, he gave me a twenty-pound note.

"To help you along the way."

I shook his hand. "Thanks, John. It was really great traveling with you. I hope someday our paths cross again." Of course I knew that was highly unlikely since I was planning to continue on through India and Southeast Asia toward Australia.

As I walked out of the truck camp I mulled the math over in my head. Since leaving Scotland, I hitched and walked well over 3,000 miles. The next leg of the journey to New Delhi, India, was roughly 1,500 miles. The biggest problem, according to most of the lorry drivers I had spoken with, was that "Tehran is the last civilized outpost to the East." I had been warned to expect to see very few vehicles on the road beyond Tehran.

Fine. I accepted the fact that the next part of the journey would be lonely, but I was not discouraged. Walking into the unknown did not frighten me. My search—whatever its actual goal—superseded fear of all the elements, of the wilderness, of hunger. The battle I fought now was within myself, no longer with the street drug lords. By now, I realized that my world, once contained neatly in a uniformed package, was disintegrating before my eyes. Now I walked in search of something lost long ago. My journey was a search for self-understanding and love in a world that seemed completely psychotic.

I headed east toward Mashhad, the last large border town before Afghanistan. For days I saw no vehicles at all. The only things moving on the flat expanse of the desert were camels and nomadic tribesmen. Here, it seemed, neither the people nor the scenery changed for the past thousand years. I remembered back to my Sunday school days as a young boy, seeing pictures of Jesus and his disciples wandering the desert. Jesus and his disciplines reminded me of my surroundings now. In fact, after a week, I began to feel as if I were hallucinating or, perhaps, had stepped into a time machine and dropped several thousand years into the past. Only the occasional passing bus or an airliner flying overhead brought me back to reality.

Whenever I came upon a village, I purchased yogurt and flatbread from roadside stands or farmhouses. To avoid dysentery I drank only hot tea.

I walked until I finally arrived in Mashhad, the second largest city in Iran, a bustling place filled with historic buildings and lots of traffic. It was a relief to once again be surrounded by humanity, not to mention many of the modern conveniences I had missed since leaving Tehran.

That afternoon, I found myself in a tearoom sipping some of the finest Iranian tea money could buy at the equivalent of five cents. The tea was served with a plate of flat bread and all the raw rock sugar you could pile into a cup. As I sat there, it seemed that all eyes were upon me. Of course, it was not possible for me to fit easily into the crowd there. For one thing, I stood about twelve inches above the tallest Iranian in the room. For another, most of them wore close-cut hair, shaved about once every two or three weeks. My blue eyes and long sun-bleached hair added up to one thing: an infidel.

Judging from the looks I received, foreigners were not a common sight in these parts.

After finishing my tea, I stepped outside. I walked a block when two large Mercedes-Benz sedans came to a screeching halt just in front of me. The doors flew open and four machine gun-carrying men surrounded me. One of them pushed me to the ground. I knew better than to resist. In fact, a sudden calm came over me.

I was handcuffed and picked up by two of the guys. A third one opened the door to the rear Mercedes, and I was thrown into the back. Two more guys jumped in—one on either side of me. A moment later, we were speeding away from the scene.

None of the men spoke a word of English, so I just kept my mouth shut.

Five minutes later, the vehicles pulled up at some kind of government compound. The men pulled me inside and pushed me into what looked like an interrogation room. I still didn't have a clue who these guys were, but clearly they were with the government.

I sat at a large table with eight armed men standing there staring at me. "Any of you guys speak English?" I asked.

No reply. I chose to look back at the men serenely. No benefit in antagonizing eight men armed with automatic weapons.

About thirty minutes passed, then the interrogation room doors flew open and a heavyset man strode in. All the others bowed. The newcomer wore a pair of slacks and a heavily starched, short-sleeved shirt. His short black hair looked as if it were slicked down with a handful of used car grease. One of the guards pulled a chair out from the table for him, and he seated himself next to me.

"Tell me, are you American?" he asked with only a trace of an accent.

"Yes," I politely replied.

"Are you CIA?"

"No."

He barked something in Arabic, and seconds later, my passport was laid on the table in front of him. He opened the cover to my photograph that was taken when I was still a cop and looked every bit the part.

He examined the picture carefully and thumbed through the following pages. No doubt he reflected on the fact that my just-passing-through visa stamps added up to several months of time spent between Turkey and Iran. I could see his mind going a hundred miles an hour.

He asked the same question several more times, with slightly different phrasing: "Are you with the Central Intelligence Agency?" Each time, I answered no.

Suddenly he rose from his seat and began speaking in furious Arabic. He clapped his hands, and two guards ran from the room. I heard the Mercedes start up and speed off.

About fifteen minutes passed, and the sound of screeching brakes could be heard. The door flung open and a brown paper package was handed to the chief. Moments later the guards removed my handcuffs. As I sat there rubbing my wrists, the head guy announced: "I am Chief Mohammed Fathy, Head of SAVAK."

This was confusing news. I knew of Iran's dreaded secret police, feared by their countrymen for their ruthless tactics in dealing with subjects disloyal to the Shah and the country. I also knew that the CIA and American government were on cooperative terms, but I wasn't quite sure what to expect next.

Chief Mohammed clapped his hands and two glasses appeared on the table. He carefully removed the brown paper wrapping from the package, and suddenly there was a quart of scotch whiskey sitting on the table. All I could think was: I wonder if he got it from John.

All eyes in the room were upon the two of us as the chief opened the bottle and meticulously placed the cap on the tabletop. He looked at me as if he were about to administer a super potent truth serum and then poured whiskey into the two waiting glasses.

The first round was a good four ounces. He raised his glass and ordered me to drink. To his surprise, I raised my glass as if in a salute, downed the drink in two sips, and placed the empty glass squarely on the table. Mohammed's eyes widened. After a few seconds, he belted down the remaining contents of his glass.

Clearly, he was not going to be outdone in front of his security forces by a man who might be an infidel secret agent. I started smiling as he poured a second round.

"You sure you are not with the CIA?" he asked.

"I'm sure."

"You are not with the CIA?"

By the end of the second round, I decided to stop denying it. Instead, I said, "I can't tell you if I'm with the CIA."

This seemed to satisfy Chief Mohammed, as if the whiskey actually loosened my tongue. When he began jabbering away to his security forces, I imagined he was bragging about his highly effective interrogation elixir.

By the third round, Mohammed was practically inebriated. Now that he established in his mind that I was with the CIA, we were practically best friends.

"Well, Mr. Owen," he said, "I am going to have to deport you out of the country. Before we do that, however, the Shah's uncle wants to have a going-away party for you."

"What?"

"Yes, yes. He is also the Governor of Mashhad. Come along. We must not keep him waiting."

So I left the building accompanied by eight armed escorts and jumped into one of the waiting Mercedes. After racing through the streets of Mashhad, our convoy reached what could only be described as a hilltop-secluded mansion on the outskirts of town.

Our guards did not accompany us to the door. Mohammed rang the bell, and a servant escorted us inside, leading us to an enormous living room where a party was well underway.

Mohammed took me around and introduced me to many of the guests, all Iranians. A few minutes later, the Governor entered. Mohammed approached him, bowed, and kissed his hand. Then he introduced me in what seemed to be a rambling dissertation. The Governor extended his hand, and I shook it. I didn't really know what else to do.

The Governor began to speak to me in Farsi, and Mohammed translated, "The Governor says you can have anything you wish. Would you like some women?"

"No, that's okay."

Mohammed relayed my response to the Governor. "Do you prefer young boys?"

"No, no, that's okay. Please let the Governor know that I'm fine at the moment."

Mohammed conveyed my message, and the Governor followed with more questions. "The Governor says you can have whiskey, hashish, or opium." Mohammed leaned over and politely whispered into my ear, "He personally prefers opium."

Clearly my host wasn't going to let up until I accepted something from him. "Please thank the Governor for this fine party. If he wouldn't mind, I'll have some more of his fine whiskey and perhaps something to eat from the beautifully arranged food on the table."

The Governor seemed delighted with my request. With a clap of his hands, I was hauled away to the dining room.

The table was at least twenty-five feet long and piled high with fruits, meats, cheeses, and vegetables. There was enough food there to feed a 150 people. I was hungry and had not eaten a solid meal since leaving Tehran. I stood around the table and grazed. Mohammed became a social butterfly for the evening, and for the first time I felt that I wasn't his prisoner but his colleague.

The party lasted all night and into the morning. By sunrise, I consumed more whiskey and food than I had thought possible.

"The governor wishes to go with us to the border," Mohammed said. "He wants to drive by the Great Mosque of Mashhad. It is beautiful in the early morning as the sun shines upon the turquoise stones embedded on the towers."

I took the hint that the party was over. We walked outside and climbed into one of the limousines. Security agents packed themselves into a second black Mercedes behind us.

As predicted, when we passed by the grand Mosque of Mashhad, the turquoise glittered like jewels in the morning sunlight. It was breathtakingly beautiful. A short time later, we arrived at the border of Afghanistan. As the limousines drew close, the guards on the near side of the frontier began shouting and running around. By the time Mohammed and I climbed out of the limo, every soldier in the outpost was standing at attention and rigidly saluting.

I turned to Mohammed and extended my hand. "I'll never forget your hospitality. I'm grateful to you and the Governor. Please convey my deepest gratitude."

"I will do so. Have a pleasant journey."

As I turned to walk away, I muttered just loud enough that only Mohammed could hear, "I'll also let the guys back at my office know how well I was treated by you and your officers."

And I meant it. Underneath it all, Mohammed was a street cop. He instinctively picked up the fact that even if I looked like a smuggler or hippie infiltrator of some sort, I was actually a figure of authority, not unlike himself. CIA? To him, that seemed the best possibility. But regardless, he understood that I was, like him, an officer of the law.

To enter Afghanistan, I walked across a long bridge. Of course, the guards at the other end observed all the commotion on the Iranian side of the border, the black limousines, the saluting, and the running about. By the time I reached the crossing gate on their side, the guards were saluting me as though I were a general in the Afghan army. They waved me through as if I held diplomatic privileges. It was by far the easiest border crossing I ever experienced.

One mile later, things stopped being easy.

Ninety-nine miles after that, I found Afghanistan to be one of the most callous, unforgiving places on the face of the earth.

It was a rugged country—all barren mountains, rock, rough brush, and frigid scouring winds. I walked through numberless Afghan villages, all the same—no electricity and no running water. In fact none of the conveniences associated with the twentieth century were present. Except for an occasional country bus belching blue smoke and dragging a blanket of dust behind it, vehicular traffic disappeared. The buses themselves were almost a comical sight—antiques overloaded with livestock and passengers, many of whom hung out the windows or clung to the roof.

As I ventured farther into the interior, even the buses stopped passing. Nothing interrupted the steady crunch of my footsteps, except the hollow note of wind blowing through rocks and sand.

By then, a mantra of three four-letter words ran constantly through my mind: food, cold, and dirt. Fortunately for me, the rural people of northern Afghanistan proved to be as warm and friendly as the surrounding terrain was cold and inhospitable.

In one of the villages, I purchased a wool coat that hung down to my boots. Such a coat was the primary clothing item worn by most men in this part of the world. I immediately found out the reason. The coat not only protected me from the bitter mountain winds, but it also allowed me to blend into the landscape, at least from a distance.

Up close, matters were somewhat different. I became the center of attention in every mountain village. Few Afghanis ever socialized up close with a Westerner. What seemed to mystify them most was that, although my height, hair color, and eyes gave me away as a foreigner, I dressed similarly to them and blended in other ways.

I even took on many of the local mannerisms. For instance, in the larger towns, when the mosques' religious criers called out for worshipers to pray, everyone fell to their knees and bowed toward Mecca. I did the same, not because I worshipped the Muslim god but out of respect to their faith.

In the smaller villages, it was not unusual for someone to invite me into his home. They were very curious about who I was and where I was from. Since we didn't speak the same language, our thoughts were communicated with hands and heart. There were never any women at these meetings, but I knew the women were behind the scenes—not only raising children, cooking, and washing, but working the fields and contributing to many of the physical tasks of survival as well.

The mountain people of Afghanistan were among the most physically tough individuals I had ever seen. Still, the harshness of life took its toll. Village elders were seldom over fifty years of age, and one of the most common physical features was a pockmarked, scarred face: the telltale signs of smallpox. Sadly, some of the scars were very grotesque, but planted in the middle of the ravaged face would be a smile.

If I had thought that my walk through the deserts of Mesopotamia would take me back in time a thousand years, Afghanistan took me back even further. For entire weeks, I did not see a single hint of the present century. I survived mostly on yogurt and bread. When the villagers invited me into their homes, I was usually given hot stew.

This stew was generally served with a huge chunk of animal fat floating in it. The men reached into the bowl, took the fat, rubbed it all over their face and hands, and then dumped it back into the communal stew pot. I took up the custom. The natives informed me that adding a thin layer of animal fat to the body helped protect one from the cold. I can't say it did much for the taste of the stew, but then I was in no position to be picky.

Often, when sitting with villagers, I was offered a small pot of burning coals. I quickly learned that this was the equivalent of a heating pad. The Afghans sat on their haunches and placed the pot between their legs, which were covered by the tails of their long coats. I quickly learned to appreciate any offer of warmth, since sleeping out in the elements left me achingly frigid most of the time.

After a full month of walking the dusty mountain trails with layering animal fat on my skin, and having hunched over pots of coals that basted me in smoke, my body turned almost as black as charcoal. Yet, the worse my physical appearance became, the more interest and kindness the locals showered upon me.

Early one morning, I came across a frozen stream with a partially melted oval area. The water flowed through the gap slowly, reflecting the throbbing blue of the sky. For the first time since leaving Scotland, I sensed that winter was at last easing its grip on the world.

I stood on the bank of the stream and stared at that pulsing blue oval. I had not seen flowing water for three and a half months, or bathed during that time. I looked around. A fair amount of brush and wood stuck out of the surrounding snow. I hesitated, then dropped my backpack, and began gathering kindling. Most of it wasn't what you'd call dry but rather frozen solid. But I was determined. I made a pile of fuel and then dripped hot candle wax on it until it began to smolder.

Soon the flames were roaring, and I basked in the warmth for a while before digging into my backpack for a bar of soap. I found it on the very bottom, unused.

After hanging my backpack from a nearby tree, I started the difficult process of removing my clothes. I was wearing everything I owned: my ankle-length Afghan coat, a foul weather jacket, sweater, shirt, two pair of jeans, two sets of T-shirts, and two pairs of underwear. The entire first layer of underclothing was a uniform gray-brown color. I peeled it off. Maybe I would clean the garments in the stream while I was working on myself.

I started to tug off my innermost T-shirt and halted in horror. The fabric literally bonded itself to my skin, glued there by a buildup of grease and filth so thick I could scratch my initials into it with my fingernail. I worked the T-shirt off carefully. It made a sucking sound as it detached, like Scotch tape being pulled off a blackboard, and left a woven fabric imprint upon my skin.

That T-shirt was the dirtiest piece of clothing I had ever seen—too dirty for even me to put back on again. Turning, I tossed it into the fire. When it landed, the T-shirt burst into a fireball so powerful I toppled backward in the snow. I sat up, staring in disbelief, too stunned to feel the cold. A few minutes later, I added my underwear to the flames, this time pitching it in from a distance. It burned rather than explode, and I wished I had tried using it for kindling in the first place.

Finally I climbed naked and filthy into the water, breaking through the ice along the banks. Within seconds, I decided that if I were right about the Afghans layering animal fat on their bodies to insulate themselves from the cold, they were wasting their time. As I immersed myself in the ice-free area, the water was so cold my body utterly failed to function for fifteen or twenty seconds. When I finally regained some control of my muscles, I quickly discovered something else. Ice water and soap are not the best way to clean grease and road grime off one's body. I used the edge of my Buck knife to scrape away the filth.

After my bath, I washed one layer of clothing and roasted the garments over my bonfire until they were dry. It took so long that I decided not to repeat the process with the rest of my clothes. I'd freeze to death before the job was done.

Finally stepping back onto the road I felt like a new man. No wonder my mother used to remind me that cleanliness is next to godliness.

A few days later I arrived in Kabul. After a week I found myself at the border of Pakistan. I arrived on the outskirts of Islamabad, Pakistan, a city nestled at the base of the mountainous territories of Kashmir. Sitting on my sleeping bag at my campsite, I stared up at the endless stony peaks and felt a sense of foreboding. My primary reason for taking the northern route to India was so I could trek the lower Himalayas. The mountains passes were covered in deep snow.

The next two days, I spent talking with locals. I learned that there were no real roads open through the mountains, only a few paths across glaciers and iced wasteland. I was equipped to handle neither the low temperatures nor the altitudes. I needed a lot more than two layers of jeans, a couple of sleeping bags, and an Afghan coat.

Although this was very disappointing news, reality dictated flexibility. It's simple to know which direction one must take when the decision is made in the context of survival. I would have to go around the base of the Himalayas.

TRUTHS OF A SADHU

A few days later, I arrived at the Indian border. Surprisingly, there was no line of tourists or vehicles, only a small station house with a half dozen soldiers standing between one of the oldest cultures in the world and me. I was eager to step over that line. It would mean that I had traveled halfway around the world. Symbolically, India marked the beginning of the second half of my journey.

I walked up to an Indian sentry who waved me into the station house where a customs officer asked to see my passport. He spoke in British English with an Indian accent. The combination was rhythmic and melodious. While my paperwork was processed, I walked outside onto the broad grassy area adjacent to the station, took off my shirt, and lay down. Basking in the sunshine, I began to feel that the long, cold winter ended.

About a half hour into my nap, I heard movement and opened my eyes enough to see a young Buddhist monk sitting down near me. Despite his shaved head, soft off-white robe, and prayer beads, he looked distinctly Anglo-Saxon.

I sat up. "Do you speak English?"

"Yes, I do." His accent was dusted with French. "I am from Switzerland."

"Where do you plan to go in India?"

"Oh, I am finished with India. I have been here for about one month, traveling and visiting Buddhist monasteries. I am going back to Switzerland now."

As I looked at him more closely, I realized he couldn't be more than eighteen years old: slender, smooth-faced, with large gray eyes. I was impressed that such a young man was on a spiritual path. His thinking and conversation inspired me.

I finally remembered to introduce myself. He responded, "I am Madelaine."

"Madelent?" I asked.

"No, Madelaine," he said in a soft but determined voice.

We talked about our separate journeys until the guards called me into the stationhouse. "Okay, you are free to enter India now. You have a six-month visa."

He handed me my passport, and I returned to say goodbye to my new Buddhist friend. "Owen," Madelaine said, "if you ever come to Switzerland, please look me up. Here's my address."

I thanked him and took the note he had written even though I had no intention of ever going to Switzerland. I had just left Europe, after all, and was heading the opposite direction. "It was nice talking with you, Madelaine. Good luck on your journey."

"And you on yours, Owen."

At dusk, I spread my sleeping bag in some bushes a hundred feet from a two-lane road—just a single sleeping bag tonight. It was an amazing sensation. The air felt almost tropical compared to the mountainous regions I just left. Exhausted, I plunged immediately into a deep sleep.

Somewhere around midnight, I partially woke from a dream of something cold crawling up my pant leg. I shifted my body, scratched at my leg, and fell back asleep.

Although I was determined to cover a lot of distance before sundown, I stopped the next day in the city of Amritsar. While reading on the *Eros*, I learned that this part of the Punjabi area was considered the seat of Sikhism, the youngest and perhaps least known of the world's monotheistic religious traditions. Personally, I found Sikh beliefs intriguing. They lived by a code of conduct that required them not to cut their hair. It also required them to carry a comb at all times, to carry a sword or knife, and to wear a steel bracelet. As far as I could tell, baggy clothing was also necessary. They all seemed to add the word "Singh" to their names. Sikhs were the warriors in the Hindu race and often supplied the applicants for police officers and soldiers of India.

Amritsar was the home of the Golden Temple, a great square building and the holiest shrine of the Sikh religion. I walked around it for most of the afternoon. Built so the building reflected in a manmade lake, the structure was deliberately left open on all four sides to express the unusually inclusive philosophy of Sikhism.

Open, inclusive—and yet the Sikhs were the warriors of the Hindu people.

Somewhere between Amritsar and the city of Jullundur, I decided to set up camp for the night. I found a clearing away from the road that was surrounded by trees. There I dropped my backpack, spread out my space blanket, and unrolled my sleeping bag. As I pulled back the flap, a monstrous blood-red centipede sprung out and lunged at me, with gaping jaws. Screaming, I fell backward into the dirt. The centipede was at least twelve inches long and as thick as my thumb. It reared up in fury, its front legs moving as if beating its chest.

I scrambled to my feet, jumped back and watched. After about a minute, the creature lowered its body and began to speed away. Now, suddenly feeling weak, I sat down. I realized that the previous night was no dream. That creature had made itself at home inside my pants while I slept. I couldn't believe the poisonous monster didn't bite me. India was a land of cobras, scorpions, and strange creatures. From here on out I reminded myself I would have to check my sleeping bag before crawling into it.

Stopping in the next village, I marveled at the crowd milling around the train station. To my amazement, India was still using coal-powered, steam-engine trains. I sat on a bench and watched two stokers loading water and shoveling coal into the giant firebox in the engine. The main stoker was a small Indian man dressed only in a turban and blackened baggy pants that had once been white. The sweat rolled off his upper body as he feverishly shoveled coal into the train's fire-eating belly. Steam poured out of fittings here and there.

Once the firebox was loaded, the conductor sounded his whistle and the engineer started pulling levers, with his turban-covered head hanging out of the massive locomotive. The great drive wheels moved each time the engine made its explosive exhalation and then stopped. Moved, stopped. Moved. Stopped. Moved. Stopped. Chunks of burning coal spewed onto the ground, and the platform shook as the train accelerated off down the track under a cloud of black smoke.

At the ticket window I purchased a third class ticket to Delhi for the equivalent of a couple dollars. There I handed my ticket to the conductor and jumped onto what can only be described as a passenger-carrying boxcar. It contained no seats, and the only views offered were pane-less window openings in the walls.

I sat on the floor with my back against a wall and waited as the car began filling with people. Everyone tried to claim his or her own sitting area quickly. Before long there were at least a hundred people, pushing and tugging for space. I began to feel nostalgic for the unpopulated wilderness of northern Afghanistan.

The train gave a jerk and pulled away from the station. Although I didn't know how long the journey to Delhi would take, it was apparent that my companions expected quite a trek. One stranger after another leaned against me and then slumped on me with all their weight. Within an hour, people's heads rested in my lap, against my shoulders, all over me. I became a big pillow for at least a half dozen heads. I was in a car with a sample of India's poorest and most untouchable, or lowest-class citizens. The stench of body odor was overwhelming.

I arrived in Delhi where the streets were narrow and packed with people. I knew Delhi boasted over seven million citizens, which gave it a population similar to that of downtown New York City or London. The difference, though, was that this city was not of high-rise skyscrapers, but of low-built structures of modern and ancient lineage.

By sundown I was lost. Beggars and children scrambled around me like hungry mosquitoes, tugging at my clothes, with hands held out for charity. No matter how fast or far I walked, if someone fell away from the pack, others filled the gap. I realized that I had thrown myself into an absolute sea of human suffering, hunger, and pain. I knew that I had to escape from the herds of people following me before darkness set in.

I eventually found a hotel in the Old Delhi section of town, clearly the low-rent non-tourist district. But it was well worth the couple dollars. A simple room with one door and one window, a tiled floor, and unpainted cement block walls to give the space a nice prison ambiance. There was no bathroom, electricity, or running water.

I opened a window and watched the sun descend upon the battered city of Old Delhi. The smell of car exhaust, diesel fumes, and baked dust filled the air above the cacophony of bustling people and traffic. I thought about how I struggled for weeks and months to get here, walking alone on what was commonly called the Hippie Highway to India. And now I was here, submerged in the depths of one of the most ancient and crowded civilizations on the planet. Could this possibly be where I, like so many other seekers before me, would find what I was looking for?

The next morning, I arose before sunrise and looked out the window. The city was already alive with people hustling around in the semidarkness. I decided to go out and get a better feel for the place. Two blocks from my hotel, as I rounded a corner, I found the sidewalks on both sides of the street full of sleeping people, sprawled bodies as far as I could see. For the first time I realized just how many of the people in Delhi were homeless. They owned nothing but the clothes on their bodies. Compared to them, I was wealthy with my backpack and pouch of traveler's checks.

Like a kid playing hopscotch, I jumped and sidestepped over sidewalk sleepers. An hour later the sun was up, and the sidewalk people were starting to move. Across the street, a man pushed a big two-wheeled cart through the crowd. I wouldn't have given him a second glance if it were not for the pair of human legs I saw dangling off the side of the cart. I slowed to watch as the man stopped and bent down to shake the shoulder of an elderly man lying on the sidewalk. When the old man did not react, the younger man picked him up and tossed him into the wagon. Then he moved on down the road.

I walked over and looked into the cart to check on the old man. He was certainly dead, as was the man lying beneath him. I stepped back in horror and watched as the man moved along down the sidewalk, occasionally bending over to shake a shoulder or lift a limp body. In fewer than three blocks his cart was full of corpses. He turned to wheel it down a side street. Shivering at the thought of the corpses within several blocks, I walked on.

Beggars. Beggars on every street and every corner. Beggars, each looking more pathetic and downtrodden than the other. I found it impossible to get some of the body mutilations and smallpox-riddled faces out of my mind. Several times, there were young children with no legs or arms, their bodies propped against a wall with a little begging can in front of them. I saw lepers with rotting flesh wrapped in soiled bandages and beggars with horrific birth defects. It was sad to see—every corner hosted bizarre and hideous forms of life.

For the first time on my journey, I could not adjust to the local conditions. I couldn't deal with all the hands in my face, fingers hooked and pleading. Nor could I adjust to the ravaging effects of smallpox and leprosy. I always believed that those diseases had been wiped out years ago. The next morning, I paid my hotel bill and set out for the next town to the north.

Late that morning, I arrived at a small nameless village. It was quiet without anyone on the streets, I noted. I stood in the sun for a while, staring around in wonder and relief of the tranquility. This was the first place I had been in India where hordes of people didn't follow me.

Everything felt good—the warmth of the sun, the emptiness, and, above all, the peace. And then I heard laughter. I looked around, surprised. In my experience, Indian people didn't laugh much.

But suddenly a small crowd of people poured around a corner, dancing and shouting and spinning around, clearly celebrating something. I smiled. It was nice to see people actually having a good time in this depressing country.

The crowd drew near, and soon I saw an old man walking in the midst of it. He was dressed in an amber-colored robe and had a white beard. He wore his white hair in a ball on top of his head. With a long staff, he marked out his steps, with a small beige pouch swinging against his hip. He walked directly toward me as if he expected to find me there. Ridiculous, of course. Any moment now he would veer off to continue down the dirt road.

But he didn't. He walked right up to me.

"I say," he said, "are you English?"

The crowd instantly fell silent. Everyone stared at me.

"No," I said. "Actually, I'm American, from California."

"Jolly well, you're quite a way from your home. Are you lost?"

"No, I'm hitching and walking and using whatever means I can to make my way around the globe."

His teeth flashed a brilliant white in his dark face. "Wonderful! And might I ask which direction you are going now?"

I pointed northeast. "Lovely, that's the same direction I am going. Would you like to join me?" I couldn't believe my good fortune. Here was a guy who spoke perfect English, seemed to be well liked by the locals, and wasn't begging or trying to sell me something.

"I would be delighted to come along with you," I said. "I'm Owen. What's your name?"

"Everyone calls me Baba. You too may call me Baba."

I extended my hand and we shook. Although he appeared to be a fragile old man, his handshake was powerful, and his skin felt like cracked leather. When he smiled, I was almost blinded by the radiance against his near black face. The next thing I knew, I was walking out of the village surrounded by a herd of deliriously dancing people. When we reached the outskirts of the village, people began to break away from the crowd until Baba and I were on the road alone.

"Your English is amazing," I said.

"Ah, that is because I was educated in England, you see. I was an electrical engineer for most of my working life." We walked in companionable silence. Baba moved much more slowly than I was used to, so I strived to match his pace.

In the next village, another cheering crowd appeared and surrounded us. Baba stopped walking and spoke to the people in his native language. During his discourse, several folks approached with bowls of rice, beans, and items I didn't recognize. Baba sat down on the spot and began eating. I sat near him.

More food showed up. Baba said what could only have been prayers over the dishes and split the food between two plates.

"Owen, do you like Indian food?"

"Sure," I said. The truth was I would have eaten that centipede since I hadn't eaten all day.

The food Baba gave me was basically beans mixed with rice and some kind of sauce so spicy that, when I took my first bite, I almost spat it out. Baba noticed but smiled and continued eating without comment.

Eating a couple more bites, I was sweating. But I was so hungry I didn't dare return any of this fiery food. After a month-long diet of yogurt, bread, and cheese, it was agonizing to swallow the food.

Meanwhile Baba finished his meal and continued talking with the gathered crowd. Many of them were clearly inquisitive about where I came from. Baba never stopped laughing as he answered all the questions about his new friend from America.

I figured out the situation soon enough. Baba was an itinerant holy man, a *Sadhu*, as I was to learn walking from place to place, dispensing words of wisdom in exchange for food and, when necessary, shelter. It seemed a curious existence, but so many people believed there was something to learn from him. I began to realize that I too could learn from him.

"Baba," I said as we left the second village, "would it be okay if I traveled with you for a while?"

He grinned, as always. "Sure, but first we have to visit a shop in the next village."

When we got to the village, Baba walked me directly into a fabric store—an old, musty place where rolls of dusty cloth lay on the floor or stood in bins along the wall. There was not much of a selection: white cotton, orange cotton, yellow cotton, and a few multicolor cotton prints.

Baba talked to the proprietor, and in a moment the man threw a large roll of amber cloth to the floor and anxiously unrolled and trimmed off a ten-foot length. He folded it and handed it to me.

Baba said, "Please give him some money."

I hesitated and then handed the man a hundred and twenty rupees. Baba asked him if we could go into his back room. Once there, Baba asked me to remove my clothing, then showed me how to wrap the long cloth that was about to become my new wardrobe around my body. He also tore several pieces off the strip and showed me how to make the Hindu equivalent of a jock strap.

"Please leave your boots on," he said, "but put the rest of your clothes into your pack."

Looking in the mirror, I stood shocked at the transformed longhaired, bearded mystic standing before me. The combat boots did look a bit out of place peeking out from under the bottom hem of the robe, but that didn't seem to matter to Baba.

We walked together for several blocks until we came to a large building built of weathered stone. We entered a temple where Baba spoke to a man I assumed was a Hindu priest. We then were directed to an office where we met the head-master of the monastery.

"Please give him your pack," Baba told me. "It will be safe here. To travel with me, you have to leave everything behind. You won't need clothing, money, or sleeping stuff."

"But—"

He smiled. "Do not worry. You can come back whenever you wish and pick your things up again."

I did everything he instructed me to do. Why not? If I were going to travel with Baba, I would have to look and live the life of a *Sadhu*.

Until now, I prided myself on how little I needed to carry with me. Now I carried nothing but my passport. Here I was twelve thousand miles from home in a strange land, culture, language. I was walking through a time and space that seemed light-years from my past.

As Baba and I left the monastery, I realized that my life was about to move on to yet another adventure. Just outside the village was a small stream where Baba announced, "It is time to stop, rest, and bathe. A *Sadhu* must bathe daily if possible."

I suspected that meant that from now on we would pass very few streams, rivers, or water buckets without indulging in some kind of religious bathing ritual. But that was fine with me. I had spent far too many months without even dampening my skin, let alone bathing.

Baba walked to the stream, removed his robe and placed it on the riverbank. He was perhaps in his middle sixties, with very dark skin that showed no tan lines at all, so he was either naturally dark or spent a lot of time in the sunshine without clothing. He didn't have an ounce of fat on his frame and looked very muscular for his age. He waded into the stream until he was waist deep and then started washing without benefit of soap or a washcloth.

Following his lead, I removed my robe, jumped into the water, and started washing in the same fashion as Baba. By the time I finished, Baba was seated on the riverbank and scrubbing his robe between his fists. After several minutes, he wrung out the material and carefully laid it out on a bush for drying. I followed suit. Then we found a pair of large rocks and sat down to wait until our clothes dried. Baba seemed pleased that I learned to follow his lead and, perhaps also, that I didn't talk much.

After getting dressed, Baba said, "Well, Owen, do you have any destination in mind or some place that you need to be?"

"Not at the moment, why do you ask?"

He shrugged. "I have come from the south. *Sadhus* usually walk north to avoid the monsoon season this time of the year."

"Do you ever get up to the Himalayas? That's where I was originally heading."

"Well, then, we will go north. There are many holy shrines and temples in the north that I have not visited in a long while."

Late that afternoon, we arrived in another nameless little village. As before, people swarmed around us but were unbelievably respectful to Baba. They bowed deeply and held their hands together at their foreheads as if in prayer and said, "Namaste."

"What does this word mean?" I asked.

"It is Hindi for I salute the divinity within you."

In all the different countries through which I had traveled, I always tried to learn the survival words first: food, water, directions, hello, good-bye. But this was the first time I had learned a word with such a lofty meaning. Very cool, I thought. I would use it frequently.

Soon we were in the heart of yet another village. This time people actually threw themselves at Baba's feet, burying their faces in the dirt. Some of them actually kissed Baba's feet. I stood back and watched in awe. I never before witnessed such a spontaneous outpouring of love and respect for another human being.

Baba sat himself down alongside the road, and a small crowd gathered around him. I sat as well and listened as Baba spoke in Hindi to the group. Of course I couldn't understand a word, but I took the opportunity to watch Baba's small audience. All of them looked spellbound. An hour into his talk, someone brought Baba two bowls of rice cooked in some kind of green sauce. Baba motioned for me to sit closer to him.

A young Hindu woman placed one of the bowls in front of me. "Namaste," she said.

Baba picked up his bowl, raised it to his forehead, and then lowered it. He said, "Eat."

I watched as he scooped rice from the bowl with his fingers. That was pretty much what I had expected. I ate with my fingers most of the time since leaving Istanbul. So, I followed suit. The moment the rice hit my lips I felt my eyes bulge from their sockets. My mouth felt as if it were stuffed with burning red-hot coals. I started to spit the food out but then noticed that the entire audience was staring at me benevolently. Although my face broke out in a sweat and I cried crocodile-sized tears, I swallowed what was in my mouth with a mighty effort. The crowd laughed. Baba looked over and smiled.

"They want to know if you like it."

I wiped the sweat from my forehead. "Yeah, it's great!"

Baba apparently repeated my words to the crowd in Hindi, and they went wild. "Eat up, Owen. This food was a shared effort of the women of the village. It is all they have to give."

I looked warily into my bowl. Clearly, if I didn't get used to eating this kind of food, I would starve to death. There were nine or ten more two-fingered portions left to go. By the time I finished the second one, I felt blisters forming inside my mouth. The third scoop brought blisters to my tongue. After that, the pain became indescribable.

It must have taken me a half hour to finish that small bowl of rice. The whole time, the crowd watched me with delight. I tried to give the impression that I was enjoying the meal rather than struggling not to faint.

Baba had long finished his own food and was enjoying the moment as the crowd watched me eat every last grain of rice. When I placed my empty bowl on the ground, the crowd cheered as though I hit a homerun. Then Baba said a few more words, and we rose to our feet. My belly raged with fire. I suspected I was going to have a bad night.

After the last member of the adoring crowd left us a mile outside town, I said, "Baba, that was the hottest sauce I have ever eaten. What was it?"

He didn't give me a direct answer. "This is how we eat our meals in India, especially in the poorer households. You see, we don't have refrigeration, clean water, or the same sanitation standards as in your country. So our people use many types of hot sauces to kill the bugs that would cause dysentery and food poisoning." I nodded. I could feel the blisters thickening in my mouth.

We walked until the sun set. When Baba announced it was time to stop for the night. He simply sat down just off the roadside and crossed his legs, going into what looked like a meditative state. After a moment I lay down on the ground about ten feet away. I felt naked without my space blanket and sleeping bag. Pulling the top of my robe up enough to provide a bit of a pillow between my head and the dirt, I reflected that this would probably have to serve as my one-sheet bed during the time I would be on the road with Baba. Lying there listening to my stomach rumble and hiss, I fell asleep.

Morning arrived before sunrise with a host of singing birds—unanimous behavior throughout the world. Within minutes, Baba and I were walking down the road again. I felt optimistic. My stomach felt like churning surf, but I had made it through the night okay.

As always, Baba moved along at a much slower pace than I was accustomed to. Of course, he was in no hurry, with nowhere to go and nothing to do at any particular time. His daily routine focused only on the moment. That was going to be a hard lesson for me to learn, especially right now. I needed to relieve myself. When we came upon a stream, I informed Baba. He just nodded. I found a secluded pile of rocks, squatted, and lifted my robe. I tried not to scream, but the burning sensation was so horrific that I felt I might pass out.

By the time I rose from my squat, my legs were shaking so badly I could hardly use them. Baba looked at me and laughed. "You walk like someone put a hot poker up your ass!"

"Funny you should say that," I muttered, and hobbled to the stream. I waded in boots, robe and all, dipping my lower half into the fire-squelching water.

A couple of minutes passed before I could raise myself from the water. "I'm sure I've got blisters on my rectum," I said.

Baba grinned. "It is a good habit to relieve yourself daily."

"This is not funny," I said, wide-stepping out of the water like a cowboy who's been on the rodeo circuit too long. "Baba, are all our meals going to hurt just as bad coming out as they did going in?"

They didn't, at least, not all of them. Eating food as hot as coal and dealing with the occasional fiery diarrhea session became just another part of my journey north with Baba. After two weeks, Baba and I were fully relaxed with each other. Unlike the adoring citizens of the towns we passed through, I saw the old man as pretty much just an ordinary guy. Other people prostrated themselves before him as if he could walk on water and turn water into wine, but I spent most of my time arguing with him—or, as he liked to call it, "having spiritual discourse."

The more I hung out with Baba as an individual, the more I began to understand the Indian people as a whole. When we met upper-class Indians,

Baba often gave his spiritual discourses in English. I felt certain that this was done to impress them, not me. At other times, we met with lower-caste Indians, and even untouchables. It all seemed to be the same to Baba, which impressed me.

As far as I could tell, Baba's basic lectures were the same with every group. Sometimes he would lecture in great detail, depending on the listener's ability to comprehend. The essence of his message was that God is unlimited and has many names. Man's identification and attachment with the physical body, sensual pleasures, material possessions, and ego pollute and cloud man's true consciousness. Sometimes the *Sadhu* spent much of his discourse talking about the divinity of man. His message was straightforward, simple, and compassionate. While his message wasn't really profound and provided no great revelations, his audiences always seemed respectfully moved by his words.

The *Sadhu* system had some real benefits for an old man. It was certainly better than the social welfare systems of Europe and America, which often discarded their old people when they were no longer part of the workforce. In India, older men who completed all their earthly responsibilities and duties to their families were able to redefine their lives and purpose, inspiring coming generations with words and deeds.

Indian culture dictated that if a distant traveler came, it bestowed great honor upon the family that provided him with food and shelter. Consequently, Baba would tell me, "This family would like to take you home to feed you. Please go. I will be here when you come back."

In one such instance, I walked to a peasant farmer's home and was seated at the family's small wooden table in a two-room mud hut. The family—including husband, wife, and two small children—watched as the usual plate of beans and rice was placed before me. No doubt this was all the food the entire family could provide. In order to do so, they would not eat for that entire day. These selfless situations always touched my heart. Here was a family that was starving, yet giving away the last food they possessed. I could not reject their offering, which would have been a severe insult. To accept the food in an unpretentious fashion gave them happiness and honor.

It sure was a very humbling experience. Hinduism, according to my understanding, was the world's oldest existing religion. Many other contemporary religions could trace their fundamental truths and spiritual laws to any number of the Hindu beliefs. For example, in the early thirteenth century, Saint Francis of Assisi said, "It is in giving that we receive." Everywhere we traveled, I observed this practice of giving in order to receive—a form of hospitality Baba called Puja.

After more than a month with the *Sadhu*, we were making our way into a forested area at the base of the Himalayan Mountains. The view was unbelievably majestic.

One evening Baba left with another *Sadhu*, so the two could discuss religion on some nearby lofty mountainous setting. I sat alone in the solitude and darkness, inhaling the crisp air of 8,000 feet of altitude. Overhead the stars were as bright as the clear sky at sea. From a distance came the melodic thunder of drums and the smell of burning incense. On occasion, I could also hear faint chanting. All the chanting, the smells, and sights overwhelmed my senses. The beauty and the religious devotion of the Indian people overcame me, and I wept. Baba returned to camp and was surprised to see that I was wide-awake and in a state of wonderment.

"Baba, what is this that I hear?" I asked.

"These are the sounds of devotion and prayer from a monastery in the valley below us. These prayers have continued in this area for thousands of years."

I sat motionless throughout that evening, enthralled by the power and beauty of the moment. I felt a similar sensation entering the ancient cathedrals in Europe. I was overwhelmed by the feeling of reverence created by the immersion in an atmosphere of a thousand years of religious consecration and fidelity.

The beauty of the Himalayas had the same exhilarating effect, magnified by thousands of years. The culture here, the people, the language, and the philosophy were foreign to me, but the love of God or the realization of one's connection to nature is universal. It was in these moments that I began to marvel at the bridges that connected East and West.

The word "Baba" is a respectful term that means "father" in Hindi. Baba was also called a *Sannyasi* by many of the Hindu people. A *Sannyasi* is a religious ascetic, one who has renounced the world by abandoning all claims to social or family standing. The *Sannyasi* or *Sadhu* sometimes also belong to a monastery associated with a particular order, but most of the *Sadhus* I met simply wandered the country alone or as part of a small group. Other *Sadhus*, Baba told me, isolate themselves in huts or caves. They generally take vows of poverty and celibacy and depend on the charity of householders for their food.

There were lots of *Sadhus* out on the road, and it was not unusual to meet up with some every couple of days. They weren't hard to spot: thin men with long, matted hair knotted on the tops of their heads. They usually wore ochre-colored robes and carried a few possessions: prayer beads, an alms bowl, perhaps a pot for boiling water. They made me feel materialistic.

Over the next two months, I lost track of time and even specific locations, knowing only that white-tipped mountains were beginning to rise over the northern horizons: the Himalayas. Three months earlier I had passed by the base of these mountains in Pakistan. I already knew that the range extended from Kashmir eastward to Tibet and contained thirty mountains rising to heights greater than twenty-four thousand feet above sea level, including, of course, the world's highest peak, Mount Everest at its towering height of 29,028 feet.

Baba said, "In Hindu mythology, the Himalayas are considered the golden dwelling of the gods. They are the site of many of the important shrines of Hinduism and Buddhism."

As Baba and I worked our way higher into the foothills of the Himalayas, we entered a tiny village overrun with buses and Indians from other parts of the country. Baba explained that all these people were embarking on a pilgrimage to Amaranth Cave, which according to legend was the birthplace of the Lord Shiva.

"Shiva, is one of the primary Hindu deities," Baba said.

"What does he represent?" I asked.

"Shiva is both the destroyer and the restorer, the symbol of sensuality and the wrathful avenger. In the Amaranth Cave, he is said to have imparted the secret of immortality. So this is one of our most holy sites and that is why we have come here to pay our respects. We will begin here, and go there." He pointed high into the mountains. "It will take a couple of days to arrive at the cave."

I gazed up at the peaks. At least they weren't covered with snow, which was more than I could say about their big brothers just behind them. How could I pass up the chance to see the birthplace of a god?

While ascending a mountainous pathway one afternoon I blurted a thought I had been mulling over silently for the past several days.

"Baba, I have decided to become a *Sadhu*."

Baba looked at me and laughed. He turned away and composed himself. But the second he glanced back at me, he started laughing again. "Owen, you can't become a *Sadhu*."

"Why not? I've listened to your lectures, and I feel I could deliver them as well. We can journey together, and I'll be your apprentice. I'll learn to speak your language. I'll learn to like Indian food. I'll learn the ways of a holy man.

I'm willing to renounce all worldly possessions, to become celibate and take vows of poverty. Don't you think I would be a worthy *Sadhu*?"

He'd gotten his lined face composed. "Not just yet, Owen. You see, there are certain stages one must go through in order to become a *Sadhu*." He gestured around him, taking in both the spectacular mountains and all the people ascending and descending. "For nearly two thousand years we Hindus have recognized four *Asramas*, or stages, of life. They are as follows: a male member of the three highest classes should first become a student, then get married and have a family, discharge his debts to his ancestors by begetting sons and to the gods through sacrifice and service. Only then can he retire to the forest to devote himself to contemplation and, finally—but not mandatory—become a homeless wandering ascetic."

"But I—"

Baba held up a thin brown hand. "You are now only the student, Owen. When you are finished here, you must return to your home and find a good wife, marry, and have children. Once you have provided completely for your family after the children have left home and you have taken proper care of your wife, then you can become a *Sadhu*."

We argued about it for the rest of that day and into the next. Why shouldn't I be able to forget all the family stuff and just skip to the rank of *Sadhu*? I was so deeply engrossed in the disagreement that I stopped pleading my case only to sleep. Even eating didn't slow me down because we ate only when a fellow pilgrim shared what little food he possessed. Even then I barely thought about my hunger. I wanted to make Baba understand my point of view.

But he just kept shaking his head.

Late on the second day of climbing the trail, we arrived at the mountaintop. I stared around in surprise. There were hundreds of people on a rounded knoll only a few acres across, as well as food stands and vendors and people hustling things. It reminded me of an American fairground or carnival.

According to Baba, we were now 8,500 feet above sea level. I could hardly believe that all these people climbed to this mountaintop, in some cases bringing along ponies laden with goods to sell. Throngs of people were gathered in an open area at the mouth of the Amaranth Cave. We settled in among the crowd. Baba spent that evening giving *satsang*, and I sat and listened. A small group of English-speaking Indians asked Baba to lecture to them in English. I learned that this group came from an upper, wealthier caste. They gave Baba enough of a donation that he was able to purchase beans, rice, and some bread for himself and me. We ate a wonderful meal under the glaring brow of the Himalayas.

I awoke the next morning and asked, "What will all these people do at the Cave?"

"Most will never enter it. They will stay outside, chanting hymns and offering prayers to a stalagmite in the ice cave, which lies deep in the mountain. Many priests will lecture and give *satsang*. Only very few people will be allowed to go into the cave."

"Why can't everyone go?"

"It is a very small place already filled with holy men and priests. They decide who gets to enter. But just being here is special. It is like sitting at the feet of our Lord Shiva."

Restless, I walked to the edge of the peak and gazed down into a great plunging valley. Its walls were sheer stone, converging thousands of feet below on a floor of heavy jungle with a stream rushing through the valley floor. The clear blue water shone as intensely as a sapphire. Beyond the valley rose the next section of mountains, much higher than the peak we pilgrims were on, with snowy caps tinted golden by the morning sun. I looked back into the valley for some time, contemplating and then returned to Baba.

"How long are we going to stay here?" I asked.

"I have no plans. We can stay as long as you like."

"Then I'm going to take off for a few days to explore the valley on the other side of this mountaintop."

He regarded me for a moment and smiled. "Have fun. I will be here when you return."

No one seemed to notice when I started down the far side of the mountaintop and into the valley. Nobody else was heading in that direction. I found a trail, but it was practically vertical in places. I took my time hiking down. I was no rock climber or mountaineer, but the sapphire blue stream was luring.

After several hours, I reached the floor of the valley and found it worth the trip. The temperature dropped ten or fifteen degrees, and just ahead of me began a forest of tall, lush trees and tropical undergrowth. To one side cascaded the stream, perfectly clear from this angle and, as I soon found out, almost as cold as ice. It was clearly the product of the Himalayan snowmelt. I took a long, grateful drink from it. It was the first time I had dared drink from a stream since leaving the mountains of Afghanistan.

It was an odd contrast. Down here the air was hot and humid while the water felt achingly cold and pure in my throat. I removed my robe and washed it, then laid it over some exposed stones to dry. Sitting naked in the afternoon sun, I listened to the sounds coming from the jungle and gave more thought to my desire to become a *Sadhu*.

"You must give up the earthly pleasures in order to obtain spiritual awakening," Baba was always preaching. Well, I certainly gave up all the material and physical amenities I could think of. That wasn't the problem. The problem was Baba's secondary argument that I had to "go back and find a good wife, and start a family." Personally, I felt I was ready to move on to a path of total spiritual awakening, but Baba argued that first I needed to fulfill my duties as a husband and as a father.

But why? That was the question he did not yet answer to my satisfaction.

I ended my contemplation after about twenty minutes, as my robe dried. Wrapping it around myself again, I began to move along the streambed deeper into the valley. I found a trail leading under the forest canopy, which was so dense the air immediately cooled down again. Here and there a ray of sunlight cut through the trees, painting distinctive bright patches on the valley floor.

I walked downstream for hours, the valley narrowing steadily on either side. Seeing no signs of humanity, I was awestruck by a silence broken only by the ever more energetic splashing of the stream.

Finally, the valley walls dropped into a rocky gorge no more than fifty feet in width. While contemplating the depths and wondering where to go next, I saw a very old Hindu man sitting crossed-legged on the cliff side no more than thirty feet away. The mouth of a cave yawned behind him.

Moving slowly, I climbed across the rocks into the middle of the stream and sat down on a rock. The man seemed not to have noticed me. He was seated in the lotus position, legs crossed and tucked in tight against his groin. His eyes were closed, his hands resting on his knees. After a moment, I realized he was chanting almost inaudibly under the clatter of the stream rushing into the gorge.

It was an almost stereotypical image of the Hindu mystic: the isolation, the cave, the lotus position, the chanting. I did not wish to disturb his meditative state, so I closed my eyes and breathed deeply. The sounds of wind in the forest, of running water, and of the steady chanting hum swept over me in waves. I found it impossible to keep my body upright, and soon my meditation deteriorated into the urge to sleep. I kept nodding, catching myself just before falling off my rock. I must have been putting out some pretty awful vibes, because after my last nod I looked up and saw that the old Hindu was staring into my eyes. I felt humiliated, busted for my beginner attempt at meditation.

Raising my hands to my forehead, I said, "Namaste."

He responded with the same gesture but no words. I hesitated, then got up, and moved closer to him, sitting down and again showing a certain degree of humility. Baba told me that many *Sadhu* and *Sannyasi* men retreated to the forest for twelve years or more in the final stages of their lives to achieve full self-knowledge. Many did not speak at all during that time.

"Namaste, Baba," I said. "Do you speak English?"

The dirt surrounding the old man was stained black, as if with used engine oil. Clearly the Hindu had not moved from this spot in some time, perhaps years?

Then he smiled. It was a genuine, pleasant smile, and I got up and once again raised my hand to my forehead. The *Sannyasi* raised one arm and pointed for me to go back up the valley.

"Okay, Baba," I said. "Good-bye."

I turned and started working my way back up the slope in the direction from which I came. I knew that with or without the *Sannyasi*'s blessing, I would retreat to the opposite direction. Although the stream provided plenty of fresh water available, I was without food. Worse, I was moving upstream in thin mountain air. There was no way I could get back to the mountaintop before nightfall. I heard that some mountains were home to man-eating tigers and other large animals. I figured with all the visitors to the near by sanctuary, that would not be a problem in this area. Yet, as I continued, the nature became more secluded.

At dusk, I made shockingly little progress up the valley, but I found a grassy area next to the stream and turned it into a bed by breaking a dozen large leaves off some nearby shrubs to use as covers and camouflage. Tigers or not, I was exhausted and fell immediately into a deep sleep.

In the early morning darkness, I woke to a thunderous roar. I sat up, heart racing. The roar came from the upper valley. It was followed immediately by wild screaming. I thrust myself into the underbrush at the base of a tree. The screams were continuous and getting louder. Clearly they came from more than a single throat. My God, what was it that was headed my way?

The roaring and screaming grew steadily louder and closer until the trees themselves began to quiver. Twigs and leaves rained down on me. Then I glimpsed swift movement in the canopy overhead, looking up I saw dark shapes flashing across gaps in the trees where the bright sky seeped through. All at once I realized I was being overrun by a troop of monkeys, screaming and hurtling from tree to tree. I withdrew even deeper into the bushes as they passed overhead, moving with such energy that the ground itself shook. Hundreds, perhaps more, passed overhead as debris cascaded down on me.

Suddenly, a lone monkey landed on the ground not fifteen feet away. It was a big animal, the size of a German Shepherd, with long canine teeth protruding from a fierce muzzle. It stood there and scratched itself, and I could not help thinking how easily a pack of such animals could tear a human apart. I tried not to move or even breathe. But the monkey suddenly noticed me, picking my human shape out of the darkness.

We looked closely at one another for a moment. Then the monkey let out a horrific scream and vaulted back up into the trees. Within seconds, it was lost in the mob of animals stampeding overhead.

I waited for the animal to notify his friends about the quivering pile of human flesh on the ground, but the noise and vibration gradually subsided. The soft morning sunlight began to glimmer through the settling leaves.

What a horrific wakeup call, I thought.

Gravity wasn't my only enemy in ascending the valley. I could not seem to find the path I had used to come down through the jungle. Sometimes the underbrush was so thick I pushed my arms through it in order to part it for my body to move forward. Finally I retreated back to the stream where I moved from stone to stone, applying all my concentration and focus to keep from falling into the fast-moving water.

I slept under a blanket of leaves again that night and awoke not to the screams of apes, but to peaceful sunlight filtering through the jungle canopy.

All that day I walked and climbed and talked with myself, much as if Baba were with me. I discussed why I should become a *Sadhu* while the part of me that acted as Baba's advocate relentlessly pointed out that I must first return home and start a family. Both the walk and the dialogue were tiring, particularly since I had not eaten for two days. By evening, I was near exhaustion and still had not reached the foot of the mountain.

The morning of the third day, the avalanche sound of screaming and roaring warned me of another monkey stampede. Knowing now what to expect, I was not as fearful. I sat up against the tree and just watched the troop thunder overhead.

At midday, I at last came to the crystal pool at the foot of the trail leading up to the Cave of Amaranth. Resting there I was thinking how foolish it seemed climbing down into this valley with no plan and no food. Now I faced the long, steep climb back up the mountain.

Better to start now than later. I drank some water and placed a small, smooth stone in my mouth. I'd learned that if I craved food, this trick offered a slight psychological satisfaction. Also, unlike chewing gum or tobacco, the stone never lost its flavor.

I reached the mountaintop just before noon, literally crawling the last few hundred yards into the midst of at least a thousand people. Following my recent solitude, this was an unbelievable sight.

Several Hindus spotted me and ran up to me. "Where have you been?" one of them demanded in English.

"In the valley," I said, pointing the way I came. The little group gasped, turned, and began waving others toward us. In a moment, a much larger crowd gathered. I began to fear I had violated a taboo. I asked an English speaker what was going on.

"My friend," he said, "you have been in the Valley of the Cobra. We do not go into this valley at this time of year."

"Why not?"

"At this time, the king cobra are mating, and they become very territorial and, therefore, even more dangerous."

"Really?…" I frowned, wondering if I was being made the victim of some kind of inside joke.

But the man seemed sincere. "The king cobra tracks down the scent of anything that comes into its territory," he said urgently. "It is a miracle that you are here. No one has gone into this valley at this time of year and lived. Yet, you were there and the cobras allowed you to pass."

He spoke to the surrounding crowd in Hindi, and suddenly I was a celebrity. People began jumping and patting my back. A miracle? I didn't mention the fact that I had hopscotched along stones in the river much of the time. I doubted any animal could have followed my scent there. On the other hand, I had also slept in the jungle covered with leaves and brush, and I never saw a single cobra.

Finally, parting with my admirers, I walked to where I had left Baba and found him still sitting there. "There you are, my dear Owen," he said. "It seems that the entire camp is talking about you."

"Word travels fast up here."

He smiled. "Have you eaten yet?"

"No, not for four or five days."

He rose and extended his hand. "Come with me."

We walked to a little booth where an Indian man was cooking food. Baba spoke and soon a plate of beans and rice in a strongly spiced curry sauce sat before me. Baba gave the man some money and handed me the plate.

Looking at the paltry portions, I was sure I would be back for seconds. But I barely managed to finish what was there. My stomach all but disappeared. When I was finished, Baba suggested that we sit down and rest. We found a shaded spot. Despite the noise and commotion, I fell fast asleep.

A few hours later, Baba gently awakened me. "Owen, please get up. The priests inside the holy Cave of Shiva wish to speak with you."

"Me? Are you kidding?"

"No, they have asked me to escort you to them."

"Have you ever been inside the cave, Baba?"

"This will be my first time. It is an honor to be invited inside by the priests."

I got up and we worked our way through a mass of bodies that packed closer and closer together as we moved forward. Finally, we came to a group of men standing at the narrow mouth of the cave. They reminded me of bouncers outside a crowded bar.

Baba spoke with them, and they allowed us to pass. After removing our footwear, we stepped into the cave. Within a few steps, the walls and roof began to shrink and shortly after that Baba and I were bent over, creeping into a dark, narrow tunnel. Cold water ran over our feet, and the walls developed ice-smooth stalagmites. The tunnel narrowed and shrank so much that I began to consider crawling.

A smell of burning incense reached us and a soft glow of candlelight appeared ahead. Baba and I entered the heart of the cave, a small chamber where a group of priests sat in a candlelit semicircle, chanting a prayer. They were dressed in bright red and yellow Hindu robes, draped with beads and flowers, each facing one priest who sat above them on an altar-like rock platform.

I sank to a seated position beside Baba. No one spoke. The trickle of water and the glow of candles and incense created an extraordinary effect. I wondered how many centuries priests sat in this chamber in prayer and meditation. I still was not sure how I gained the honor to be there. I was humbled by the experience.

Soon the prayers stopped and the altar priest began talking with Baba. Baba related to me that the priests heard about the western white man dressed as a *Sadhu* who went into the Valley of the Cobras, and they wanted to give this man their blessings.

The high priest asked me to come forward. The ceiling was so low that I could not stand, so I approached him on my knees out of necessity as well as respect. He leaned forward, tied a piece of red nylon cloth around my head, and then chanted a prayer. I thanked him by clasping my hands together and touching them to my forehead in the traditional Hindu greeting. Then I returned to Baba's side. They continued to talk with Baba. Several times they all laughed and seemed to be in a very merry mood.

Finally, Baba raised his hands to bid them thanks and farewell and then turned and began crawling out of the cave.

Back in the sunshine, I asked, "Baba, that was amazing. But what was everyone laughing about?"

"I told them you'd decided to become a *Sadhu* yet wanted to skip the most fundamental duties of a holy man. They thought it funny." And he smiled as if to say that now the days of arguing this very point with me were confirmed by those who should know.

We made our way back down the mountain and began walking south again. Baba decided to head for Allahabad, a city just south of Delhi. I thought about civilization with its smoke-bellowing buses roaring through streets loaded beyond maximum capacity, the busy open air markets packed with bustling crowds of people, the beggars posted on every corner. It did not appeal to me. For once, I did not mind Baba's snaillike walking speed.

"Why Allahabad?" I asked.

"Every twelve years, Allahabad becomes the focus of one of the largest religious gatherings in the world. It is on the Ganges River, considered by most Hindus to be the most sacred spot in all of India." He paused. "It is known for its great healing powers."

I nodded and said nothing. After a few steps, Baba continued, "Your body is breaking down, Owen."

"What do you mean?"

"You have lost a great deal of weight these past three months. You are moving slower and slower. Have you not noticed? The waters of the Ganges are highly prized in rites of healing and purification."

He described in elaborate detail many Hindu traditions and customs. I barely absorbed any of it. It was like having the radio on while driving down a long stretch of highway. I kept thinking about what he had said about my health. I didn't given it much thought, but he was right. My body was melting away. Obviously, I was not adapting well to the Indian poor man's diet of beans and rice smothered with chili peppers so hot I cried every time I ate the stuff.

And then, I would cry again every time I had a bowel movement. Worse, I started having trouble urinating. Baba was right. If there was one thing I could use, it was some healing and it was only a two-week walk.

The Ganges River was a wide band of water as brown as coffee with cream. By the time we got there, I was urinating blood when I could go at all. Baba instructed me to remove my robe and submerge myself into the holy river waters. I did as he asked, wading into a brown flow as warm as piss and about as pleasant to smell. And there I sat waiting to be healed.

We remained on the riverbank for several days while Baba gave *satsang* to anyone who passed by. Many of the pilgrims were so poor they had nothing to give in return, except kisses upon the feet of an old *Sadhu*.

Baba was certain the river would purify and heal my illness. After several days with no apparent improvement in my condition, however, he decided that a new plan was in order.

"Owen, you need to buy medicines and perhaps see a doctor. It is time to go back to the monastery where you left your belongings." I was too weak to object.

A few days before arriving in New Delhi, we came upon a small building in the country. The structure was not much larger than a two-car garage constructed of white-painted mud under a thatched roof. A big red cross was painted on the side. Baba led me into the building, which was packed with eight to ten people. I sank onto a wooden bench while Baba spoke with a man wearing a white shirt above a traditional skirt-like wraparound cloth.

Waiting, I looked around. Almost everyone in the room was dressed in filthy rags and smelled of decay. I looked closer and saw missing digits and rotting features. Lepers. The man in the white shirt walked over to the far end of the bench, carrying metal tongs in one hand and an amber bottle in the other. He spoke with some of the lepers while he used the tongs to pull off their dirty bandages. I watched in amazement as the filthy strips of cloth dropped to the dirt floor, often bringing with them chunks of decaying tissue. No one cried out. The lepers sat motionless with their destroyed faces fixed in expressions of sadness and despair.

The doctor poured what I assumed was hydrogen peroxide onto the raw wounds. The liquid boiled, and more pieces of flesh spattered against the floor. Still no one cried out. I turned away and held my breath.

After the lepers were tended to and re-bandaged, the doctor worked his way down the row again, this time administering a shot to each of the lepers. I didn't pay much attention to what he was doing. My eyes were fixed on the heap of bandages scattered on the floor. They were covered in puss and blood, and the hydrogen peroxide continued to bubble on the rotting flesh.

Suddenly, I felt a sharp jab in my shoulder and looked to see the doctor withdrawing a needle. He refilled the syringe and proceeded to give the leper sitting next to me a shot, with the same needle!

"Baba!" I shouted. "He just shot me with the same needle that he used on the leper next to me. Ask him why he did that?"

Baba spoke with the doctor and nodded. "It is the only hypodermic in the hospital and, therefore, the only tool he has for administering shots." I stared at Baba in dismay. "Is this how they practice medicine in India?"

"You have to understand this is a country outpost, not a real hospital. The gentleman who administered the shot is not a real doctor. Life is quite difficult in India if you become ill. We do not have the same medical standards that you might find in Great Britain or the United States. Here, we have to make do with what little we have."

"But Baba, I could become infected with…." I stared at the stinking pile of bandages on the floor.

"We must see if this shot will help you in the next several days," Baba said in an uncharacteristically serious voice. "If not, then you may have to consider leaving India to get back to modern medical practice."

We left the clinic and continued on our slow way back to New Delhi. When I awoke the next morning, I could barely hear. My ears were impacted and aching. I suspected an infection from the filthy water of the Ganges. By the evening of the next day, green puss was draining steadily from both my ears. Worse, my urine was now bright red, and I lost control of my bladder.

"You must get back to England, Owen," Baba said. "There they can take care of you. Later, you can come back to visit me. I said nothing as I did not want him to think I had so easily given up on being a *Sadhu.*

When we finally reached the monastery, Baba took me to a courtyard and asked me to be seated while he talked with the priest. As I slumped in the sunshine, I noticed that my arms and legs now took on a pronounced yellow hue. Jaundice? Or a sign of hepatitis?

I pondered my physical condition. My ears were now steadily oozing both blood and puss. I pissed scalding urine the color of cranberry juice. And now, to top it all off, the rest of my body was slowly turning yellow. A few more colors and I might pass for a rainbow.

Baba returned with the priest and my backpack. Small as the pack was, it looked like a moving van next to the wallet-sized pouch Baba carried at his waist.

I didn't bother to open the pack. Although my *Sadhu*-style robes were filthy and stained with blood old and new, I knew that the only clothing inside the pack was some Afghan pajama pants and a long-sleeved shirt. Since these were traditional Muslim garments, I decided not to change.

I thanked the priest for storing my belongings and followed Baba outside. I leaned weakly against the wall. "Where we going now?"

He stared at me with his great dark eyes. "I am taking you to the bus station."

"Why the bus station?"

"Because you must leave India now, my dear brother. If you don't get modern medical help immediately, you will die here in India."

I opened my mouth to object and then closed it again. It seemed as if I had done little but argue with Baba during the entire time I had been with him. But I realized he was acting in my best interests and did so all along.

I let out a long breath. "Baba, I know you're right, but it saddens me to leave you. I feel as if I have failed you…and myself. If I leave, I will never become a *Sadhu*, and I will never even complete my original task of traveling around the world."

"Perhaps these are not your true tasks in life after all. I think it is said somewhere in your Christian Bible that the Lord works in mysterious ways. You must work with Him now, Owen, and listen when he tells you what to do next. You will be guided, my dear brother. Keep your faith. You must live, so you can continue your journey to find what you seek."

We walked to the bus station where Baba sat me down on a vacant bus bench and then returned with a bus ticket.

"This will get you to the border of India, Owen," he said. "There you must find a way to return quickly to England for good medical help."

I stared at him. How he came up with the money for this? I didn't know.

Tears welled up in his eyes. We hugged each other. His body felt strong and hard. I'm sure mine felt more like a bag of bones.

"Namaste," I whispered.

"Namaste."

The bus door clunked opened, and Baba gently pushed me on. By the time I fell into an empty seat, the bus was already rolling. I looked out the window, but Baba was gone.

FACING DEATH

As the bus jolted along the rough roadway, I sat in a half daze, reflecting on my long walk with Baba. He was very much an Easterner, and I was equally a Westerner. His skin was black-brown, mine white-tan. He looked at the world through spiritual eyes. I perceived it through physical eyes. He was old and wise, and I was young and impulsive. Yet, we were connected by the love and respect we shared for life and the fact that we were both seekers of enlightenment. The fact that I argued with him only strengthened his resolve. He appreciated what I said because most Indians revered the *Sadhu* so much that they never disagreed with him. Our relationship became the epitome of ideological fusion between East and West. In the final analysis, we both simply recognized the divinity within one another.

I closed my eyes and crossed my arms over my stomach to quiet the inside of my body and waited to see what God planned next. The bus stopped many times, lastly on the outskirts of a village on the Pakistani border. I hobbled off the bus and crept to the main intersection of the village where I saw a sign indicating that one of the roads led west to Lahore, Pakistan.

I opened the much-folded map in my mind and calculated that as the crow flies—4,500 miles separated me from England. For a moment I reeled. It took me half a year to cover that distance the first time. I could never do it again, not feeling the way I did. I decided to stop thinking about it. I would do what Baba would do, to take things one moment at a time. One step at a time if need be.

Buses, trucks, and cars passed in an unsteady trickle. Most of the cars were European, but they ignored me. After four hours, I struggled to my feet. There was no other option. I would just have to walk as far as I could. That turned out to be less than a couple steps. Dizziness drove me straight back to the ground. My ear infections worsened, affecting my equilibrium.

I rested a few minutes, then clenched my jaw, and pushed my feet under me. I rose unsteadily. When I was sure I would remain vertical, at least for a while, I heaved my pack on my back and started walking. I wasn't surprised that nobody stopped to pick me up. I found it almost impossible to walk in a straight line. Any observer would conclude I was either drunk or high on drugs. My skin was the color of a lemon peel, and my beautiful *Sadhu* robe was stained a shocking combination of red blood and brown dirt. And there was nothing I could do about it.

By the time I arrived in Lahore, my condition was grave, and I knew it. In the city's main bazaar, I looked around for a pharmacy. With a hundred and fifty dollars left, I figured on purchasing antibiotics and medicine. But antibiotics were unavailable. All I was able to find in the bazaar were vendors of herbs and homeopathic nostrums. I had no idea what might be suitable to treat all my various illnesses, which, for all I knew, included leprosy. I couldn't communicate with the vendors to ask for their advice.

At midday, I found myself standing outside the main hospital of Lahore. It looked to be a far better facility than the leprous, mud-floor, and thatched-roof facility in India. I shuffled to the hospital entrance and into the lobby. Suddenly, my legs gave out, and I took a seat on the floor. There I was resting with my back against the wall when a Pakistani gentleman approached me and started speaking Arabic, punctuated with one word I recognized. "British, British." I nodded.

He disappeared. A moment later, a young English-speaking doctor came out to the lobby.

"Good day, sir, what seems to be your problem?"

"Doctor, I'm glad to see you. I don't know exactly what my problem is, but I have so much abdominal pain that I can hardly sit up. I'm pissing blood and have no control over my bladder. My ears are infected, and I think I have hepatitis. I need some medicine, so I can make it back to England."

"Medicine, eh? Well, come now. Let me help you up, and we'll go back to the admitting area."

"Admitting?"

"Well, yes, unless of course you wish to die."

In a back room, I was laid out on a table where a group of doctors and nurses stripped me of my clothing and put me in a hospital gown. From there I was wheeled to a ward containing a dozen other patients.

The doctor said, "Mr. Owen, we will run some tests on you to determine if there is anything that we can do to help clear up your condition. This may take several days. In the meantime, the rest here will do you much good."

Over the next week, I gave urine and blood like a damaged fountain and was rolled in and out of the X-ray room almost daily. The doctor, who was educated in Europe and spoke three languages fluently, visited me each morning. Based on his restrained but compassionate behavior, I realized he was a devout Muslim. In the Middle East, most educated people I observed tended to be discreet about their religious viewpoint. It was the uneducated ones who tended to be vocal about their religious beliefs.

I was given two meals a day, breakfast and dinner consisting of bread, rice, and tea. Although I didn't have much of an appetite, the doctor and staff encouraged me to eat and drink as much as possible. So far, compared to what I had experienced in the past many months, my hospital stay was a jaunt in a five-star hotel. If only I felt well enough to enjoy it.

On the seventh day, the doctor came in earlier than usual, pulled up a chair, and sat next to my bed. "Owen, I have some bad news for you. I'm afraid that you are too sick for us to help you here. Please understand that it is not because I don't wish to help you. It is due to the fact that we don't have the medical supplies or technology to heal you here. I am afraid that if you don't get back to England and a modern medical facility, you will die."

I was so weak I could hardly sit up. "Doctor, I'm grateful for all you've done for me, but I've spent almost all the money on medications. I can't afford a plane ticket home. I don't even have enough money left to buy a third-class bus ticket."

He looked at me solemnly for a moment and then stood. "Please get dressed and come with me."

Limbs shaking, I put on my Afghan shirt and pants. The doctor and a male nurse helped me up. "Come with us, Owen. We are going to take you to the bus station. It is several blocks from here."

I ordered my body to step forward, but I literally couldn't lift my legs. Finally, with one arm over the shoulders of the doctor and the other arm over the shoulders of the nurse, I got moving. Even with the two men supporting most of my weight, the walk that followed was the most exhausting of my journey. By the time we stepped outside into the chaotic whirl of traffic and air pollution that was Lahore, my eyes sagged shut.

They opened again when I realized we stopped moving, and the doctor was saying something in rapid-fire Urdu. We were at a bus station, and the doctor was speaking to a man standing in front of one of the vehicles. After about five minutes of passionate gesturing, the driver gave a nod.

The doctor turned to me. "I told him you are very sick and trying to get to England. I also told him you are out of money and that, if you could not get to England soon, you would die. He will take you as far as he can drive to the west. Once there, I asked him to transfer you to the next bus going west. I told him that this was a religious duty to the Almighty and most benevolent Allah—for him and all the drivers after him. He has agreed to take you."

Before I could reply, the doctor and nurse heaved me onto the bus, which steamed with the warmth of bodies compacted beyond any legal limit. I was half-dragged to an occupied seat, which the man quickly abandoned once he got a look at me. My escorts eased me into the seat and put my backpack on the floor at my side. I looked up at them and tried to think of something to say.

"May Allah be with you, Owen," the doctor said. "I pray that you will be okay on the long journey before you." With that, he turned and exited the bus, the nurse behind him. Seconds later, the bus lunged forward toward yet another destination I knew nothing about, except that it lay to the west. The bus was dirty, loud, and jammed. But none of that mattered to me. That it was moving was all I cared about. On this bus I would cover more ground in one day than I could walk in a week.

Still, it was all I could do to hold my body upright. Finally, I gave in and slumped sideways onto the seat. Every time the bus hit a bump or hole in the road, which was often, my insides felt as if they were being ripped out. Wrapping my arms around my stomach, I held myself together as best I could.

Lying there with many curious eyes staring down at me, I wondered for the first time if I could actually make it back to England. For the first time since the hurricane off Mexico, I started thinking about death. I removed a pen and a piece of paper from my backpack and wrote my last will and testament in a shaky, almost illegible hand:

I wish the following things be done with my body following my death. Please keep my corpse for a period of seventy-two hours. If possible, I wish candles burnt continuously around my body. After this time, I wish my body to be cremated and the ashes to be sent home to my family in California. I am a Christian by faith. A priest or minister could be called if available to perform rights, but I ask that the ceremony be simple and in a spirit of joy, not sorrow. I have been a religious man for a number of years, so my requests are not without reason. I am grateful to whoever will see to it that these things are done. Bless you, my brother or sister, and God's peace be with you always.

At nightfall, the bus arrived in a dusty, no-name village, and the seats slowly emptied. The driver came back and started speaking Arabic to me. I didn't know what he was saying, but when he extended his hand I guessed he was telling me this was his final stop. I gave him my hand, and he helped me off the bus.

He half-supported me as we walked to an old building. He laid me on the concrete floor of an otherwise empty room. He left without a word. One window, one door, and four walls were all that I could see. It could have been a monastic cell, but I suspected it was some kind of storage area.

I laid my head on my backpack and fell asleep, praying that the Lord would give me the strength to deal with the destructive force at work in my body. At dawn several men entered the room and stood over me, talking. I opened my eyes as two men reached down and pulled me up, placing each of my arms over a different man's shoulders. I couldn't move my legs, so they hauled me outside with my boots dragging behind me. My chin thumped against my chest.

I couldn't see much along the way, but I could hear people talking excitedly. Apparently the sight of me was causing a commotion in town. The voices faded, as I was hoisted up onto the steps of a bus, dragged to the back, and laid on the floor between seats. My backpack was placed gently under my head. People stood or sat all around me, chattering in Arabic and ignoring me as if I were a piece of luggage.

The bus lurched forward. Once again I prayed, knowing that the pain within was about to consume me. Days passed—or perhaps weeks—all floating on the rumble and chatter of one bus after another. One time I opened my eyes to see the udders of a goat slapping my face. Another time I found chickens standing on my chest. Occasionally a kind soul would hold my head up to give me water or offer food, but I could swallow nothing solid. There was no doubt about it—I was dying.

I could not differentiate between an hour and a day. I heard voices, but they were distant, dreamlike.

"What's your name?"

For once, this voice was not distant. I opened my eyes. A woman with blue eyes knelt beside me on the floor of the bus. "What's your name?" she asked again.

I made a whispering noise that even I didn't understand.

"Where are you going?" she asked.

I tried to say, "I'm sick and trying to get back to England," but that came out even worse than my name.

Soon a second voice, a man's, spoke, also in English. I opened my eyes. "Who are you?" I whispered.

That seemed to come out better. "I'm Chris," he said, "and she's Helen." He gestured toward the woman. They both started talking, apparently in English, but this time I couldn't follow what they were saying. Helen gave me sips of water from a canteen and held my head in her lap. She ran her fingers through my hair. Although I was filthy with puss and blood oozing out of every orifice, I was too far beyond self-consciousness to care.

I wondered if this lady was an angel.

Suddenly, the bus jolted to a stop, and I let out a wheeze of agony. Helen and Chris raised me from the floor and struggled to drag me off the bus.

"Where are you taking me?" I asked when my feet hit the ground.

"To the hospital."

"Are we in England?"

"No, we're in Mashhad, Iran."

An unfamiliar male voice broke in, speaking English with only a hint of a Middle Eastern accent. I heard a name, Radhim-Ahmdi. The rest became garbled. I couldn't even understand Helen and Chris when they replied to him. I just hung there on outstretched arms, waiting for the quietness that would precede the arrival of the Angel of Death.

The newcomer listened to Helen and Chris, then turned toward the street, and began shouting and waiving his arms. A moment later, my three benefactors were pushing me into a taxicab. Radhim climbed in beside me, and the next thing I knew the taxi was roaring through the streets of Mashhad. Radhim asked me questions and I tried to answer, but I could barely stay conscious, never mind coherent.

Finally, the cab pulled up in front of a building with a sign written in both Persian and English: Shahreza Medical Center. Radhim hurried inside and returned moments later with a rolling gurney. He and the driver helped me out of the cab and onto the gurney where I lay there while Radhim disappeared again.

Next, he returned with a group of people in white coats, presumably doctors. They began to argue—Radhim on one side, the doctors on the other. Radhim shouted so loudly I opened my mouth and tried to ask what was happening.

He placed his hands on my shoulders. "Owen, the doctors have refused to take you because they feel you are too sick. They don't want the responsibility of you dying here. I have told them that I am going to get the SAVAK Police. I will return with them shortly."

The doctors started yelling again. Radhim shouted them down, and the next thing I knew I was being rolled into a private hospital room. Radhim followed.

"These doctors fear the Shah's secret police," he said as the nurses began removing my clothing. "I know them well. To avoid trouble they agreed to admit you. I will be back tomorrow to visit. Meanwhile, you must rest."

I could hardly open my eyes, much less say thank you. Soon the room was abandoned, except for me and the lights dimmed. For the first time in days, I was alone in a world not rocking and thumping. No goat udders hanging over me. No chickens.

But in this place of peace and quiet, I could actually feel the life drifting out of my body. Inch by inch, my limbs became cold and limp. The already dim light faded into complete darkness; the hush became absolute silence. I lay in a state of complete surrender, waiting. Not afraid this time. My only regret was that the first thing my parents would know of my demise was when they received a small wooden box containing my ashes.

Then I stopped even thinking about that. I drifted in a space of silence and peace. The doorway of death stood wide open, and I was about to cross through it the way Baba probably would some day, not kicking or screaming or fighting, but in a state of accepting surrender, devoid of all thought, worries or....

Suddenly, a fierce white light jolted my eyes open. The room shone with the brightest, clearest illumination as intense as an arc from a welding torch, yet somehow soothing to the eye. It emanated from the foot of my bed. There stood a woman, her face beautiful and gracious and her eyes piercing. The light flowed all around her.

This was not the bird-headed woman, not the Angel of Death. Yet, I said to her the same thing I had said during the hurricane, "You've come to take me."

She smiled, an expression that intensified her radiance. Without moving her lips, she said, "You have fought gallantly on the battlefield of life, faced death and corruption, hunger, the elements, and the valley of death. Yet, you still live. But you have yet to find your purpose."

I stared at her.

She smiled. "You must go on. You still have much to do and much to learn."

She reached into the radiant lighted area of her heart and, with both hands, brought forth a five-pointed silver star. She raised it toward me, and instantly a bright red laser ray poured over me striking deep into my heart. My cold and empty body immediately began tingling with warmth.

I didn't realize I had closed my eyes again until the light began to dim beyond my lids. I opened them. The being was gone. So was the burning pain in my stomach, and I felt my ears pop as the air equalized inside them for the first time in weeks.

I raised my hand and looked at it in the dim light. It was tan and brown, not yellow.

Smiling, I closed my eyes again and instantly fell into a deep sleep, knowing I would live to see the light of the next morning and many mornings yet to come.

The next morning, a group of nurses rolled me down the hallway to another part of the hospital. The nurses spoke to one another Persian while giving me sidelong looks as if they were surprised that I survived the night. In my new room, they began poking needles into my arm, and soon I was being fed intravenously.

As the day progressed, the routine of taking blood and urine started up once again. There was a steady flow of people in and out of my room, but no one spoke English.

On the second day, Radhim visited. "Don't worry about nothing. They have moved you into a special disease ward. Here they will take good care of you." His words were reassuring, but I already knew that the angelic guardian of light healed me. I was not destined to die in this hospital.

The days passed by slowly. The small, square room with its barren walls numbed all my senses. I couldn't tell the time of day or night. I could only hazard a guess by the timing of the two meals that were served to me each day. The Iranian nurses couldn't speak a word of English, but they came into my room several times a day to marvel at my long blonde hair and blue eyes.

Another regular feature was the appearance of a doctor who took up the habit of visiting my room once a day. He spoke some English. He diagnosed my medical problem as a nasty concoction of viral hepatitis, dysentery, systemic infection, and kidney malfunction.

After I had been in the disease ward for about a week, the doctor sent me down the hall to an ear specialist, who prescribed antibiotic drops. Days later my ears stopped bleeding, and the oozing diminished. The doctors were less successful with my kidney situation. After a week in the hospital, I was still in pain and still could not control my urination. But at least the blood in my urine had ceased.

After another week, I began to spend more hours awake than asleep. Two weeks later, my only excitement was anticipating the arrival of my next meal. It was incredibly boring, but I realized that my body needed the time to implement the healing initiated by the angelic force and medical science.

The Shahreza Medical Center was one of the most modern medical facilities in the Middle East, but it was apparent that I reached a point where there was not much more they could do with me. In fact, I suspect that my angelic visitor was responsible for most of my healing, with the unwitting support of the doctors and nurses. I was deeply grateful of this, but I knew the time came for me to leave.

That afternoon I tried to get my nurses to understand I wanted my clothing and backpack. I sensed that they knew what I was asking, but they were reluctant to comply. Finally, one of them nodded and gestured for me to get out of bed. I managed it after a couple of tries and followed the nurse into the hallway. She pointed to a locker, waved good-bye, and walked off down the hallway.

I opened the locker and found my backpack and clothes neatly folded inside. I grabbed everything and walked back to my room where I struggled to control my shaking as I dressed. I also noticed that the tips of my boots were worn off by my being dragged from bus to bus between the cities of Lahore and Mashhad.

I found a stairway and descended through an emergency exit. I suddenly was standing on a busy street. Behind me, the door shut and locked. I stood there momentarily. The sounds of cars and buses filled my senses, along with the smell of vehicle exhaust. It was the first time I had seen sunlight in over a month. Everything was so bright and intense. I bowed my head and said a prayer of gratitude for the special blessings I received. I was alive, thanks to the efforts of those who gave so much, so selflessly. The Hindu, the Muslim, the Christian, even the nonbeliever each gave something of themselves. I was certain the beautiful tapestry woven of these threads of beliefs, ideas, and religions would influence my life until the end of time. I took my next step with the idea that I was blessed beyond all reason.

Two blocks later I was sitting on the sidewalk, exhausted, unable to go a single step farther in any direction. Pedestrians simply walked around me. I must have looked like a homeless beggar sitting there.

Clearly, I gravely overestimated the extent of my recovery. When darkness arrived, I could not find the energy to rise and walk to a nearby alley to find a place to sleep off the main street. Instead, I leaned against a wall, pulled out one of my sleeping bags, and covered myself.

THE WAY BACK

The next morning I got up and started walking again. A half hour later, I came upon a bus station where I bought a third-class ticket to Tehran, cutting my money supply in half.

We arrived in Tehran late that afternoon. I got off the bus just outside the city limits and started hitchhiking to the truck camp. I arrived just as the sun was beginning to set. Nothing changed. There were thirty or forty rigs with European plates parked around the perimeter. I walked slowly into the restaurant.

"Owen, is that you?" I heard an excited voice shout. I looked across the room.

"Damn, I can't believe it. John, are you still here?"

"What do you mean 'still here,' mate?" He stood and grabbed me by the arm. "I drove to Europe and back since I last saw you—what, almost six months ago? Christ, you look like shit."

"I'm exhausted and sick."

"Hell, why don't you sit down here, and let me get you something to eat and drink?"

"That would be great. I haven't eaten in two days."

He pulled me over to his table and introduced me to four Europeans I didn't recognize. "Guys, this is that Yank George Lee was talking about during out last trip here. The one that took on six Arabs attacking George's lorry"

He turned back to me. "I'll be back in a minute. I'm going to get you some food."

I sat at the table. The truck drivers stared at me as if I were a ghost. Then one of them said, "So, where the hell you coming from?"

"I was in India."

"What the hell did you do in India?"

I thought for a moment. "I did a little sightseeing," I said. "And a lot of dieting."

They all started laughing.

They all were very interested in my journey, but I wasn't sure if it was something I wanted to talk about on a superficial level. What I really wanted to do was eat and go to sleep.

John placed a large bowl of stew in front of me. "Try this, Owen. I think it will pick you up!"

I stared into the bowl. "This will be the first time since I left India that I've eaten anything with meat in it."

I was stuffed before the bowl was half empty.

John laughed. "Well, you not only lost a little weight, but you lost your appetite, too. Don't worry, Owen. You hang around here for a few days, and I'll help you find it."

The following morning, I awoke at sunrise, lying in my sleeping bag on the edge of the camping area. I thought about the next leg of my journey.

As the campsite came to life, I got up, packed my gear, and walked to the bathroom and showers. A few guys were already involved in the morning routine of showering and shaving. The place looked like a high-school locker room. I jumped into the shower and rinsed about six to eight weeks of dirt and grime off my body. For the first time, I really noticed how much weight I lost. My waist was the circumference of a basketball.

Frightened, I finished showering and stepped onto a big upright scale like those found in doctor's offices. It registered sixty-two kilos: about one hundred thirty-five pounds. God, I had lost over fifty-five pounds since leaving San Diego. Crews of truckers came and left the bathroom before I finally finished. The simple joys of taking a shower were never more gratifying.

In the restaurant, I found John and most of the same guys I had met the night before sitting at the same table playing cards. "You guys are still here?" I said.

One of them laughed. "You bet, mate. You have to keep yourself entertained around here. Otherwise, you'll go stark-raving mad."

The European truck drivers were a special brand of people, particularly, in my opinion, the drivers from Great Britain. I considered them the cowboys of Europe. They smoked, cussed, drank, and loved to play practical jokes on one another. In their own ways, each was driven by a thirst for adventure and travel.

I pulled John aside. "I need to find a trucker who's heading west in the next few days. Could you keep your eyes and ears open for me?"

"I'll do that, but you know how long it takes to get anything rolling in this country. I don't think any of these mates will have anything lined up for at least a week."

"I'll do some scouting around myself. If you hear of anything, please let me know."

"You got it, mate."

After eating breakfast, compliments of the truckers, I stopped off at the showers and started washing some of my clothes. My stuff was riddled with two months of blood, puss and road dirt.

Finally, my clothes were as clean as they were going to get. I put them on wet and headed out into the sunshine. For the first time in months I was fed, washed, and rested all at the same time. Yet I could barely stand up from exhaustion. I returned to my sleeping bag, lay down, and fell asleep.

The next several days passed quickly. I had just come from an environment completely devoid of outer stimulation, and suddenly there was boisterous activity all around me. Each morning and evening, I returned to the restaurant to find out if anyone was heading back to Europe.

Finally at dinnertime, I wandered into the restaurant to find John playing cards with a half dozen other guys.

"Owen," he said, "I got some news for you. Jimmy and Frank here are heading out piggyback in the next few days. I told them about you needing a ride, and they want to talk with you."

Jimmy, an older black-haired man, shook my hand and said, "Why don't we move over a couple of tables where we can talk a bit?" he said with a heavy Irish accent. He and his companion, Frank, got up and escorted me about fifteen feet to a vacant table.

"So," Jimmy said, "you be wanting to head back to England, might you?"

"At least in that general direction."

"Well, we have a proposition for you, lad." He looked at Frank and smiled as if about to make a bet. "You see, we're kind of stuck here for the moment and low on funds. We're supposed to be heading out to Istanbul to make the next pickup, but we need some help financially to get there. Are you willing to share some of the expenses?"

"I'm pretty much broke at the moment. I have about fifty British pounds left to my name. How much do you figure a ride to Istanbul would cost me?"

"About seventy-five pounds in fuel, I figure."

"When are you guys pulling out?"

"We're ready to leave right now, but we can wait a day if you're willing to put up the money."

"Let me think about it, Jimmy…Frank. How about if we get together tomorrow?"

"Sounds good, mate." Both Irishmen stood and extended their hands. We shook and they made their way back to the card table. It was obvious how they had gotten "low on funds," sitting around the poker table for days on end.

Later, I met with John. "I spoke with the two Irish guys, and they would be willing to take me back to Istanbul for seventy-five pounds."

"That sounds reasonable," John replied.

"The problem is I only have fifty pounds."

"Shit, Owen, I'll spot you the extra funds just to help you get out of here. Besides I've taken twice that much from them in the past few days at the poker table," he said with a grin.

Later that evening, I walked up to the table where Jimmy and Frank were elbow-deep in a card game and belting down whiskies.

"Well, did you give our proposal some thought?" Jimmy asked when he saw me.

"Yes, and I've decided to take you up on your offer."

"Great!" Jimmy elbowed Frank in the ribs. "Frank and I have been piggy-backing for the best part of a week now, and we're ready to go. I figure we can pull out at around six tomorrow morning. Would you like to place your deposit with me now?"

I looked at them for a moment. The table in front of them was adorned with small change while the truckers on the opposite side of the table sat behind piles of sterling notes. "I'll turn it over when we're at the diesel pumps."

I saw John suppress a grin.

I stretched. "Well, guys, I'm going back to my camp to get ready for my trip back to civilization." I shook hands with each man at the table and thanked John for all his kindness. "I hope to see you on the road someday," I said. "Just remember to look at every roadside hitchhiker. You never know where I'll show up next."

He laughed and slapped me on the back. "That's for sure."

I turned and walked out of the restaurant.

On the road one learns to adapt to the rhythm of nature, including those indicating the start of a new day. The birds begin singing as the first light glimmers on the eastern horizon, after which the countryside quickly ascends from dead stillness and darkness into song, movement, and magnificent light. Outdoors, sunrise is the natural time to start the day. I was dressed and packed before the sun was halfway over the horizon and walked to Jimmy and Frank's tandem-back lorries. I sat on a grassy area to wait.

Before me laid a new day and the beginning of the final part of my journey, I thought. It was hard to believe that only five days had passed since I shuffled out of the Shahreza Medical Center and collapsed on the sidewalk after only two blocks of walking. With about twenty-five hundred miles left to cross, I felt hopeful. At least this time there would be fewer obstacles like snowed-in mountain passes and homicidal Kurdish guerrillas. It was possible we would reach Istanbul within a week, maybe less.

The rattling thunder of a diesel engine starting up broke my stream of thought. Daylight was spreading over the distant mountaintops, and Frank was walking around the rig checking tires and tie-downs.

I found Jimmy under the flatbed inspecting the spare tire. He grinned at me as he crawled out. "Top o' the morning, lad."

I figured he was in his early fifties and probably lived the trucker's life for more than half that time. His skin was weather-beaten, and his jeans and T-shirt looked as if they needed an oil change. Also, his suntan was reversed. Most English lorry operators drove vehicles built on the Continent, which meant that the steering wheels were on the left side, the opposite of English vehicles. As such, Jimmy's pasty-white right arm and suntanned left arm were the reverse of the average English driver.

"Cheers, Jimmy," I said. "You guys ready to roll?"

"Right, we're just checking on a few last-minute things. You got any fags on you, mate?" His morning breath was as foul as a barroom floor on Sunday morning.

"No, Jimmy, I don't smoke."

"Oh, bloody hell. I don't need a fag. I need a drink." Foamy crescents coated the corners of his mouth as if he fell asleep with an antacid lozenge in his mouth. Although the bloodshot appearance of his eyes could have been the result of hours of driving in the blaring sun, I suspected it was actually due to a long night of drinking and chain-smoking at the restaurant poker table.

"A drink?" I said. "This time of the morning, you'll be lucky to get a sugar-laced spot of Iranian tea."

"These fucking Arabs spoil their tea by dumping loads of sugar in it. It's like drinking a hot soda pop without the bloody bubbles."

Frank finished his part of the inspection and joined us. He was a light-skinned, rather thin man in his late forties. He appeared to be Jimmy's gopher. His one-armed tan gave him truck driver status, but in his case, both arms were encased in tattoos. Most of the artwork had a maritime theme—skulls and crossbones, anchors, flags, and lightly clad ladies. Some of the tattoos looked professional while others had the look of prison-yard quality. He hadn't shaved in a week, and his short-cropped hair looked as if it were long overdue for a bushing. In straightforward trucker fashion, he said, "Let's get the fuck out of here, Jimmy."

I felt a bit dubious. They both looked worn out even before we started. "You might as well crawl into the back of the cab, mate. It will be a bit cramped but it's the best we can do," Jimmy said. He pulled the driver's seat forward for me, and I tossed my backpack onto a narrow bench seat loaded with clothing, sleeping bags and trash. When I climbed back, the noise I made was like a ground squirrel pushing mounds of dirt aside.

Jimmy jumped behind the wheel and Frank into the passenger's seat. In seconds, the lorry was pulling out of the Tehran truck stop. The windows were rolled up, and the cab had the familiar stench of a prison cell: a combination of foul armpits, dirty socks, and stale cigarettes. Clearly, Jimmy lived in the cab of his lorry for months.

Resting my back against the rear window and my knees against the front seat, I breathed through my mouth and decided that, if Jimmy took care of his engine as well as he did his cab, it would be a miracle if we made it to Istanbul.

We drove about 350 miles before reaching Tapirs, the last major city in Western Iran. Jimmy pulled into a filling station on the outskirts of town. "Well, Owen, it's time that we load up our tanks. You able to make your first payment?"

"You bet," I said. We all climbed out of the cab, and moments later Jimmy and Frank were haggling with an Iranian attendant over the cost of diesel fuel. Apparently, the price changed daily based on fluctuations in the local currency. We drove for another hour or so before darkness fell and Jimmy pulled off the road for the night. Once the rig was parked, I jumped out, laid my backpack and sleeping bag close to the lorry, climbed into the bag, and immediately slid into sleep.

By sunrise, the following morning we were up and back on the road. Jimmy and Frank didn't talk much. Both seemed desperate to put miles under their wheels and get to Istanbul. Unfortunately, the terrain was turning mountainous, and navigating the constant switchbacks was tediously slow. Our elevation averaged between five and nine thousand feet. After approaching the Iran-Tur-key border, Jimmy chose the southern road to Maku to avoid the higher route through which George Lee and I had originally driven. The road couldn't have been more than 400 miles long, but it consumed eighteen hours of solid driv-ing.

On the fourth day, we found ourselves on some rough dirt roads. It felt like driving over miles of washboard. Gradually, as the shuddering continued, I began experiencing incredible stomach pain, worse than what I had in India. Soon I was doubled over on the back bench with so much pain I was certain that my kidney was about to burst. Sweat streamed down my face, and I felt faint and nauseated.

"Jimmy," I gasped, "you have to stop the lorry. I feel as if I'm about to rup-ture inside."

"Oh, hell, we have to keep moving. We can't stop here in the middle of nowhere."

"Jimmy, slow down at least. I think the washboard is about to do me in."

Surprisingly, Frank spoke up. "Christ, man, can't you see the bloke is bloody well sick? Slow down before you kill him."

Jimmy slowed the lorry down a bit. Although the pain in my intestines less-ened, I stayed doubled over with my head in my lap until, several hours later, we were back on asphalt and the discomfort passed.

The drive to Istanbul reminded me of the ride I had shared to New York with the two junkies. Jimmy and Frank often argued. From what they said, it was clear they should have been in Istanbul days ago. They informed their office back in England that they left Tehran a week earlier than they actually did. My payment for gas was their only ticket out of the Middle East.

Frank explained that, once they got to Istanbul, they both had shipments waiting for them to haul back to England along with some wired funds.

On day six, the lorry broke down less than one hundred miles from Istan-bul, in the town of Izmit. We spent the rest of the afternoon unloading Frank's lorry from Jimmy's flatbed, after which the drivers unhooked their flatbed trailers and roped the two lorries together.

Frank towed Jimmy's tractor rig to a truck repair shop in town, and then we returned to the tandem trailers, hooked them to Frank's rig, and drove to a truck camp a short distance from downtown Izmit.

Frank and Jimmy made telephone calls to their main office and explained the situation. The company agreed to wire money to them for the repairs, as well as a little extra to help tide them over until they reached Istanbul. They figured the repairs would not be finished for three or four days, about the same amount of time it would take for the wired funds to arrive. So here I was again waiting around a truck stop.

The days of waiting passed slowly. My sickened body now seemed defenseless against the insects. For the first time in two years, my body became their host. On the tenth day, Jimmy's truck repairs were completed, but we waited three more days before the wired funds arrived.

They dropped me off in Istanbul early that afternoon. They were going to hang around Istanbul for a couple more weeks since their company arranged for them to haul goods back to England. I preferred to leave than hang out with two unpleasant people for another couple weeks.

I thanked them for the ride and, within minutes, was back on the road, walking.

Despite the delays, I covered almost fifteen hundred miles in two weeks. Riding in the back seat of the cab turned out to be, perhaps, the best thing that could have happened. My body was considerably stronger now, so walking didn't wear me down as quickly as it did fourteen days earlier.

I reached the Turkish border town of Edirne in three days, a distance of 130 miles traveled on foot and with the help of a couple of rides.

Crossing into Greece was another milestone. I was back in Western society, with its dramatic differences in language, clothing, food, and religion. With the noticeable increase in vehicular traffic, I figured I could cover a lot more distance during the passing days.

I was wrong. As it turned out, although the roads of Greece were well-traveled with many private cars, the hitchhiking was not particularly good. So I walked. For the first time I felt discouraged. I needed to get back to England, but at the rate I was going, that would take another two months.

My luck changed five days later when a young Belgian guy on a holiday road tour of Greece picked me up in Thessalonica. Derrick was an easygoing guy in his late twenties, who, like most Europeans, took his one-month vacation during the summer. We hit it off and immediately became friends. I wasn't sure why. Our appearances were complete opposites. Derrick was clean-cut and well-groomed—future management material—while I looked rather like Jesus Christ, with the beard and my hair hanging past my shoulders. Worse, I was dressed in Hindu attire and a pair of tattered combat boots. Still, hit it off we did. Maybe that was because I had been starving for meaningful conversation since leaving India, and I finally found some with Derrick.

During the next few days we stopped at all the ancient ruins along the eastern coast of Greece. During the drives in between, we discussed everything from God to war. Although we didn't always agree, we respected one another's points of view. Instead of trying to win the other man over, we simply shared our perspectives.

After spending an entire day in Athens looking in awe at the magnificent structures of Greek antiquity, we headed out of town and camped that evening on the beach. Derrick's plan was to continue north through central Greece and then head for Hungary and Austria. My plan, of course, was to keep going west. As we studied the map that evening, I realized my best bet was to take a ferry from Greece to Italy. From there, I could continue hitchhiking to England.

In the morning, Derrick drove me to the seaport town of Patra, where there was a ferryboat to Italy. I was overwhelmed by the hectic activity of the town. Everyone seemed to be either coming or going. Derrick and I exchanged mailing addresses, and he drove off.

I sat down along a busy boardwalk. For the first time in over two years of traveling, I felt as though I were on a vacation. Finally, at dusk I boarded a ferryboat. Sixteen hours later, I debarked in the bustling seaport village of Brindisi, Italy, and immediately held my thumb out in hopes of catching a ride from someone leaving the ferry. Although a lot of traffic passed, no one stopped to pick me up.

After all the vehicles unloaded, I once again stood alone on the roadway. I took stock of my situation. Fifty dollars was all that was left in my pocket. Also, I was facing the reverse of the "no vehicles on the road" problem I experienced in the Middle East and Central America. Although there was traffic everywhere, all the drivers seemed to be in a road race, where no one dared to stop to pick up a weary hitchhiker.

In the next eighteen hours, I traveled only seventy miles, most of it on foot. My body was not ready for so much exertion, and it let me know. Exhausted and overheated, I found a spot next to the on-ramp of the major highway going north to Naples and Rome, and put out my thumb. I stood there all day. Not a single car or truck stopped. I was exhausted and did not have the energy to keep walking. By sunset, I crawled into some brushes and slept.

The next morning, I got the same results. No one even slowed down. They simply stared while passing. So did the people who passed me on foot, evidently walking to their jobs.

By noon, I felt so weak I sat down. I made a sign out of cardboard that said UK and held it up. Still, no one stopped.

By late afternoon, the same pedestrians who passed me on their way to work were returning home. They seemed amused to find that I was still there after more than eight hours. At nightfall I crawled back into some bushes and laid out my sleeping bag. All the goodwill in my heart was expended. So was my water. And I felt as if I were getting a fever.

In the morning I returned to the on-ramp. I felt hot and dizzy and in no condition to walk. I was worn out and too weak to walk further. Again, a dozen or so pedestrians walked by me on their way to work and looked at me with astonishment. When they returned that afternoon and found me still there, they passed me not individually but in groups of two and three, chattering to one another. Maybe they had an employee gambling pool going, wagering on how many days I would last. I was exhausted, but I knew I would eventually get up and start walking.

At the end of the third day, I crawled back off the roadway exhausted, forlorn, burning with fever, and dehydrated. What a strange place to be stuck—beside a busy highway within a thousand miles of my destination. I had prayed most of the day that someone would take pity on me and pick me up while, at the same time, swearing deliriously at every car and truck that passed by.

On the fourth morning, I barely found the strength to walk back to the roadside, but I did. By now I was out of food, water, and severely dehydrated. I was also without any hope that someone would give me a ride. I sat on the roadside out of sheer stubbornness.

Then, suddenly, to my amazement, one of the gentlemen who passed me on foot each morning approached me and began speaking in Italian. He was a short, bald man in his fifties who probably weighed 250 pounds. He wore dark slacks, a white short-sleeved shirt, and thick black-rimmed glasses. I could not understand what he was saying, but his gestures made it clear he wanted me to follow him.

Getting up, I heaved my nearly empty pack onto my back and walked along with the man. We left the highway and entered a main street that we followed for a half dozen blocks. There, at a bus stop, my escort stopped and gestured for me to do the same. A few minutes later, a city bus pulled up, and the fat man grabbed me by the arm and led me on board.

The bus drove for about fifteen minutes and stopped at another bus station. My escort led me to a bench and approached the ticket counter. A few minutes later he returned and handed me a ticket. I looked at the destination, ROMA. The man stayed with me until a bus pulled up, and then he gently pushed me onto the steps.

As the bus drove away, I looked through the windows and saw the man waving at me. I watched until he was out of sight, then turned back to the driver, and handed him my ticket. Everyone stared at me as I shuffled to the back seat. I sat in an empty seat and tried to figure out what had just happened. That little man answered my prayers. It was as if God himself came to me disguised as a fat little Italian man. He gently shoved me in the direction I needed to go and disappeared before I could even understand what had happened. He saved my life no less than Baba had or the doctor in India or the doctor in Pakistan.

I was ashamed of myself. Back at that highway on-ramp I had been so caught up in my personal suffering and weakness that I had given up hope. And I had been wrong.

The bus arrived in Rome at six the following morning. I purchased some sodas and water and was able to recover a bit.

Rome itself was a nightmare of traffic, congestion, and people. I made my way through the chaos toward the outskirts of town. Along the way I stocked up on water and bread. I was down to ten dollars with half of Italy yet to cross.

At the edge of town I took off my boots and examined them. Although I extended the life of the soles by stuffing the bottoms with cardboard and paper, things reached the point where wearing these boots was like walking barefoot with ankle lacings. I discarded them.

Barefoot, I continued north for another two weeks. Often at night I would enter a small village, find the Catholic Church in its center, and beg for food and a night's rest. The priests always took mercy on me, and either gave me bread and water or the money to buy them. Sometimes, I was allowed to sleep inside the church. At other times, the priest took me to a nearby youth hostel and arranged for me to spend the night without charge.

This generosity was still not shared by drivers. In two years of roadside travel, I never met a general population so disinclined to pick up a hitchhiker. It was ironic. Here I was in the most Catholic country in the world, and I still couldn't get a ride even while I looked like the portraits of Jesus found in every church and home. Lord, have mercy on Christ if he ever came back to Italy as a hitchhiker. The problem was that by now, my very life depended on the help of others. My health deteriorated to the point where I could walk only ten or fifteen miles a day before having to stop from exhaustion.

One evening at dusk, I ducked off the roadway to find a place in the bushes to sleep. In the darkness, I felt something as hard and sharp as a fang sink into my foot. I screamed in pain and, balancing on one foot, lifted the other and pulled out a two-inch thorn that sunk at least a half inch into my heel.

I pulled it out and took a couple of staggering, limping steps in the dark. I stepped onto a second thorn. This time I dropped to the ground, sobbing from the pain. I wandered into a briar patch. Both my feet oozed blood, hot and oily in the darkness. With shaking hands, I pulled the second thorn out and then sobbed even louder. Now it was real and undeniable. I couldn't go any farther. After all this time and all these miles, I was finally defeated. I was ready to lie down and let the Angel of Death come and collect me at last.

Then, out of the darkness, a voice shouted: "Hey, man, are you okay?"

At first I thought I was hearing things. I held my breath and listened hard. There it was again, "Hey, man, are you okay?" Someone was speaking English to me in the middle of Italian nowhere. That couldn't be.

Yet, I said, "No, not really."

"Hold on. I'll be right there."

Within a minute, a young man stood before me in the darkness. I could just make out the shape of a backpack on his back. He knelt beside me and said, "You need some help, man. What the hell are you doing out here?"

"I'm trying to get back to England."

"You don't sound British." He extended his hand. "I'm Pete, from Ohio."

I wiped the blood off of my hand and reached up. "I'm Owen from California."

His teeth gleamed in the shadows. "Well, that explains everything."

Slipping his pack off his back, he sat down alongside me and explained that he had just gotten off the airplane a few days earlier. His plan was to hitchhike around Europe for the summer.

"Good luck," I said. "Evidently Italian cars aren't able to stop."

He laughed. "Listen, I'll set up camp and then we can talk. Is that okay?"

"Great. I haven't spoken English in almost three weeks."

In the light of a flashlight from his pack, Pete gathered wood and started a fire. In its supple glow, I saw that my newest benefactor was about twenty-five years old, clean-cut, and muscular.

We talked about our travels while Pete cooked up a can of beans and dried meat. He shared his water with me, as well as some fresh bread he had picked up earlier that day. For me, it was like a full-blown gourmet meal. "What are the odds," I said around a mouthful of bread, "that in all of Europe, two American hitchhikers would happen to meet in the darkness alongside a country road at this precise day and time?"

"Not great," he said, and seemed contented with that.

I told him I was barefoot because I had used up my boots about 300 miles ago. His eyebrows rose. "You really walked through the bottoms of your boots? Listen, I have an extra pair in my backpack. What size do you wear?"

"Thirteen."

"Oh. I wear a ten, so I guess that's no help."

"It was a nice thought, though."

I woke at daybreak and started gathering my things. Pete was still sleeping, but I figured he would soon fall into the sun's rhythm if he stayed on the road. He must have heard me stirring because he sat up with a big smile on his face. "Hey, you can't take off without joining me for some breakfast."

Reaching inside his backpack, he pulled out a can of peaches, some more bread, and jerky. "I'd say we have enough here for a feast. What do you say?"

"Unbelievable, Pete, you're a godsend."

He shrugged. "What goes around comes around. I think is how the saying goes," he said and began opening the can of peaches. "After listening to your stories last night, I think you've gone through some amazing experiences. Who knows, I might need some help on my journey." He held out the can. "The first half is for you."

"Thanks." I took the can and drank some of the syrup. Then I reached in with my fingers, pulled out half a peach, and swallowed it whole. It was the first peach I had eaten in at least a year.

I handed the can back half empty.

After the peaches were gone, Pete broke a bread roll in half and tossed part to me. "You know, Owen, I was just looking at your feet. I've got an idea."

He reached into his backpack and pulled out his second pair of shoes. "I know it's going to look kind of ridiculous, but if I cut the toes off these, you could wear them."

"You're kidding."

"Look at your feet. They're a mess. This has got to be better than nothing." With the blade of a folding knife, he sawed the toe off one of the shoes and handed me what was left. "Try it on."

I slipped into the decapitated shoe carefully. My toes hung over the sole, as expected, but most of the ball of my foot was protected. I grinned. "Shit, Pete, this could work."

He started work on the second shoe, and in a few minutes I was lacing my new footgear. I stood and walked back and forth. "Amazing. They feel great." I wiggled my toes. "If any of the locals ask, I'll call them 'Hang Ten' footwear, the latest California fashion statement."

Pete stood and extended his hand. "Congratulations, Owen. You'll surely turn some heads, but I don't recommend you do any dancing in those shoes. You may end up in the same condition I found you last night."

Back at the roadway, we shook hands again. "Thanks, Pete. I hope our paths cross again someday."

"So do I. Meanwhile, here's a little something to help you on your way." He shoved a twenty-dollar American bill into my hand.

"Pete, I can't take this," I protested.

"Yes, you can. I insist. Good-bye and good luck." He turned and walked south. I watched until he was out of sight. I realized that traveling connected me to humanity. The daily innumerable acts of kindness, love, and sharing of so many kind souls brought consolation to my afflicted heart and gave me hope. I turned and started walking knowing my vision of humanity and the future were irrefutability transformed by my journey.

The day was cooler than those before, and I was now fed, refreshed, and invigorated. I had waited less than an hour when a vehicle with French plates towing a small trailer pulled off the road. A teenage girl rolled down her window and said in a heavy French accent, "Would you like a ride?"

"Thank you very much. Yes, I would appreciate it."

The passenger spoke in French to the two occupants of the front seat. The driver's door opened and an older gentleman got out and walked around to the rear of the car, where he straddled the trailer hitch and opened the trunk. He spoke quickly in French, gesturing for my backpack, which he placed in the trunk.

I slid into the back seat next to the girl. "Hello," she said, "I am Michelle."

She introduced me to her mother and father in the front seat. They didn't speak a word of English and had apparently pulled over because Michelle saw my 'UK' sign and figured I was English-speaking. I got the impression she wanted to use this opportunity to practice her second language.

"We are going to Switzerland," she said. "You are welcome to ride with us to Lugano."

"Please thank your parents," I said, and wondered why Lugano sounded familiar. I had never been to Switzerland in my life and never intended to go.

Michelle's family dropped me off at the train station in downtown Lugano, obviously assuming that was where I would want to go. They drove off as I looked around. I immediately observed that Lugano was situated on the banks of a large Alpine lake, in a setting of picture-perfect beauty with a stunningly deep blue sky, emerald water, and gardens overflowing with yellow and white flowers surrounded by mountains. Enraptured, I strolled around. For the most part, I tried to avoid large cities on my journey because crowds and traffic were of no interest to me. Cities were hostile places, full of noise, polluting traffic, and people following me around, either out of curiosity or in the hope of taking something from me. But Lugano was different: neat, orderly, peaceful.

Still, there was a price to pay. The Swiss folk stared at me openly as I walked along their pristine streets. Although I had tied my bushy hair back in a ponytail, the Indian shirt and pants I wore did not exactly blend into the local suit-and-tie crowd. Then there was also the fact that my toes hung over the soles of my custom-cut shoes.

I wondered how the hitchhiking would be in Switzerland. Would I be able to get out of the city in time to find a campsite for the night, or would I have to look for an alley to curl up in? I found a bus bench and sat down to study my road map. The name Lugano still resonated for some reason. I met someone from here on my travels—a Sufi, perhaps? Or—

Opening my backpack, I dug down to the very bottom and found a slip of paper that sunk there months ago. On it was written the name and address of the young Swiss Buddhist monk I had met in India the day I arrived there. The young man with the odd name of Madelaine.

I was right. He lived in Lugano. I wondered if he would mind my dropping in. How could he not, as a Buddhist dedicated to living in the moment? Well, since I did not have his telephone number, there was only one way to find out.

At about five in the afternoon, I stopped in front of an old, two-story residential building in a Lugano suburb called Lauizzari. For a couple of minutes, I paced back and forth, rehearsing what to say. Then I gave up and knocked on the door. A beautiful young blonde woman opened it.

"Good day," I said. "Is Madelaine here?"

"Yes, she is, wait just a minute, please," the blonde replied in a very pronounced French accent. And she messed up the pronoun, calling Madelaine a "she."

A minute later, a young woman with very short brown hair stood in front of me, eyebrows raised quizzically. "I am Madelaine."

There was some kind of mistake. The Madelaine I had met in India was a guy. Yet, there was something about the face. I swallowed. "Um, do you remember me? We met at the Indian border some time ago."

Her face broke into a smile, and now I knew this was definitely the same person I had met in India, now sporting about three inches of hair. And he was a she.

"Owen from California!" she said. "Please come in."

She hugged me and led me down a long hallway into a kitchen. "Would you care for some tea?"

"That would be kind," I said, placing my backpack on the floor and sitting at the table.

Madelaine opened a cabinet and reached to the top shelf for the tea. She was wearing a pair of cut-off jeans and a T-shirt that clearly revealed small but pronounced breasts. How could I have ever mistaken her for a guy, hair or no hair?

She put a pot of water on to boil, came back, and sat at the table. She laughed at the expression on my face. "Don't be so surprised. When I was in India, I realized it would be nearly impossible to travel around as a single woman. So, I decided to shave my head and wear a monk's robe. People thought I was a Buddhist monk and left me alone. I was able to travel throughout most of upper and central India totally unimpeded that way." She swiped a hand over her scalp and smiled. "Of course it has taken a while for my hair to grow back, but it's getting there."

We talked for the next several hours, drinking tea and eating bread and cheese. Madelaine was very interested in my experiences in India. As for me, I simply enjoyed sitting in a relaxed atmosphere with a woman. I loved just listening to her talk.

Finally she said, "Owen, do you have any plans for the moment? We have a spare room, and you are welcome to stay with us for a few days if you want."

"Thank you. I really appreciate the offer."

"Good. Why don't you let me show you to your room? I have to do some shopping and will be back in about a half hour, is that okay? If you like to use the shower or take a nap, please make yourself at home."

The last time I had a bath was a quick dip in the Aegean Sea in Greece. A warm bath in a tub sounded great.

I found the bathroom and undressed. There was a mirror over the sink. When I glanced into it, I staggered in shock. This was the first time I clearly saw the ravages the road and illness had inflicted on my body.

There was a scale on the bathroom floor. I stepped on it and watched it register sixty-four kilograms—about 140 pounds. I weighed 185 pounds when I left California, already lean for a man standing six feet three inches tall. Jesus, no wonder I was always hungry. I had some catching up to do, that was for sure.

I soaped and scrubbed, mesmerized by the warm water—all the warm water I wanted. When I finally climbed out of the tub, I was a bit waterlogged but invigorated. Best of all, I was clean. I dressed, combed my hair, and returned to the kitchen.

Madelaine greeted me from the stove where she was preparing a meal of something that smelled so good my mouth instantly filled with saliva. Before I could speak, the young blonde who greeted me at the door joined us. Madelaine introduced her as her roommate, Frances.

I said, "How is it that you both live in the Italian speaking part of Switzerland, but you speak French?"

"Ah," Frances said, "we came here because of school. We're both in language school."

"How many languages do you speak?"

"Three: French, German, and English. Now I'm learning Italian."

"What about you, Madelaine?"

"The same. It's not too difficult here since we have four national languages in Switzerland. In addition to German, French, and Italian, about ten percent of the Swiss people also speak Romanish. It is a language from the olden days. And now most of us learn English in school as well. That is because the English language is the language of business and science."

I could barely concentrate on the conversation in any language. Wonderful aromas wafted around the kitchen, and soon I sat down to the first home-cooked meal I had eaten in a long, long time.

That evening I did something else. I slept in a bed that wasn't in a hospital room. It was heavenly.

The past twenty-four hours seemed like a dream. I had gone from crying helplessly by the side of a road to living in luxury in the company of two beautiful women. Although I had made an effort to convince my hostesses that I found all this quite ordinary, the truth was I had been away from Western civilization for so long that it was impossible to take anything for granted.

The following morning, I woke before sunrise, strictly out of habit. I lay in bed for as long as I could, then got up, entered the living room, and read for about an hour before Madelaine came in.

"Do you like coffee?" she asked as she walked into the kitchen.

"Sure." I started to rise. "Would you like some help?"

"Oh, no, this is the kitchen, and we Swiss women take care of the kitchen. Please, just relax."

A short while later, Frances came into the room, her eyes half-open. Madelaine smiled. "Frances can hardly talk until her first cup of coffee."

Without comment, Frances poured herself a cup and joined me at the table. I watched her take her first sip of coffee. It was like watching a child smell a fragrant flower.

Finally, she set the cup down and spoke. "Owen, Madelaine and I were talking last night after you retired to bed. We have some friends who live in a small village called Indemini, up in the mountains almost on the Italian border. They told us that there is an American guy working there. He's from California. Would you like to go up and meet him?"

"Sounds great. When do you want to go?"

"We were thinking that we would leave after breakfast. We will probably spend the weekend there, so you may want to bring your backpack.

"I'll go get it."

Some decisions seem so frivolous, so casual. One often does not know when one's life is about to change.

FINAL CALLING

Madelaine was kind enough to give me the front seat in Frances's tiny Renault although, even with the seat all the way back, my knees were pinned against the dashboard.

Southern Switzerland is a beautiful place in summer. Green pastures dotted with Swiss cows blanket the countryside as it rises to the Alpine peaks on all sides. We drove to the base of a particularly large peak and began climbing along a steep, narrow two-lane road.

"Does this road bother you, Owen?" Frances asked.

Thinking of George's wild driving through the deadly mountains of Turkey, I smiled. "Not at all."

We drove for another hour, climbing steadily. We passed through a pine forest and crossed small bridges and open pastures. I didn't see more than two other cars the entire time.

Finally, Madelaine leaned forward and pointed. "Here comes Indemini."

I sat up and saw a small, picturesque village perched on a steep slope. We parked on the main road just outside town and got out. All the houses I could see were built of gray stone. To the rear, a dense Alpine forest lined the slope. Down below, a vast grassy pasture plunged into blue distances. It was a breathtaking panorama.

I followed Madelaine and Frances along a narrow cobblestone street that wound into the village. Every building stood directly against the curb and leaned overhead. I felt as if I were walking back in time.

After a couple of minutes, we arrived at a two-story building where Frances stepped up and knocked on a massive oak door. While we waited, I examined the surrounding stonework. There was no visible sign of cement; the stones were perfectly fitted. It looked more like art than walls.

The door opened to reveal a short, black-haired woman in her early thirties. She was, to put it bluntly, one of the least attractive Swiss women I had ever seen. She wore a red bandanna on her head. Her olive complexion looked slightly bruised. When she smiled I noted that she didn't have a straight tooth in her mouth, and the hair on her upper lip resembled a teenage boy's first attempt at a mustache. But Madelaine and Frances hugged her with joy and then introduced me to her as "Owen, the guy we told you about."

"Hi, Owen, I am Bianca," the woman said in a strong German accent and extended her hand. "I am happy to meet you."

Crooked as it was, her smile radiated a genuineness that was difficult to describe and impossible to resist. I smiled back.

As I stepped over the threshold of the house, my head thumped into the upper edge of the doorframe. I staggered, and the women gathered around me and jabbered to one another in Swiss-German. Madelaine translated, "Bianca says that these homes were built five to six hundred years ago. Back then the men weren't so tall. So be careful because everything in the house is much shorter than you."

"I'll remember that," I said, rubbing my scalp.

The interior of the house was decorated just like I imagined it might have been half a millennium ago: simple, heavy furniture, wood-beam ceilings, and a stone floor. A huge wooden table, a copper sink, and a wood-burning stove dominated the kitchen. The ceiling was adorned with bundles of herbs, dried fruit, and sausages.

Bianca and the girls kept speaking in Swiss-German, looking sidelong at me, and smiling. "Owen," Bianca asked, "are you hungry?"

I grinned. "I'm always hungry."

It was as if I had tickled her. Her laugh reflected so much warmth and love that I didn't know what else to say.

She reached into a cupboard and took out some bread, sausage, and three or four different cheeses. From another location she grabbed a bottle of red wine. "Start on this and I will cook you some dinner."

"You don't have to go through so much bother, please."

"No, no, it is my pleasure to feed you."

The three women laughed and conversed in Swiss-German again. Then Bianca made several telephone calls. I couldn't tell what she was saying, but it was obvious she was excited. Meanwhile, Frances sliced bread and poured wine. Bianca hung up the phone and made a pushing motion at me with her hands. "Please, Owen, start eating."

Ten minutes later, I heard a knock at the front door, and several women called out. Bianca called back, and soon three more women were standing in the kitchen. Bianca introduced me as if she had known me all her life. In a moment I discovered that all the new arrivals brought gifts of food for me. I couldn't understand why all Swiss people weren't obese.

The women were putting food out on the table and begged me to eat. I couldn't believe it. For almost a year, I practically starved to death. But now, suddenly, food was piling up in front of me faster than I could shovel it down. Bianca was busy making more.

The next few hours, I sat eating and laughing with six beautiful women. The more I ate, the happier they became. If ever my plate was half empty, the women took turns shoveling more food on it. After two hours, I could barely sit up. I pushed my plate aside. The women laughed.

After Bianca cleared the table, she said, "Owen, would you like to take a walk through the village and meet the other American who is working here?"

"That sounds great."

When we went to the front door, I remembered just in time to lower my head. Bianca laughed.

Outside, Bianca gave me a quick history lesson. "When this village was built, most of the residents were shepherds, caring for goats and cows on the mountainside. There weren't many people living here."

"What's the population now?" I asked.

"Fifty-four people live here fulltime."

I noticed that all the buildings were two stories tall. Bianca explained that in the early days, farmers kept their livestock on the ground floor and their families on the floor above. "The streets are so narrow because, in the early days, the villagers closed the gates at either end of the village at night to keep the wolves out. When wolves did get in, the farmers cornered them on the narrow streets and clubbed them to death."

Soon we arrived at yet another stone building. "This is Papa Al's place where James, the California guy, is working." Bianca approached the door and knocked. Soon it opened. Standing before us was a short, portly gentleman in his sixties, with neatly combed gray hair. "Owen," Bianca said, "this is Papa Al. He speaks English and is also originally from the U.S."

"Good afternoon, sir," I said. "As Bianca might have mentioned, I'm from California. She said that you have another Californian working for you. I was hoping I could meet him."

"I'm sorry, but James has gone into town to get some supplies. Perhaps you can try back later." His accent was German, but not the same dialect as Bianca's.

"Papa Al," Bianca said, "we're having a little get-together this evening at my place. Perhaps when James returns, you could ask him to stop by, so Owen could meet him."

"Okay, Bianca, I'll pass along your message."

We turned and headed back through the village.

"What's the little get-together?" I asked.

"We always have some type of Saturday-evening party. Up here in the mountains, life is fairly boring unless you make your own entertainment."

"It's hard for me to believe anyone could find this beautiful place boring."

Bianca smiled. "I agree, of course. And some very interesting people have come to live in the village. My husband and I are musicians. There are other musicians as well, one or two artists, at least a half dozen society dropouts, and a few spiritual hippies."

"Well, that makes the place even more interesting," I said.

By the time we reached Bianca's house, several more people gathered in the kitchen. One of the newcomers was a very animated Swiss guy, the center of everyone's attention as Bianca and I entered the room. Bianca grabbed his hand.

"Owen, this is my husband, Charlie."

He was like a combination of Albert Einstein and Beethoven. His hair looked electrified, standing up as if he had just plugged himself into a 220-volt outlet. His skin was a pale white with pink undertones, his frame very slight. His voice was as animated as his appearance. He was dressed as if he had just stepped out of the eighteenth century with his blue jeans, sandals, and a white hand-embroidered blousy shirt adorned with Swiss cows. He wore a paper-thin pair of silver bifocals that further highlighted his pinkish complexion.

The conversation, in German and French, was lively. Madelaine translated for me from time to time. Apparently, several of Charlie's friends and fellow musicians would be joining us that evening to put on a concert in the living room.

Bianca placed a hand on my arm. "Owen, you can stay with us if you like. We have several extra rooms."

"Thank you, Bianca. I would love that."

I followed her into the rear portion of the house. "Charlie owned this place before we were married," Bianca said. "He is a fanatic about preserving the building in its original state, inside and outside, as you can see." She pushed open another miniature door. "This is your room. The bathroom is just down the hall. We'll see you in the living room later."

The room was only marginally larger than my monk's cell at the Benedictine monastery and furnished similarly with a single bed and a small desk and chair. One difference was that a colorful quilt covered the bed. On the back wall, a window looked into a courtyard. On another wall hung a black-and-white photograph that depicted the valley and mountains as viewed, I guessed, from the second floor.

I sat on the bed and kicked off my ridiculous custom shoes. Then I lay back and contemplated recent events. It seemed my luck was changing—and rapidly. For tonight at least, I had my own bedroom and would be surrounded by very nice people in one of the most picturesque places I had ever seen. In addition, for the first time in as long as I could remember, I was fully fed. Everything was perfect.

And yet it wasn't. Something inside me was still unsettled, nagging, complaining. Despite all my journeys, all my seeking, all my struggles—despite all these things and after nearly dying on more than one occasion, something was still missing.

A gentle knock sounded on the door. "Owen, are you up?" Madelaine's voice called.

I opened my eyes. "Yeah, I'm up." I swung out of bed and opened the door.

Madelaine smiled. "We're all wondering when the guest of honor is going to come to the party."

"Shit, I'm sorry. I must have dozed off. I'll be out in a few minutes."

She left. I grabbed the small Tupperware box containing my toothbrush, comb, matches, and nonessentials and carried it to the bathroom. There I combed my hair, brushed my teeth, and threw a little water on my face. I decided not to wear my ridiculous shoes, and instead opted to go barefoot and put on my worn Indian garments. For me, that qualified as getting dressed up for a party.

As I approached the living room, music began playing—a chorus of instruments. I stopped in the doorway. The room was crowded with twelve to fifteen people, all young and hip-looking. Half of them were playing instruments—and playing them very well. Charlie sat at a grand piano, accompanied by several women playing violins, a guy on bass, a woman on cello, and a guy on trombone.

They were playing a piece by Beethoven or Bach. I could only guess which since I was unfamiliar with this kind of music. There were numerous pictures of both composers hanging in the hallway. I had been raised on country-western and rock-and-roll. Now I stood in awe. The acoustics of the stone house were surprisingly warm and clear, the music mesmerizing.

After a few minutes, I glanced toward the fireplace and noticed a petite woman with long dark hair sitting on the bench. As I looked at her, she raised her head, and our gazes connected. She immediately looked down, the blush on her face visible even in the primitive lighting of the room. I didn't look down. I couldn't take my eyes off her.

When the music ended, everyone clapped. Charlie rose to his feet. "Owen," he said in English, "I am happy you can join us. Please come in and make yourself at home. Everyone, this is Owen from America."

Everyone smiled, nodded at me, then turned away, and continued their conversations. I immediately crossed the room to the fireplace and approached the young dark-haired woman. "May I join you?"

She smiled. Her eyes were big and puppy-dog brown. I gazed into them for several seconds before it dawned on me that she had not answered my question.

"May I join you?" I asked again. Upon receiving another smile, I realized she might not understand English, so I gestured with my hands and body to mime my request. She laughed.

"Yes, please," she said, her Swiss-German heritage stamped strongly in the two words. But I was already sitting. As strange as it sounds, I found her laugh so sweet my knees simply buckled. I stared at her and couldn't think of a thing to say. Besides, I wasn't sure how much she would understand. So I said the only thing that came to mind, "I'm Owen. What's your name?"

"I am Christina." With the nearness of the fireplace, the warmth of the young woman's smile, and the sparkling light in her eyes, I felt as if I had caught fire. She looked about eighteen, but you never could tell. So the second profoundly stupid thing I said was, "How old are you?"

She laughed again. "I have twenty-eight."

I couldn't believe it. How could she be just a two years younger than I?

Bianca came around with a glass of red wine. "Here, Owen, try this. I think you will like it. It is our village wine."

"Thanks, Bianca."

"I see that you have met Christina." She started talking with Christina in Swiss-German. Charlie was now back at the piano. Soon the room filled with a symphony. It was beautiful, but not as beautiful as Christina's smile.

I sat there the entire evening, as if Christina were the only other person in the room or, for that matter, on earth. We talked very little—and not just because I spoke no German and she very little English. We just seemed to understand one another.

Eventually, the other local American, James, made his predicted appearance. It took him a while to get through the crowd to my part of the room and shake hands. "Well," he said, "I see you managed to meet the most beautiful girl in the village and the only one not taken."

I did not have to wonder why he didn't move on Christina himself because it was obvious that Frances and James were already a pair. We chatted about California for a few minutes. Christina's eyes moved back and forth as she avidly followed the conversation. Finally, James said, "Owen, do you know anything about construction by any chance?"

I found myself remembering the Sufi farm in England. "This doesn't have anything to do with a barn, does it?"

He looked startled. "How did you know?"

"Never mind. Yes, I do know a little bit about construction."

He looked from me to Christina and back. "The thing is, I'm going to be taking off in about a week, and Papa Al will need someone to finish up the work we've been doing. Would you be interested?"

"Absolutely." I didn't even ask what the work entailed. I didn't care as long as it would give me an excuse to stay in the village for a while.

He grinned. "Good. How about stopping by tomorrow, and we can talk more?"

"I'll come over in the morning."

I looked at Christina. She smiled.

The party came to an end around midnight—three to four hours past my normal bedtime—yet the entire evening buzzed past as if it were only minutes. Before the final moment came, I moved next to Christina on the bench and took her hand in mine. Her hand was as small and soft as a flower in my leather-tough, suntanned mitts.

Christina and I watched silently as the guests began to leave. Finally, she looked at me and said, "Owen, I must go to my home."

I stood up. "May I walk you?"

She smiled. "Yes."

She rose. I could not believe how small she was. She barely came up to the middle of my chest, and probably didn't weigh a hundred pounds. We thanked Bianca and Charlie for the evening and walked outside together.

The Alpine air was cool and crisp, the stars exceedingly bright. Christina and I walked along the cobblestone street for about five minutes, saying nothing, until we reached an old building with steps leading up to a porch and front door.

At the top of the steps, we halted. I faced Christina. There was nothing I could say in such a perfect moment, so I simply leaned down and kissed her as if it were the first and last kiss of my life. She met my lips with exactly the same intensity.

When we finished, I held her head against my heart, which was racing as if I had just finished a marathon. I knew she could feel it because she placed her lips gently on my chest and looked up at me. "Thank you, Owen. I see you tomorrow?"

"Yes, yes, most definitely."

She smiled, turned, and walked into her house.

My world caught fire that night. The passion of love was lit. I sensed that this was the purpose of my journey—to travel three quarters of the way around the world just to find my way here, to this stone house on the side of a Swiss mountainside. Christina's home.

The next morning, I was out of bed at daybreak. No one else was up, so I took a stroll around the village.

It didn't take long. In less than an hour, I had covered every street and pathway. When I returned to Bianca and Charlie's house, they were sitting at the kitchen table with Frances and Madelaine, speaking in Italian. As I walked up, the conversation automatically switched to English. "Well, how did you sleep last night?" Frances asked.

"Heavenly."

"You looked like you were having a great time with Christina," Charlie said.

"She's amazing," I said.

"You just caught her," Bianca said. "She lives in the city and only got here a few days ago. She usually stays for a few months."

"What does she do for a living?"

"She's a photographer, among other things. For the past several days she has been going into the forest and collecting plants for making dyes to color the hand-spun wool she uses for making sweaters."

"You mean she knows how to knit and sew and all that?"

"Of course, she is Swiss." Bianca and Madelaine laughed.

Bianca started feeding me, beginning with a half-cup of strong black coffee topped off with steaming milk. Then she placed a wood cutting board in front of me and handed me a round loaf of homemade bread.

"Here, cut some bread and try these cheeses."

I helped myself, knowing that if I didn't she would do it for me.

An hour later, I was stuffed and excused myself. "I have to go see James this morning about a possible job working for Papa Al."

I started to clear my plate off the table and quickly got reprimanded. "That is a woman's job," Bianca said. "We'll see you later."

"James said that you might be stopping by this morning," Papa Al said with a smile. "Please come inside." I walked into the house, reminding myself just in time to duck. The living room opened onto the kitchen, where James sat eating breakfast.

Papa Al asked, "Do you care to join us?"

Before I could reply, Christina stepped into the kitchen from a back room, carrying a basket of wet clothing. "Owen," Papa Al said, "have you met Christina yet?"

Christina and I smiled at one another, and I felt my heart accelerating. "Yes," I said, "we met last night."

"Whenever she comes to the village, she always helps me with laundry and cooking. I have absolutely no interest or talents in those departments."

Christina came to the table and poured me a cup of coffee. I stared at her. It was all I could do to focus on anything else.

"James is leaving in a few days on his motorcycle to finish his tour of Europe," Papa Al said. "He's been doing some stonework and repairs here on my house. I'm hoping to get everything finished before winter comes. He says that you might be interested in working for me."

I didn't take my gaze off Christina. "Yes, I am interested, but I thought it was a barn that needed work."

Papa Al lowered his gaze. "Well, yes, that too. I am afraid that by Swiss standards the pay isn't that good, but you'll get a room and three meals a day."

"What is the pay?" I asked.

"Eighty francs a day."

I nodded, with no idea how much a Franc was worth, but it didn't matter. I would have worked for room and board alone if it meant being near Christina.

"There is one other thing. I work in Zurich and can only be here during the weekends, so I hope that you won't mind house-sitting during my absence."

"That's no problem."

After we finished our coffee, James and Al took me outside and outlined the tasks to be completed. My last glimpse of Christina was seeing her bend over the table to clear it.

Al gestured overhead. "As you can see, James is working on finishing the roofing of the house. He has taken all of the old stones off, put plywood over the beams and coated it with a rubberized material for weatherproofing." He pointed at rows of flat stones stacked neatly beside the house. "Next these will have to be placed back on the rooftop. It's a big job, wrestling them all into place. Is this something you think you can handle?"

"Oh, I've got plenty of roofing experience. It shouldn't be a problem to have this done within a month or so."

He nodded and again avoided my gaze. "Excellent, but I have a slightly more pressing job to finish first."

He led me and James to the street level of his home. "This is the barn," Papa Al said as he started unlocking the weather-beaten oak door. "For centuries, Swiss farmers kept their livestock under the house in the winter. The cows and goats provided food and dairy products, and also helped keep the upper story warm.

The last lock snapped open. James stood back as if he already knew what was going to greet us as Al swung the door open. I stared into a room about the size of an extra-large one-car garage, filled wall-to-wall and clear to the ceiling with what looked like lumpy black cement weeping with moisture.

Al stood back. "There's probably a hundred years of goat waste here. I want you to clean it out and paint the room, and we'll open it as a boutique. Plenty of tourists visit the village during the summer, and it will be a way for me to make a little money on the side. Someday I intend to quit working in Zurich and live here fulltime. Well, do you think you can handle this job for me?"

Now I understood why James decided it was time to finish his motorcycle tour. "None of this is…fresh?" I asked.

"No, no. There have been no goats for the past thirty years now."

I looked at my toes poking through the front of my shoes and thought about what it would be like to stand in centuries of goat dung.

"That's eighty francs a day plus room and board," Al said quickly.

He had misunderstood my hesitation. The fact was that I would wade chin-deep in the contents of this room if it meant even a single extra day with Christina. "You've got a deal," I said.

He grinned. "That's great. When can you start?"

"How about today?"

"No, no, the Swiss would be unhappy to have you working on a Sunday. Could you start tomorrow?"

"Absolutely."

That afternoon, I returned to Bianca's house, hugged Madelaine and Frances goodbye, and then carried my scant belongings to Papa Al's. James was now talking about leaving in a few days instead of waiting until the end of the week. I suspected he was determined to avoid any involvement in the barn muck. Papa Al would depart in the morning and not return until the following Friday evening. It occurred to me that, for the first time in almost two and a half years, the only person in my immediate vicinity who was not going anywhere was me.

In the morning, Papa Al and James were having coffee when I came down from my room. Al was already dressed for Zurich in a white shirt and tie.

"I hope you'll have the barn cleaned and painted by the time I return Friday evening," Al said.

"Don't worry. I'll have it finished."

"James decided to leave on Wednesday, so it might be a good idea to have him show you what you need to do on the roof as well before he's gone." Al finished his coffee and rose. "Well, gentlemen, I'm off to Zurich. James, I wish you well on your motorcycle trip, and thank you for your help. Owen, I'll see you Saturday morning."

"Sounds good, Al. Have a safe trip."

James led me around to the side of the house. "I have some shovels and a wheelbarrow over here. Al wants you to wheelbarrow the shit you dig up out to the end of that pathway there and dump it into the ravine. No one will say anything. I guess the villagers have been cleaning out their barns like this for centuries.

"Here's a square-tipped shovel. Don't wear it out. It's the only one we have. I'll be up on the roof if you need anything."

I laughed. "How about some shoes?"

He looked at my feet. "I have to admit those convertible shoes of yours might be better for a grape harvester than a shit shoveler. Man, I'm glad you agreed to take this job. Papa Al asked me to do it when I first got here, but I declined. Shoveling shit isn't exactly what I came to do in Switzerland."

"Just what did you come to Switzerland to do?"

"I was touring Europe, got a little low on cash, found this place. And the rest is history. Papa Al has been real easy to work for. He doesn't have a clue how to do anything with his hands. He's a book man."

I nodded. "Well, I'll see you later, James. I'm going to hit the shit."

"Owen, seriously, don't you have any better shoes than those?"

"They're all I've got."

"Man, you'll have the stuff oozing between your toes."

I didn't tell him that, as a cop, I waded nightly through human pain and suffering. Compared to that, I didn't fear a little goat shit between my toes. "I can handle it," I said as I started off with the wheelbarrow.

"Better you than me."

I got to the barn and stood outside the door for a moment. Everything looked normal from here. But as in life, sometimes things are not what they appear to be.

I reached for the door handle, conscious of how symbolic the chore in front of me was. For over three years, I had been trying to shovel the accumulated shit out of the cellar of my soul in hopes of ridding myself of the debris and waste I allowed my psyche to collect during my life as a warrior. The question was: Could I do the job?

There was only one way to find out.

I pulled the door open and stepped forward. Surprisingly, the smell was not unlike that of any old barn. Papa Al explained that, in the old days, residents threw straw and lye down along with the waste in order to keep the stink from overwhelming them during the summer. In the winter, it wasn't an issue because everything froze solid.

I parked the wheelbarrow, grabbed the shovel, and shoved it deep into the wall of dung. It was softer than it looked, and I withdrew a heaping shovel full and dropped it into the wheelbarrow.

In two minutes, the wheelbarrow was full, and I trundled it down the village street, the front tire bouncing on the cobblestones. Two hundred meters later I arrived at the ravine and tipped the wheelbarrow forward, sending its contents into the depths. I watched it slide down and away, then turned, and pushed the empty wheelbarrow back up the hill.

Each load became a symbolic and physical purging.

A couple of hours later, I came back from dumping one of my wheelbarrow loads and found Christina standing by the barn door. She held a pitcher of ice-cold lemonade in her hands and a beautiful smile on her face. "You thirsty Owen. Here, have drink."

"That's very kind of you," I said. I took the glass and emptied the contents in three swallows.

She filled it again.

"Would you care to sit down?" I said, pointing to a low stonewall adjacent to the barn.

We sat, and I cleared my throat. "Well, what do you think about my new job?"

"You are hard worker."

Amazing. She clearly did not think about the menial aspect of the job, or the menial guy doing the job—just the end result. I stuck my feet out in front of me. "You know, when I get my first paycheck, I'm going into town to buy a new pair of shoes. Will you come with me?"

She smiled. "I can drive you."

We talked a bit longer, and I announced that I needed to get back to work. Christina rose. Despite the fact that I was slathered in sweat and dirt and worse, she gave me a big hug.

My heart flew into high gear again. "Can I see you tonight?" I blurted into her hair.

"Yes, Owen." And she turned and walked away.

I shoveled shit like a madman until sunset.

When I entered Papa Al's place, James was seated at the kitchen table having a glass of wine, and Christina was in the kitchen cooking. "Hey, Owen," James said, "you're supposed to take a lunch break and two coffee breaks during the day. Don't tell me you've been at it since this morning!"

"Yeah, and it looks like I barely made a dent in the pile."

He polished off his wine. "Well, I'm going to hit the road. I've got a date with Frances. Christina came over because she knew you wouldn't be in the mood for cooking after a hard day of shoveling the shit."

"I appreciate it. But if you don't mind, I think I'll go take a shower first."

For a few seconds, I watched Christina bustling around the kitchen. She was a woman on a mission. When she saw me staring at her, she smiled. The dimples in her cheeks became so pronounced that the sight of them made me smile as well.

I took a long, hot shower, then brushed off my only pair of pants and put them back on. I removed my shirt at the start of the shoveling project, so it wasn't too soiled.

When I returned to the kitchen, James was gone and Christina set the table just as one might imagine out of a Swiss picture book: home-baked bread, cheese, vegetables, mushrooms just picked from the forest, sausages. It was a simple meal but prepared and presented with pride and love.

She served me as if I were royalty. When she sat at the table, I was so overwhelmed by the moment that she had to remind me to start eating. But first I picked up the bottle of wine.

"May I pour you a glass, Christina?"

"Yaw be so good."

The meal was perfect. Afterward, she cleaned the kitchen while I set a fire in the fireplace.

We sat on the couch, and I talked for hours. Although I was sure Christina didn't understand every word I spoke, I was just as sure that she comprehended exactly what was inside my heart.

As fire turned to scarlet embers, I pulled her into my arms, kissed her, and whispered, "Christina, would you care to come up to my room?"

Without a word, she rose from the couch and took my hand.

But as we climbed the stairway a wave of anxiety overcame me. It had been so long I wondered if I would be able to love her physically in the manner she deserved. With each step toward the bedroom, I grew more fearful. In the past, I made love to women because of various urges—to satisfy my ego and lust, out of selfishness, to try to fill a sorrowful emptiness. Now, something was different.

Christina must have sensed my apprehension. As we entered my bedroom, she climbed onto the bed and said, "Come, Owen, lay here with me."

I did so. It felt so right that soon I clutched her and felt her heart pounding against mine. When our lips touched, I was transported into the depths of the present moment—the exact now. I was no longer absorbed in thoughts about myself and my uncertainties. I was hyperaware of Christina's smell, her soft hair, her wet warm lips, her heart, her soul.

I awoke the following morning to find Christina still in my arms. It was not a dream. The window over my bed was wide open, and sunlight filtered into the room. Birds sang, trumpeting the start of the new day. For the first time in almost three years, I felt no desire to get on with my journey. I felt that I found my destination.

Christina's skin was white and delicate in the mountain light. She was simply the most beautiful woman I ever knew. Looking at her, I realized that I loved her from the moment I saw her. I knew that she would be with me for the rest of my life. I knew she would be the mother of my children.

And then I remembered the admonition of Baba, the venerable *Sadhu* in India: a man could not embark on a holy life until he understood the importance of marriage and family. I argued with him endlessly about it then, but now I understood what he meant. How could a man be whole without knowing the happiness that came from total surrender to love?

When Christina's eyes opened, it was like watching the sun rise all over again. I kissed her. "Christina, I love you," I said, feeling no fear.

Her dimples appeared, and she touched my cheek. "Owen, I love you one hundred times infinity."

We both started laughing.

As I hauled wheelbarrow after wheelbarrow load from the upper end of the village to the lower, the local residents began to come out and socialize with me. Even though none of them spoke English, they were clearly pleased to see my making improvements to the neighborhood. Most of the folks spoke Italian. I found that if I spoke Spanish, they were able to understand many of the words. At noon, Christina brought me cold lemonade and a sandwich.

On Wednesday, James packed his stuff and left. By that time, the cellar was nearly empty of the many years of accumulated waste. On Thursday, Christina came with me into the barn, and we washed it down, scrubbing the walls with soap and water. To my surprise, the room was transformed into a place of beauty: hand-hewn rafters made of huge logs hundreds of years old and hand-cut stones laid with the same precision that gave Swiss watchmakers their reputation.

On Friday, Christina and I painted the interior walls of the cellar white, and I finished the final cleanup late that afternoon. As the sun set, Christina appeared with a couple of glasses and a small jug of the village wine.

"We must celebrate the finish of your job, Owen," she said.

We sat outside the cellar doorway in the twilight, and I thought about how the past several years of searching and wandering delivered me to this perfect moment. Spared in the Pacific by the Angel of Death, then given life in the Middle East by my own guardian spirit for what? To be a warrior? At last, I knew what I was really fighting for. My quest for explanations, my journey in search of truth and understanding had reached its conclusion. I had realized the truth: there is no higher cause, no higher purpose, than love.

978-0-595-36431-2
0-595-36431-4

Printed in the United States
44065LVS00005B/109-510